Drive and Determination

by Kara Louise

© 2006 by Kara Louise
Cover Image by Kara Louise

ISBN 978-1-4303-1792-0

Published by Heartworks Publication

Printed in the United States of America

All rights reserved. No part of this publication my be reproduced, stored in a retrieval system, or transmitted in any form or by any means -- for example, mechanical, digital, photocopy, recording -- without the prior written permission of the publisher. An exception would be in brief quotations in printed reviews.

Library of Congress Cataloging-in-Publication Data

Kara Louise
Drive and Determination

A Note from the author -

Many thanks to all those who helped and encouraged me with
this story. Thanks to Sharni, Terie, Linnea Eileen,
Denise, Debbie, and Mary Anne,
who each contributed in their own unique way as I
attempted to put this story in writing.
Thanks also to those who made such positive comments as they read
the story and those who encouraged me to publish it.

I also wish to thank Jane Austen.
When she wrote her novel, *Pride and Prejudice,*
little did she know how deeply it would touch people
two centuries later.
While this is a modern story and a great deal *unlike* her story,
she is behind the inspiration for the characters
and some of the plot development.
Thank you, Miss Austen!

I hope you enjoy *Drive and Determination.*

Prologue

Elyssa Barnett stepped into the white steepled church and looked around her. It was of moderate size and had a warm, inviting atmosphere. Light diffused through the stained glass window at the back, casting its glow among the pews, the altar, and the couple that was standing up at the front.

It was dusk, and the rehearsal had just begun for her sister's wedding. Janet was about to marry the man of her dreams, Chad Blakely. Elyssa smiled as she thought back to the excitement in Janet's voice when she called and told her she had met the most wonderful man. Elyssa had been skeptical at first and wondered of the viability of a relationship with someone her sister had merely met on an airplane and who lived half way across the country. Janet lived in Los Angeles and Chad lived in Chicago.

Elyssa was pleasantly surprised that they made their long distance relationship work. Chad and Janet had dated by way of phone, email, snail mail, and an occasional plane flight. After three months, Janet made the critical decision to move to Chicago to be close to him. She was easily able to secure a transfer within her company and moved immediately. It seemed to Elyssa to take them forever to announce their engagement, but they finally did. That was four months ago and tomorrow was the wedding.

As long as Elyssa could remember, Janet had been considered by everyone she met to be undeniably beautiful. Yet Janet was not one to be affected by it and was oftentimes oblivious to the attention she drew. She was also the kindest person Elyssa knew. Being her best friend, it had been difficult when Janet moved away. Despite their separation, Elyssa would never have wanted to deny her sister the happiness she found, and she shared her sister's joy.

The wedding was to be small, but elegant. Elyssa was Janet's maid of honor and their younger sister, Lynette, and one of Janet's friends were her bridesmaids.

Everyone who had a part in the wedding had assembled to run through all the elements of the ceremony. Janet was not one to be distraught if someone made a small mistake, but the wedding coordinator, Dani Cooper, went over every precise movement, cue, and position to ensure that the wedding would be perfect. Elyssa wondered if she required perfection for her own sake or for the sake of the bride.

Dani was quite put out, therefore, that the best man had not made a point to attend the rehearsal. He had informed Chad that he would not be able to join the others until some time during the rehearsal dinner.

Elyssa had never met the man, William Denton, and only knew that he and

Chad had long been good friends. He was the president of a family owned coffee company, Pemberleo Coffee, where Chad was a sales manager. Although the two men rarely saw each other outside the office, Janet told Elyssa that Chad held him in the highest esteem and often relied on his wise advice. Elyssa wondered just how much this man valued his friendship with Chad if he could not even make the time to attend the wedding rehearsal. Apparently, Chad's sister, Carolyn, had permanently elevated him up on a lofty pedestal as well as herself, as she was the only woman he had dated in the past several months.

Dani asked the whole wedding party to come up front and get into their positions. As Elyssa watched her sister closely from her vantage point standing at her side, she could see how obviously in love she and Chad were. Elyssa was suddenly gripped with a fleeting pain in her heart with the realization that her father would have been very delighted with his first son-in-law. Unfortunately, he had not lived long enough to see this day.

Their father died unexpectedly two years earlier from a heart attack. His sudden, premature death devastated Elyssa with grief for well over a year. She and her father had always shared a special bond. She had been his favorite daughter and she greatly admired him.

She blamed his death wholly on his boss, who had demanding expectations and continually pushed his employees beyond what was reasonable. She resented the fact that her father's health was exacerbated because of the hours he spent at work and the undue pressure he was put under there.

Elyssa was convinced that her father's boss was a man who preferred work over his family. Her father, therefore, was expected to work a great deal of overtime and in the end, was able to spend little time with his own family. She knew that the hours took their toll on him, but was reassured often of his love for her. He made vain promises that the overtime would soon cease once this project or that project was completed, but it never was to be, and suddenly he was gone.

Elyssa's way of dealing with his death and her anger toward this all consuming life style around her was to move as far away from the big city as possible. She moved north of Los Angeles and found a small college that offered a degree in interior design, something in which she had a great interest.

She was now 21 and looking to finish in another year. She lived about 20 minutes from the college, outside of town in a rented house that overlooked some of the most beautiful sights in the Santa Ynez Valley. Moving here had given her a new perspective on what she wanted out of life, strengthened her conviction about what she didn't want, and filled her with an abundant sense of contentment.

At the rehearsal dinner, Elyssa sat beside Janet at one of two tables reserved for the wedding party, while her mother and younger sister were seated at the other. The chair next to Chad was noticeably vacant, as that was to be for his best man. Next to it sat Chad's sister, Carolyn. The meal was finally served and while everyone ate, Elyssa talked with Chad, teased Janet, and visited with the others around her.

While enjoying her meal and the conversation of others, Elyssa did not notice a gentleman walk quietly into the private room. She did hear a squeal of delight and turned towards Carolyn, watching as she stood up and walked over to the newcomer. Elyssa narrowed her eyes as Carolyn possessively put her hands through the gentleman's arm and brought him over to the empty seat between her and her brother. He quickly took his seat without offering up any sort of apology for his tardiness.

Elyssa cast a critical glance at the man, William Denton, who had been one of the top 50 most eligible bachelors for two years running in a well known publication. She had to admit he was handsome and she was well acquainted with his significant affluence. She knew, however, from what she had read about him and heard about him personally from Janet, he was most likely a man consumed by his work. No doubt he expected nothing short of total dedication from his employees, often at the expense of their families. She felt an all too familiar sense of indignation as she recalled the man who behaved similarly and destroyed her father's life.

As Elyssa quickly assessed him, she readily noticed his immaculately tailored imported suit and the way he carried himself with an air of distinction and importance. She thought it curious however, that he avoided any and all unnecessary eye contact with others in the room. Elyssa immediately recognized the look of someone who felt his time could be utilized more proficiently somewhere other than a wedding rehearsal dinner.

Introductions were made at their table and she greeted him with a bitter taste in her mouth as she watched Carolyn draw him more closely to herself as if warning Elyssa to keep her distance. Elyssa almost laughed to think that Carolyn most likely did not trust him to make any lady's acquaintance.

As the meal ended, several toasts were offered up and just when Elyssa thought that everything had been said, William Denton stood up and walked over to the microphone, which had been set up in the center front.

Holding up his glass, he turned toward the couple. "My good friend Chad is about to venture on a journey that, I do hope and pray, becomes one of great joy for him and his wife."

Several cheers rang out and Elyssa watched him as he took in a deep breath. "I have never met a better man than Chad, and as for his bride, even though I know you only slightly, Janet, I am convinced you are going to make him very happy." Several more cheers were heard, but as Elyssa watched him, his smile seemed forced, as if he was not truly happy about his friend's marriage.

"I do bring you more than my blessing and kind words, though; particularly to you, Chad. I must add that this will undoubtedly affect you as well, Janet." He lifted his glass and eyed Chad with a piercing stare. Everyone listened intently as he continued his speech. "Chad, I have a wedding gift for you, although I must admit that I would be offering this to you even if you were not getting married." He paused a moment before announcing, "Chad, I am happy to say that tonight I am giving you a promotion!"

Gasps went up and Elyssa saw Carolyn look with great satisfaction toward her brother.

"Chad," he continued, "I am giving you the position of vice president of sales of Pemberleo Coffee in Guatemala."

Elyssa heard the words he said, but barely heard her own anguished cry out, "No!"

She glared at the man standing up front who only turned slightly in her direction to see this young lady, who had been sitting across from him, and who had the gall to utter that dissenting outburst. Several people in the room gave Chad a rousing "Congratulations!"

Under the table, Janet took Elyssa's hand and gave it a gentle squeeze while looking at Chad, giving him an approving smile.

Elyssa tightened her other hand into a fist. *How dare he barge in like this and make this kind of announcement! Who does he think he is that he can control their lives like this and order them out of the country?*

Elyssa took in a deep breath, fighting off the tears. Somehow, she knew that if they were to move to Guatemala, life would never again be the same for her and Janet.

She clenched her teeth as she watched him walk back to the table, accepting the round of thanks from Chad and Janet. Her eyes bore into him and she was quite certain he did not meet her glare because he knew the degree of her anger. She listened in astonishment as people came up and offered their congratulations to the couple. She watched in fury as he leaned back in his chair and finally glanced over at her with a triumphant gleam in his eyes.

Later, as people began to leave, Elyssa lingered around waiting for Janet. She suddenly felt someone's presence behind her and turned, finding herself staring into the chest of William Denton. She let out an exasperated sigh and slowly looked up.

"I take it you were not happy with my announcement about Chad's promotion." His eyes met hers and pinned her with a pointed look.

"Janet is my sister and my closest friend. She is about to be married and you are sending them off to Guatemala? How can you do this? They will have enough adjustments as it is without having to move to a completely different culture with a different language."

"I am sorry you feel that way, Miss Barnett."

"It's Elyssa."

"Elyssa. But an opportunity like this doesn't come up often. Chad is the best man for the job, he speaks the language fluently, and he knew there would always be the possibility that he would go there. I must differ from your assertion that it will be difficult. I like to think of it as an adventure the two of them can enjoy together that will only lead to bigger and better things. Besides, I understand your sister can speak the language well enough to get along."

"Well you don't know my sister! She is very close to her family; at least to me! This is highly unfair of you!"

He was unsure whether he was more angered by her insolence or affected by the magnetizing pull of her eyes. "Certainly you are aware, Elyssa, that she has lived half way across the country from you for some time now. The distance to Guatemala is miniscule when you consider flying there," he challenged her with a haughty glare.

In provoked anger, Elyssa's hands gripped together tightly. "If you will excuse me, Janet and I have plans tonight. And I plan to enjoy this evening, even though you did your very best to ruin it for me, Mr. Denton!" Tears pooled in Elyssa's eyes and she was grateful her sister was occupied saying goodnight to her guests so she could sneak off to the ladies' room and deal with her emotions that were so blatantly displayed across her face.

"It's Will," he said softly as he watched her march away.

~~*

The next day, Elyssa was in no better frame of mind as her anger at William Denton had not dissipated. Janet had given her sister reassurances that as long as Chad was happy, she was happy, and that she was actually looking forward to it. Although she told her that it was something that they both had been somewhat expecting, Elyssa could not look with any pleasure upon it.

As everyone was readying themselves for the wedding, there were several times that Elyssa found herself having to redo her face because of tears spilling over and eye makeup running. She wished she could honestly say they were tears of joy, but a much stronger, more unpleasant feeling had intruded; all because of one man's announcement.

As the time for the ceremony was finally upon them and they were lining up outside the chapel doors, Elyssa turned and looked at her sister. She saw how beautiful Janet looked and all she could do was smile. "You are at least five times more beautiful than any bride I have ever seen, Janet." Elyssa leaned over and kissed her. "I am so very happy for you!"

"Thank you, Elyssa." Janet looked back at her with a radiant smile. "And I have never seen you more beautiful! Did I not do well in selecting the deep teal for the bridesmaid dresses? I did it for you, you know!"

"For me?"

"I have always thought it to be the best color on you, bringing out the blue in your green eyes."

"This is *your* wedding, Janet. You were not to make *me* look good!"

"I just thought if there were any irresistible, single men here today, they would not be able to take their eyes off of you! I only wish you could be as happy as I am."

"Janet, I never believed you to be so scheming! You know that I am perfectly content living where I do... and *alone*!"

"And I am happy, too, Elyssa. Truly, I am."

Janet and her bridesmaids waited in the hallway outside the chapel. Each young lady had pulled her hair up, allowing one single strand to curl down either side of their face. Janet's gown was a simple white dress with a number of pearl beads sewn throughout. Their uncle, Edward Garner, had the honor and privilege of stepping in for their late father and bringing Janet down the aisle on his arm.

The music soon started and the bridesmaids individually began taking slow steps up the aisle. As Elyssa stepped out, the first person she saw standing up front was William Denton, who stood tall and rigid next to Chad. A wave of anger clouded her face until she turned her eyes to Chad, who was simply beaming, waiting anxiously for the first glimpse of his bride.

She came down to the front, found her position, and then turned as the bridal march began. She saw Janet begin her promenade up the aisle and at that moment she heard Chad whisper, "She *is* an angel!" Elyssa smiled joyfully as she proudly watched her sister come toward them.

The ceremony was simple but meaningful. As the couple was declared to be Mr. and Mrs. Chad Blakely, the ecstatic groom leaned over and kissed his wife in a clearly passionate kiss. Elyssa surmised that he most likely had just unintentionally embarrassed sweet, innocent Janet in front of all these people.

With a contented smile upon her face as she was contemplating this, she looked past the embracing couple and caught William Denton's eyes upon her. She felt a warm flush permeate throughout her and she quickly looked away, forcing her attention back to the couple as they turned and began to walk back down the aisle together. She was so caught up in watching the newlyweds and masking her response to having Will's eyes upon her, that she missed her cue to step toward the center and take his arm, as they were to walk out next.

A clearing of his throat accomplished its goal in securing her attention and she was dismayed to see that he had already stepped toward the center and was waiting for her. She suddenly felt foolish, chiding herself for forgetting those simple instructions Dani had given them yesterday. An unreasonable anger against Will rose in her chest due to the fact that he knew what he was supposed to do when he hadn't even attended the rehearsal.

She looked to him and recognized the condescending look in his eyes and for a brief moment considered bailing, but forced herself to smile derisively, walk toward him, and place her hand around his extended arm. Under his breath, he whispered, "Everyone's eyes are you now, Elyssa, so swallow your pride, restrain your anger toward me, and keep smiling."

Her hand inadvertently tightened around his arm at the same moment his arm tensed, allowing her fingers to feel the well muscled arm that was cloaked underneath. They had to stand together, arms linked, until the bride and groom were almost completely down the aisle before they began their exit.

Elyssa had never before felt so trapped as they slowly made their way down the aisle. She looked out at the smiling faces as everyone's eyes were now upon them and it was all she could do to smile in return. While she wanted to rush out, William kept a very firm grip on her arm and kept a very slow stride. When they finally reached the end of the aisle and stepped out into the hall, Elyssa quickly let go of his arm and turned to her right, wishing to distance herself from him as speedily as possible.

~~*

Later that day at the reception, Elyssa was talking to her friend, Charlene Lukas. The band played a specially requested song and the bride and groom were asked to come to the dance floor and have their first dance together.

"She does look happy, doesn't she, Charlene?" Elyssa said to her friend.

"Uncharacteristically so! I have never seen her display such an outward expression of joy. She seems quite happy!"

They were silent for a moment and then Charlene continued, "You were quite the envy of many a young lady today, Elyssa."

"And why is that?"

"William Denton, of course! I dare say you must find him as irresistible as everyone else does!"

"Irresistible? Heaven forbid! That would certainly present me with a great misfortune, as I am quite determined to despise the man."

Elyssa noted Charlene's eyes widen and quickly dart to the side as she finished her sentence. She was therefore, quite stunned when she turned and noticed Will standing next to them.

Barely meeting his eyes with her own, she said, "Yes?"

"They are calling the wedding party to the dance floor to join Chad and Janet. I believe this is *our* dance."

"I... uh..." The last thing she wished to do was dance with this man. She should have anticipated this dance with him, but it had not even crossed her mind. Turning to Charlene and giving her a pathetic look of dismay, she extended her hand to Will. He grasped it and led her to the dance floor.

They danced for some time in silence and Elyssa was resolved not to break it, which was highly uncharacteristic for her. When it dawned on her, though, that Will preferred to dance without speaking, she suddenly decided it would be much more fun for her and punishment for him to break that silence.

"Was it truly necessary for you to send Chad and Janet down to Guatemala?"

She felt his arm tighten around her back as he easily moved around the dance floor. He pulled back and looked at her with one prominently raised eyebrow. "You like to be confrontational as a rule while you are dancing?"

"Only when I am dancing with someone whose actions I strongly disagree with. Since we have nothing else in common, if I did not speak of that, heaven forbid, we would dance entirely without speaking a word to one another."

He seemed at a loss for a retort, but only for a short while. "And do you think you know how to run a business so that it utilizes people's gifts and abilities for the benefit of the company?"

Now it was Elyssa's turn to pull away. "Benefit of the company? What about the benefit of the employee? Do you ever consider that?"

"There are things about running a successful business that you do not understand, Elyssa."

"And there are things about consideration for others that *you* don't understand!"

The effect was immediate. A deeper shade of hauteur overspread his features but he said not a word. For the rest of the dance, they each danced in angry silence.

As the song came to an end, however, Elyssa realized that this was the first time she had ever danced in perfect union with a man. She had not given one thought to her steps as he led her about the floor. She attributed it to his being an excellent dancer, but she decided to make one final silent declaration.

As the final note of the song was played, Elyssa planted her foot firmly and decisively on his. They stepped apart and she looked at him. "I'm so sorry," she said sarcastically and turned and walked away.

~~*

Later, as Elyssa walked through the hall outside the reception area, she stopped in front of a small table that she had seen several times that day. It was situated in front of a mirror and each time she had walked past, she had fought the overwhelming urge to rearrange the items that were displayed upon it. This time she acquiesced to that impelling force within her. Picking up a vase of flowers, she moved it back a few inches while bringing a dish of potpourri up and to the right. Tilting her head and narrowing her eyes as she looked at it, she still felt something was not right. She took one of three candles and brought it towards the center and to the right. Stepping back, she looked at it and felt quite pleased.

She blamed her keen eye for placement in design for this odd propensity of hers as she felt a strong sense of restlessness if things were not arranged properly. Her biggest enticements were items on a table that she could easily rearrange. Poorly placed pictures and décor on walls were much more difficult for her to discreetly rearrange. As she looked at the table with a sense of contentment, she heard two men talking who were just around the corner of the hall. She knew immediately that one of them was William Denton.

"So are you and Carolyn a serious thing?" asked someone unknown to her. "Do I hear wedding bells for the two of you?"

Will Denton had let out a huff. "Marriage is not something I have the time to think about at this stage in my life."

"And what about Carolyn? Is she quite content to put up with your long hours and busy schedule?"

"She understands the demands of running a successful business."

"You bet she does!" The man let out a hearty laugh. "And she understands all the benefits, too. She is lavished with all the gifts that you bestow on her to make up for your absence."

As Elyssa heard this, she laughed to herself, as that was exactly the way she imagined their relationship to be.

"It's not like that," countered Will.

"Sure it's not," the other voice said sardonically. "Heavens, Denton, you have women falling at your feet! Why settle for just one? Particularly *that* one!"

Elyssa was about to walk on when she heard her name mentioned. "You know, if I were not already married, I would do my best to attract Janet's sister's attention. Now that's one fine looking lady, that Elyssa, don't you agree? You looked stunning together out on the dance floor."

"Hmmph. She's tolerable I suppose. I find nothing noticeably striking about her."

Elyssa's eyebrows shot up. She found herself frozen to the spot, unable to will herself to move away as the men's footsteps grew closer.

"Only tolerable?" the other man laughed. "Nothing striking about her? Come, William."

"She's just a naïve, opinionated little girl who lives in an idealistic world, thinking that everything revolves around her. She lives in a fantasy where friends and family are never separated. She has no idea what running a business entails and should keep her ignorant opinions to herself!"

Before Elyssa could even respond to what she heard, the two men turned the corner of the hallway where she was standing and they found themselves face to face with the object of their conversation. The look she flashed them gave them both the impression that she had overheard everything. Silence seemed to overtake everyone and Elyssa archly walked past them, with not so cordial feelings toward the man building up within her. Consequently, neither Elyssa nor Will spoke to one another again for the rest of the day and they wouldn't see each other again for two years.

Chapter 1

Two years later

Elyssa's hands were shaking as she tried to put on the finishing touches of her makeup. It suddenly seemed a trivial thing to have to do. Everything now seemed inconsequential and meaningless. Her eyes were red from endless tears. She had very little motivation to do much of anything since she had received the news and now, when she felt completely inadequate, she was expected to give a eulogy.

Chad and Janet had been driving on a highway during a rain storm and their car skidded off the road. There was no one else involved and because of the poor visibility that night, very little information about how it happened could be gleaned from the few eyewitnesses. The car had overturned twice and by the time an ambulance had come and they were taken to a hospital, both were gone.

Elyssa closed her eyes tightly, deciding that people would have to accept her red and swollen eyes and tear-stained face. They would have to accept her shaking hands and quivering voice. She felt that any eulogy she gave would never be able to do Janet justice, and even though she felt completely incompetent to give her the kind of eulogy she deserved, Elyssa knew she had to do it. She had to tell the world what a wonderful sister and friend Janet had been to her.

Her aunt, Maddy Garner, tapped lightly on the bathroom door. "Are you about ready, Elyssa?"

Elyssa swallowed. "Yes, Aunt. I'll be right there."

She gave her long, rich, dark brown hair one last thorough brushing and opened the door. Looking at her aunt, she gave her a slight shrug of her shoulders. "I guess that's about as good as I can make myself look."

As tears filled her eyes again, Maddy pulled her close. "You poor girl. You have been through so much; first losing your father, and now dearest Janet and her husband." She drew away and looked at her. "Are you quite certain you want to read the eulogy? You know your uncle or the pastor would be more than happy to read the words you have written in your place."

"No, no. I must do this for Janet." Elyssa took a deep breath.

"Come then, Elyssa. Your mother and sister are ready and the limousine that Mr. Denton sent for us has arrived to take us to the church."

Elyssa felt her heart grip with anger at just the mention of his name. *Mr. Denton*, the high and mighty president of *Pemberleo Coffee. Mr. Denton,* who was responsible for sending Janet and her husband, Chad, down to Guatemala in the first place, thereby separating Elyssa from her beloved sister, dearest friend, and closest confidant. *Mr. Denton*, who thought only of his business and gave no consideration as to what either Chad or Janet wanted; and now, because of that decision, they were both gone. *Mr. Denton*, who put his business first, and woe to anyone who countered him. *Mr. Denton*, whose disparaging remark about her two years ago still stung.

Elyssa found herself gritting her teeth thinking back to all he represented to her.

She shuddered in contempt as she considered that this man's means of showing his devotion for his supposedly good friend and compassion to the grieving family was merely to provide the limousine for them and order a large floral display for the funeral.

Elyssa shook her head. No, most likely he had his secretary order it.

He was giving the eulogy for Chad and she imagined he would be very good at it. He would be very businesslike, unemotional, and detached. Elyssa had very little gratefulness in her heart for the meager, superficial actions of this man.

Elyssa came downstairs and joined her mother and younger sister, Lynette. The family had come to Chicago, where the funeral was being held. This was where Janet and Chad had lived before getting married and only briefly as man and wife before they set out for Guatemala. The Barnetts had all been flown out and put up in a hotel at the expense of Pemberleo Coffee and Mr. William Denton.

When Janet moved to Chicago several years ago, Elyssa missed her terribly and even more so when she and Chad moved to Guatemala. She had seen her only three times in the two years they lived down there and that was only when they came back home on extended visits.

How she wished she had taken the time to visit the Blakelys in Guatemala. But she never had and now she would never again have the opportunity to see Janet in the country that had become her home these past two years.

When Elyssa came downstairs to the lobby, her uncle drew her into a hug. "Now, Elyssa, just say the word and I'll do the eulogy for you. I think Janet would be pleased simply that you wrote such a moving tribute to her."

"No, but I thank you, Uncle. If I don't do this, I know I will regret it."

He took her by the hand, patting it. "I'm sure you'll do just fine, Elyssa."

"Thank you," she said softly.

They walked out to the stretch limousine and Elyssa cringed at the somewhat stifled "Wow!" uttered by Lynette as the door was opened for them. Elyssa turned to reprimand her sister for her thoughtless reaction, but stopped, reminding herself that she was only 17 and still very immature. Her sister was so different from herself and Janet that she knew the young girl's grief did not reach the depths of her like it did Elyssa.

Elyssa could not help but wonder, as well, of her mother's grief. While she had initially cried, Elyssa now saw her display very little emotion. The only difference in Mrs. Barnett's demeanor was that she was more subdued than normal. Elyssa wondered how to even reach out to her, but she and her mother had never been close and she hoped that Lynette, who was more like her mother in temperament, would be there for her.

They all settled into the spacious vehicle and departed for the church. Elyssa looked out the window and found herself pondering how everyone was going about their usual business. *How can they carry on as if nothing has happened?* she asked herself. She could rationally tell herself that Janet meant nothing to these people, but she felt the loss so powerfully that she felt that everyone else should feel it, as well.

The funeral was in honor of both Chad and Janet. Chad's family consisted of his two sisters, a brother-in-law, and a handful of distant relatives. Janet's family consisted of her mother, sisters, their Aunt Maddy and Uncle Edward Garner, Aunt Laurel and Uncle John Phillips and several cousins. The Barnett and Blakely families were each given private gathering rooms of their own before the funeral. The two families were not particularly close, so they felt more comfortable grieving separately.

When the limousine pulled up to the church, they all walked in silently, which was exceedingly difficult for Lynette, who was usually inclined to comment on everything and everyone around her. They were shown into the room that was reserved for them to gather before the funeral. Their Aunt and Uncle Phillips had already arrived and everyone greeted one another warmly and with fervent hugs.

While everyone seemed to be bearing up under the strain and grief of it all, Elyssa was unexpectedly and unusually quiet. Her Aunt Maddy lingered closely, keeping a pulse on Elyssa's demeanor. Elyssa gripped the piece of paper on which she had typed out Janet's eulogy, nervously folding and unfolding it, curling it, and pressing it flat. Her aunt wondered whether the paper would survive the remaining 30 minutes before the funeral service began.

"Elyssa, how are you doing?" her aunt asked.

"I was just thinking that the last time I was here at this church…" her voice trailed off and fresh tears came to her eyes. She took in a deep breath as she continued, "Janet and Chad were getting married. And now…"

"I know it is difficult, Elyssa." Her aunt took her hand and patted it reassuringly. "I'll be praying that you'll find the inner strength and command of presence to do this."

They both grasped hands and Elyssa took in some more deep breaths. "Thank you. You know I appreciate that."

Soon guests began to arrive. The two grieving families were escorted into the chapel once all the guests were seated. When they walked into the church, Elyssa gasped at the multitude of people. She was amazed at how many had come to pay their respects to the young couple. Elyssa tried to glance about her and see who had come, but tears began to fill her eyes again and it was a useless attempt. She reached into the pocket of her skirt and pulled out a handkerchief she had earlier placed there, dabbing her eyes.

The pastor -- the same one who had married them -- welcomed everyone, thanking each one for coming, and extended comforting words to the families.

A mutual friend of Janet and Chad was asked to play and sing one of Janet's favorite songs during the service. As she sang, Elyssa steeled herself for the daunting task that lay ahead of her. She barely heard the song and suddenly felt a hand upon her shoulder. She looked back to see her Aunt Maddy, who was seated behind her, and was reassured by her gentle touch and warm smile. In her grief, she barely heard the pastor say, "And now, Janet's closest sister and dearest friend, Elyssa, will give her eulogy."

Elyssa took a deep breath, wiping her eyes one last time with her well used and crumpled up handkerchief before walking up to the front of the church. Each step seemed an encumbered effort. Finally, she reached the podium and turned. Standing before everyone, she took in a deep breath and proceeded to tell everyone what a wonderful person Janet Barnett Blakely had been.

William Denton was seated behind the Blakely family members. If there was anything he disliked more than being in social situations with people with whom he did not have a previous acquaintance, it was sitting through a funeral. He would have preferred to sit in the back, giving him an opportunity for a quick exit, but considering he was giving the eulogy for Chad, that was not possible.

He shifted in his seat as the song came to an end. It was when Elyssa came up to the front that he was suddenly attentive. He eyed her curiously. She had grown up a bit since he had last seen her two years ago at the wedding. She had been beautiful then, a 21 year old with a lively personality and deep, engaging eyes. But, in a manner most typical of him, he had blurted out some inane remark about her that was unkind and she, he was quite certain, had overheard.

Now he looked up and watched Elyssa as she struggled through the eulogy. She was deeply emotional, but through her words she was able to paint a picture of her sister that was moving to everyone in the church. She had to stop several times to regain her composure, taking the time to wipe her eyes and catch her breath. He sat mesmerized as he watched and listened, realizing that he was beginning to feel the depths of her loss as everyone around him was, as well.

She concluded with, "What more is there that I can say to all of you here that would help you get to know my sister Janet perhaps a little better? There was none finer, none sweeter, and none more caring than Janet Barnett Blakely." Elyssa stopped and looked down, her breathing labored. Stifling the threat of an onslaught of tears, she finished, "I will miss her more than I can bear to imagine."

Elyssa walked slowly back to her place, her tears falling freely. Sniffling could be heard throughout the church because of the depth of emotion that was evoked through her words.

Will shook himself out of it. He could not allow himself to feel this way. It was now time for him to give Chad's eulogy and he needed to remain composed and steady. Ever since his mother's death, he had been taught by his father that it was wrong for a man to display any sort of emotional feeling. When his father died 7 years ago, he had pushed aside all feelings and unflinchingly taken over as president of *Pemberleo Coffee*, making it one of the premier family owned coffee companies in the world.

He looked down at his notes about Chad. Suddenly he felt foolish. Elyssa had returned to her seat and most everyone had been moved to tears by what she said. Now it was his turn and he knew he would sound cold and unfeeling, just as he always did. Exactly as he wished to be.

He was introduced and walked up to the front. He made a vain attempt to smile at the Blakelys, trying his hardest to avoid Carolyn's gaze, as he had broken things off with her a little over a year ago. In her grief, she seemed intent on pursuing him again, calling him several nights in a row after they had received word of the deaths, wanting to get together and talk. He knew what that would mean and politely and repeatedly declined.

He looked over to Janet's family and noticed Elyssa's head turned down, handkerchief pressed tightly to her eyes, and shoulders shaking violently.

He took in a deep breath, made an attempt to moisten his mouth which had suddenly gone dry, and he began. He talked about Chad in their university years together, how he had been a loyal and good friend; how he had been an excellent employee and, from all he heard, a loving and supportive husband. As he spoke the words he had written, he knew that they were lacking the feeling that Elyssa's words held. When he was finished, he gratefully and slowly returned to his seat, taking note that most people seemed unstirred.

Elyssa heard every word of his eulogy, although she never once looked up at him. *Yes*, she thought to herself. *Cold and heartless; just doing his duty. Precisely as I imagined. He will never change*

After the service, the Blakely family and the Barnett family gathered in the courtyard of the church and accepted the words of sympathy from everyone as they filed out. Elyssa was counting the minutes before this would all be over.

Feeling as though every word she spoke and every action she took were strictly a mechanical response or a forced effort, she received everyone's kind words of sympathy, making a concerted effort to smile and show a brave front. She noticed that several people from *Pemberleo Coffee* were now coming through the line, many of whom she had never met.

Among them were John and Shelley Walker, who worked with Chad and Janet in Guatemala and who could only say wonderful things about them.

There was Bill Collier, the company's employee relations man and chaplain, who had been the one who had to fly from Chicago to California, bringing the Barnett family the news of the accident.

"Hello, Miss Barnett. Your words about your sister were such a blessing to each person here. Everyone who knew Janet now knows a little more about her and those who did not know her… well… I am sure they wish they had."

"Thank you, Mr. Collier."

He nodded and offered a, "God bless you." He lingered but a moment longer, as if he wanted to say something more, but then moved on.

He was followed by a man who introduced himself as George Westham. He informed the Barnetts that he was a sales person who spent most of the time in Guatemala. He was most charming and cordial to Elyssa. "Miss Barnett, I knew Chad and Janet quite well, and I do not know of any couple more generous or kind than they were."

"Thank you, Mr. Westham."

He reached out for Elyssa's hand and held it firmly in his. "If there is anything I can do to help you through your grief, I would be most happy to offer whatever assistance I can give."

"You are too kind."

George Westham reluctantly released her hand and walked on. Elyssa only barely noticed the giggling response Lynette gave him when he approached her and spoke to her.

As Elyssa accepted and released the hand of another kind person who had more thoughtful words of praise for Janet and Chad and sympathy for the family, she turned toward the next person in line and unexpectedly found herself face to face with William Denton.

He extended his hand to her as Elyssa flashed him a darting glare.

"Miss Barnett, I am truly sorry for your great loss."

She merely looked down at his hand and then back up to meet his eyes with a piercing stare. "Yes, well, perhaps if they had not been forced to move to Guatemala, they would still be here with us today."

Will tensed and withdrew his hand as Elyssa did not seem inclined to accept it. "Well," he started awkwardly, "if there is anything we at Pemberleo can do to make it easier for you, let us know."

"Thank you, but I think we shall manage just fine without any of your assistance."

Will walked on and gave a simple word of sympathy to the rest of the family and quickly made his exit, avoiding Carolyn, avoiding the large gathering of people, and avoiding Elyssa's accusatory stare. For some reason that he could not fathom, her censure disconcerted him immensely.

Elyssa took in a faltering breath as the last of the guests moved past her. She looked up and noticed the tall, dark, and meticulously dressed man, who so enraged her, quickly make his exit. His duty was done and all this would now be behind him. She did not think she would ever be able to forgive him.

Chapter 2

Two months later

Elyssa pulled her car over to the curb of her modest home, stopping in front of the mailbox. Scooting over to the passenger side of the car, she opened the window, reached out her arm, and took out the collection of mail that had been delivered that day. As she pulled into the long, cracked, and irregular driveway toward the garage, she flipped through the letters, rolling her eyes at each bill and piece of junk mail that made up the majority of the bundle.

She had just completed her last final in the small college she attended north and inland of Santa Barbara in the Santa-Ynez valley. Here the green hills and valleys beckoned her to take walks, ride her bike, or to simply go for long drives of solitude. She looked forward to the three months of summer and more time to do those things she enjoyed.

"Bills… junk mail…" She muttered to herself, shaking her head. It was always the same. She was hoping one of these envelopes contained her final grades. Her eyes widened, however, and her chest unexpectedly tightened around her rapidly beating heart as she looked down at the return address of one very formal looking letter. Her foot unwittingly slammed on the brake and her hands began to shake.

Two months ago she would have excitedly opened a letter bearing the return name *Pemberleo Coffee*, hoping to hear from her sister, Janet. That changed with Janet and Chad's deaths; each stark reminder seemed only to reinforce Elyssa's unrelenting grief and pain.

After a few moments, she lifted her foot from the brake and lightly stepped on the gas. Pulling into the garage, she turned off the motor. Sitting still for several moments just staring at the letter, she attempted to regain her composure. With the death of her father four years ago, and her mother's instability and unwillingness, Elyssa was the one who had to deal with all the details after her sister's death. She wondered what information this letter would bring.

Getting out of the car was suddenly an impossible effort. She walked slowly toward the house, keeping her eyes fixed on the letter while fingering her set of keys. Upon finding the right one, she opened the door and walked in, dropping all the mail onto her kitchen counter but the one that had her attention.

She slowly walked into her living room and sat down on her overstuffed chair. She closed her eyes and took in a deep breath as she tried to calm herself. *No tears. No tears*, she commanded herself. *I can do this.*

She ripped open the envelope to find a neatly typed letter. Glancing quickly to the bottom, she saw the meticulous signature of William Denton, President.

This caused another rise of consternation within her as she wondered what it was he wanted.

Bringing her eyes back up to the top, she began to read the letter.

Dear Miss Barnett

I would like you to know that all of us at Pemberleo Coffee grieve with you in the deaths of your sister, Janet, and her husband, Chad. They were two very warm, caring, and giving people. Chad was not just an employee, but a close friend, as well. Although I cannot claim to feel the loss as deeply as yourself, I grieve for them also.

I wanted to inform you that we have not done anything with their belongings in the townhouse Pemberleo provided for them in Guatemala. If you would like, we could pack up all their belongings and send them to you so you could sort through them at your own leisure. In talking with both of Chad's sisters, they informed us that there are only a few items they want. We are sending those things to them as they do not wish to go down there to retrieve them. I would not wish to have you make a trip down there if you are not inclined to do so.

Therefore, I am willing to have them shipped to you if you just say the word. However, we would be willing to fly you down there on our private jet, if that would be convenient for you. Please advise me and I will do the best to accommodate your wishes.

Again, my deepest condolences,
William Denton

Elyssa blinked her eyes several times to diminish the tears that were pooling up in them. She knew that having to sort through their things would be an agonizing and difficult task. It was something she had not wanted to think about. She certainly didn't want them to ship all their belongings to her. She would be more than willing to donate most of their things to some charitable agency in Guatemala that could use them, but she knew there could be some things her sister owned that she would want to keep as a memory. She wouldn't know what those things were, though, unless she went down there herself.

She walked over to her desk and opened the drawer, pulling out an airline ticket she had purchased just before Janet died. She had planned to fly out on June 30, which was only two weeks away. She reasoned that she might as well go ahead and use the ticket and get this over with. Going through their things would not be easy, but there was really no other way. She would go down to Guatemala.

~~*

Back in his office, William Denton was glancing over the end of the month figures and was just about to pick up his phone to call his cousin, Richard, who was Vice-President of Pemberleo, when his secretary, Mrs. Reed, buzzed. "Yes, Mrs. Reed," he said in a detached way, more from automatic response than interest.

"Miss Elyssa Barnett, Janet Blakely's sister, is on the line for you."

Will looked over to the phone. After a slight pause he asked, "Pardon me, but who did you say it is?"

"Elyssa Barnett. She is Janet Blakely's sister."

He noticed an increase in the pulsing of his heart and wondered of its root. "Do you know what she wants?" He unwittingly winced when his voice produced a most annoying and uncharacteristic crack.

Without giving any indication that she noticed, Mrs. Reed answered, "She received the letter I wrote for you and is responding, Sir."

"And what did we say in that letter?"

"You had mentioned that we needed to do something about the Blakelys' personal things. I wrote to her that we would be willing to ship them to her or, if she preferred, we would fly her down to Guatemala so she could go through the items herself at a suitable time and per her convenience."

"Hmmm. And, uh, you said it is her sister, Elyssa?"

"Yes, Sir. The one that was closest to Janet and is handling her affairs. The one who gave her eulogy at the funeral."

Will pursed his lips together, disturbed by the tension he felt just in anticipation of speaking to her. "Mrs. Reed, would you please apologize to her and tell her I'm busy. Just find out what her wishes are and tell her we'll be more than happy to accommodate them. Would you do that for me?"

"Certainly, Mr. Denton."

Mrs. Reed hung up from him and picked up the blinking light. Will looked at the speakerphone in silence. He planted his elbows firmly on his desk and brought one hand up to his face, clasping it over his mouth as he eyed the light on the phone line. He knew he was taking the easy way out, but at the moment, he did not feel like dealing with an emotional woman who harbored anger and resentment toward him. Particularly Elyssa Barnett.

Will kept his eye on the telephone and watched until he saw that the light had gone out. He buzzed Mrs. Reed back.

"Yes, Mr. Denton?"

"Did Miss Barnett say what she wanted to do?"

"Yes, Sir. She told me that she had previously purchased an airline ticket a few weeks before Chad and Janet's deaths that she had planned to use for a visit. She said she would fly out there on her own, using that ticket."

"Did you tell her we will do everything we can to accommodate her down there?"

"Yes, Sir. I also told her to send us the amount of the ticket and we would reimburse her for it, although she really did not wish to accept any compensation from us."

"See how much a ticket costs and reimburse her anyway."

"Yes, Sir."

"Thank you, Mrs. Reed."

Will hung up the phone, but quickly called Mrs. Reed back.

"Yes, Mr. Denton?"

"You might want to send her a letter with some advice on what she will need to take down there and what she might expect. Tell her we will have someone pick her up and take her wherever she needs to go and that we will make reservations for her at the hotel if she would rather stay there."

"Yes, Mr. Denton. Is there anything else?"

"No, I don't think so."

"Thank you, Mr. Denton," Mrs. Reed replied with a curious tilt of her head. He was behaving in a most uncharacteristic way. He was usually so businesslike and precise, getting everything he wanted in one phone call. She looked at the phone and pondered to herself, *This is really interesting, indeed!*

Will stood up and began pacing around his office. He felt something stirring inside him that he tried to push down into the depths of him. While uncharacteristic of him, it seemed to be a combination of nerves and restlessness. His pacing became more determined and he felt as if he were spiraling out of control. He did not like that feeling at all.

He looked around him at the diplomas adorning the walls, a Bachelors degree in economics and a Masters degree in business. He had always succeeded easily in school, grasping even the most difficult concepts, acing the tests, and impressing his teachers and professors, but he had never really learned how to empathize with his peers.

He was easily considered by everyone to be one of the more popular students because of his looks and athletic abilities, but he was never forced to make any sort of effort in developing and sustaining a friendship.

Reserved by nature and reinforced by the same behaviour in his father, he had always found it difficult to get close to people. Very few people really knew who he was, save for his younger sister, Gina, and his cousin, Richard. Even Chad, who had been a good friend since university days, had not really known him all that deeply. His friendship with Chad had always been based on his friend's outgoing nature and ability to strike up conversations with just about anyone. That complimented Will's own lack of natural ability in that area. Chad looked to Will for wisdom and guidance, as he enjoyed life so much he sometimes found it difficult to make a decision if it committed him to something at the expense of something else.

William Denton could talk business and articulate his goals and direction for his company, taking the leadership with a youthful, but mature confidence. He found it difficult, however, to share his deepest feelings. He could be in a room full of people and still feel disconnected and flooded with a sense of loneliness. He wanted something more but had no idea how to go about getting it.

When he broke things off with Carolyn, he had come to the realization that she had simply been happy with the *idea* of him. She knew little about *who* he was and really didn't seem to care. She liked the attention of being with someone who was incredibly wealthy, who was thought to be handsome, and who was well respected. But after a little over a year, he found that the two of them had very little in common and consequently he ended their relationship. She took it hard, but he doubted that she would miss *him* that much, only those things that *came* with him.

He had dated very little after that relationship. The magazine that named him one of the top 50 most eligible bachelors without any consideration whether or not *he* wanted that title, gave him cause to be suspect of any woman who tried to secure his attention and affections. He wondered whether it would ever be possible to enter into a relationship with a woman who was interested in him and not his wealth.

He recalled watching his father when his mother had died. Although he knew his father and mother loved each other deeply, his father barely shed a tear and he admonished his son to bear up under it like a man, even though he was only 15 years old at the time. Ever since then, he had pushed his emotional side down as deep as he could. As a result, he found it difficult dealing with people who were emotional themselves. He now questioned whether that truly was a positive trait.

He thought about his sister, Gina. She was almost twelve years younger than him, but she was the one person who could readily reach down into the depths of him and she made every attempt to do so. Ever since their father had died and he had been given guardianship of her, she had touched places in his heart that he had thought were sealed shut. But she was the only one who could evoke such feelings and responses.

Will walked about his office and casually picked up a picture of Gina. He sat down on the edge of his desk and looked down into her sweet, smiling face. His heart lurched as he considered what it had taken to make him realize he had been neglecting her due to his misguided sense of priorities. Even though a little over a month had passed, it still shook him. He vowed never to let that happen again -- even if it meant getting up and leaving an important business meeting to be by her side if that's what was needed.

In the fall she would begin her first year at Stanford University. It had been her desire to attend this college in California and despite its distance, he made her, as well as himself, a promise to keep in close contact with her. He was proud of her, maybe a little protective of her, and he loved her as much as any father would love his own daughter.

He replaced Gina's picture to a prominent place on his large, mahogany desk and walked around to his leather chair. He was on the eighteenth floor of a building that overlooked Lake Michigan. Pemberleo Coffee owned five complete floors in addition to office buildings in Texas, Guatemala, and Columbia. He owned a private jet, a couple of limousines, several company and personal cars, a townhouse and two homes. Yet he had to admit that even with all these things, he was still not happy.

He shuffled some papers as he looked down at his calendar. He had much to do before the weekend. He could not afford to idle his time away thinking of things that were not as he wished them to be.

~~*

Elyssa sat in her living room eyeing the ticket that would take her to Guatemala. She knew sorting through her sister's things would be difficult. It had only been two months since their deaths and she was still frequently overcome with grief at some thought or reminder of her.

She looked around her at her comfortable home. She had been renting it and hoped to someday buy it with her savings and little bit of money her father had left her when he died. An insurance policy had provided money for each of the girls, in addition to a larger sum left to her mother.

She worked part-time at the public library while attending college and was now full-time. She thoroughly enjoyed her job and often wondered how they could pay her when she enjoyed reading as much as she did, but her great love and dream was to become a full-time interior designer.

While still working on a degree in interior design with an emphasis on historical decor from the nineteenth century, she'd had several opportunities to exhibit her natural talent. While living in Los Angeles, she had been able to secure occasional work on movie and television sets that dealt with historical periods. Her good friend, Charlene Lukas, was a set director who had made a name for herself and often called Elyssa to help out when she worked on period movies. Knowing how talented Elyssa was, Charlene also freely handed out her friend's business cards when someone was looking for an interior designer.

Many people recognized Elyssa's talent and she was tempted to forego college and work full time in the studios. But she disliked the traffic, crowds, and smog too much to want to stay there, so she moved up to the beautiful Santa Ynez Valley. Besides, she reasoned, she wanted to use her talents for people to enjoy, not just for a temporary set that would be torn down after the filming was complete.

Here, she was close enough to LA so that if she were occasionally called to work on a movie set, she could easily drive down there and stay with family during the course of the time she was needed. She had done some small decorating jobs in and around where she lived, but it was not enough to consistently pay the bills. So her job at the library was one way to solve that problem. There she had a job she loved and they were willing to let her take time off when her own business demanded her time.

Looking around her, she was proud of her living room. It was this room that she had put the most time and money into designing and redecorating. She figured that this was the room most people would see when they came to visit her, and hopefully, would recognize the talent she had in the area of design. Her eye for placement demanded that every item on a table or shelf and every picture or knick knack hung on the wall had its perfect place.

She knew all about how the eye must be drawn to one object, how you must decide what you want that focus to be. She knew how to make things look balanced, even when they were not. She knew how to hang odd shaped and sized pictures without them looking as if they were just stuck on the wall. Unfortunately, there was not a lot of demand for her work and she was just not willing to move to a big city; at least not if she didn't have to.

She stepped outside onto the large porch and walked over to the porch swing that was hung out there. When she found this house and its porch swing, she knew this was the place for her.

She had fond memories of visiting her Aunt and Uncle Garner in the Midwest and how in the evenings when the weather was mild, they would sit together on their porch swing. They would talk to each other about their day, her aunt working on some needlework or crocheting and her uncle smoking his pipe and reading the newspaper. But the one thing Elyssa noticed was that they talked and listened to each other. Elyssa came to believe that the happiness in their marriage was due in large part to that porch swing.

She picked up a pillow and sat down upon the swing, plopping the pillow down onto her lap. She brought her legs up and the movement caused the swing to sway as she wrapped her arms around her legs. She leaned her head forward against the pillow and felt her grief begin to spill out again. The creaking from the swing's long chains seemed to echo her anguish with mournful cries.

While Janet was in Guatemala, when either of the sisters needed a word of encouragement, they would be on the phone with one another and Elyssa would always be rocking soothingly with her cordless phone in hand. When Janet visited Elyssa the previous year on a trip home, the two sisters spent hours catching up with each other on this very swing.

She loved it here. She loved the slow pace and the appreciation everyone had for the beauty that surrounded them. She thought of her father down in Los Angeles and how he traveled an hour both ways to get to work and then spent over ten hours a day there. He would come home tired and irritable, with little time for anyone. He virtually had no free time to enjoy his own pursuits. While Elyssa and he once had a very special relationship, towards the end she saw what his job had done to him, but it was too late for a change.

When he had a heart attack at the young age of 54, she could only blame it on the high pressure tactics of his boss and swore that she would never marry a man who was so consumed by his career. For some odd reason, she thought of William Denton.

Here was a man who most likely worked 24 hours a day, 7 days a week, and demanded the same from his employees. He was a man who most likely would not be able to take the time at the end of his day and enjoy the serenity of a porch swing in the presence of a wife and family.

An angry tremor passed through her as she placed him in the same sphere as her father's boss. Both men were responsible for the deaths of people she had loved dearly. She hoped that once she had gone to Guatemala and taken care of Janet and Chad's things, she would never hear from William Denton again!

Chapter 3

Elyssa sat comfortably on the plane, occasionally glancing out the window down to the world below. Her eyes closed as she listened to classical music through the ear phones the plane provided. Her seat had been bumped up to first class and she was fairly certain she knew who had done it and why. William Denton's meager attempts at assuaging the anger and bitterness she harbored towards him didn't work in the least. Whether it appeased his conscience or not, that was something only he could answer. She really didn't care.

The movie had just finished and the lights came on. It had been a comedy, she had gathered, from the pratfalls and silly antics she noticed when she occasionally looked up, but she was in no mood for humor. She was on her way to go through the belongings her sister and brother-in-law had in their home in Guatemala.

For the past two weeks, in preparation for this trip, Elyssa had forced herself to look through scrapbooks filled with pictures of herself and Janet growing up. She had read and reread letters that Janet had written to her. She thought that the more she immersed herself with memories of her sister, the easier it would be to go through the things in their home and not continually dissolve into a flood of tears and heartache at every turn.

She made arrangements for her friend, Katy, to look in on her home and occasionally check her messages on the answering machine. She would not wish to let an offer for a decorating job slip by. Not that she anticipated much business living where she did, but there was always the chance that someone might call after picking up one of her business cards. Elyssa left several in various stores around town and her good friend Charlene liberally handed them out.

She looked out the window as the captain came on over the loudspeaker announcing they would be preparing for landing. The sun was low on the horizon and lights were beginning to sparkle throughout the sprawling city below. A tremor passed through her as she contemplated getting off the plane in a foreign country where they spoke a language she knew only slightly and had customs and a culture she most likely would not understand. She had been informed in a letter from the Pemberleo offices that Shelley Martin would be picking her up. She hoped that one of them would recognize the other.

After a smooth landing, Elyssa gathered her carry-on items and once off the plane, she retrieved her luggage at baggage claim and easily made her way through customs. Stepping out of the airport, she looked over the crowd of people waiting to pick up friends or family who had just arrived. It was growing dark and the air was warm and moist. She glanced around her and suddenly heard a voice call out her name.

She turned her head in the direction of the voice and saw a familiar face. It was definitely not Shelly Martin, but a man. He had been at the funeral, but she could not recall his name.

"Elyssa! It is good to see you again! George Westham!"

"Ah, yes. George. It is very nice of you to pick me up."

"I wouldn't have had it any other way!"

He took the suitcase from her and pointing with a nod of his head, said, "I am parked this way. It's a lengthy walk. If you wish, I'll go back for the car while you wait here and I'll come back for you."

"Oh, no, thank you, George. I have been sitting idle far too long. I could use a good walk."

George laughed. "That's what I like to see; a woman who is not afraid of a little exercise."

He put his free hand gently against her back and gave her a nudge. "Shall we go?"

Elyssa smiled. "Thank you."

As they walked, George congratulated himself on offering to pick Elyssa up and take care of any needs that arose while she was in Guatemala. He just happened to be in John Walker's office when the phone call came from Mrs. Reed telling them that Miss Barnett was arriving and needed someone to pick her up, take her to the Blakelys' apartment or a hotel, and help her with whatever else she might need.

Remembering this pretty young lady with a very fine figure, he figured it would be a most pleasant chore.

The Walkers gladly accepted George's offer when they had some guests unexpectedly drop by and this made it much easier for them.

As George looked down furtively and watched Elyssa walking along by his side, he thought how much prettier she looked tonight than the day of the funeral. He recalled how she had been crying and did not look her best that day, although his attention had centered mainly on her younger sister, who seemed to have a very flirtatious personality and a lot of energy. He often thought he would like to have gotten to know that sister a little better.

As he looked at Elyssa, he believed that if he really poured on the charm, there might be some sort of reward from her in return. Considering the reason for her visit, however, he reminded himself that he would have to take it slow.

"You know, Elyssa, your sister Janet was certainly well liked by everyone that knew her. Just the other day, I talked with a lady who lives down the street and she could not stop talking about what a sweet, generous young lady she was."

"That is very comforting to hear, George. I am so glad she had such an impact on people's lives here."

Elyssa felt that all too familiar lurch inside that indicated an onslaught of tears was on its way. She turned her head away from George and gave a slight tremble, which did not escape his notice.

"I can only imagine what a difficult time this is for you." He pulled out a clean handkerchief he had pocketed just before leaving for the airport and handed it to her.

"Thank you." Elyssa wiped her eyes. "And I'm sorry. I just never know when the grief is going to spill out again."

"No need to apologize to me." George brought his hand up and gently squeezed her shoulder. "You will come through this, Elyssa. I can see there is great strength in you."

"You are too kind."

They came to George's car and he popped open the trunk, putting Elyssa's suitcase inside and then closing it. Walking over to the passenger side of the door, he unlocked it and opened it for her, taking her elbow in his hand as he handed her in.

George walked around to the driver's side and slid in. He started the engine and turned to her, "Now, where would you like to go? Do you want to go by Chad and Janet's townhouse, should I take you to a hotel, or would you like to stop somewhere and get a bite to eat?"

"If you don't mind, I think I would prefer to stay at their home. That way I can start early and work as late into the night as I want. I don't want to be a bother to anyone having to drive me back and forth."

"Are you sure? Pemberleo has a very nice suite in a nearby hotel for our clients and it wouldn't be a bother at all for me to drive you back and forth. I'm available any hour of the day… or night."

"I am quite sure. Thank you, George." She reached down to fasten her seatbelt. "I understand they lived in a townhouse with the Walkers living next door."

"That's correct. Pemberleo Coffee -- or *PC* as we call it -- owns a whole townhouse complex on a street in a nice, quiet part of Guatemala City. I live there too, when I am in the country. If you need anything, just give me a call. Occasionally I have to travel to Colombia or back to the States, but at the moment, I don't have any plans to leave."

"I appreciate that."

"It will only be about a twenty minute drive to the duplex. Are you sure you don't want to stop somewhere first for something to eat or drink?"

"No, thanks. We had a meal on the plane. I'm more tired than hungry."

He nodded, feeling a bit disappointed, but smiled and said, "Your wish is my command."

They drove in silence for awhile and then Elyssa turned and asked him, "How long have you been down here in Guatemala, George?"

"On and off for a couple of years now. Unfortunately, I don't get back to the states now as often as I used to. Denton prefers that I do the sales in the Central and South American countries since I am more fluent in Spanish than anyone else. That keeps me pretty busy here."

"Do you have any family?"

"Not married. I am an only child and my father passed away several years ago. He worked with the elder Mr. Denton as his right hand man, so I was able to begin working at Pemberleo as soon as I was old enough. Mr. Denton saw great potential in me and my promotions in the company were due largely to his influence. Unfortunately, William Denton harbors some jealousy towards me and I can't help but wonder where I would be if his father hadn't died." He turned and looked at her with a wry grin. "Heck! I could have been vice-president by now!"

"That doesn't seem fair." The sympathy in Elyssa's voice was easily detected by George and he turned and smiled at her.

"He's now the boss. He chose to give the position to his cousin, who had never even worked for the company! What am I to do?"

Elyssa looked at him, searching the darkness for his expression; the tone of his voice suggesting he did not get along well with his boss.

"You sound somewhat resentful of him."

"Of Denton?" He let out a huff. "We have known each other too long, but we actually have a very good working arrangement. He leaves me alone to do my job and I leave him alone."

Elyssa's eyebrows raised in a quick movement. "Hard to work for, is he?"

George looked at Elyssa, wondering whether her questions about William Denton were because she was as taken by him like every other woman or because she was truly interested in George's opinion of him. "He has a tendency to want to control everyone's lives and if he can't, he makes life miserable for you."

"So he doesn't come down here to Guatemala very often?"

"Can you imagine Denton down here?" Westham pointed out the window as they passed run down businesses. "They may grow great coffee beans here, but Denton won't lower himself to come here unless it is an absolute emergency."

Elyssa took in a deep breath, thinking how callous he was to force Chad and Janet to come down here to live and yet he would not even consider stepping foot in the country. Yes, she could see how he had the power to control other people's lives and she felt that all too familiar anger start to boil up inside her.

"It must be a big help to the company to be able to speak fluent Spanish."

"Yeah. Especially because the man himself speaks only enough to ask how much profit has been made, when something is going to arrive, or where the bathroom is."

Elyssa laughed along with George. "I'm rather surprised, being as how his company has so much interest in Guatemala."

"Well, he can afford not to bother himself. He lets others do it. He's the president and he can do or not do anything he wants."

She decided to change the subject. "What about your mother? Is she living?"

"My mother lives in Chicago. We were never really close, so…" George was silent for a moment. "All in all, living here has proven to be quite pleasant."

As they drove through the streets of Guatemala City, Elyssa enjoyed the warm, moist air reviving her face and her spirits as it came through the open window. She loved the feel of it course through her hair. George looked over and took in how striking she looked with her long hair dancing in the wind.

"If it's too windy, I'll close the windows." He was hoping she did not mind.

"No, no. It actually feels quite refreshing."

"We're just out of the rainy season, but there's always the chance for rain. I hope you're prepared."

"Yes, I was told it would be wise to bring an umbrella, boots, and a raincoat."

"Good. We can get some real downpours here that come upon you with little warning. The temperature remains consistently mild, so you'll probably need nothing more than an umbrella."

George turned down a side street and nodded his head toward a large building. "These are our Pemberleo Coffee offices. We occupy two of the five floors, leasing out the rest."

"It looks new."

"It was built about three years ago; same time as the townhouses. They're just about three miles from here."

A short while later, George turned and pulled into a driveway. He came up to a gated entrance and pushed in a code, opening the gate. Elyssa looked around her and took in the beauty that surrounded them.

It was in the style of a hacienda with large trees and flowering bushes everywhere. George pulled into a parking space and hopped out. As Elyssa reached for the door handle, George was already on her side opening the door.

"Thank you," she said, returning his smile with one of her own.

He pulled out her luggage and they began walking toward the building. We have an elaborate security system here. You need to enter a code to get in; both into the main complex where we drove in, and into the courtyard." He looked at her. "The code is 1220. The big man's birthday." He pushed the buttons and the gate to the courtyard opened. They walked in and Elyssa gasped.

"It is beautiful here!" She looked around and took in the vast array of flowers. "There are so many flowers!"

"Yes, they grow quite abundantly here." He pointed off to the left. "Over there is a pool. I hope you brought your swim suit. We have a Jacuzzi, too."

"I just might have need of that."

George smiled as he thought of soaking in the hot tub with her by his side. "Heals many an ailment, from stress to achy muscles to just plain weariness."

"I'll remember that."

"I'll hold you to it! It will be my responsibility to ensure that you see all the sights and experiences of Guatemala City." He laughed and then his voice turned serious. "Elyssa, I know that the task ahead of you won't be easy, but I do hope you will intersperse your time with some periods of pleasant distraction."

"Thank you, George. I believe it will probably do me a lot of good."

"Good. Here it is," he said, pulling out the key.

As he opened the door, Elyssa steeled herself to walk into the room. She knew it would be a reflection of her sister and she needed every ounce of courage to walk in.

George watched her as she slowly stepped inside. Even though she had never been here before, she knew immediately that it was her sister's home. When she walked in, she almost expected Janet to step out from the kitchen and greet her.

Her eyes glanced upon the wall and lit upon an enlarged portrait of Chad and Janet at their wedding.

Elyssa suddenly felt a wave of dizziness pass over her and began to sway. George quickly reached out both hands and grasped her shoulders to steady her. "Elyssa, are you OK?"

She took a deep breath. "I… it…" She was unable to say anymore. George grabbed her as she fell against him in a flood of tears.

~~*

William Denton walked into his outer office at the end of a very busy day and greeted Mrs. Reed. She handed him his messages as he walked past her, opening the door to his private office. He collapsed into his chair and put his head back, not wanting to move. He had been up practically the whole night before, getting ready for the board meeting he just returned from and although it went very well, he was exhausted. He casually looked down at the messages, making mental notes of whether he needed to respond with a call, a letter, an email, or not at all.

Suddenly his head came up abruptly. "What…!"

He stood up and walked back out to the outer office. Mrs. Reed looked up, "Yes, Mr. Denton?"

"Mrs. Reed, do you know why Westham has taken matters into his own hands with Miss Barnett? I thought the Walkers were seeing to her needs."

"I understand the Walkers had guests come visit and George offered to do it for them."

"I'm sure he did. Why would they allow him to do such a thing?"

Mrs. Reed narrowed her eyes in response to his question. Was he actually displaying a rather protective stance regarding this young lady? "I do not believe they know Westham as you do, Sir, and therefore they had no reason to question his ability nor his integrity in helping Miss Barnett out."

"I don't question his ability either… his ability to deceptively charm and worm his way into a young lady's confidence, woo her and flatter her with his puffed up attention, all with purely selfish, lascivious motives."

Mrs. Reed sat quietly, allowing him to vent his anger. Very softly, she said, "You could always fire him."

Will closed his eyes tightly. "Perhaps I should have and someday I will. If it weren't for the promise I made to my father to take care of him, he would have been gone long ago! At the moment I feel like I have more of a pulse on him if he's in my employ… in Guatemala." He took in a ragged breath, "and as far away from Gina as he can possibly be!"

"I'll take care of it for you, Sir, with a quick phone call."

He turned abruptly to enter his office but stopped short in the doorway. "No… no."

Still looking at the message, he uttered a very concise directive to Mrs. Reed, "Cancel all my appointments for a week. Reschedule them for… no, just cancel them. We'll set them up again when I return."

"Excuse me?" she asked, completely surprised by this impulsive and unusual request.

"I'm going to Guatemala. Find out how soon the jet can get me there. I'll be ready in the afternoon immediately after my meeting with Jenkins. Let me know what time it's available."

He walked into his office, never really looking at the woman who had served him and his father so faithfully for well over 25 years. He knew this was out of character for him and he was not even sure why he was doing it, but he did not want George Westham anywhere near Elyssa Barnett. He only hoped he would get there before he did anything to tarnish the name of Pemberleo Coffee!

Or take advantage of Elyssa Barnett in any way.

Chapter 4

Elyssa awoke the next morning and looked around her. She was grateful for George's calm and reassuring presence last night when she emotionally broke down. He sat with her late into the night as she spilled out her grief. He had been a sympathetic and eager listener as she pointedly put the blame on William Denton for sending Chad and Janet here and ultimately, for their deaths.

He had been more than willing to stay with her through the night, but she collected herself after a while and told him she would be fine. The guest room in Janet and Chad's townhome had been cleaned up and prepared for her arrival and she gratefully fell into bed that night, wishing herself to fall asleep and not dwell on the empty bedroom that was just down the hall.

The sun was now shining brightly into her room and an array of birds could be heard singing outside. She pulled herself out of bed, preparing herself to face the task that lay before her. After showering and putting on some jeans and a short sleeved cotton blouse, she walked back out into the living room. She stepped up to a small table that sat inside the door and fixed her eyes at the items displayed; some that Janet had obviously bought here and others that were from home. Without thinking, Elyssa began rearranging them into a more eye appealing display. When she was satisfied with the way it looked, she went into the kitchen to brew a cup of coffee.

Last night before he left, George told her that the townhouse complex had a distilled water tank that went to each of the units through a special faucet in each sink. Everywhere else, she had been told, she needed to remember to drink bottled water. She walked up to the sink and saw the small faucet. She pressed the lever and filled the coffee pot.

George arrived shortly after, with some fresh rolls and the most delicious display of fruit she had ever seen. There was some variety of fruit on the plate that she had never seen in any of the stores in California.

"Here," he said, as he held one out to her and slowly brought it up to her lips. "You must try this."

Elyssa smiled and took a bite. "Mmmm," she said and took it from him. "It's delicious!"

"They grow the best fruit here! Try the pineapple. Unless you've been to Hawaii, you've never tasted better."

Elyssa was grateful for George's thoughtfulness and offered him a cup of coffee. The two enjoyed a morning meal together.

"So what do you think of Pemberleo Coffee, Elyssa?"

"It is delicious." She closed her eyes and took another sip. "Very rich," she added. "Every Christmas, for the past two years, we all received an ample supply from Chad and Janet."

"Do you know what makes the coffee from Guatemala so rich?"

Elyssa shook her head as she spooned out more fruit onto her plate.

"The volcanoes."

"Volcanoes?"

"Yes, Guatemala has several. Since you came in at night, you weren't able to see the one that overlooks Guatemala City. If we're lucky, it will put on a little display for us."

Elyssa looked at him in alarm. "You mean erupt?"

"No, it merely lets out a little steam now and then."

Elyssa smiled at him, a little more reassured. "I think Janet may have mentioned the volcanoes in her letters, but I had no idea they were active."

"Not all of them are active. If we can get out to Lake Atitlan, you'll see three volcanoes that surround the lake. None are active, but they make a beautiful sight."

"Didn't Chad and Janet also have a little place there?"

"Yes. You'll find some of the best coffee fields in the country there because of the volcanic ash in the soil."

"How far away is it?"

"It will take a few hours to drive there. You'll want to see it before you leave; not just to go through their things at their home there," he lowered his voice to a husky whisper, "but because it has to be the most romantic place in the country, if not the world."

Elyssa smiled at George, his eyes sparkling as he softly informed her of this, causing her to blush slightly.

"I would be more than happy to take you there." He paused, and then added as an afterthought, "Janet loved it there. I'm sure you would, too."

Elyssa felt her eyes pool again with tears when a realization hit her. "That is where they were returning from when they had their accident, wasn't it?"

George looked at her and then looked down. "I'm sorry, Elyssa. I should not have mentioned it."

"No, no, it's quite all right." She reached behind her to pull a tissue out of a box and brought it up to her eyes. "It was inevitable that it would come up. I would very much like to go if there is time. My airline return reservation is for Tuesday."

"That should give us plenty of time to go up there for a few days," George assured her.

Elyssa quickly composed herself and when they had finished their meal, she looked around her. "I think I ought to begin. Do you think you can find me a medium sized box? I don't think I'll need anything too large. From what I've seen, there are just a few items I think I may want to take home. But I won't know until I go through everything."

"Your wish is my command." He bowed as he repeated last night's words.

George left and a short time later he reappeared with a couple different size boxes. I brought several over so you can have your choice, depending on how much you find."

"Thank you, George. I do appreciate all you have done."

"It's nothing." He stood with his hands folded across his chest, watching her. "I need to go in to the office for a little bit this morning."

Elyssa looked up at him. "I'll be fine."

"I have no doubt of that, but what do you say about taking a break this afternoon and seeing some of the sights? I can show you the underground market place that has every Guatemalan handicraft you could ever want to buy. I can take you to the old town of Antigua and see some ancient ruins or we can just go out and take in a delicious Guatemalan meal."

"That's sweet of you, George. They all sound delightful. I'll let you know when you come back. How about that?"

"Sounds great. Now if you need anything, the Walkers are next door." He took out his wallet and pulled out a card from it, handing it to her. "Here's my business card. My cell, home, and business phone number are all here. Feel free to call. I can return in a heartbeat."

"Thanks, George."

George left and Elyssa set her mind to the task. She casually went through the kitchen drawers, knowing most things there would be general items that she would have no use for. She found a set of hand embroidered Guatemalan placemats and a tablecloth that she thought were pretty and placed them neatly in the box.

She spent the rest of the morning finishing going through the kitchen and then moved to the living room. It was early afternoon when she came upon a stack of pictures. She steeled herself to look through them, but upon feeling a terrible weight come upon her heart, she placed them directly into the box after only looking at two of them. As the afternoon wore on, so did the heaviness in her heart. She was about to burst into tears when there was a knock at the door.

Grateful for a diversion, she went to answer it.

A vaguely familiar looking couple met her, holding a large steaming pot.

"Hi, Elyssa," the woman said. "We're John and Shelley Walker from next door."

"Come in," Elyssa said.

"We're sorry we haven't come by sooner. We have guests and were just now able to get away."

Elyssa smiled at the friendly couple. "That's quite all right."

"I made a pot of chili for you. I wasn't sure how long you would be here, but feel free to eat this whenever you like. We want to have you over some evening while you're here, but I thought it would be good for you to have something on hand if sudden hunger pangs hit."

"Thanks, Shelley."

Elyssa took the pot from her and set it down.

Shelley clasped her hands together and looked around. Elyssa could sense the awkwardness the couple felt; that they really didn't know what to say to her. Elyssa decided she would broach the subject, as most people didn't know whether she would find it difficult to talk about Janet; although George seemed to understand her need to talk about her sister.

"Is there anything you can tell me about Janet that perhaps I might not know about her? I feel as though she lived this very different life down here and I have no idea how she spent her time."

John noticed the tears that began to fill Elyssa's eyes and he picked up the tissue box and handed it to her. "Apart from being a delightful neighbor and wonderful wife to Chad, she was very much involved in a preschool."

Elyssa's eyes widened. "Can you tell me about it?"

"Yes, Casa de Esperanza runs a preschool for underprivileged children. She went down three mornings a week to help out. From everything I have heard she was a natural with the children. She loved them and they loved her."

Elyssa thought back to her sister's letters. She had only casually mentioned working with some children in a preschool and Elyssa assumed it was with the children of people working with Pemberleo Coffee. She had no idea they were underprivileged children.

"Do you suppose it could be arranged for me to visit this preschool?"

"Yes! They would love to meet Janet's sister!" Shelley exclaimed.

Elyssa let out a contented sigh. It made her feel good to know that Janet was doing something that she truly enjoyed and that she was helping others.

They talked a few more minutes and Elyssa asked them about Lake Atitlan. "It's a bit more rustic there than here," John told her. "When Chad and Janet were there, they lived in a very simple, one bedroom home."

"George and I talked about it. Do you think I could go there?"

"Elyssa, if you're one who is used only to the finest things in life, you might not find it to your liking. It's a very rural village."

Elyssa laughed. "Believe me; I am not afraid of roughing it. I really would like to see it. George thought perhaps he could take me."

John and Shelley exchanged glances. "I am sure he would. Elyssa, just make sure…"

At that moment there was a knock at the door and it slowly opened. George peered his head in. "I'm back!

He came striding in, greeted the Walkers, and saw the pot sitting on a table. He lifted the lid and sniffed its contents.

"Mmmm, this smells good. Nothing better than the Walkers' chili."

The Walkers smiled and before long excused themselves to get back to their guests.

George eagerly turned to Elyssa. "Are you ready for a break? If you are, I have a surprise for you."

"You do? What?"

"When I left the office, the volcano was steaming. We can't see it from here. We'll have to drive a few miles to get out to the other side of the hill to get a good view."

"That sounds great. Let me put a few things away and then we can be off!"

George briskly rubbed his hands together. Things were progressing just as he planned!

~~*

William Denton gathered up his briefcase as his meeting with Jenkins came to a close. They had met in his favorite restaurant just across the street from the Pemberleo Coffee offices and he now anxiously waited for the light to turn green so he could cross the busy street. He looked at his watch and figured if the jet was ready within the hour, he would get into Guatemala at a reasonable time. He hurriedly crossed the street and entered the building, taking the elevator up to his office. He walked in to find Mrs. Reed on the phone.

He waited for her to finish the call and then asked her when the jet would be ready.

"I'm so sorry, Sir, but there is a slight problem."

Will listened in frustration as Mrs. Reed relayed to him the news that the jet was having some repairs done. Most likely it would not be ready for his use until first thing the next morning.

He almost uttered those words he disliked so much, "Book me on a commercial flight," but thought better of it. He disliked flying commercially almost as much as he disliked attending funerals or social functions with people he didn't know. No, he would wait one more day and hope that Westham would not have the audacity to do anything reckless!

~~*

Elyssa did not realize how much she would enjoy getting away from the house. It had been an emotionally draining day and she looked forward to seeing a little bit of the city. As they drove along the streets of Guatemala City, Elyssa could not believe the difference from last night, when there had been hardly any traffic. Now, the streets were heavily crowded with cars zooming in and around each other at frightening speed!

"Driving in this would definitely take some getting used to!"

"I am sure you would do fine, Elyssa. I would be glad to give you a personal driving lesson if you want to give it a try."

"Oh, no! I have no intention of driving these streets! I won't be here that long, anyway."

Elyssa smiled and George returned one. It made him feel good to know that he was able to cheer up someone as grief stricken as Elyssa.

She could now see the city below her. It was a sprawling city and she was amazed how large it was.

The area in which the PC complex was situated was in a somewhat hilly area. As they came down the hill, Elyssa was in awe over how green everything was and the variety of flowers that grew everywhere.

George suddenly swerved to the side of the road and came to a stop. He turned toward Elyssa, putting his right arm on her shoulder and pointing with his left hand across her to her right. "Look!"

Elyssa turned her head and saw the volcano rising from the edge of the city and spitting out smoke. "That's amazing!" she said.

"Just for you!" George laughed. "I ordered it special!"

"You must have an inside contact, George."

They sat quietly in the car, Elyssa's eyes fastened to the volcano and George's eyes fastened on her. Finally, he clasped his hands together. "Now! What are you in the mood for? A nice mall to shop for some of the finer things money can buy or are you in mood to do some bartering for handmade items at the marketplace?"

"I would prefer to see the handmade items, I think."

"Excellent! Then to the marketplace we will go!"

George looked behind him at the traffic and pressed his foot to the gas pedal, quickly placing himself between two cars that were speeding down the hill.

Elyssa gulped, but did not say a thing.

"Now, Elyssa, a word of advice. No one expects you to pay full price. Look at the listed price and then offer something lower. They'll actually be offended if you don't."

"Janet told me that bargaining was something she had a hard time getting used to."

"Well if you don't want to do it, I'm an expert! I can wear down anyone's defenses. Just leave it to me!"

They drove into town and along the way Elyssa asked George if he knew about the preschool where Janet helped.

"Sure! It's a few miles from the marketplace. If you like, we'll go there tomorrow. The preschool only has classes in the morning so there would be no use in going now."

"I would really like to if you don't mind…"

Placing a hand again on Elyssa's shoulder, he said, "Elyssa, whatever you want, I'll do."

"Don't you have work to do?"

"I have stuff I have to do, but as long as I get it done, it doesn't matter when I do it. We'll do that tomorrow morning and then in the afternoon you can get back to work going through your sister's things while I go in to work."

"That sounds like a plan," Elyssa smiled.

"But…" George quickly glanced at her and then turned back to the road. "Tomorrow evening, we go out to eat. There is one restaurant that I really want to take you to."

"I'd love it!"

George thought it would be a good time to press his luck. "The next day, we can visit Antigua. If you like history, you'll find the monastery ruins fascinating!"

"I do love history. I would really enjoy that."

"That's settled, then. On Friday, I thought we'd drive out to Lake Atitlan. I have the weekend off and would love to show you around."

"I really don't want to inconvenience you, George. Don't you have to work on Friday?"

He leaned in towards her. "Like I said, I have work to do, but as long as I get it done, it doesn't matter when I do it… or where. Besides, I have contacts there. I'll do a little work and can write off the expenses!"

They arrived at the market place and walked around the large square before going down the steps that took them inside. People bustled about everywhere.

"Now stay close to me, Elyssa. I don't want us to get separated."

He put his arm about her, drawing her closer. They walked in and she saw booth after booth of people selling their wares. There were things made of leather, ceramics, and brightly embroidered fabric. She loved the carved wood, hammocks, and the wide variety of jewelry.

Just as George promised, when she found something she liked, he put his persuasive powers to work to bargain down the price. Elyssa took him at his word that the seller would be insulted if they didn't try to talk down the price, but she felt uncomfortable doing so. She would have willingly paid the price as it was such a reasonably marked price in the first place.

When they finished shopping, her goods included a beautifully embroidered vest, a leather purse, a pair of earrings, and a carved wooden box.

Upon returning to the apartment, Elyssa was tired. George suggested a swim or some time in the hot tub, but Elyssa turned him down. "I think I'll just have some of the chili Shelley made me and call it an evening. But I do appreciate all you've done for me today."

George smiled. "I'll come by tomorrow and we'll go to the preschool. Let's plan on getting there around ten thirty. I have an early morning appointment, but we should still have plenty of time to see what they do there."

"Thank you, George."

"Then don't forget tomorrow night, I'm taking you to dinner."

"I won't. See you tomorrow, George."

"Yeah, tomorrow. Good night, Elyssa."

Elyssa was grateful to spend the evening by herself. While George was fun and certainly well acquainted with Guatemala, she was beginning to feel that he was getting a little too friendly. There was something about him that made her hold back a little, although she couldn't figure out what it was.

She sat down on the large sofa and looked about her. She shook her head and let out a breathy chuckle as she considered how Janet could have arranged the furniture in a much more efficient and eye pleasing way that would have given them more room and had a more fluid movement to its look. She was tempted to get up and make the changes herself, but held herself in check. There was no sense in doing that, she told herself. Janet was gone. For the first time that day, she gave in to her tears.

Chapter 5

Elyssa crawled out of bed the next morning and put on some sweatpants and a T-shirt. When she was dressed, she came out to the kitchen to make some coffee and eat some breakfast. She wanted to be decent in case George unexpectedly came by before leaving for work.

She pulled out the remaining fruit and rolls from yesterday. George didn't come by, but the Walkers did. They asked her if there was anything she could use as they were going to the store. Elyssa looked in the refrigerator and then the pantry, shaking her head at the disorganized array of items. As much as she loved Janet, the two of them were decidedly different when it came to organizing a household. She told them she could use some fresh milk and eggs, but that there seemed to be a good variety of things she could eat.

When they left, she sat down to enjoy her fruit, rolls, and a cup of Pemberleo Coffee.

After taking a quick shower, she went to the small closet in the guest room and pulled out a simple skirt and cotton blouse. Elyssa had asked Shelley what would be the best thing to wear to the preschool and Shelley told her that she ought to dress simply but nice. The children usually came to school wearing hand-me-downs and clothes that they had greatly outgrown so she cautioned her about wearing anything too lavish. The teachers all wore dresses, so it would probably be wise for her to do the same.

She walked down the hall of the townhouse to the open door of Chad and Janet's bedroom and looked in. She had done this several times since arriving, but she could not yet bring herself to go in. In this room would be more personal items and she did not think she was ready to tackle that. Perhaps this afternoon after going to the preschool she would consider it, but she would wait and see. For now, she decided to work on the living room.

A little later, she decided to go out for a walk around the complex while waiting for George to arrive. It was such a beautiful day and she thought it would do her some good to walk around and enjoy the sights and smells.

The flowers were exquisitely beautiful and she watched in delight as a trio of hummingbirds gathered the nectar from them. She sat down on a bench that overlooked the courtyard and pool and thought how tranquil it seemed. While she loved the view of the green hills and valleys at home, this was beautiful in a different sort of way.

As the time drew near for George to arrive, she returned to the house and grabbed another piece of fruit from the kitchen. A few moments later, she heard a soft knock at the front door. She walked into the living room and opened the door for George.

"Good morning, Elyssa," he said with a mischievous grin. He was holding something behind his back.

"Good morning, George." She looked down at his khaki slacks and up to his dark green polo shirt and commented, "You look nice. That color really suits you," her outstretched hand waved across his shirt.

"Thank you, Elyssa, but I must say that you look stunning yourself!"

She tried to look around him. "What do you have there?"

"Oh!" he laughed. "I almost forgot!" He pulled out from behind his back a huge piñata. "You mean this?"

Elyssa's eyes reflected the glee she felt. "Is that for the children?"

He nodded. "Filled with candy and little gifts. The children will love it."

"That was so thoughtful of you!"

"It was nothing." George could not have thanked one of his co-workers enough for his idea. When George mentioned they were going to the preschool, his co-worker told him that the children loved piñatas more than anything. Stopping by a store on the way back took very little time and he hoped it would only improve him in Elyssa's favor.

He walked in, closing the door behind him. Looking around the room, he saw that she had begun to put things into a box. "I see you've made some progress. How are you doing?"

"I'm doing fine, thanks."

"Good. Are you ready to go?"

"Yes, I guess I am."

Elyssa went back to the guest room to collect her purse when there was another knock at the door.

"I'll get it!" shouted George.

As Elyssa slung her purse over her shoulder, she heard George bellow out a disgusted curse and exclaim, "Of all the... what are *you* doing here?"

"Who is it, George?" Elyssa called out as she hurried back into the room.

She blinked her eyes repeatedly in astonishment when she beheld William Denton standing at the door. She was so stupefied by his presence that she was unable to even utter a greeting.

Will's eyes went from George to Elyssa; refusing to enter until he was invited in.

Elyssa was finally able to find the strength to utter the words, "Come in."

He stepped inside, bypassing George, and nodding a thank you to Elyssa. He found himself staring at those eyes that again seemed to be icy with anger, but frustratingly attractive, all the same.

"Mr. Denton," Elyssa began. "This is a surprise."

George walked over to Elyssa, almost in a possessive sort of way. "You bet it is! You hardly ever come to Guatemala! What are you doing here?"

"I have come to see to Miss Barnett's needs." He turned to George. "And *you* are needed in Colombia!"

"Colombia! Why do they need me there now?"

Will peered at him through narrowed eyes. "Something has come up that needs your immediate attention. When I heard the Walkers were unable to see to Miss Barnett, I decided it would be best if I came personally."

Elyssa did not know if she was more confused or angry. She could easily see that the two men did not get along, and she could definitely understand why George had such strong feelings against him.

George raked his hand through his hair. He knew that to argue with his superior in front of Elyssa would not put him in a good light, but he did not want to give up this opportunity of being with Elyssa!

"Look, Denton. Whatever they need, certainly it can wait. Elyssa and I have the next three days planned out for us."

Will raised his eyebrows at that comment. "I am sorry to have to spoil your social life, George, but this is work and you are being paid to work. The company jet is at the airport this very moment waiting for you. I suggest you get a bag packed and set out immediately."

George let out a frustrated breath and looked over to Elyssa. "I'm sorry, Elyssa. Maybe next time. I'll try to make it quick."

"Sure, George. Thanks for everything you did."

He nodded and then turned to Denton, giving him a livid scowl before stomping out.

Both pair of eyes watched Westham, each somewhat reluctant to turn to the other, now that they were the only two in the room. Will finally turned his eyes back to Elyssa, who was now looking down and biting her upper lip.

"Miss Barnett... Elyssa, I am sorry to have barged in this way. I know I'm the last person you wanted to see, but when I heard the circumstances, I felt I needed to come."

"Well you need not have bothered, Mr. Denton. I can manage quite well on my own!"

"You were on your way out?"

Elyssa gave a sarcastic laugh as she looked over at the immaculately dressed man in his designer suit. At least she was fairly certain it was a designer suit. *Was it Armani?* she wondered. "Yes we were. We were going out to visit a preschool Janet worked at."

"I've got my driver here. He'll be happy to take us."

"Us?" she asked, looking incredulously at him.

Will looked away and then back at her. "I was hoping..." He paused and seemed unable to go on.

Elyssa shook her head adamantly and let out a sarcastic laugh. "You cannot possibly go!" she said pointedly to him.

"Excuse me?"

"Dressed like that. Can you imagine what these children would think seeing someone like you walk in?"

"Why? What's with these children?"

Elyssa rolled her eyes and closed them, shaking her head. "It's a preschool for underprivileged children, Mr. Denton."

"It's Will."

"Will." She had a very bad taste in her mouth as she spoke his name. "They have very little and it would just not be in good taste for you to show up dressed as you are."

"We'll stop by the hotel on the way, then, and I'll change. Would you agree to that?"

"You really do not need to do this."

"I insist on it."

Elyssa let out a frustrated sigh, seeing his refusal to yield. "If you insist on tagging along, I suppose you best change then," Elyssa said disdainfully.

Will held the door open for her, watched as she picked up the piñata and walked past him with an air of irritation, and then closed the door snugly behind them. They walked out toward the parking area and Elyssa could not prevent a gasp from escaping.

"Is there a problem?" Will asked.

"I am not quite sure you want to drive *that* into the part of town where we will be going!" she said as she pointed to the new shiny black car. It was not quite a stretch limousine, but a limousine it was.

Now it was Will's turn to roll his eyes as he wondered what he had willingly allowed himself to get into.

"It is perfectly good transportation!"

"Not when you're going where we're going!" She inhaled slowly to calm herself. "Look, Mr. Denton… Will… I don't think this is going to work out. Obviously you rarely come down here and when you do, you most likely stick to your office and hotel. Am I correct?"

Will shifted uncomfortably. "Look, I am only trying to do my best to make your time here a little easier. This is the car that I happen to use when I'm in Guatemala."

She was tempted to tell this man with too much money on his hands and no clue as to how the real world lived to just go back to Chicago and let her finish her task alone. Another more appealing idea, however, came to her mind. She would absolutely love to see how Mr. Denton handled himself in an environment like the one where they were about to head.

She smiled. "Does your driver know the way to Casa de Esperanza preschool?"

He looked over to his driver, Manuel, who was standing within earshot. Giving him a questioning glance, Manuel nodded his head. "She is correct, Sir. If that is where we are going, we best take another car."

"See if you can get one from the Walkers, Manuel."

Manuel sprinted off to the Walkers, and in a few moments he returned with a set of keys jingling in his fingers. "The Walkers said we could take their extra car, Mr. Denton. They'll use their van to get around if they need it."

"If it has to be, let's get started."

"Their car is over here, Mr. Denton."

Manuel spoke with a Guatemalan accent and Elyssa smiled at him. So this was how the great Mr. Denton got around when he was here; a man to drive him and interpret for him, all in one. They both followed Manuel and Elyssa caught up to him, introducing herself.

"Hello, Manuel. I'm Elyssa Barnett."

"Nice to meet you, Miss Barnett. I am told you are Janet's sister. We all liked her very much. We were sorry to have lost her and Chad."

"I appreciate that, Manuel."

"Manuel, we're going back to the hotel first so I can change." Will increased his pace and his stride and easily caught up with them.

"Sure thing, Sir!"

Manuel unlocked the car doors and opened the door to the back seat for Elyssa. She slid in and thanked him, looking curiously over to Will as Manuel then came around and opened the back door on the other side for him.

She placed the piñata conveniently between the two of them and looked out the window away from him so he would not see her roll her eyes. He obviously had this mentality that Manuel was the chauffeur so he had to ride in the back seat, even if this wasn't their limo!

They hadn't been in the car more than a few minutes when Will pulled out his mobile phone. He made a call and informed the person at the other end that he would like to be informed of the results of the sales report as soon as it was completed. As he talked, Elyssa entertained herself by watching the scenery pass by and trying to imagine how she would fare living down here and having to drive these chaotic streets. It gave her a greater respect for her sister accomplishing such a feat!

By the time they arrived at the hotel, Will had made three phone calls. With each call he made, Elyssa's ire rose as her assessment of him was being completely confirmed. He was a man whose sole objective in life, whose only source of satisfaction, was in his work. Forget that Guatemala was a beautiful country with flowers one would never see in the States. Forget that the hillsides were so green because of all the rain. Forget that the volcano was sending out secret messages in its plume of steam. He seemed completely oblivious to it all.

Stopping at the front of the hotel, Manuel came around to open the door and Will hopped out. He inquired of Elyssa if she'd prefer to wait in the car or come up to the room. As much as her curiosity tempted her to see what his opulent room must look like, she opted to remain with Manuel in the car.

Once he was out of sight, Elyssa opened her door. Manuel quickly ran around to help her out.

"There is no need for that, Manuel. I let myself in and out of cars all the time."

"It is my job, ma'am."

"I know, and I appreciate that." A sly smile crossed her face. "Would you mind, Manuel, if I rode up in the front with you?"

His eyes widened in surprise. "Up front?"

"I should like to get to know you better and as Mr. Denton seems inclined to only carry on conversations with his phone, I would enjoy it so much more."

Manuel smiled. "I am not sure if my boss would approve."

Elyssa propped her hands onto her hips. "Would he not wish for you to do all that I ask?"

"I think so, yes."

"Good! It's settled, then," Elyssa said as she opened the passenger side of the front door. "This is what will make me happy!"

Manuel laughed under his breath as he rushed over to assist her in getting in, wondering just what his boss would say when he returned.

Elyssa was amazed at how quickly Will reappeared. His long legs carried him swiftly to the car, and Elyssa watched him through the side mirror as he came to a halt when he realized she was seated in the front. She could not prevent the smile that came across her lips.

Manuel opened the door for him and he slid in. "So, Elyssa, do you have a problem with motion sickness that requires you to sit in the front?"

She turned to look at him with a furrowed brow. "No, Mr. Denton. I just wanted some conversation and I think Manuel is just the one to provide me with it!"

Will began a retort, but was halted by the ringing of his phone. The look Elyssa gave him with her sharply raised eyebrow said more to him than any words she could have spoken.

As they drove to the preschool, two conversations were being carried on. The one in the front seat between Elyssa and Manuel dealt with their families and interests. Elyssa enjoyed getting to better know this man who was a husband and father of four children. The conversation in the back seat of the car dealt with sales figures, profits and losses, and a sundry of other business particulars.

When they arrived at the preschool, Elyssa directed a sly grin at Will when he inadvertently gave it away that he had not been paying any attention to where they were going. He had just finished his call and put his phone away when he looked out the window.

The street was filled with buildings -- if you could call them that -- propped up and supported with any piece of metal or sheeting that could be found. Many were vacated and boarded up, and it made you wonder whether people lived in them. Small children dressed in ragged, dirty clothes, observed them curiously with their dark, wide eyes as they pulled over to park. There was a stench in the air that permeated everything.

Will's eyes flashed as he looked out. "Would someone please tell me just exactly where we are and what in blazes are we doing here?"

Chapter 6

Manuel looked back at his boss, attempting to remain dignified and not give in to the smile that was threatening to escape. "La Casita de Esperanza."

"*This* is the preschool? What is that dreadful stench?"

"The dump, Sir. It is just a few blocks away. Most of the people who live around here survive by sifting through the dump and using whatever they can find in whatever way possible. They keep some of their treasures or try to sell it or recycle it. Depends on how vigilant you are in retrieving the stuff after the trucks dump it."

Elyssa looked in awe at Manuel. "And the children?"

"They've learned that's their survival, too."

Elyssa had no idea. The tightness within her belly rivaled the pain she felt in hearing of Janet's death.

Manuel was quickly out of the car, but both Elyssa and Will had opened their doors. Elyssa gave a sly glance at Manuel who only shrugged his shoulders at observing Will letting himself out of the car.

"Let's get inside," Will ordered. "I don't want to dawdle out here any longer than I have to."

Elyssa could see that he was uncomfortable, but she had to admit that she was, too. She had hoped that his coming with her today would make him ill at ease and she had succeeded. She had to admit, though, that anyone would feel that way coming down here and seeing the way the people lived. It wasn't so much being afraid for herself, but the wrenching pain deep inside knowing that people had to live this way.

Manuel retrieved the large piñata from the car and hopped up the steps, ringing the bell outside a heavy wooden door. As they waited for the door to be opened, Will glanced up and down the street. Elyssa wondered if he felt he might be some sort of target for thieves. She had to stifle a laugh as she considered how he would have felt if he had worn his expensive designer suit and they had come in the limo.

The door was opened and a small woman peered out. Manuel addressed her in Spanish and she opened the door, letting them enter.

Bowing slightly as they came into a reception area, she uttered an, "Un momento, por favor," and stepped out through a door. Elyssa looked around her and saw a small table with crafts that the children made in the corner of the room. Elyssa walked over to it and picked up one at a time, looking closely at each one and then setting it back down in another place.

Will watched her curiously, as she did not seem to be setting them back down randomly. Instead, she seemed to be purposely rearranging the whole table display. He was about to say something to her but was prevented in doing so when another woman returned to the room.

"Good morning and welcome to Casita de Esperanza," she said with a slight Hispanic accent as she came toward them. She took Elyssa's hands in hers. "You must be Janet's sister."

Elyssa nodded. "Yes, I am Elyssa Barnett."

"It is indeed a pleasure to meet you. I am Rosa Martinez." She turned to Will. "And you are Mr. Barnett?"

Will quickly shook his head and stammered, "No, no, my name is William Denton, an… an acquaintance."

"I'm glad you have come. Shelley Walker called to let us know you would be coming this morning. The children are looking forward to it as well. We'll take you through each of the classrooms and let the children sing a song for you and then once you've done that, the children will come out to the courtyard and have a great deal of fun with that piñata you brought."

Looking at Will, she said, "That was so thoughtful of you. The children will love it!"

Elyssa looked derisively at him. George was the one who deserved the thanks for the idea of the piñata and he knew it!

As they walked out, Elyssa asked Mrs. Martinez about the children that came to the preschool.

"They all live within a few blocks of here. Two years ago several local people felt that something needed to be done for the children that lived around here. This preschool was built to give the children an opportunity to learn and play in a more positive environment."

"The parents must be most grateful!" she exclaimed.

Mrs. Martinez drew a pensive look about her. "You would think so. But unfortunately, some don't even allow their children to attend because that takes precious time away from their only source of family income."

"Sifting through the dump?" Elyssa was horrified.

Mrs. Martinez nodded.

"I cannot imagine!"

"It is difficult to comprehend, and yet these children know nothing else, so to them it is normal." She smiled. "The children are as precious as any you will find. I am sure you will discover that for yourselves.

As they walked through the hall, Elyssa was amazed at how colorful and bright everything was -- and clean, too! They came to the first classroom and the children all wore brightly colored smocks over their tattered and worn clothes. The teacher said something to the children in Spanish and they all looked at Elyssa with wide eyes and sad looks upon their faces.

Manuel, who had joined them, informed Elyssa the children had been told that she was Janet's sister.

It was apparent the teacher did not speak any English, so her attention remained on the children. She had them stand and they sang a song. As they did, Elyssa was amazed at how well behaved they were. They had a joy in their faces that belied their living conditions. She snuck a glance up to Will to see how he was faring. He stood rigid and expressionless, almost as if his thoughts were elsewhere. Elyssa swallowed hard as she made a vain attempt to keep the tears from pooling up in her eyes and she knew their time here was only just beginning.

There were four classrooms and each was the same. They each had a song prepared. One class had made a large card that read, *"To Janet's sister, We are sorry. We loved Janet very much!"* and was signed by each one of them in large, scribbled letters. It was obvious that the teacher had written out the words in English. Elyssa was touched to think that Janet had made some sort of difference in these children's lives; children who lived in conditions that she would never be able to fathom and yet they seemed surprisingly content.

When they went out to the courtyard, Manuel had hung the piñata and the children squealed when they saw it. The children sat down on the benches that lined the courtyard from youngest to oldest and Mrs. Martinez brought out a large stick. The children wiggled and squirmed in eager expectation and Elyssa openly admired each one.

One by one, the children were blindfolded and given the opportunity to give a few swings at the large, papier-mâché bird. Manuel, who must have done this dozens of time before, pulled the string to which the piñata was attached to make it swing wildly and rise up high off the ground.

Will stood off to one side. It seemed to Elyssa that he was busy looking at everything but the children. She watched as he pulled out his phone and stepped around the corner of the building. She shook her head in disgust as she realized he allowed his work to interfere with every moment of his waking hours. Most likely he was asking for a car to be sent to pick him up as quickly as possible!

Elyssa sat down and once the children had taken their turn swinging at the piñata, they came over to her; some more tentative than others. A few climbed right into her lap, others touched her long, pretty hair, and a few simply stood back timidly and watched.

After a while, Will finally returned and Elyssa watched him walk over to a bench across the courtyard from her, sitting down next to the last child in the line. Elyssa had to laugh when he unexpectedly found himself the object of unwanted attention as children began to climb up into his lap, much like they had hers. She waited for him to shoo them away and remove himself from their midst, but instead, he leaned down to talk to them, tickled them, or simply held their hand.

Elyssa continued to watch in amazement as he pulled out a pair of sunglasses from his pocket and put them on a little boy. The children around him began to giggle and laugh, and soon they all wanted to try them on. He passed them around from one to the other, getting the same gleeful response from each child. Elyssa wondered if they were an expensive pair, as his actions totally surprised her.

Her attention was drawn back to the piñata, which was becoming more and more tattered, but still holding tight to its treasures. As the older children were now the ones taking swings at it, Manuel maneuvered the ropes to a greater extent to make it more difficult for them to hit it. The piñata swung high and low and from side to side. Elyssa hoped that all the children would get a chance to take a swing. She was certain each child wanted a turn, but she was amazed at how they cheered each one on and waited patiently for their own opportunity to break it open.

One of the last, older boys gave the stick a hefty swing, striking the piñata full force and it broke open, spilling candy and little toys all over. Suddenly all attention was drawn to the center of the courtyard where the children scrambled for whatever their little hands could gather. Elyssa walked over to make sure each child was able to get some treasure of their own. When she looked up over the crowd of children, she saw a little girl off to the side standing by Will.

The little girl seemed hesitant to throw herself into the melee. Elyssa was about to go see to her when Will suddenly picked her up and said something to her. The little girl nodded her head shyly and he walked into the crowd of children with her, reaching down and picking up a handful of candy and toys that had not yet been claimed.

Holding tightly to the priceless treasures, he walked back over to the bench with her and sat down. When he opened his hand, the little girl reached for something immediately. It was a pink plastic toy ring. She slipped it on one of her fingers and looked up at Will and smiled. She held out her hand as if it was the most beautiful thing she had ever seen.

After admiring it for some time, she tentatively reached into his hand for one of the pieces of candy, tore off the wrapper and ate it, remaining perfectly content in his lap.

Elyssa observed this all with conflicting messages assaulting her. He could not behave like this! He was not that type of man! She had expected him to come here and be appalled by what he saw and withdraw, wanting nothing to do with these children. She had half expected him to wait out in the reception area of the school. The last thing she anticipated was for him to take to the children as he seemed to have done.

Once every little toy and piece of candy had been claimed and snatched up, the children all returned to the benches to assess and enjoy their bounty. Elyssa's attention was drawn back to some of the other children coming up to her to show her their treasures. The joy the children had was contagious and she found herself enjoying herself more than she had in a long time. Even though she spoke very little of their language, she easily conveyed to them how special each one was with her engaging smile.

When it was time for the children to return to their classes, even though they had been with the children for barely an hour, Elyssa found herself reluctant to part with them. There were several children who had easily wound their way into her heart and she realized she really didn't want to leave. As she leaned over to give hugs to the children or clasp their little hands in hers, she looked across the courtyard to see how Will was faring. She saw that the little girl was still happily seated upon his lap, but his attention was not on his new friend. It was riveted back upon her.

As the children proceeded to line up and bid farewell, Will placed the little girl on the ground in front of him. He leaned over and whispered something in her ear. Elyssa watched as the little girl's eyes lit up, giving him an enthusiastic nod, and then she ran to find her place with the other children.

Even more difficult than leaving the children was stepping back outside the walls of this haven and realizing these little ones only spent a few mornings of the week here for only a few years of their life. Elyssa, Will, and Manuel all walked out in mutual silence; unable to formulate the words to describe what each was feeling.

Manuel opened both the front and back seat door. Before getting into the front seat, Elyssa stole a look at Will who was looking up and down the street. Could he possibly be wondering how these children lived here and whether they had any sort of hope for the future? Or was he merely concerned that they stood out and might become easy targets for some unsavory character?

Elyssa looked back at La Casita de Esperanza, *Little House of Hope*. Maybe there was a little bit of hope that existed within these walls for them. She had to trust that there was.

~~*

As they drove away, Will said something to Manuel that sounded like a Spanish name. Manuel responded with a, "Yes, Sir."

Before long, Manuel was pulling to a stop in front of a restaurant, bearing what she assumed was the name Will had spoken.

"What are we doing here?" Elyssa asked.

"Having lunch. It is way past lunchtime and I am hungry!"

"You don't have to..."

Will put up a hand to stop her. "I know I don't, but I am. So there will be no discussion about it."

Elyssa's eyes darkened as she saw traces of the William Denton she had heard so much about begin to emerge.

Manuel had already jumped out of the car and was opening the doors for them. Elyssa found herself walking reluctantly at Will's side. At least she had Manuel to keep her company.

The outside of the restaurant was rather drab and Elyssa thought it odd that Will would come here, but when they walked inside, Elyssa could not believe her eyes. It was filled with tall plants, beautiful flowers, and exotic birds that flew in a large, glassed-in aviary at one end of the room.

The host greeted Will by name and soon they were walking to a small table. He held out the seat for Elyssa and she sat down. When she looked around her, Manuel was gone.

Will ordered *agua pura* for the two of them and two bottled waters were brought to their table along with some chips and salsa. Elyssa looked across the table at Will. "What about Manuel?"

"He's eating on his own."

"But why?" Elyssa asked with an accusatory stare.

"Because that's the way it is. It's what he expects as well as prefers." He looked down to his menu. "Now, everything is good here. It's written in Spanish and English so you can pretty much know what you're getting."

"Do you come here a lot when you're down here?"

"I make every effort to come here at least once each visit."

Elyssa narrowed her eyes. "And just how often do you come down to Guatemala?"

He looked up from the menu, his eyes just peering over the top into hers. "Is this an interrogation?"

"No, I was just under the impression that you didn't come down to Guatemala that often."

"I guess how often I come down is a relative issue. For some, I probably come down too often and for others, not often enough."

The waiter returned and Will ordered something in well spoken Spanish. When they both looked to Elyssa, she looked back at the menu and shook her head. "I really don't know."

"Make it two of them, Miguel."

"Sí, Señor Denton."

With an arched eyebrow, Elyssa asked, "So what am I getting?"

Without any hesitation, Will replied, "Sautéed tongue wrapped in a deep fried tortilla smothered in cheese and salsa."

Elyssa's eyes widened. "No!" she exclaimed. "I will not eat that!"

"Good," he replied, taking his napkin in hand and placing it in his lap. "More for me."

Elyssa folded her hands in front of her and scrutinized the man sitting across from her. She was unsure whether he was teasing or not. There was a look in his eyes that she could not describe, but since he had not the slightest trace of a smile, she felt she should take him at his word. The thought of sautéed tongue, however, did not sit well with her. She decided if she was going to ease her hunger pangs, she would have to do it with the chips they brought.

Will seemed content to sit quietly and occasionally pick up a chip, drown it in the salsa, and pop it in his mouth. Elyssa practically devoured them; she had never tasted chips so fresh and tasty. The salsa was perfection; not too mild, but not too hot.

"Hold your horses, Elyssa! Save some room for your lunch!"

"I think perhaps this *is* my lunch!" she retorted.

His lips broke into a small smile, revealing for a short moment, a small dimple on his cheek. "You'll enjoy it. Trust me."

When they brought the order, Elyssa looked it over. It certainly looked delicious, but she was hesitant to try it. Will turned his attention to his food and Elyssa watched him cut into the filled tortilla on his plate.

"Mmmm," he replied in an exaggerated way when he looked up and saw Elyssa watching. He looked down to his plate and finally said, "It's not tongue, Elyssa. It's shredded beef. I really didn't think you would believe me."

She was greatly relieved and took a bite. It was heavenly, but she was reluctant to admit that to Will. Instead, she concentrated on her food.

Will appeared perfectly content to forego any further conversation in lieu of eating. Elyssa was not usually one to eat in silence. She loved to talk with people and get to know them. She loved to discuss the latest books she had read or music she had listened to. It seemed as though something was holding her back. She wondered if she still blamed him for her sister's death, although she really had not thought about that at all since the preschool.

Well, if he doesn't want to talk, that's fine with me, she thought.

At length, it was Will who started the conversation.

"What did you think back there at the preschool?"

She looked at him and wondered if he truly wanted to hear her thoughts or was he merely making polite conversation. "I applaud what they are doing. It's heartbreaking to think the children don't know life isn't supposed to be that way." She felt a wave of sadness come over her and fought off the tears that were threatening to spill out. "It… it makes me ashamed of how much we have and how little contentment it gives us. Those children had such pure joy!"

Will looked up at her. He felt the same way, but had not known how to articulate it. He felt the shame in a greater degree, knowing how much more he had than even Elyssa. His successful business, the homes, private jet, and every convenience available had not given him the contentment he felt was so lacking. He had wondered whether that kind of contentment was even attainable.

Elyssa believed his silence to be from the lack of any sort of feeling that may have been produced there. She decided to broach the subject she had been wondering about since being at the preschool.

"I must confess I was surprised to see how well you took to the children. You seemed to be able to reach that shy little girl. What is it, Will? Do you have a secret life with a wife and a dozen children somewhere?"

He put his fork down on his plate and picked up his napkin, wiping his mouth. Waving his hand in the air he said, "Nothing so dramatic. I have a younger sister. She is almost twelve years younger than me and has always been quite shy herself. I merely treated that little girl as I often treated Gina."

"Oh." She wanted to hear more about this sister of his, but was prevented from saying anymore when his phone rang.

"Excuse me, Elyssa. I am expecting a call from the national office."

He pulled his phone out and stood up, turning to walk toward the front of the restaurant as he brought it up to his ear. Suddenly all those warm and fuzzy feelings that had begun to surface began dissipating as she reminded herself who he was and what he represented. Life with a man like him would take a second seat to his business; his family would suffer at the expense of some deadline, meeting, or crucial decision that had to be made. He obviously was one who could not leave his work at the office. It went with him everywhere he did.

When he returned, he noticed instantly her change in demeanor. Sitting down, he asked her, "Is everything OK?"

"Yes, I think it is, now." She could not help but think that if she had judged the man by what she had seen today, her thinking could have been swayed in favor of him despite everything about him that disgusted her.

"What about you? Is everything OK? Was that the call you were expecting?"

"Yes. The news isn't quite what I wanted to hear, but things are progressing. I need to get back to the office here to fax the national office some things. We'll drop you and the car off first."

Elyssa only nodded, but was surprised by his next comment.

"So what was it that you had planned for tomorrow?"

Her eyes widened and she looked at him suspiciously. "Excuse me?"

"George said you had made plans for the next few days. What were your plans for tomorrow?"

She thought for a moment. "I think he was going to take me to Antigua to see the ruins."

"Then Antigua it is. We'll come by around 10:00 in the morning. Does that sound reasonable?"

Elyssa's mouth was suddenly dry as she eked out a measly, "Yes. I suppose that would be fine."

Chapter 7

Elyssa returned to the townhouse, still trying to reconcile the Will she saw today and the Will she had known about for the past two years. While she knew she should focus on her task of going through Chad and Janet's belongings, she paced about the living room. Her feelings fluctuated as she recalled his arrogance at the wedding rehearsal dinner and reception two years ago. As she considered the glimpses she caught today of a man who actually had shown an ability to care, she found it increasingly difficult to hold on to her resolve never to forgive him for sending Chad and Janet here, ultimately leading to the accident that took their lives.

Folding her arms in front of her and going to the window to look out, she could not decry the accommodations Chad and Janet had while they lived here. It was simply beautiful and they had everything they could have wanted. From all she had heard, Janet had been content here. She had been happy and had made the most of everything.

She walked over to their bedroom and stood at the door. Looking in, she felt she was not yet ready to step over the threshold to begin going through their more personal things. Perhaps she would tackle it tomorrow afternoon when they returned from Antigua.

Looking inside the master bedroom from the frame of the door, she saw a picture of the two of them over their bed. She tentatively took a few steps in to get a better look. In it, they were surrounded by beautiful, large flowers. She was sure it had been taken somewhere here in Guatemala. She glanced about her and knew that there would be things in this room that she would want to take home with her; things that didn't really have monetary value, but purely sentimental value. At the moment, however, she was not ready to sort through the things in this very personal sanctuary of her sister who was now gone.

A knock at the door interrupted her musings. Walking into the living room, she saw Shelley Walker through the open door. Elyssa went over and opened the screen door, inviting her in.

"Hello, Shelley."

"Hi, Elyssa. When Manuel returned our car, I knew you had come home. How did your day go?"

"It was incredible."

"That preschool is something, isn't it?"

Elyssa nodded. "I had no idea."

"Janet loved going there. She only hoped that the little time she could devote there would make a difference in at least one small child's life."

Elyssa sighed. "She was always that way, wanting to help out someone who was hurting, take in some stray or lost animal, or just be there to listen." A single tear appeared in Elyssa's eye and trailed down her face, prompting her to quickly wipe it away. "Do you have some time to talk?"

"Why do you think I came by?"

Elyssa and Shelley talked for a good part of the afternoon. Most of it dealt with Chad and Janet. Elyssa was grateful for the insight Shelley had on their life in Guatemala. She appreciated the light she shed on how happy Chad and Janet seemed together.

At one point, the conversation drifted to William Denton.

"I don't know him well at all, Shelley. Just what kind of man is he?"

Shelley looked intently at Elyssa. "He is a man of integrity. He demands it from all of us. I heard there was some incident recently regarding one of the employees that really had him steaming mad. I don't know who it was or what they did, but Will quickly took care of things."

"In what way?"

"I really don't know. One of his greatest dictates regarding Pemberleo Coffee's employees is respect and privacy. If he hears any gossip, it infuriates him, particularly gossip about him or his family." She took a sip of coffee and then continued. "I would imagine that's because he is such a private person. He doesn't want talk of him or anyone else being bandied about."

"I have heard his whole life is Pemberleo Coffee; that he lives and breathes it. Is that true?"

"Well, I can't say whether his whole life is Pemberleo Coffee, but I know he puts a lot into it. He's actually kind of a mystery to most of us. Even Chad, who was his best friend in college, was concerned about how little Will ever got out. What he does with his time I can't conjecture. Sometimes he just disappears. Whether he's locked up in his office working twenty-four seven or jet setting about the globe, is something that only he really knows."

When their conversation ended, Shelley invited Elyssa to join them for dinner that night. She agreed, as she was eager for lively companionship. She was grateful to be able to spend that evening with the Walkers and their guests. She hadn't enjoyed herself as much in months.

Elyssa went to bed that night trying to figure Will Denton out. In attempting to rationally evaluate his character, she was dismayed to discover that she might be vulnerable to him if he continued to behave as he did today. His compassion for the children, particularly that little girl, had touched Elyssa's heart.

However, all she had to do was recall the rude behaviour that she had been witness to, and his dealings with George Westham, and she was fairly sure she would be able to keep her head on her shoulders and view him as she should.

He was the same sort of man as her father's boss, who pushed his employees beyond what was reasonable for the sake of the company. As he apparently had no family other than a much younger sister, he would not put a high priority on the time others would want to spend with their loved ones.

She finally drifted off to sleep after repeatedly and most vehemently reminding herself who the man, William Denton, was and what he stood for.

~~*

The next morning Will arrived promptly at ten. When he walked in, Elyssa felt a most disconcerting flutter as he strode past her dressed in a crisp muted pastel shirt and slacks. His aftershave wafted across her nose and she looked away, suddenly wishing he was a short, overweight, ogre of a man who smelled like disgusting body odor. She had to make a determined effort to ignore the effect he was having on her senses.

"Good morning, Elyssa. Are you ready?"

She nonchalantly gave him a nod of greeting and murmured an affirmative, looking around her for her purse while he stood patiently waiting.

"Here it is." She picked it up and he walked her to the door.

They walked out to the parking area and Elyssa noticed Manuel standing next to a nice sedan, instead of the limo.

"Good day, Miss Elyssa! How are you today?"

"I am fine, Manuel. How are you?" Elyssa answered cheerfully. She looked over at Shelley Walker, who was just walking over. "Good morning, Shelley," she called and waved.

It did not escape Will's notice how different her greeting was to them than it had been to him.

"Good morning, Elyssa," Shelley replied. "Good morning, Will."

Will nodded at her. "Good morning, Shelley."

Shelley looked at Elyssa. "Are you all set to step back in time and spend a little money?"

"Spend some money?" Elyssa asked.

"Ah, yes. Some of the finer stores are located in Antigua. If you want any jade jewelry, this is the place to buy it."

"Thanks for letting me know, Shelley. I'll keep my eyes open."

They walked toward the sedan and Manuel opened the back door, waving his hand toward the car for Elyssa to step in.

Elyssa looked at him and then back to Will, who was eyeing her also, curious as to whether she would again insist upon sitting up front. While she certainly did not cling to this whole "chauffeur" arrangement, she obligingly slid into the back seat, joined by Will.

They drove away from the apartment complex and within a few minutes, Will's phone rang.

He briefly looked to Elyssa and offered what seemed to be a sincere and regretful, "Excuse me."

Elyssa turned her head to look out the window on her side of the car. She took in a frustrated breath as she heard only his end of the conversation.

"Can't your find who owns it? Well do what you can. I really want this! No, that is not acceptable… Have Marlowe get on it then. I don't care if the weekend is coming up. I want a contract and this finalized before I leave Guatemala!"

Elyssa's eyes widened as she continued to look away from him. As he issued his orders, she thought of all the family members of these people who would suffer because of his demands. It reminded her just how much her family suffered at her father's long hours at work to comply with the orders of his demanding boss. She was sure the intense stress he was under contributed to her father's heart attack and most likely all for a measly increase in profits!

A fleeting thought crossed her mind that sent shivers up and down her spine. Could Chad have been tired when he was driving the night of the accident because Will demanded he put in extra hours? Was he in a rush to return to Guatemala City from the lake because of Will's insistence? She stole a glance at him as he raked his fingers through his hair in frustration at something that was being said to him. Looking up in the rear view mirror, she caught Manuel's eye. He gave his head a minuscule shake and shrugged his shoulders slightly.

She turned her attention back to the scenery as they drove through Guatemala City. Looking out the window on Will's side, she noticed that the volcano was now in sight and a steady stream of smoke trailed out. Each time she had seen this sight, it didn't cease to impress her. *How often*, she thought, *does a person get to see an active volcano?* But it obviously meant nothing to Will as he seemed solely intent on dealing with his business, oblivious to the scenery passing by, and certainly not inclined to carry on any sort of conversation with her.

The drive to Antigua passed quickly for Elyssa as Manuel provided a more entertaining distraction from the front seat than listening to Will's end of the phone conversation in the back seat.

Sensing Elyssa's frustration with her back seat partner, Manuel began giving her a brief history of Antigua, which at one point had been the seat of Spanish colonial government. Several major earthquakes destroyed the city in 1773.

By the time they reached Antigua, Will had completed several phone calls. Elyssa noticed the tightening of his jaw as he turned away from her and stared out the window. If Elyssa had learned how to read men at all, she knew his body language was telling her he was not happy with something.

She cared little about the demeanor of the man next to her, as the cobblestone roads, old buildings and ruins, and the Agua volcano outside the window captured her attention. The main street was lined with little shops that were most inviting. She was determined to embrace this charming town and try to forget her pain and grief for a short time! He could stay behind in the car for all she cared, with his scowl, his thoughts, and his blasted cell phone.

No, she mused as an afterthought. It was most likely a satellite phone as he seemed to have constant accessibility wherever they were. She groaned inwardly as she considered that with that phone there would be very few places he could go where he wouldn't be able to easily connect with the office and his *Pemberleo Coffee* world.

Manuel found a parking space on the street and adeptly pulled into it. He turned off the motor, removed the key, and turned back towards them. "If you walk up this street, you'll find the best shops. Up at the end you'll find the restored palace, although it is not as grand as the original. Down the side street in that direction you will find the ruins of Las Capuchinas, a convent. If you walk through any ruins at all, these are the ones to see."

"Thank you, Manuel." Elyssa looked over at Will who had unbuckled his seat belt and without saying a word opened the door and stepped out. Before Manuel had even had the chance, Will walked around and opened Elyssa's door.

"You didn't have to do that," she said a little more defensively than she liked.

"I know," was all he said.

Elyssa raised one of her fine brows in surprise. *He certainly doesn't want to tag along with me again, does he?* she wondered to herself. She looked back at Manuel and gave him a questioning look which was answered by a bemused smile and a raised eyebrow of his own.

Elyssa began walking toward the rows of shops with Will walking alongside. Neither had spoken a word since getting out of the car. She felt weighed down by his presence and could not make herself understand why he was so intent on remaining at her side.

They came to a jewelry store and both stopped simultaneously to look in the window. The display of jade items was beautiful.

"Shall we go in?" Will asked.

"Yes," Elyssa answered. "I would like that."

They walked in and were greeted in by an American clerk behind the counter. "May I help you?"

"You're an American!" Elyssa was surprised.

"Yes! I'm here for a year living with a family and learning to speak the language. This job gives me practice, but I do so enjoy helping an English speaking person. Can I show you something?"

"I would like to look around a little first," Elyssa answered.

Elyssa walked away from Will and was amused to hear the young girl gush over him. "I would be more than happy to help *you* find something."

"I think I would like to browse, too, thank you."

That didn't seem to stop the young girl from coming out from behind the counter and standing closely at his side. Elyssa chuckled as she saw her look at him most admiringly. Elyssa turned her attention to the display in front of her, but easily overheard the conversation.

"Are you interested in buying something for your wife over there?"

"Uh, no. She is not my wife."

"Oh, I see. A gift for your girlfriend then?"

"No, she's... no, thank you."

Elyssa thought he sounded somewhat abrupt and soon the young girl returned to her place behind the counter. The salesgirl didn't cease gazing at him, giving him a hopeful smile each time he looked in her direction.

Elyssa shook her head at the poor girl's instant infatuation. Her gaze drifted over to Will, and she had to admit he was truly a handsome man. He was tall and had a lean, sturdy build. His dark curly hair framed his face and complimented his dark eyes. When she thought about it, the young girl had every reason to be infatuated with him. At least with his outward appearance.

If you only knew what he was really like! she thought to herself. She turned back to look at the jade and grit her teeth tightly together. *He may be handsome,* she thought, *but he has to be the most inconsiderate and arrogant man I have ever met!*

Elyssa turned her attention back to the display of jade and finally saw a pair of oval drop earrings that she liked and that were reasonably priced. She noticed that Will was also making a purchase on the other side of the store.

When she had paid for her earrings and joined him, she inquired about his purchase. "You didn't buy that jade letter opener I saw, did you? I was tempted, but couldn't bring myself to pay the price."

"As a matter of fact, I did not."

"Then it certainly had to be the pen holder. I am sure it will add just the right touch to your desk."

"No," he answered, a smile twisting upon his lips, believing that her mocking of him was preferable to her just ignoring him.

"Then what? Please don't tell me it was a pair of jade cufflinks."

"No again. Nothing for myself."

"Then something for your new admirer?" Elyssa looked over at the young girl behind the counter. "I am sure she would be pleased with anything you bought her."

Will narrowed his eyes at Elyssa. The intensity of his gaze made her shudder. She turned away as she realized that this man most likely had a volatile passion in both love and anger.

"Actually, I bought a little something for my sister."

His words surprised her and she looked back at him. The intensity she had just seen in him had suddenly and surprisingly been replaced with a look of tenderness. Rather than allowing herself to be drawn into that gaze, Elyssa thought this would be a good opportunity to find out more about his younger sister.

"Ah, your sister. Tell me about her."

"You want to hear about Gina?"

Elyssa nodded. They walked out of the store and continued up the street.

"Well, I think I mentioned to you that Gina is almost twelve years younger than me. Quite a surprise for my parents, I think." He let out a soft chuckle. "But a nice surprise. She has always been a real sweet girl. I couldn't have asked for a…" His voice trailed off as he realized what he was about to say. The last thing Elyssa needed to hear now was about how sweet a sister she was.

Unfortunately, he heard the catch in Elyssa's breath and was confident she knew what he was going to say. He quickly continued on. "In the fall Gina begins her first year at Stanford, in northern California. Just north of where you live, I believe."

"It's a real nice campus. And what is she majoring in?"

"Business Management."

"Of course, I should have guessed," Elyssa said. "Does she have plans to oust you and become the first woman president of Pemberleo Coffee?"

Will smiled. "I think not. While she hasn't outright said so, I believe her interests lay in a completely different field."

Hearing Will talk about his sister stirred her again. She could easily comprehend from his words and expression that he was fond of her.

Talk of Gina, however, was suspended as they came upon some of the old ruins. They were transported back hundreds of years walking through them.

After walking through several, Will waved his hand up the street.

"The convent is down this way. Did you wish to walk through it?"

"Yes I would like to."

When they came to the convent, they approached a small window outside where Will walked up and ordered two tickets. Elyssa began to reach for her wallet, but was stopped when Will firmly put his hand up. "I'll take care of this."

From the insistent look in his eyes, she knew she dared not argue with him.

When they walked inside the doors, they were greeted with a contrast of beautiful gardens and decaying ruins. Elyssa let her hand run along the dusty exterior of the building, imagining what it would have been like for a young woman to have lived in this convent and to dedicate her whole life to her faith.

They walked past novice cells that were not much larger than her kitchen at home. She paused at one and looked in the doorway, wondering what it would be like to forgo ever marrying. She suddenly wondered whether she would ever marry. Things did not look too promising at the moment.

She turned her head and saw Will pull out his phone and turn a corner. He was quickly out of sight. She shook her head and determined that if she ever were to have even a fleeting flutter of attraction for the man, to quickly extinguish it. He would never be able to completely leave his work at work!

Elyssa let out a long sigh and turned in the opposite direction. This place wasn't that big. She figured she would meet up with him again eventually.

Elyssa strolled about the ruins, peering in rooms and wondering what they had once been used for, what type of furniture had filled them, and what, if any, accessories decorated the place. She walked in and out of the beautiful gardens, breathing in the fragrant flowers and reveling in their bright colors.

Up ahead, she noticed a tour group and caught up with them. The tour guide spoke English and she listened attentively to his description of how life was here for the women. They came upon a large domed room and were told that historians were not really certain what it had been used for, but possibly for worship ceremonies.

The guide ushered everyone in and told them to spread themselves around the dome and against the wall. He then singled out a lady and had her whisper something to the person next to her. When she did, everyone on the other side of the room laughed.

"The acoustics in this room allow one to hear what someone is whispering on the other side!" He had a few others try it before he continued on.

"Now, if we have anyone here who can sing, we shall have a real treat, for the acoustics created by its domed shape will give it a beautiful rich sound!"

He looked around and everyone shook their head. "No singers? Certainly there must be one!"

Elyssa had taken singing lessons when she was younger, but felt awkward volunteering since she wasn't part of this touring group.

When no one volunteered, the guide asked again. This time, Elyssa meekly raised her hand. "I am not a part of your tour group, but if that doesn't matter, I could sing for you."

"Splendid!" the tour guide exclaimed. "Sing anything you like, but face toward the center."

Elyssa swallowed, moistening her mouth which now felt dry. She suddenly wondered what made her do such a thing as to volunteer to sing! Her mind swirled for a song and the only thing she could think of was hers and Janet's favorite song, *I Will Wait for You*, which she had recently sung at a Community Center Talent Night.

The song was from the movie, *Umbrellas of Cherbourg*, which she, Janet, and Charlene had watched late one night on television. Since none of the girls knew French, they had to read all the sub-titles as it was done completely in French and sung the whole way through. They cried at the end of the movie, but of course had to watch it several more times. They still cried each time it came to its same grievous ending.

She closed her eyes and lifted up a prayer, "Help me do this!"

As she began singing the words, she noticed the effect immediately. It was as if she was singing into a microphone and the sound monitor was reflecting her voice back to her. The dynamics of this domed room carried her pure voice in every direction. She opened her eyes to see everyone's eyes riveted upon her.

As she continued to sing, she thought how Janet would never have to wait for love anymore. She had found her love and was now with him for eternity. As she began to sing the chorus, she noticed Will walk into the domed room and look around, finally resting his eyes upon her.

Will had heard the singing off in the distance and was drawn to the angelic quality. When he came to the domed room, he had a difficult time discerning where the voice came from, as it seemed to pour forth from every point in the room. However, when he turned to follow everyone's gaze, he was amazed to find that it was Elyssa whose voice he heard.

As Elyssa finished the song, Will stood in awe, lost in the clarity and tone of her voice. The words haunted him as the song had been about having to wait for love!

The words seemed to radiate from Elyssa's heart and yet the words spoke of the condition of *his* heart toward *her*. He wondered whether she had any idea of his admiration. He could not tell her yet as she would not accept it... accept him. How long would *he* have to wait for her?

When Elyssa finished, there was much praise from everyone.

A gentleman standing next to Will turned to him and whispered, "Now that's one beautiful lady and one fine voice if you ask me."

Will nodded while keeping his eyes on Elyssa.

"I saw you with her. Is she your wife or a special lady?

Will turned to face the man and whispered rather abruptly, "No. I guess right now you could say she's a major project!"

Glancing back at Elyssa, he was met with fiery eyes.

He turned and walked out. The quality of her voice affected him. The words had stirred him. He greatly appreciated good music and now this was added to her appealing traits. He shook his head and scuffed the ground with his foot, asking himself why he had to fall for a woman who was so decidedly bitter towards him… a woman who would never be able to love him.

Elyssa finally walked out after accepting some words of appreciation from those in the group. "I'm ready to go," she said, and strode briskly and determinedly past him.

Chapter 8

The next day, Elyssa awoke with a heaviness in her heart. She attributed it to knowing that today she would finally have to sort through the things in Chad and Janet's room. She refused to credit Will's remark as having such an effect on her.

The words Will had used to describe what he was doing had hurt deeply, although she really wasn't sure why. *A major project!* That's what he called her. Just like drawing up the details for a merger or a business transaction, she was a major project!

Sure, he had complimented her on her singing. While driving home, Will praised her performance, but his words did little to ease the pain she felt because of his businesslike reference.

A frustrated huff escaped. She shouldn't care what he thought of her! Earlier, she had vowed never to allow herself to be captivated by this man.

He is certainly good looking, she warned herself. *But his charms,* she added with a laugh, *they are quite another matter.* She had no reason to fear being captivated by his charms because he had none!

She was grateful that today was one free day to spend without him. He had business this afternoon and most likely would not be stopping by. When they had returned from Antigua yesterday, Elyssa was anxious to bid him farewell and afterwards did not feel inclined to begin sorting through the bedroom and decided to put it off one more day. That major task still lay ahead of her.

She hoped that she'd finish going through the townhouse today and somehow she would be able to go to Lake Atitlan tomorrow. George had promised her he would take her. Now she wondered whether that would happen. Since she hadn't seen him since Will arrived and sent him away, she assumed his work in Colombia was keeping him busy.

She poured herself a freshly brewed cup of coffee and wrapped both her hands around the warm mug. As she took a sip, she smiled as she heard the birds noisily greet her. She walked over to the window and took great delight in watching the hummingbirds that made their appearance every morning visiting the plethora of flowers. Despite the feelings she had when she awakened, those things managed to soothe her unsettled spirits.

She finished her coffee and decided to take a shower before starting her task.

She felt much better when she stepped out of the shower and put on a pair of jeans and cool cotton shirt with short sleeves. She brushed out her hair and applied some light makeup. When she had finished, she looked up at herself and took a deep breath.

"Well," she said to her reflection in the mirror. "I guess the time has finally come! I can't put it off any longer."

Going to the door of Janet and Chad's room, she stood with her hands braced on either side for several moments, steeling herself for the inevitable. She knew she was behaving irrationally. She may not find anything here that would distress her. It was just that everything here would be so personal and she could almost feel Janet's presence. Coming into this room, she felt that Janet would walk in at any moment.

The first thing she did when she walked in was to take a closer look at the pictures on the walls. "Oh, Janet," she said aloud to herself, "You never did learn to group your pictures well." There were some framed prints as well as framed photographs haphazardly dotting the walls.

Elyssa walked up to the photograph of Chad and Janet that was mounted over the bed and found herself smiling. They were both peeking out from behind a large bougainvillea plant and were framed themselves in flowers. She took it off the wall and put it next to the box of things she would take home with her. It was too large to fit inside.

Inside the box, she placed several other pictures of the two of them. In went a small jewel box holding a few nice pieces of jewelry. She found a pile of books and sat down to begin looking through them, losing all track of time. She finally placed all of them in the give-away box, hoping someone here could use them.

There was a pile of papers on the night stand, and upon scrutiny, Elyssa decided they were not of any sentimental value or importance and crumbled them up in her hand. She went into the kitchen and retrieved the large trash can, bringing it back to the room and placing it next to her. She dropped the wad of papers inside.

Elyssa began opening the drawers of the dresser. The first drawer contained some folded knit blouses. Elyssa picked up the neatly stacked pile and brought it tightly up to her chest. Leaning her head down, she could barely discern the scent of Janet's favorite perfume. Her eyes closed as tears began to fill them.

She removed only one blouse that she had remembered Janet wearing and put the rest in a pile to give away. Going to the next drawer, she pulled out some sweaters. As her hands tucked under the sweaters to pull them out, something that had been placed underneath them caught her attention. She pulled it out and saw that it was a journal.

She felt a tremor pass through her and stood staring at it for several minutes before willing herself to open it. She knew that it would be emotionally difficult to read her sister's most personal thoughts. She would never have stolen into her sister's room before to sneak a peek into her diary or journal, although they always shared everything together. Now she harbored hopes that there might be something in it that might give comfort to her.

Her hand began shaking as she slowly opened the thick leather covered book. Her lips curved in a bittersweet smile at Janet's meticulous handwriting. She laughed as she saw little smudges of writing, presumably by Chad, adding his own enlightening comments -- in bold, smeared strokes -- to Janet's. So much for being private! Janet let her husband not only read it, but write in it himself!

She flipped towards the back until she found the blank pages, and then began working her way back to the last entry. She only wanted to know what Janet had written in her last few days.

She finally came upon the last entry. Looking at the date, Elyssa saw that it was written two days before their accident.

She closed her eyes and took a deep breath. Then she began reading.

May 23, 2005
Today began as every other day began. The sun awakened me with its bright rays pouring into our room, as if impatient for us to begin our day. I looked over at my sleeping husband **(that's me!)** *-- a notation obviously from Chad -- and thinking to myself how much I love him and how, in just a few hours, we might know for certain what we have been waiting so long for.*

Elyssa gulped. Her hands began trembling as she continued.

It was such a beautiful morning that we were both very sure we knew what the result would be.

We opened the package and read and reread the directions so we wouldn't do it wrong. The few minutes we had to wait for the results were excruciating. We both wanted to peek, but decided that might only give us false hope or disappointment. When the time was up, we held our hands tightly and looked. And guess what! I am pregnant! Chad and I are going to have a baby! **Am I a proud papa!?! Yes!**

We'll be going to our home at the lake to celebrate for a few days before we tell anyone!

Elyssa felt the room was swirling around her. "No, Janet! No!" She fell toward the bed and then crumpled down on the floor, sobbing uncontrollably.

Strong hands unexpectedly came around her and picked her up from the floor.

"Elyssa, what is it?" Will had impulsively stopped by and was just about to knock on the door when he heard Elyssa cry out. Rushing in, he found her collapsed on the floor sobbing. Instinctively, and without thought, he reached down to gather her in his arms.

The concern in his voice and tenderness of his actions were disregarded by Elyssa as she began pounding his chest with her tightly clenched fists.

"It's not fair!" she cried out. "Why? Why?"

He sat down upon the bed with her and cradled her face with both of his hands, turning it towards him. Her eyes were closed and tears were flowing freely down her cheeks. He drew aside a strand of hair which was clinging to her face, and with a great sense of regret, wondered if Janet and Chad's death would ever cease to come between them.

He did not know what to say to her, however much he wanted to say something; anything that would take away the pain she was feeling and the anger she harbored toward him. He felt a surge of compassion swell within him and wondered what he could do to ease her pain. All he knew to do was to simply hold her.

After a few moments, Elyssa pulled away. She stood up and reached for some tissues, avoiding any and all eye contact with Will.

A weak, "Excuse me," came forth from her lips as she left the room, and Will heard the hall bathroom door close.

He looked around and spied the journal lying on the floor. He clenched his jaw as he presumed it was Janet's, and that Elyssa had been reading it. He picked it up, knowing this was not something he would normally do, but curiosity prompted him to see if he could determine what had been the cause of her anguish. Knowing Elyssa as he did, he was quite certain it could have been something as minor as reading about Janet going to the hairdresser.

He reached down for the book and found it open to the very last entry. Glancing down to read it, the words that lay before him pierced him as profoundly as if he had been struck with a knife. Janet had just found out she was pregnant.

He closed his eyes and shook his head, taking in a deep breath and then letting it out in an exasperated groan. He slowly stood up and walked back into the living room, taking a seat in one of their two matching recliner chairs. He chose not to recline, but leaned forward and rested his elbows on his legs, clasping his hands in front of him.

When Elyssa finally walked out, her face was still streaked with stains from her tears and her eyes were red. Will stood and looked at her with a feeling of helplessness gripping him.

"I am sorry, Elyssa. I read in the journal that Janet was pregnant."

She walked over to a window and silently looked out. Her arms were folded tightly in front of her and Will wondered whether she would even acknowledge him.

She finally spoke; her words shaky and almost distant. "Janet and I use to lie in our beds at night and talk about what our life would be like when we grew up." She took in a deep breath to steady herself. "We talked about how we would have children and love each other's children as much as our own; how all the cousins would be so close." She slowly shook her head. "Now that will never happen and I'll never even know if Janet's child was a boy or a girl."

Will's lips pursed together tightly. "I wish there was something I could do."

"It's too late for that. What's done is done." Elyssa's words came out like daggers.

Will came up to her and spun her around. "Look, Elyssa, that accident could have just as easily happened in Chicago, or Los Angeles, or Santa... whatever it's called where you live! Perhaps it was just their time and no matter where they were, it would have happened."

Tears pooled in her eyes again and she closed them, forcing the tears to escape down her face. "I would have loved to have been an aunt to her child." She began to say more, but her choking sobs consumed her again. Will drew out a handkerchief and handed it to her, then drew her against his chest. He wrapped his arms around her as she let out another release of grief. Mumbling against him she cried out, "I miss her so much!"

He tightened his hold about her until he felt her begin to pull away and then he let her go. "I am sorry, Elyssa. I am truly sorry."

After regaining her composure, Elyssa walked into the kitchen dabbing her eyes with Will's well used handkerchief. "Would you care for a cup of coffee?" Her tone was terse and her eyes avoided his.

"No thank you, Elyssa," he replied. "I've had enough this morning."

"If you don't mind, I'm going to pour myself another."

She casually glanced about her for the mug she used earlier. Not seeing it -- not really seeing anything -- she reached into the cupboard for another one. Will came up behind her and took her hand, placing the mug she had been looking for in it. She glanced down at it, murmured a soft "Thank you," and poured coffee into it. She then walked over to the small kitchen table and sat down.

Will came and sat across from her. He watched silently as with each sip, Elyssa closed her eyes. He would like to believe it was because she was savoring the rich blend of Pemberleo coffee -- and his company -- but realistically he knew it was her way of dealing with this new wave of grief. He found it odd that each time she closed her eyes, he waited expectantly for her to open them again. Even though her eyes were red and swollen and flashed bitterness and anger toward him, he thought them exceptionally fine.

Elyssa wrapped her shaking hands around the mug and took a few more sips of coffee. "Why did you come by this morning? I thought you had work to do."

Will looked down and noticed his fingers tapping on the table. He quickly clasped his hands together to prevent any further nervous movement. "I… uh…" He looked back up at her. "I wanted to see how you were doing."

"Oh." Elyssa shook her head slowly. "Well, you certainly came upon me at the opportune time."

"I'm sorry, Elyssa. I wish there was something I could say or do to make you realize…"

Elyssa looked up at him through tear stained eyes and interrupted. "Getting over Janet's death is just going to take some time. That's all."

"Are you going to be OK today? I'll see if I can send someone over."

Elyssa waved her hand through the air and shook her head. "There's no need for that. I'll be fine." She took a long sip of coffee. "I was hoping, though, to leave for Lake Atitlan tomorrow and see the village where Chad and Janet had a small home. George was going to take me…"

Will let out a disgusted groan. "I am quite certain he won't be able to do that now." It was Will's turn to be terse. "He has too much to do in Colombia."

Will closely watched Elyssa's face as he said, "I'll make the arrangements to take you myself."

Her eyes darted up to meet his. "I really don't think you have the time nor the desire to do this and you certainly don't have to feel obligated. I'll find some other way on my own."

"Go to this small village by yourself?" Will leaned in. "I don't think so, Elyssa. You have no idea where you'd be going. Manuel will drive us. We'll leave in the morning and return on Monday. I don't need to be back to the States until Wednesday afternoon for my board meeting. That will give us plenty of time."

Elyssa finally glanced up at him, looking at him oddly. She quietly acquiesced, but her mind was in turmoil as to why he was so insistent on taking all this upon himself. Her flight home was scheduled for Tuesday morning, so getting back from the lake on Monday would suit her as well. However, she was not as certain how his presence would suit her for the duration of her time spent in Guatemala.

When Elyssa finished her coffee, she stared into the empty mug for a moment and then, with little expression, excused herself. She returned to the bathroom to freshen up, putting a little extra makeup on her face to hide the blotchiness that resulted from her tears. As she looked at herself in the mirror, she wondered why Will seemed so inclined to linger. She knew he had work to do and she certainly couldn't believe *she* was the attraction. She looked terrible! Maybe if she stayed in the bathroom long enough, she would find him gone when she finally came out.

Will remained motionless at the table when Elyssa left. His hand slowly made its way to his face and he clasped it over his mouth and jaw. He had noticed the sudden transformation in Elyssa's demeanor. She no longer had the flash of anger in her eyes directed at him. Even the grief she experienced earlier was gone. A look of resignation had wiped away all traces of any other emotion. Was it resignation over the fact that she was being compelled to remain in his presence?

He was suddenly gripped with the odd notion that he would rather have her feel anything toward him but indifference. He would welcome her sly comments that mocked him or even her heated words that accused him; but not indifference.

He stood up and walked over to the window. Stuffing his hands in his pockets, he gazed outside in bewilderment. Most women threw themselves at him and now the one woman who seemed to have somehow, unwittingly captured his heart would most likely never forgive him; never want anything to do with him. He had come to Guatemala with the hopes that Elyssa would get to know the real William Denton and find him to her liking. Instead, each day was proving to sink him further in her estimation rather than raise it and he was at a loss to know what to do about it.

When Elyssa walked out again, she saw that Will was still there, standing at the window staring out. His hands were tucked in his slacks pockets and she watched as he pulled one out and began raking it through his hair. He appeared to be miles away and didn't seem to notice her. For a moment Elyssa wondered whether he was actually feeling some compassion for her, but quickly credited it to him pondering over some highly important business concern and how things were being handled in his absence.

Elyssa cleared her throat.

He turned around and abruptly straightened up, bringing both hands to his side. Elyssa readily noticed him tighten them into fists.

When he saw her, he desperately felt the need to do something to change the tone between them. He did not want to leave her in the state things were in.

As he looked at her standing across the room from him, Will searched his mind for something to say or do. Then he suddenly had the most absurd idea! He figured it would either relieve some of the tension between them or completely end his chances with her.

"Elyssa," he said, looking around him. He walked over to her purse and picked it up. "Here's your purse." He handed it to her and gently took her elbow. "I have someplace I'd like to take you."

Elyssa shook her head and dug in her heels to keep from moving. "Exactly what makes you think I want to go anywhere with you?"

"Oh, you just wait and see. I am quite sure you won't regret it!"

Chapter 9

"I am in no mood to go anywhere with you, Will. Just leave me be."

His hand on her elbow tightened. "We won't be long, and like I said, you won't regret it."

She looked up into his face fully expecting to see his features determined and set. Instead of seeing the face of a ruthless man issuing a command that she better not refuse, she saw the light of encouragement in his eyes and a reassuring, albeit small smile on his lips.

She looked down and grudgingly took her purse from him. "Then let's get this over with."

They walked out to the parking area where Manuel was standing by the limo. He seemed surprised when he saw Elyssa returning with his boss and greeted her cheerfully. He then looked back at Will with a question on his face.

Will said something to him in Spanish and Manuel seemed even more surprised but nodded. They continued to speak, and Elyssa was only able to pick out a few words here and there that she understood. But there was one thing for certain -- Will could certainly speak the language and he could speak it well. The words easily rolled off his lips, and Elyssa, despite her novice ears, thought he spoke well enough to have been born here.

She did not realize that she was gaping at him, quite capriciously enjoying the sound of his voice as he spoke, when he stopped and turned to her. "Is something the matter, Elyssa?"

"I didn't think you could speak Spanish." She blurted it out before she even thought.

Elyssa was met with a look of disbelief on Will's face. "Why would you think that?"

Elyssa suddenly wished she could take back those words. How ridiculous it was to believe that!

Not wanting to appear as foolish as she felt, she muttered, "I had only observed you speaking English to Manuel. I thought that was because you couldn't speak Spanish."

Manuel laughed softly. "No, Miss Elyssa, he speaks English for my sake, so I can improve my language skills."

"Oh," she replied sheepishly.

Will was staring at her incredulously, his arms folded across his chest.

"So you were under the impression that I don't speak the language."

Elyssa bit her lip and looked down. She murmured an affirmative.

Still grinning over this whole situation, Manuel said, "You'd have a difficult time around here, wouldn't you, Señor Denton, if you didn't speak the language as well as you do."

Elyssa was more than eager to put this conversation behind her when a thought occurred to her. She looked back up at Will. "Wait a minute! Why were you speaking Spanish to Manuel just now?"

Manuel raised his eyebrows and laughed. "He told me where we were going and swore me to secrecy not to tell you." A more subdued look passed over Manuel's face. "He also told me what you just found out. Lo siento, Señorita Barnett. I'm sorry. It must have been very upsetting."

Elyssa nodded. "Thanks, Manuel."

"Well," Will began. "Shall we go?"

Elyssa looked at him sharply. "I would still like to know where we're going."

"You'll find out soon enough," Will answered.

Manuel walked over to the car and opened the back seat door. Elyssa decided she was in no mood to argue about where she was going to sit, so she stepped in. She looked in and saw two rows of plush seats facing each other. She surmised this was so that if there were four people in the car, they could easily carry on a business meeting.

How convenient! she thought to herself. *Is that why I'm here? For a meeting? About his project?*

The inside of the car was very spacious and elegant and as she slid in, her hand swept over the supple leather seat cover.

Will slid in after her and sat on the seat across from her and at the other end.

He leaned back into the seat and drew his hands together, entwining his fingers slowly. He seemed content to just silently watch her.

Elyssa swallowed hard. When she looked up, their eyes met and she could suddenly feel the pace of her heartbeat increase. She was struck with the absurd thought that his deep brown eyes were very soft.

She shook her head to rid it of its unwanted wanderings. "Will you tell me now where we're going?"

"If I did, you'd just tell me to turn right back around and take you home."

Elyssa sharply turned her face away from him so she was looking out her window. *He can be so infuriating!* she thought.

It was more than just his wanting to take every situation into his own hands. She had no idea how to deal with this conflict of feelings she was beginning to experience. She found it more and more difficult to hold on to that anger towards him that had previously so consumed her. In the last few days she found that she had to remind herself that she was angry at him and to jog her memory as to all the reasons why. She was annoyed that she was gradually seeing little things in him that actually attracted her to him. She grit her teeth tightly together. Now *that* made her angry!

The look of annoyance that swept swiftly across Elyssa's face did not escape Will's notice. He very briefly considered throwing in his "trump" card, but just as quickly dismissed it. He was certain she would be pleased with what he desired to do in Janet's memory at the pre-school, but details were still being worked out. The owner of the property next door was not to be found. Until he could tell her it was a done deal, he would have to wait.

Besides, he thought, as he looked over at her, he wanted her to like him for who he was and not what he -- or his money -- could do.

They drove for about fifteen minutes in silence; Will never receiving or making a call and neither speaking to one another. Both were lost in their own thoughts and the streets of the city passed by in a blur.

Manuel finally pulled the car over and Elyssa looked out in surprise. All she could see was a small amusement park. It had the kind of rides the traveling companies had that would pull in for a special weekend and set up for a few days and then leave.

"What are we doing here?" she asked.

"You'll see," was Will's only answer.

Manuel got out and opened her door while Will let himself out.

"I am really in no mood for an amusement park!" she said firmly, remaining in the back seat. "If you think I will receive any amusement at such a place -- particularly after what just happened -- you are sorely wrong."

Will walked around and reached in for her hand. "We'll only be here a short while. Trust me."

He took her hand, wrapping his fingers around it a little too warmly for Elyssa not to feel a shiver go through her. He gently pulled and Elyssa reluctantly stepped out.

"We'll return shortly, Manuel."

Manuel chuckled. "Yes, sir."

They walked into the small park with Will still holding lightly to her hand. Elyssa looked around at the children squealing on the rides. Concession stands sold food and drink and everyone seemed in a most jovial mood. This was certainly *not* what she was in the mood for.

"Are we here because they have the best tacos in Guatemala?" she asked mockingly, trying to rid herself of the feeling that it felt very right for her hand to be wrapped in his.

"No," he answered and walked up to a ticket window. "Dos, por favor," he said, ordering two tickets and he finally released her hand.

"I don't do roller coasters," she lied. While she truly loved them, the ones that looked like they were just thrown together like a set of children's building blocks didn't sit well with her. She clasped the hand he just released with her other and noticed how warm it felt.

"No roller coasters," he said. He seemed to know exactly where he was going and all Elyssa could do was follow.

He gently nudged her to a small line. "Here," he said, extending his hand toward the ride opposite them.

"Bumper cars? We're going on the bumper cars?"

He turned and looked down at her. His face grew serious as he said, "If we are to spend the next few days together, something has to change. You, obviously, are still quite angry with me. So…" and here he paused and looked toward the ride, "I want you to take out all your anger and pummel me to death in there."

Elyssa's eyes widened and her jaw dropped.

The ride stopped and everyone stepped out, allowing those in line to scramble in and find a car. This also prevented Elyssa from responding. That was fine with her, as she had no idea what to say to him. Something resonated deep within her that he would recognize her feelings toward him and actually want to do something about it.

"Let's go." Will looked at her, encouraging her to go along with this with his eyes.

Elyssa found a vacant car and climbed in, feeling a surge of anticipation. *Yes,* she thought, *I will gladly take out my anger and bitterness towards you! Just you wait, Mr. William Denton!*

Once settled and buckled in, she watched as he climbed into another small car. His legs were so long that his knees practically came up to his chin and Elyssa struggled to stifle her giggle. He already looked uncomfortable and the ride hadn't even begun.

When everyone was secure in their cars, the ride began. Elyssa turned her car in Will's direction and applied her foot to the pedal. She was so intent on aiming hers toward his that she was surprised when a car hit her from behind, lightly jostling her. She began laughing and somehow knew she was going to really enjoy this.

Will sat in his car, with seemingly no intention to try to aim for her or even avoid her. She was grateful for a fairly open space between her car and his and she sped towards him. He looked at her and lifted up his hands in surrender as she hit him soundly on the left side of his car. It jerked him back and he allowed his car to remain where it stopped.

Elyssa turned around and drove away from him, so she could gather up some speed for the next attack. While she was going, she pointed Will out to the others, hoping they might join her in the assault.

Again and again she hit his car as others joined in. While the ride was perfectly safe and fun, she knew he was being jostled with every hit. Each time she rammed his car, she found herself inexplicably laughing more and more.

When the ride finally came to an end, Elyssa triumphantly, but quite gingerly, stepped out of the car. She had suffered enough hits from others and felt the effects, but her slight discomfort did little to erase the victorious smile upon her face. She watched as Will struggled to climb out of the car, his cramped limbs rejoicing at their sudden freedom; his body aching slightly from every hit. His eyes met hers as he stretched out, and he did not seem inclined to turn his gaze away.

His intense gaze unnerved her, so she resorted to levity. "I see you survived the assault." She couldn't prevent a laugh from escaping.

"Barely. I'm sure I will feel even worse tomorrow." He rubbed his side vigorously. "You were quite ruthless out there."

"You didn't put up much of a defense."

He only shrugged and they returned to the car.

Manuel laughed as he watched them coming towards him. Will walked with a slight limp and his hand vigorously rubbed his side.

"It looks like a hot bath is in store for you tonight, sir. And should I arrange a massage?"

"I can think of only one or two things that sound better than that, but unfortunately I have work at the office to do first."

He glanced at Elyssa, grateful that both the anger and distant look in her eyes had been replaced by a playful liveliness. He hoped that was a good sign.

Manuel looked at Elyssa. "Your face is luminous, Elyssa."

"Why, thank you, Manuel." Elyssa's heart was also beating erratically, but Manuel could not know that. She wanted to attribute it all to the fun she had just had, but she began to wonder if it was because of Will.

They rode in silence for a while. For Elyssa, it was due to her surprise at such a seemingly uncharacteristic scheme on Will's part. Did he truly care whether she harbored resentment toward him? If so, why? A smile intermittently tugged at the corners of her mouth, as hard as she tried to prevent it.

She looked away, conflicted in her feelings. What he had set out to do by taking her on the bumper car ride had done exactly what he had desired. She was now angry with herself for the tender feelings that his actions had prompted to grow in her. She had to tell herself he chose to do this only because he was not used to women behaving in such a way around him. Like the young girl in the shop in Antigua, the majority of women most likely pampered him and fawned over him.

A voice broke her reverie. "Is that a smile I see, Miss Elyssa Barnett?"

She tried to wipe it from her face before she turned to look at Will, but she found it to be too difficult. "And what if it is?"

"It's nice to see," Will answered. "I haven't seen too many of them gracing your face while you've been here."

His actions just now had disarmed her. It was so unlike what she would expect from him. Looking over at him she asked, "What made you do that?"

"Do what?" he asked with an exasperatingly straight face.

"The bumper cars."

"Did you not enjoy yourself?"

"Oh, immensely," Elyssa said with a little too much enthusiasm.

"It was something my father did with me once." Will tilted his head and looked at Elyssa. *And something I had to do with Gina just a few weeks ago,* he added silently to himself.

Will glanced out the window and it seemed to Elyssa that he was drifting back in time. "My father had promised me something -- I forget what it was -- but because of something that came up in the office, he had to cancel the plans we had made. I was very upset and angry with him. I think he understood my anger and disappointment and took me to a small amusement park in Chicago. There, while standing in line for the bumper cars, he told me he was very sorry, but that occasionally there were things he would have to do at work that would cause me disappointment. He told me that he preferred I take out my anger at him with the bumper cars and not in my relationship with him."

Elyssa stared at him, touched by the story. "And?" she asked.

"I have long forgotten what it was that made me so angry with my father, but I have never forgotten what he did." His gaze drifted back to Elyssa; his intense eyes burning into hers. "I was hoping it might do the same for you."

Elyssa opened her mouth to say something, but surprisingly, nothing came out.

When she didn't say anything, Will continued, "I know you'll never forget your sister. I don't expect you to. I was only hoping you might…" He took in a deep breath. "…you might not blame me -- at least totally -- for hers and Chad's death."

Elyssa had never seen him appear so vulnerable. While she knew this must be difficult for him, she was not sure she could do that. She was not sure she *wanted* to do that. Blaming him for Janet's death ensured she would never fall for him. Despite his actions in the past hour -- and occasionally in the past couple of days -- she had to remember the type of man he still was when it came to his career. She doubted he would ever have time for his family, if he even chose to have one.

Elyssa was silent for a moment as she considered her words. "I must confess pounding you with my car back there released a bit of my anger towards you." She could not hide the smile that returned to her face. "You looked absolutely contorted in that small car and I loved it!"

"Too much, I dare say."

When they reached the housing complex, Will helped her out of the car. "We'll be leaving early in the morning for Lake Atitlan. Pack comfortable and conservative clothes enough for three days. The people in these villages are not as modern as here in the city."

Elyssa nodded. "What time should I be ready?"

Will looked at Manuel. "Manuel, what time do you think we should leave to get us there at a reasonable hour?"

"Ten o'clock would be fine. That should get us to Panajachel by about noon and then the boat ride to the village is about forty-five minutes."

Will looked back at Elyssa. "Ten o'clock it is, then. Let me see you to your door."

"No, thank you. I can manage. Goodbye, Will. Goodbye, Manuel."

They both uttered their goodbyes simultaneously as Elyssa turned to walk inside. Will kept his eyes on her and Manuel watched *him* most curiously. He had driven his boss around Guatemala for several years and had seen him interact with several different ladies. There was something very different about the way he acted with Elyssa. He took a deep breath and shook his head as he contemplated whether or not it was a good thing.

Elyssa was grateful to step back inside the apartment. She closed the door and collapsed into a chair. She needed time alone to think. Janet and Chad's apartment had a way of bringing her back to reality as she thought back to the events of the day.

The morning had brought the revelation that Janet had been pregnant when she died. Elyssa's intense grief upon making that discovery had been actually tempered by Will's sudden appearance and consoling arms. But what did he really do but put his arms around her? She pounded her fist against the arm of the chair. Why did the recollection of his arms about her suddenly seem more prominent than the memory of her grief?

Yesterday, in the car on the way to Antigua, he spoke on his cell phone most of the way. He had been upset by something and issued orders and demands as if no one else mattered. Did he even care about his employees and their families and how they might suffer from their loved ones not being able to come home for having to satisfy all his demands?

Why, when she had promised herself she would never fall for him, was that becoming more and more difficult?

And then there were the bumper cars.

Elyssa slumped down into the chair. It was true. Her intense anger and resentment toward him was waning. But she was seeing a side of him that was not his real life. Snippets of conversation came back to her as she realized he was basically cold-hearted and manipulative. Even the bumper cars had been a form of manipulation to rid her of her anger so he would not have to endure her wrath these next few days.

"I just have to remember that," she said to herself. "He will still be the same man he always was once he returns to the States."

She sat down on the floor next to the box of Janet's things and picked up the journal, gently stroking it. "What will I find in here that will help me, Janet? Will I find any answers?"

She closed her eyes as they swelled with tears. "And what will I find in this little village that you found so captivating?" She put the journal down and closed her eyes.

George had told her that the lake, with three volcanoes surrounding it, could be one of the most romantic places one ever visits. She felt her chest tighten as she contemplated spending three days there with Will. Was it because she loathed his company… or was it because she feared falling in love with him?

Chapter 10

During the night, a brief but turbulent thunderstorm awakened Elyssa. The flashes of lightning and rumblings of thunder outside kept her from sleep as she considered her own clash of feelings deep within.

She had come to Guatemala with the sole intent to go through her sister's things and bring back those items that had sentimental value. Her feelings toward William Denton had been set in stone... or so she thought. He was to blame for sending Janet and Chad down to Guatemala, thus separating Elyssa and her beloved sister. He was to blame for their deaths, for if he hadn't sent them down to Guatemala, they wouldn't have been in the accident and died. He was a powerful and forceful man whose dictates affected -- often adversely -- the lives of his employees and their families.

She shuddered as another rumble of thunder rattled the windows and resonated deep within her. Rain began pelting the window as she considered the man she had been with the past few days. Much of what she had seen of him confirmed her estimation of him, but she also had seen glimpses of someone very unlike the man she envisioned him to be.

As much as she prided herself on being able to discern one's character quickly, completely, and fairly accurately, she had to admit that there were sides of the man that did not fit neatly into the mold she had constructed concerning him. His tender actions toward the children made her question her estimation that he was heartless and cold; that he would consider it beneath him to interact with the poorest of people.

She knew he was a man who could use his power and authority to manipulate people; who seemed to know intuitively how to influence others. She was all too aware that he had used that ability with her. As the rains poured down, resentment flooded her as she considered how he seemed to know exactly what would diminish her anger towards him. She disliked the fact that taking her on the bumper cars had done just that and for a short while, had even made her forget her pain. She had to admit, though, that she had enjoyed pummeling him with her car and seeing his great discomfort far too much!

She rolled over onto her stomach, fluffing up her pillow and then stuffing her arms underneath it. She pounded her head down upon the yielding mass as she recalled the steady gaze of his eyes as they stepped out of their bumper cars. While she had thought little of it then, she wondered whether he had been scrutinizing her face to see evidence of victory. She shivered as the recollection that came to her was of eyes filled with warmth and concern.

"Don't go there, Elyssa!" she said aloud. "That's a ridiculous notion!"

~~*

As the first rays of sun came up over the horizon and birds began eagerly announcing the start of a new day, Elyssa awoke with less enthusiasm. The storm outside had kept her awake for a good portion of the night and once it had moved on, the storm within lingered.

She numbly made her way into the kitchen to make a cup of coffee. She knew that would alleviate a good deal of her grogginess. Once she started the pot, she readied herself for the trip to Lake Atitlan, packing some comfortable clothes, enough for a few days.

When she finished, the coffee was ready and she sat down to enjoy it.

With each sip, she found herself revitalized and more alert. She savored each sip until she set her cup down abruptly and shook her head.

"Even when he is not with me, he has influence over me!" she exclaimed as she looked down into the dark swirling liquid of Pemberleo coffee. Picking up her mug and defiantly downing the remainder, she said, "This is absurd. I can't allow him to affect me so! I will go to Lake Atitlan, go through Janet's things, and come back. Nothing more!"

Elyssa opened the front door of the townhouse, feeling a little more inclined to accept the cool breeze that brought in the delightful fragrance of the flowers and the cheerful song of the birds. She then returned to the kitchen to clean it up before Will arrived.

At precisely ten o'clock, there was a knock at the door. Walking over to it and looking out through the screen door, she barely recognized Will, who was dressed in jeans and a crisp, muted blue T-shirt. His dark curly hair, rather than being exactingly slicked down in place from gel, danced freely in the breeze.

She dared not speak as her heart fluttered at the sight of him. He looked nothing like a wealthy, powerful executive, but instead a handsome young man that she might…

No! She hastily arrested that thought. Looking down quickly, she muttered a soft, "Come in," and opened the door. She turned away from him to look for her purse so he would not detect the surge of sudden feelings flooding through her.

"Good morning, Elyssa. Did you sleep well?"

"Yes, thank you, I did," she lied and continued to search the room with her eyes for her purse. She took in a breath to steady her nerves at the feel of his hand brushing against hers as he was suddenly at her side handing her purse to her.

"The storm didn't awaken you, then?"

"Yes, I heard it, but it didn't keep me awake for very long."

Keeping her head averted from his gaze, she made the excuse to go into the kitchen to make sure everything was turned off.

He walked over to her suitcase which was sitting by the door. "I'll take this to the car, then."

Elyssa walked into the kitchen and then turned back. She watched as Will took her bag out and she took in another deep breath. "This is ludicrous!" she said softly. "I loathe the man!" Standing in the center of the kitchen, her fists clenched tightly as she reminded herself, "He is everything I don't want in a man! Just remember, Elyssa! Remember what he did! Remember who he is!"

She slipped her feet into her sandals and tightened her grip on her purse. Stuffing in a few last minute items, she walked out, closing and locking the door behind her. As she set out for the car, she wasn't surprised to see that they had the limousine again. It would certainly make the trip comfortable. Will was leaning against it, his arms folded across his chest, when she walked up.

A wayward thought crossed her mind affirming his good looks and she suddenly realized it was due to his uncommonly casual attire today. It almost seemed that just by wearing jeans and a T-shirt had somehow transformed him, making him look more down to earth -- more laid-back. *But it's not a permanent transformation,* she reminded herself.

She mused that perhaps it would be beneficial for her to sit up front with Manuel so she wouldn't have to be in such close proximity to Will and have these preposterous thoughts about him. She was beginning to feel far too vulnerable around him. As she contemplated this, she noticed a young boy standing next to the car.

Manuel was putting her suitcase in the trunk and as she walked over to greet him, the young boy walked over also.

"Elyssa, I would like you to meet my eldest son, Luis. Luis, this is Elyssa." The young boy nodded and extended his hand.

"He doesn't speak much English, but I'm helping him with it."

Elyssa took his hand and smiled. "Hello. Hola." Turning to Manuel she asked, "Is he... is he going with us?"

"Yes," Manuel answered as he opened the wide back seat door. "We have family in a small village close to where you will be going and I thought it would be good for him to come along."

That settles that, Elyssa thought as she realized she would have no choice but to sit in the back with Will.

"It's a rather long ride, so you two will be very comfortable."

Elyssa offered a meek thank you to Manuel and muttered a soft, "I doubt it," to herself as she stepped in, sitting down on the seat facing towards the front. Will slid in after her, and again took the seat across from her.

She felt his eyes upon her as she looked out her side of the window waiting for Manuel to start the car. Finally meeting his gaze, she said, "Will we drive this car all the way to the village?"

Will shook his head. "We will take the car only as far as Panajachel, a very popular tourist resort on the lake. From there we will board a boat for the village. It's quicker and more efficient to go across the lake. Driving to the village would take us who knows how long on extremely poor roads that may or may not even be passable. Manuel will find a secure garage in Panajachel to keep the car parked in while we are gone."

"Is that what Chad and Janet had to do to get to the village? Take a boat?"

He nodded as he adjusted his body in the seat to get comfortable. "Yes. Manuel told me that when the Blakelys first moved to Guatemala, they went to Panajachel on a little vacation. Manuel drove them that first time to help them get around and suggested they visit some of the villages around the lake. They went with him and met his family. While out there, Manuel told them about the coffee that was grown on the surrounding hillsides. Those coffee beans made some of the best coffee Chad ever tasted and he contracted many of the farmers to grow the beans for us."

"The bigger coffee companies didn't already own them?"

"No, the bigger coffee companies aren't interested in the little farmer."

"And you are?"

"We're interested in getting the best coffee beans. If that means paying one farmer who farms only one acre, we'll do it. You must remember, Elyssa, Pemberleo is not one of the major coffee companies, but many people say our coffee is one of the best."

The car started and they set off. Manuel informed them that it would be a couple hours' drive and if they needed anything to let him know.

Will thanked Manuel and turned back to Elyssa with a faint smile. "I can't help but think Manuel planned all along to take Chad and Janet to this village, hoping Chad would see for himself the flavorful coffee beans that are grown there. Growing them in the volcanic soil gives the coffee a rich, full flavor, but hillside farming really can't be done on a large scale. We were the perfect buyers."

The look on Elyssa's face and the curious tilt of her head openly displayed her surprise.

"This surprises you?" Will asked.

"I confess it does." Her voice sounded softer than it had previously in all their conversations.

Will rested his elbows on his knees and leaned over, looking down at his hands which were clasped together. "I'd thought I'd stop in and visit a couple of the farmers while we are there since Chad…" He paused and glanced up at Elyssa, compassion flooding his eyes. "Well, no one has done it in a while."

Elyssa's brows furrowed unwittingly and she looked quickly away.

Will straightened up and turned to look out the other window, wondering if he would ever be able to mention Chad or Janet's name without Elyssa turning away.

They rode in silence for a while as Elyssa contemplated why he, the wealthy president of Pemberleo Coffee, would be willing to interact with the small farmers who grew only a portion of his coffee beans.

Elyssa entertained herself for a while by watching the countryside. They passed corn and wheat fields and an occasional small town as they made their way to the lake. She thought it odd that Will seemed perfectly content in the silence, making only an occasional comment on one thing or another. Silence was something she was not used to.

She turned her eyes discreetly upon him. *He's probably wondering how he ever got himself mixed up with me and he's regretting every minute of it.* But the more she thought about it, she had to admit to herself that he did not at all seem perturbed by it.

Shrugging her shoulders lightly, Elyssa finally pulled out a book she had brought along and Will reached for a briefcase which housed a laptop computer. Opening it up, he began typing away.

Well, at least he's not talking on his phone as much, she mused. In fact, she actually found that quite surprising and wondered whether he had even brought it along or perhaps had actually turned it off. A sudden ringing about a half hour later confirmed that he had it with him and it was turned on, but he carried on only a very brief conversation.

After a couple hours of driving, they made their way along a winding road ascending a mountain. Even though the road was in excellent condition, Elyssa actually found herself grateful for the sturdy and reliable car in which they were riding.

When they reached the summit of the mountain, Manuel turned and said, "It looks like we should have a nice view of the lake from the turnout. Would you like me to stop?"

"That would be great, Manuel. Thanks."

At the next turn the lake came into view on Will's side of the car. "Slide over here and give a look, Elyssa." He pointed out the window and drew his stretched out legs in. "It's a beautiful sight."

Elyssa slid over, eager to have a better view. As she brought her legs over and looked out, she felt her knees brush up against Will's. Her subtle attempts to move her knees out of his way soon became futile and then forgotten as a grander view of the lake came into view. Two of the three volcanoes which surrounded the lake could be seen. The third was obscured by clouds. Her eyes widened at the sight in front of her and she watched as Manuel pulled into a turnout occupied by several other cars.

The car came to a stop and both Manuel and Luis hopped out. As Luis was on the side of the car where both Will and Elyssa were sitting, he promptly opened the door for them. Will stretched out his legs toward the other side of the car, allowing Elyssa freedom to step out.

Manuel came around and held out his hand to assist her. Will stepped out after her.

They were greeted by a warm breeze as they stood at the summit of a mountain. The lake was below them and Elyssa took in the beautiful sight before her.

"Those two volcanoes are Toliman and Atitlan," offered Manuel, extending his hand out toward them. "Unfortunately, San Pedro volcano is a little shy right now, not wanting to peek out from the clouds."

Elyssa laughed and then asked Manuel what the city was beneath them with all the large hotels.

"That is Panajachel, the largest city on the lake and a world class tourist resort." Looking at his watch he said, "If you would like to see a little bit of Panajachel, we probably have a few hours to spare for you to walk around. Or, if you like, you can have a leisurely visit and spend the night in a hotel there and we'll secure a boat to the village first thing in the morning."

"I do want to visit the Saturday market that Janet wrote to me about," Elyssa commented.

"You'd have time to do that even if we don't leave until tomorrow morning," Manuel told her. "It's only a forty-five minute boat ride to the village and you can catch a ride up to the market place every twenty minutes or so."

Will looked at Manuel. "*Up* to the market place?"

"Yes, Sir! It's at the top of that mountain!" He stretched out his hand toward a distant mountain.

Will cast his eyes down at Elyssa. "What's so great about this market place that you would want to go all the way up that mountain?"

"It's a market place for the locals, so you don't have all the touristy items. Besides, Janet did and she loved it!"

Looking at Elyssa with arms firmly braced on her hips and a most determined glare in her eyes, Will dared not argue; at least at the moment.

"It's quite a big deal," Manuel affirmed. "You won't want to miss it."

Will turned to Manuel. "Let's take things as they come. We'll decide whether we want to stay in Panajachel when we get down there."

This was another surprise, at least to Elyssa. She had determined that Will was most likely one who lived with a highly detailed agenda and wanted everything scheduled out. Ten minutes for this; an hour for that; then on to the next thing.

They stayed at the lookout for awhile, hoping the clouds would part and give them a picture perfect view of the lake and the third volcano. It was not to be, however, and from there they set out down the hill.

When they arrived in Panajachel, Elyssa felt as though she had been transported to a whole new land. Majestic modern hotels mingled with historic buildings; people in jeans and T-shirts walked amidst the locals in their brightly woven clothes. Beautiful flowers were growing everywhere and there seemed to be a liveliness permeating the air.

Manuel drove around and finally pulled into a parking space close to the shore of the lake. Shops and restaurants abounded around them.

They all got out of the car and Will looked at his watch. "Let's plan to meet back at the car in two hours." He looked at Elyssa. "Do you think that's enough time to take a look around?"

Elyssa nodded. "I think so."

Manuel and Luis left and Elyssa looked about her, deciding where she wanted to go first.

"Which way would you like to go?"

Elyssa's eyes widened at Will's question. "You don't have to accompany me. I'll be fine."

"I don't doubt it. But I would like some company. Besides, I'm hungry and I don't like eating alone."

Elyssa had to admit she was hungry too and they began walking in step with each other toward the shops and restaurants across the street.

"Do you see anything that looks appealing?"

Elyssa nodded. "Everything looks good."

They came to a corner and looked up and down the street. Will spied what looked like a nice sit-down restaurant about a block away.

"Come," he said, taking her elbow in his hand. "Let's try this place."

As they walked to the restaurant, Elyssa decided she had best make a pact with herself now. She would enjoy her time here -- even if it meant being with Will. She would try to get to know the man who had proven to be most puzzling to her. She reminded herself, though, who she was and who he was. Once she returned home, she would return to her simple country life and he would resume his corporate world lifestyle.

They entered the restaurant and saw that a large window on one side looked down over the lake. Although they were several blocks from the shore, the view was breathtaking. The restaurant was quite crowded with many people waiting and there didn't appear to be any tables available along the window. Will walked over to the host and spoke to him in Spanish. They were soon walking back to a small table in the corner, right next to the window. Elyssa was quite certain a little bribing -- or perhaps a great deal of bribing -- helped.

The atmosphere was more festive than romantic, for which she was grateful. They took their seats at the table and were handed menus which were written in both English and Spanish.

When they both had ordered, Will looked across at her. "So tell me about yourself, Miss Elyssa Barnett."

She raised her eyes and tilted her head. "What do you want to know?"

"For starters, why do you live way up in the middle of nowhere?"

Elyssa leaned in, her eyes flashing. "The Santa Ynez Valley is not the middle of nowhere! It's beautiful country!"

"I know. I've been through there."

"You have?" Again, she was taken by surprise.

He nodded. "A few years ago. But your whole family is in the LA area. Why did you move up there?"

The thought, *Because of people like you*, crossed her mind, but she chose to be more civil.

"The lifestyle was too crazy for me down there. I like being able to get out and walk and breathe in fresh air. I like knowing my neighbors and feeling as though they are watching out for me and care for me and I do the same for them."

"And you didn't find that in LA?"

She narrowed her eyes at him. "Can you find that in any large, metropolitan city?"

"There are other benefits to the big city."

Elyssa only shrugged. She went on to talk about her work at the library, her meager attempts at interior design, and her friends. She laughed as she told him how Charlene, who was very successful doing set designs in the movie industry, faithfully handed out Elyssa's business card to people she met anywhere. Elyssa had never picked up any business that way, but she appreciated her friend's efforts to help her business. When the meal had come, she realized she had been doing all the talking.

He had barely spoken a word and she wondered whether it was because he really didn't want her knowing about him or because he merely felt obliged to listen to her.

They ate their meal with an occasional comment about the lake, or the clouds that were accumulating, or the sound of thunder off in the distance.

As the thunder grew louder, Will suggested they finish eating as soon as they could and get back to the car.

The sudden downpour of rain outside proved Will's suggestion to be a little late. They watched as people grabbed whatever they could - plastic bags, purses, and coats, to cover their heads as they ran for cover. Elyssa had never seen such a sudden onslaught of rain before.

He relaxed in his chair and looked out. "Or… we can stay here and wait out the storm."

They slowly ate what was remaining on their plates all the while keeping an eye outside. The rain did not seem inclined to let up and the thunder roared mercilessly.

Looking at his watch, Will noticed that their two hours were almost up. "Manuel and Luis are likely back at the car. Do you want to go outside and make a run for it?"

Elyssa smiled. "A little bit of water never hurt anyone."

"Did you bring an umbrella?"

Elyssa shook her head. "I have one in my suitcase. Did you?"

"Conveniently packed away in mine."

After paying the bill, they stepped outside and couldn't believe what they saw. The street was like a river, with the water at least three inches deep, rushing down toward the lake. They stood underneath the awning of the restaurant as they both contemplated what to do.

"We have to cross that street," Will said. "But I don't like the looks of it."

"It can't be that bad," Elyssa pointed in the direction of some people running across.

"Let me carry you."

Elyssa put up her hands. "Thanks, but no. I'll do fine."

"All right," he said, taking her arm without asking first. "Let's go!"

They both stepped into the water and found crossing the street easier said than done. It was deeper and more forceful than they both anticipated and each step was a difficult maneuver.

They were almost half-way across the street when Elyssa screamed, "My sandal!"

One of her sandals slipped off and was now floating down the street in the current. Before she could even react, Will adeptly swept her up in his arms and began running to the other side of the street.

"Wait here and don't move!" he said as he put her down and set off running in the direction of the wayward sandal.

Elyssa sought shelter under another awning while she waited. Why, she didn't know, as she was already soaked through. She watched in gleeful amusement as Will jumped out into the street several times in an attempt to retrieve her sandal, but it was obvious that he wasn't having any luck. The street made a curve and soon he disappeared around the corner.

This was so ridiculous that she couldn't help but laugh. And she laughed with no restraint.

She wanted to go find him, but didn't dare walk on these streets in a bare foot, so she stayed where she was, hoping he would return soon -- with her sandal! If he was unable to retrieve it, however, she might just be forced to allow him to carry her. She folded her arms tightly across her as the thought of his arms going around her and lifting her up suddenly seemed very appealing.

When she finally saw him turn the corner, she saw that he somehow had captured the sandal. She chided herself for the initial sense of disappointment that overtook her in seeing that he had been victorious.

As he walked toward her, his hair was wet and matted down, his shirt was soaked through and she couldn't help but think he looked like a drowned rat. But a well-toned and handsome drowned rat! That thought brought a sparkle to her eyes and made her laugh some more.

He held out the sandal to her and gave a mock bow. "Shall we slip this on, Madam, and see if it fits?"

His eyes brightened as he looked intently at Elyssa. She easily caught his reference to Cinderella. He may be handsome and he may have just returned her lost sandal, but he was far from being her Prince Charming!

Then why did a shudder course through her?

She took the sandal from him and lifted up her foot to slip it on. As she began to wobble, she steadied herself with her other hand by reaching out and grabbing Will's arm. At the moment her fingers wrapped around his arm, she felt his muscles tighten as he placed his hands up around her shoulders to straighten her.

When her sandal was securely back on her foot, she let go of Will's arm, but he kept his hands upon her shoulders. She looked at him with a lively quip ready on her lips, but his eyes silenced her. Their eyes locked and Elyssa felt incapable of any sort of response, let alone a rational thought.

Will seemed to search her face for something and Elyssa's eyes traveled from his eyes down to his mouth, which suddenly seemed far more attractive than she would have liked to admit. The thought of him leaning over and kissing her had unexpectedly too much appeal and she quickly turned away.

"Perhaps we ought to return to the car." She hoped he didn't notice her faltering voice.

She began walking quickly and Will followed. Raking his hand through his hair, he knew that he only had three days to change her opinion of him. He wondered if she had been aware how much he had wanted to kiss her just now. Did she find the thought repulsive? Did she… would she… always direct her anger at him and blame him for her sister's death?

His long strides easily caught up with her as they made their way to the car, oblivious of the rain soaking them; each lost in their own thoughts.

Chapter 11

When they reached the car, Manuel and Luis were already there. Seeing them approach, Manuel jumped out and opened the back door, letting them in quickly to get out of the pouring rain.

He returned to the front seat and turned towards them. "Looks like you got caught in the storm!"

Staring up front at Manuel and Luis who were both fairly dry, Will commented, "Obviously. And how did you avoid it?"

Manuel laughed. "You get to know the sights and sounds of an approaching storm. We grabbed something to eat and came back to the car immediately to eat and wait it out." He looked slyly at Will. "I tried to call you on your phone to warn you, but was surprised to discover that you had turned it off."

"Oh," Will reached into his pocket and pulled out his phone. Looking at it, he said dryly, "It appears I did."

The sudden storm caused a brief drop in the temperature, and in her drenched state, Elyssa shivered and brought her arms about her.

Will noticed and reached behind him, pulling out a light jacket. "Here, put this around your shoulders, Elyssa." He turned to Manuel and asked, "How long do you suppose the storm will last?"

Manuel looked out across the lake and at the solid sky of clouds. "My guess would be that it will be here for most of the rest of the day."

"Perhaps we ought to find a hotel here for the night instead of taking the boat. You said we could leave first thing in the morning?"

"Yes. I'll make the arrangements."

Manuel started the engine. "There is a very nice hotel only a few blocks away. I'll have you there in no time!"

They drove to a hotel that overlooked the lake. It was about ten stories tall and looked quite nice from the outside. Manuel drove up to the covered front entrance and stopped the car so they could get out. A porter was there right away to open the doors and gather their luggage.

"I'll park the car while you check in and also see about leaving it here while we're out at the village."

"Thanks, Manuel," Will said. "Call me on my phone and let me know what time we should be ready to leave in the morning."

"Yes, Sir. See you tomorrow. Good day, Elyssa."

Elyssa murmured a soft farewell and as Manuel and his son drove off, she looked curiously at Will. "Will they not be staying here also?"

"Manuel and his son?" Will laughed. "Hardly."

Her eyes narrowed. "And why not? Why shouldn't your own chauffeur be entitled to stay in the same hotel as you?"

Will looked down at her, recognizing the blaze of injustice in her eyes. He put up a hand to calm her. "Elyssa, Manuel has a company credit card and he is entitled to use it while in my employ however he chooses. How he chooses to use it is of no consequence to me. But I am quite convinced this will not be his place of choice."

"Why not?"

"Because he feels more comfortable in places that cater to the local people."

Elyssa put her hands on her hips. "Perhaps I would prefer that as well."

Will folded his arms in front of him and met the determined glower in Elyssa's eyes. "Are you always this stubborn?"

"No," she said, and turned to follow the porter with their luggage towards the front desk. "Sometimes I'm worse."

Will's feet remained planted in one spot as he watched Elyssa march away. "I can well imagine that!" he said softly, an amused smile forming on his lips.

Elyssa marched determinedly up to the desk and began talking with the clerk. Will came up behind her and listened as she asked whether there was a moderately priced room available. Remaining behind her, Will began speaking in Spanish to the clerk. The clerk's attention abruptly shifted towards him.

Elyssa opened her mouth to protest Will's taking charge, but it was too late. The clerk quickly secured two keys as Will produced his credit card.

The transaction was quickly and efficiently completed, and when they stepped away from the desk, Elyssa vocalized her feelings. "You did not need to do that. He understood my English perfectly and I was wholly capable of securing my own room."

"I have no doubt of that."

"I truly believe you are even more stubborn than I am!" She reached out for the keys. "Now which one is my room?"

"You are not in a room. We are both in a suite."

"A suite? Different ones, I hope!" The remark escaped Elyssa's lips before the thought had barely entered her head.

"Rest your little head, Elyssa. We are in different suites. Next door to one another, but different suites."

"Well, I certainly don't need a suite. I am used to small hotel rooms and they are more within my budget. So if you don't mind, I'll get my own room!"

Will looked at the porter, who was waiting with their luggage, and whispered, "Un momento," gently wrapping his arm through Elyssa's and ushering her off to the side.

"Look, Elyssa," he said, as they made their way away from the listening ears of the porter. "I am paying for this hotel since it was not in our original plan and I would rather you not be six or seven floors down from me. You never know what may happen here, even a place as reputable as this."

"But a suite is really not necessary and I am perfectly capable of taking care of myself!"

Will took in a deep breath. "It may not be necessary, but that's what we're going to stay in tonight."

They stared at each other, Will practically holding his breath to see what Elyssa would do. It was true, he was looking out for Elyssa in wanting to keep her close by, but he was also hoping to provide an atmosphere that would offer some sort of chance at redemption with her.

When she didn't answer, he finally said, "Look at it this way. How often do you get to treat yourself to a little luxury? Besides," he said as he drew in closer. "You most likely could use a little pampering right now with everything you have been through. Allow yourself this one little comfort."

Something inside Elyssa wished to fight him. She felt her defenses wearing down the longer she was with him. As he stood only mere inches from her, he stirred feelings within her that she felt she could only combat by challenging his every word and his every action. At every turn, Will was becoming nothing like the man she believed responsible for Janet's death.

Finally, seeing he was not about to budge, she acquiesced. "All right, but don't you get it into your head that I have to stay at some premiere hotel at the village. I'll be perfectly content staying at Janet and Chad's home. If she felt safe there, I shall feel safe there, too. You can find yourself somewhere else to stay."

"I will gladly do that," he replied, "however, I am quite sure there aren't any premiere hotels anywhere near the village. Manuel has given me the name of a pension close by."

Too bad for you, Elyssa thought to herself and smiled as she wondered how he would fare in less than exceptional accommodations.

They turned and walked quietly toward the porter waiting for them; Will nodding his head to him that they were ready to proceed.

They rode the elevator up to the ninth floor. From the sign on the wall when they stepped out, Elyssa noted that there were only four rooms -- that is, suites -- up here, two on either side of the hall.

They walked down the hall on a plush carpet. Textured wall coverings with Guatemalan artwork canopied around them. Locked curios filled with Guatemalan treasures stood on each side of the hall. Elyssa didn't know whether the whole hotel was this elegant, but she had the notion that their suites would be unlike anything she had ever seen.

They stepped up to Suite 9A and the porter opened the door. Will stepped back to allow Elyssa to step in first and her eyes widened and her jaw dropped at the sight she beheld.

A huge open room welcomed them. She was sure it was larger than her whole house back in the Santa Ynez Valley. Large pieces of furniture gave the room a masculine feel, but the colorful pieces of artwork on the walls added a liveliness that was quite appealing. Fresh cut flowers filled several vases. Elyssa walked in and admired the interior decorating in the suite. While done in a Guatemalan style, it had flourishes of American and European design.

Will tipped the porter and sent him away with some final words in Spanish. He turned to her and smiled. "Is it to your satisfaction?"

"Yes. It is quite nice."

"Good. The two suites should be comparable, but you can check out the suite next door and choose the one you want. I'll take the one you don't want."

She silently admitted to herself that staying in a suite such as this was much more preferable than a small room.

Will walked over to a door on the wall next to the one they came through and opened it, revealing a completely different suite. Thinking it was still part of the one they were in and he was merely showing her more of it, she walked over to take a thorough look. When she saw that it was arranged exactly as the one they were standing in, her eyes widened.

She turned to face Will, her eyes were glaring.

"You said we had two separate suites!" she said, accusingly pointing her finger at him.

Will took a few easy strides and stood before her, wrapping her pointed finger in his hand and gently closing it as it joined the others into her fist.

"I wouldn't do that here in Guatemala, Elyssa. It is very rude to point."

With her hand now completely encased in his and his most natural, manly scent emanating from him, she didn't trust herself to look up into his face. She knew his eyes were upon her and felt her heart quicken as if she were a small bird in the clutches of a fierce cat.

"Now what were you saying?" he asked in a soft voice.

Elyssa gulped as everything but his close proximity was suddenly wiped from her mind. Frantically searching for her last thought, she finally recollected it. "You said we were in different suites!"

"Elyssa, these *are* two different suites. This is only a connecting door. You can lock it on your side if you are so worried. Now, which one do you want?"

Elyssa looked from one to the other, not really noticing any difference. "I'll take this one," she said quickly, pulling away and nodding to the suite on the other side of the door.

"Are you sure?"

"Quite sure. It suits me fine."

Will carried her small bag into the suite and set it down. "After I clean up, I think I'll go downstairs and inquire about dinner options. Will you want something to eat later?"

"I'll have to see. I ate quite a bit at lunch."

"I'll let you know what I find."

He turned to leave, but was halted by Elyssa's words. "I really do appreciate all you have done," she said as she allowed a smile to appear. "Thank you."

Her words stunned him and his heart seemed to swell into his throat, preventing him from saying anything more than, "You're welcome."

He left the room, closing the connecting door behind him. She remained fixed to one spot, her heart pounding. Feeling it was the only way to deal with the turmoil building inside, she turned the lock on the door and said softly to herself, "I am not doing this because of you, Will. I'm doing it because of me!"

She faced away from the door and leaned against it, looking about her. "So this is what he is used to," she said softly to herself. "He doesn't think twice about spending money on the finer things while all my life I've had to weigh every purchase and its price before I spend what little money I have." Then she laughed, "Unless I'm using someone else's money to decorate their home!"

She shook her head and began to chide herself. "Don't go thinking it's a lifestyle you want, Elyssa. Consider what you would have to give up being married to someone like him!" She bit her lip and wondered what ever prompted her to think of him and marriage in the same sentence!

She was anxious to get into the shower, so she opened up her suitcase and took out a pair of cotton lounge pants and top. She stepped into the bathroom and openly gawked at the immense room before her. It was tiled in rich inlayed blue and gold tile with a marble sink and tub accented with beautifully polished brass faucets. She couldn't help but feel regal.

She gratefully shed her wet clothing and turned the water on in the shower. She tested it a couple of times until it was a soothing temperature and then stepped into the pulsating water. The droplets felt invigorating as they washed over her. Taking a bottle of shampoo, she liberally poured some into her hair and began sudsing it up with her fingers.

As her fingers massaged her scalp and worked the shampoo throughout her thick, brown hair, she began humming a song. When she realized what the song was, she had to laugh at its implications. It was a song she had sung in her high school musical when she had the lead in *South Pacific*.

"Oh, yes!" she said emphatically. "I *am* going to wash that man and everything about him right out of my hair!"

Then she slowly shook her head and said, "But I'm finding it harder and harder."

After spending a good fifteen minutes washing and soaking (and singing the song through several times for emphasis), she emerged from the shower and quickly dried herself off. She pulled her hair up and wrapped one of the luxuriant hotel towels around it. She put on her lounging outfit and then released her hair from the towel, letting it flow freely.

When dampened, her thick, natural curls seemed to have a mind of their own, but they framed her face beautifully. She shook her head a few times and ran her fingers through her hair, deciding she would let it air dry for a while.

Walking back into the bedroom, her hand swept over the thick, luxurious bedspread. "This is really nice!" She sat down upon it and flopped back. Lying there for several minutes, she concluded that she had never felt a more comfortable bed.

Turning her head toward the large sliding glass door, she looked outside and noticed that the sun was trying to peek out from the clouds over the lake. She stood up and walked over to the door, opening it and stepping out onto the balcony. A light rain continued to shower down and looking far across the lake, she saw the faintest of rainbows emerging. The slowly strengthening sunlight glistened across the lake. The air was fresh and cool and she watched as the sun and clouds vied for dominance in the sky.

She gazed out at the scenery before her, and while she didn't think she could ever live here, she had to admit that it was more beautiful than anything she had ever seen. She even began to consider that Janet and Chad could have been very happy with homes here and in Guatemala City.

She looked toward the two volcanoes that she had seen earlier. They were both shrouded in a heavy mist. The third was still yet to be seen. Her thoughts went to Will and she laughed as she suddenly thought of how much like these volcanoes he was. *Prominent, yet cloaked in mystery. Firm and solid, yet hiding so much. Ready to erupt at any moment?* She shuddered.

Yes, she thought to herself. There was more to him than she had ever imagined. But did she really want to dig deep enough through the layers to discover what lay beneath the surface? What would that mean if she did?

Her eyes rested on a beam of light coming down from the clouds as it played upon the water. The large gray billows moved across and around the sun, creating unexpected shadows or sudden rays of light. She was mesmerized by the beautiful sight and therefore did not notice that Will stepped out onto the balcony from his suite.

A light rain continued to fall, but they were protected from it by the balcony above. Will walked over to the edge and grasped the railing with his hands, looking straight out.

"I have often heard how beautiful Lake Atitlan was, but other than a quick trip a while back when I was here for barely an hour, I've never had the opportunity to really see it for myself."

Elyssa turned to look at him. His sharply chiseled profile and dark, wavy hair brought a lump to Elyssa's throat. There was something in his demeanor that betrayed some sort of recollection of grief or pain.

"Why were you only here for an hour?"

Silence overtook him and Elyssa waited.

He turned to look at her and for the first time he saw compassion in her eyes directed at him. She had no makeup on, her damp curls glistened, and she was the most beautiful woman he had ever laid his eyes on. A stirring in his heart gave him reason to hope that her opinion of him was changing and that possibly this visit to Lake Atitlan would make up for the disaster that brought him here a short time ago.

He chose not to answer and abruptly changed the subject. "There is a nice dining facility on the main floor. Shall I call for you in an hour?"

Elyssa slowly nodded her head which was met by Will nodding his. He then turned to go back inside.

They each stayed in their suite until about seven o'clock, when Will rapped at the connecting door. Elyssa unlocked and opened it. Her hair had dried; she had styled it simply and had put on a little makeup. She was wearing a light cotton dress; the only one she had brought along to the lake.

Will had changed into Dockers and a long sleeved dress shirt that was open at the collar. A slight hint of the cologne he was wearing teased Elyssa's nose with an outdoorsy scent.

He looked at her and Elyssa noticed his eyes travel down to her shoes and slowly up again. He tightly pressed his lips together, and Elyssa suddenly wondered whether he was disappointed in her looks. He was probably used to women who only wore the most fashionable clothes.

Well, this will just have to do! she thought to herself, although deep down inside she regretted that she had not taken more time with her appearance.

Seated in the small restaurant downstairs, lit only by candles on the table and the setting sun, Elyssa found herself battling her feelings for Will. It came as a surprise to her that she had not really felt any anger toward him in quite a while and was actually enjoying his presence. She knew the romantic atmosphere was certainly no ally to her in helping her curb these burgeoning feelings.

An unusual curiosity about the man had taken hold of her which she fought with everything in her being to control. It left her unable to talk of even the simplest things.

Finally, after picking lightly at the food that was brought, she said, "You told me a little about your sister earlier. What about you?"

"Me? What do you want to know?" Will looked up at her with surprise.

"I don't know…" Elyssa shrugged. "I did all the talking at lunch." Elyssa gave him a disarming smile. "Now it's *your* turn."

Will took in a deep breath at the sight of Elyssa's sparkling eyes. "Well, you know I live and work in Chicago."

"Ah, yes. Do you live nearby your office?" Elyssa was tempted to ask him if he lived at his office, but thought the better of it.

"I have a condominium in the city, which is about 20 miles from the office; a relatively easy distance to travel back and forth."

"An easy distance you say! I would imagine in rush hour it could take you close to an hour to get to work. Let me have my rural country home where the only traffic we have is when the fair comes to town!"

"I think you'd like Chicago if you gave it a chance. It's a main hub for several airlines… you can get just about anywhere from there."

"I don't think that's enough incentive for me."

Will looked at her oddly, wondering if there was any incentive great enough to bring her there. At this point, he was quite certain it *wasn't* him. "You are that attached to Santa Ynez? You enjoy living in the country?"

Elyssa skewed her mouth and leaned forward. "We are talking about me again, but yes, I do. Country living suits me fine and I have no desire to ever live in a large city ever again."

Elyssa listened with interest after that as Will began to talk of his family. He told her how his father poured himself into the small family company his grandfather began when he came over from England and settled in Chicago. He talked of his father dying far too young and leaving him to run the company at an even younger age. His mother, it seems, had died when Gina was a child and his father never remarried, having been totally devoted to his wife.

During the course of the meal, Will spoke very little about himself. Elyssa wondered whether he would confess how he felt being selected as one of the country's top 50 most eligible bachelors in a popular magazine; or how many hours he usually spends at the office compared to his home; or how he spends his hard earned money any way he pleases. Perhaps, she wondered, he had nothing to say about himself because he had no life other than Pemberleo Coffee. In speaking about his family though, Elyssa had to admit that it appeared he cared deeply for them.

Elyssa found herself again and again pondering this man and why he had taken so much upon himself for her. Her heart began to swell with a cautious conviction that perhaps he was doing this for her simply because he wanted to.

When they finished dining, they parted on amicable terms and as soon as she entered her suite, she walked over to the window overlooking the lake. Looking out at the reds and golds that dotted the sky and reflected down on the lake, she didn't dare step out on the balcony. If Will joined her, she knew his mere presence in such a romantic setting would unsettle her immensely.

In the final light of day, Elyssa looked out across the lake and smiled when she was finally able to see the very tip of the third volcano peering out from behind the clouds.

Chapter 12

The next day, Elyssa awakened early. She called for room service to bring her fruit, rolls, and coffee. When she poured some coffee into her cup from the pot that had been brought, she found herself wondering whether it was Pemberleo. After a few sips, she was quite certain it wasn't. She was surprised at how easily she could tell the difference and how much more superior Pemberleo was.

When she finished eating, she took a shower and then slipped into a thick terry cloth robe provided by the hotel. She ran her hands down the plush fabric after tightening the belt around her waist and walked over to the sliding glass door. She peered out to see if the weather had improved enough for them to take the boat ride to the village this morning. A few clouds splashed the skies with pinks and oranges, announcing the sun's approach. The last remnants of the previous day's storm lingered as a dense mist. It clung tightly to the mountains across the lake, keeping the volcanoes hidden from her sight.

Opening the door, she walked out onto the balcony and filled her lungs with the morning air. She felt the heaviness that came from warm air and high humidity, but a light breeze teased her with cool wisps that played with her hair. She walked to the edge of the balcony and looked down to the street below, where a few of the locals walked, presumably to begin the new day at work. Glancing back out across the lake, boats of all sizes dotted the waters as fishermen got an early start in the hopes of catching enough fish to make ends meet.

She turned to step back inside, but was halted when Will stepped out. She instinctively pulled the robe more tightly about her.

"Good morning, Elyssa," he said. "How are things looking this morning?"

He was shirtless, wearing only lounge pants and a towel slung about his shoulders. His hair was still damp from a shower. As she gazed at his well toned form, she could not formulate even a simple answer to his question. The only view impressed upon her was of him, and she hoped her blush escaped his notice!

She turned back to look at the lake and felt him come stand next to her on his side of the balcony. She took in a deep breath as her heart began pounding relentlessly. "It's a lovely morning," she was finally able to say. "I don't think I've ever seen a more beautiful sunrise."

"It is beautiful." He looked back at her. "Have you ordered breakfast, yet?"

"Yes, I've eaten already."

"I haven't ordered yet. I'll do that now, so we can be downstairs when Manuel meets us. We have a little over an hour before he comes for us. I'll call when we need to go down."

Elyssa packed her things and sat in one of the large plush chairs in the living room as she awaited Will's call. Today they would set out for the small village for a couple of days. She would stay in Chad and Janet's modest home while Will would be forced to find something else. A smile appeared as she contemplated him staying in a pension filled with bugs and peeling paint and who knows what all else. *Now that will be interesting!* she thought.

Will finally called and said the porter would be coming up for their bags. Elyssa gave one last look around the room and made sure she had everything packed. An appreciative sigh escaped as she beheld what had been her accommodations for the night.

Going to the connecting door, she turned the knob and it opened. Will immediately walked over to her and picked up her bag, bringing it into his suite.

"Manuel said he would be waiting for us outside the hotel. It is a short walk to the dock."

She walked into his suite and distracted herself by walking to the window and looking out.

"Were your accommodations adequate?" Will asked her.

Elyssa chuckled to herself. "Oh, yes," she assured him with an appreciative nod of her head. "They were *more* than adequate."

"I'm glad," he replied with a satisfied smile. "I hoped you would like it."

Manuel met Elyssa and Will outside the hotel. He and his son had already walked down to the dock, where he had deposited their luggage. His son remained there to watch over it until they all returned. Manuel insisted on carrying Elyssa's luggage and Will carried his own.

When they reached the dock, they were both rather surprised by the boat. It was certainly not a luxury yacht. They could easily see why traveling in it during a rainstorm would not have been advisable. It was completely open to the elements and seemed somewhat primitive.

Their luggage was taken and stored in a small hold while passengers gathered and waited. They were finally allowed to board and Elyssa took a seat. Will came and sat down beside her.

She and Will were two of only three on the boat who were not locals and were looked upon with friendliness but perhaps a bit more curiosity. Elyssa doubted that many foreigners would embark away from Panajachel to a small village whose name she didn't even know. The other person seemed to be a typical tourist, happily taking pictures of the scenery around him.

They arrived at the village after a rather disconcerting forty-five minute ride in this boat that one could hardly believe would remain upon the water. Elyssa wondered whether they even had lifejackets for everyone. She was most grateful to Manuel for insisting they not venture out in the storm yesterday.

The boat pulled up to a small dock, and after everyone gathered what little belongings they had, they stepped out. Elyssa felt the boat sway and had a little more trepidation than everyone else in taking the giant step out of the boat. Will reached out and took her hand to steady her, making sure she was safely on the dock before he let go.

Manuel gathered their two small bags as well as the one he and his son were sharing and began to lead the way. "It is a short walk this way."

Elyssa and Will followed, and as they passed small shanties with little more than one room and a tin roof, they cast glances at one another several times. Elyssa was shocked that people had so little and she wondered whether the look on Will's face reflected a disgust at even being here or empathy for the people and their living conditions.

As they walked through the small dirt streets, Will took it all in. He knew the small farmers would live somewhere around the edge of the hillsides and he depended on Manuel to take him there. He had seen the poorer parts of Guatemala City, but had never actually come this close to simple life. His morning with Elyssa at the pre-school was about as close as he'd ever been to it.

He looked over at the edge of the lake where people were washing their clothes. He wondered whether they could even be getting them clean. His glance unwittingly went down to the clothes he wore and even though it was a T-shirt and jeans, he knew they were clean and probably cost him more than some of these people made in a month, if that.

Elyssa looked at the faces of the people they passed. They smiled at her and seemed to have an inner contentment that defied their living conditions, much like the children at the pre-school. They lived simply and were happy. They had none of the stress and worries of modern day, big city life to bring back to their home. They may have had to worry about enough money for food, but many had small gardens in their yards and she was quite sure they looked out for one another.

They reached a side street and Manuel stopped, looking at Elyssa. If you want to go up to the market square, this is where you will come for the ride up. It will cost you only a couple quetzals."

"How often does it run?"

Manuel shrugged. "Whenever it gets here and fills up with people." Manuel looked up at a mountain that edged the village. "It's up there. Are you sure you want to go?"

Elyssa nodded. "If Janet enjoyed going to it, I am sure I will too."

"And Sir," Manuel said, as he turned to face Will, who was walking behind them. "Will you be going with her?"

Will looked at Elyssa and then back to Manuel. "I suppose so."

A satisfied look spread across Manuel's face and he vigorously rubbed his hands together. "Good," he said and he turned to continue on towards the house.

They finally came to a small white house, complete with a not so white picket fence around it. The garden looked as though it had once been well tended and Elyssa wondered how much time Janet had spent tending it. But it had been neglected for some time, and although frequent rains kept it watered, the weeds seemed to be overtaking what had a short while ago been a nice, manicured garden.

They walked up to the house and Manuel pulled out a key. He opened the door, allowing Will and Elyssa to step through and he then stepped back out after handing Elyssa the key.

He turned to Will. "The pension I told you about -- *La Vida* -- is just around the corner. It's nothing like you're used to, but it's clean." He pulled out a small piece of paper and handed it to Elyssa. "If either of you needs anything, you can reach me at this phone number. We'll be in another village a ways down the shore, but I can be here fairly quickly."

"Thank you, Manuel," Elyssa said appreciatively.

He turned back to Will. "I will come by tomorrow to take you to visit some of the farmers. What time should I come by?"

"How about one o'clock?"

"One o'clock it is." He turned to leave, but stopped. "Oh, by the way, I made arrangements for us to take the boat back at nine o'clock on Monday morning so we can get back to Guatemala City that afternoon."

Now it was Will's turn to thank the young man. Manuel and his son said their goodbyes and left.

Elyssa stepped in and looked around the living room in the small home. It was decorated very simply which made it feel more cozy. Will merely stood there with his gaze upon her and she suddenly felt awkward.

"Do you want to look around?" he asked.

Elyssa chuckled. "That won't take very long."

She was grateful she wasn't feeling the overwhelming grief upon coming in here. While she knew Janet and Chad had lived here, she felt a little more composed than she did when she first stepped into their townhome in Guatemala City.

She walked through the living room and down the hall toward the single bedroom. When she stepped in, she felt a tightening around her heart as she looked in, but it was brief and she was soon able to smile as she looked around her. On the wall, photographs and pictures were hung in the most haphazard way.

Will remained in the living room and began to sit down in one of the chairs when he heard Elyssa cry out, "Oh, Janet!"

Will's heart leapt and he jumped up from the chair. As he rushed back to the bedroom, he wondered what it was that triggered her outburst this time. He came to the door and braced both hands against the frame; a concerned look upon his face. He saw Elyssa staring intently at some pictures hung on the wall.

"What happened?" he asked as he looked to her and then followed her eyes to the grouping of pictures on the wall. "What are they? What do they mean?"

Elyssa turned and without understanding, asked, "Excuse me?"

"You cried out. You said, 'Oh, Janet.'"

Elyssa shook her head. "Janet knows better than to hang her pictures like that! You never hang four pictures on the wall in such a random way. Your eye doesn't know which one to look at."

Will looked at Elyssa with more than a little incredulity. He had expected to find her in another sea of tears, but instead, she was critiquing her sister's decorating style.

Elyssa continued, "Janet never had an eye for placement, but she ought to have known you never place pictures on the wall that way. You must have a semblance of balance and a focal point."

Will's eyes widened as his face transformed from panic to disbelief. "You cried out like that because she had hung her pictures wrong?"

Elyssa walked over to the wall and removed a couple of pictures from their nails. "Sure. Can't you see? This one should have gone here, with these two on either side. And this one," she held it up to the wall because there was no nail upon which to hang it, "would be perfect here."

Will rocked back and forth on his heels as he looked at her with a gleam in his eye. "So that's what that was about at the pre-school."

"What are you talking about?"

"You walked over to the table and began rearranging things. You didn't like the way they were placed."

A sheepish look made Elyssa's face look annoyingly irresistible to Will. "Guilty. Sometimes I do it without realizing it."

Bringing the one picture down, she held it in both hands and stared at it. "That's the curse of being a designer. Always critiquing and figuring out how you could do it better." She turned and noticed him eyeing her curiously. His gaze was deep and intense, and she quickly turned her attention back to study the work of art in her hands.

"I think I'll take this one back with me," she said thoughtfully.

A small smile threatened to burst forth from Will. He felt as though they had made a major breakthrough. Elyssa had finally been able to think and talk about Janet in a lighthearted manner instead of dissolving into tears. But he didn't dare bring it to her attention.

There was silence in the room for a moment and then Will said, "Everything has been cleaned in the house, all the linens and such, so there should be no problem for you to sleep in here."

She turned quickly, her eyes darkening. "No! No, I could never bring myself to sleep in their bed."

"Elyssa, don't be unreasonable." He wondered whether they had just taken a step backwards.

"Perhaps I'm being unreasonable -- irrational, even -- but I can't do that. I won't do that. I'll sleep on the sofa in the living room. If you want to stay here instead of the pension, *you* can sleep in here."

She turned to walk out when Will answered back, "Well, I'm not sleeping in their bed if *you're* not!"

Elyssa stopped suddenly, her eyes widened, and she turned sharply around. "What did you say?"

An uncharacteristic, but disarming blush spread across his face. "I didn't quite mean that the way it sounded, Elyssa." Normally, he carefully thought through every word that came out of his mouth. Why he didn't catch it this time, he was not quite sure.

Elyssa could not hold the smirk back any longer. "I certainly hope you didn't."

Inwardly, Will cherished the light banter that had replaced the cold demeanor and biting words that had at first characterized their relationship. He could sense that Elyssa's feelings had begun to change from bitterness to acceptance. He could only hope that would be enough to erase her resentment towards him and that her acceptance would evolve into something deeper.

After they both freshened up, Elyssa looked at her watch. "Well, if we want to spend any time up at the market square, we better leave now."

"If you don't mind, I'll leave my things here and check in at the pension when we get back this afternoon."

They each grabbed a bottle of water and placed it in a small backpack Will brought along. They walked out, easily finding their way back to the corner where Manuel had told them to catch the transportation up the hill. A few other people had begun to collect and again they were watched with curious eyes.

A short while later, both Elyssa and Will noticed the people begin to gather their things and press towards one another as if their transportation had arrived. But in looking down the street, all either of them could see was a rickety looking cattle truck. When it stopped in front of them and people began piling into the back, neither could hide their astonishment.

"We're not going up a mountain in that, Elyssa. I absolutely put my foot down!"

Elyssa looked at the truck and then back at him. "You can put your foot down all you want, even stamp it a few times…" She straightened her shoulders and stared intently at his eyes. "But I am going!"

Defiantly, she pulled out a few coins from her purse and strode up the ramp, handing her coins to a young man and taking her place on one side. She stood, placing a firm grip on the side rail. While not looking directly at him, she could see Will out of the corner of her eye as he raked his fingers through his hair in frustration.

The truck was fairly well packed with people, and the doors were about to be closed in the back. Will held up his hand to stop them and he jumped in. There were too many people between him and Elyssa to easily walk over to her. For that she was grateful, certain that she would have been the object of a very stern scolding.

As the truck slowly began its ascent up the hill, the breeze played with Elyssa's hair. She looked over the edge of the truck as the view began to stretch out below them. The abundance of greens covering the hillside and the blues of the water and sky were nothing short of beautiful. The volcanoes off in the distance stood majestically as if they were sentinels guarding the lake. A smile on her face drew all of Will's attention, despite his misgivings about what they were doing.

While he had reservations about the mode of transportation they were taking, he had no idea that this little excursion would involve about thirty sharp hairpin turns as the truck made its way up the mountain. He didn't even want to think about what would happen if they encountered a vehicle coming the other way. Several times he wondered whether the vehicle would even make it up the hill! But in all these things, Elyssa seemed oblivious as she watched with glee the scenery pass.

At one point, the truck did encounter another vehicle and had to back down the mountain a short way to allow the other vehicle to pass. Elyssa met Will's eyes briefly with concerned ones of her own, but once the tremulous maneuver was successfully completed, she turned away.

As Will's mind reeled between the absurdity of them riding this cattle truck up a mountain and Elyssa's evident enjoyment of it, he realized that this was the very reason he was so drawn to her. He would have never ridden this truck if she were not with him. If he had to, he would have sought someone out and paid them a nice sum to drive him up in a trustworthy vehicle.

From that very first evening he saw her at Chad and Janet's rehearsal dinner, he had seen an endearing liveliness in her that was so unlike the other ladies in his circle of acquaintance. They concerned themselves with always looking their best in designer clothes, being seen in the right places and with the right people, driving the most popular car, and all those other traps that were of no value, at least to him.

He chuckled to himself as he recalled how angry he had been at her for her outburst at his announcement of Chad's promotion, while at that same moment he had found her even more appealing. At the wedding, as he stood by her side and escorted her back down the aisle behind Chad and Janet, he couldn't shake the feeling that she felt so right for him. He remembered chiding himself for his completely unreasonable infatuation and determined to have nothing to do with her.

A slight jarring of the truck brought Will back to the present and he saw that they finally reached the top.

As everyone eagerly stepped down from the truck, Will stepped over toward Elyssa and helped her down, shaking his head. "It's not often that I risk my life going to the market!"

"Personally, I found it invigorating!" Elyssa replied with an unrestrained smile. "Besides, driving the streets of Chicago can't be any less dangerous!"

"When I drive in Chicago," he took her arm and guided her in the direction everyone was going. "*I* am the one in control of the vehicle."

Elyssa smiled as they followed the crowd of people to a rather large sized plaza. Here they saw vendors selling a variety of goods from garden fresh produce and baked foods to brightly colored yarns and threads, pieces of wood ready to be carved, and large sheets of leather that would be fashioned into belts, wallets, and assorted other goods. They walked around in silence, each taking in the unique atmosphere of this place. Up here there were no vendors selling souvenirs for tourists; everything was for the locals. Elyssa could clearly understand why Janet had been fond of coming up here.

A stage was set up on one side and a band played lively music. Occasionally a vocalist appeared and sang. She didn't understand one word but completely loved it.

As they meandered through row after row of goods, Elyssa found herself drawn to the yarns and fabrics. She knew she needed restraint, as she would never be able to take home everything that she liked, but she did allow herself to make a few purchases.

Something caught Elyssa's eye and she wandered away from Will. When she looked back around, she could no longer see him. Shrugging her shoulders, as if convincing herself she didn't really care, she began walking around alone. The fresh fruits and vegetables looked delicious and when she found herself staring at basketfuls of ripe, red strawberries, she couldn't help herself. As Elyssa handed over the small number of quetzals the woman asked for, she was grateful she could at least remember her numbers in Spanish. She purchased a small bag and began to enjoy their succulent taste.

She continued to wander through the plaza, occasionally looking around for Will. She walked over to a man who was selling hand carved wood. They were beautiful pieces and she began dreaming about what she could do with them.

She was about to bite into another strawberry when she felt a hand on her shoulder. She turned to see that Will had caught up with her. Rather than greet her, he asked what she was doing.

"Looking at the beautiful wood pieces," she answered rather defensively. "Why?"

"Not that!" he said firmly. "That!" he said as he pointed to the strawberries.

Elyssa could not understand his concern and decided to be lighthearted. "Now you know, Will," she took his hand in hers and closed his finger within her palm. "It's not polite to point here."

He couldn't help but smile. "I stand corrected, Elyssa." He rather enjoyed the feel of her small hand around his, but his concern for her welfare was greater. "What are you doing eating those strawberries?"

Releasing his hand, she said, "I'm doing just that! Eating strawberries. Why?"

He reached for the bag and took it from her. "Did you remember to wash these first in your bottled water before you ate them?"

Elyssa's eyes widened. "No, other people were eating them right out of the bag."

"Yes," Will answered in a rather long, drawn out way. "That's because they're used to the food and water here. Your system isn't."

Elyssa hated being treated like a young child by him but knew he was right. "I am sure I will be all right."

"Well, just in case," and here he took her hand tightly in his. "We're getting down the mountain. The last thing you need is to make all those hairpin turns with a queasy stomach."

They began walking toward the stop where the truck dropped them off, but arrived to see that it had just departed and was making a turn down the street.

"Great," he said. "We have no idea when the next one will come."

"I feel fine," Elyssa reassured him. "We can wait."

"Now you feel fine. But it won't last long." He looked around him and then told her, "Wait here!"

He quickly departed without allowing her any response. "Ohhh!" Elyssa cried out in disgust. "He makes me so mad when he issues all these orders!"

She sat down on a bench and began to wonder whether she really would get sick. *I hope not!* she thought to herself. *That's the last thing I need with him around!*

She watched for Will to return and was startled when a small pickup truck stopped in front of her and Will opened the door and jumped out. "Here, Elyssa. Get in."

She stepped into the truck and slid across to the middle of the seat, nodding at the gentleman behind the wheel. As they took off, Will explained to Elyssa that he had asked around whether anyone knew of someone willing to drive them down the hill in a car, and this gentleman said he would. The older man nodded and smiled as Will talked to her, almost as if he understood what he was saying. Elyssa was quite sure, however, that he couldn't.

The ride down was much less adventuresome than the ride up and Elyssa was becoming more convinced that there had been no need for alarm.

As Will carried on a friendly conversation with the driver, Elyssa looked through her treasure of things she had bought. Her favorite find was a brightly colored embroidered shawl that cost her almost nothing.

Leaning her head back, she felt comforted by the voices, particularly Will's. He had a very soothing voice, and as she really could not understand anything they were saying to one another, before she knew it she had drifted off to sleep.

She awakened when the truck came to a stop at the bottom of the hill. Her eyes opened slowly and none too soon did she discover that her head had toppled against Will and his arm was wrapped snugly about her. She quickly righted herself and he withdrew his arm. He opened the door and stepped out, reaching for her hand, as if nothing had happened... almost as if it had been the most natural thing for her to fall asleep up against him.

They walked the small dirt streets up toward what Elyssa thought would be considered the center of the village. Small markets, a variety of stores, and eating places lined the street. Will seemed to be looking for something as he gazed down the street.

"Are we looking for something in particular?" Elyssa asked.

Will nodded. "Manuel recommended a place to eat. Are you hungry?"

Without any warning, Elyssa paled and wrapped her hands tightly around her stomach. "I don't think so, Will. I think we better get back to the house. I'm not feeling very well."

Chapter 13

Will took hold of Elyssa's arm and began walking at a faster pace. "The house is still a few blocks away. Do you think you can make it?"

Elyssa grabbed her stomach tightly as she nodded. Presently, it was merely cramping and the situation was nothing more than bothersome, but she already felt all the mortification that her unthinking actions would lead to. All she could foresee was locking herself in the bathroom as her body rebelled against some bacteria that it was not used to.

Why, she thought, *does he have to be here to witness this?* She cast a sly glance up at him. *And why does he always have to be right?*

Elyssa's steps became slower while her sense of urgency increased. About a block from the house, she suddenly doubled over, the cramping in her stomach overtaking her. Will reached down immediately and picked her up. Her face, which was normally vibrant and rosy, was now pale and dull.

It was awkward carrying her with the bags she had purchased up at the market, but it felt good to have her in his arms. It gave him a sense of gratification being there to help her. He liked the feeling, especially when she relaxed against him and turned her head and rested it upon his shoulder. His delight in holding her was tempered, however, knowing how poorly Elyssa must be feeling.

They arrived at the home none too soon. He put her down to open the door and as soon as it was opened, Elyssa made a beeline for the bathroom, slamming the door behind her. She turned on the water full blast, hoping it would cover up some of the sound. Then she sat on the floor next to the toilet and waited for the inevitable.

Will went to the small pantry that Janet and Chad had just off the kitchen and he looked inside. Seeing a small box of crackers and a bottle of 7Up, he pulled them out. When she was ready for something to eat and needed something to drink, these would be best. He knew Pemberleo recommended that their employees in Guatemala keep them on hand for this very reason and was grateful to find them stored away.

He settled down in a recliner in the living room and waited. He knew it would be a long day and might be a long night and he had no intention of leaving her here alone.

~~*

Will made several attempts throughout the afternoon to get Elyssa to open the door, offering her crackers, 7Up, or plain bottled water, but she refused all.

"Go away!" she moaned when he knocked on the door. "You might as well check in at the pension now, because I'll be in here a long time."

"Elyssa, you need to drink some fluids. You don't want to get dehydrated."

"Just leave me alone!"

Will tried the knob to the door again, hoping it would open, but she kept it securely locked. "I'm not leaving until I know you're feeling better."

He looked down at the knob and figured all it would take was some sort of screwdriver to open it from his side. Having no idea where to even look for one, he deemed it wiser that he not attempt that unless it was truly needed. Elyssa would be even more angry with him if he opened the door against her wishes.

Telling Elyssa that he left crackers and drinks outside the door, Will returned to the living room.

Will took a seat in the recliner and picked up a book. He didn't often find the time for the luxury of reading and decided he would try now to begin the book he brought along.

After reading through a couple chapters of the book, Will put it down as his hunger began to increasingly overtake his desire to read. He didn't dare cook anything inside the house, being all too aware from experience that the scent of the food would not sit well with Elyssa considering the condition she was in. He called to her through the door to let her know he was running out to pick up something to eat.

A moan let him know she had heard him. Stepping outside, he walked quickly down the street in the hopes of finding something close by.

Elyssa listened for the sound of the door closing and slowly pulled herself up. She looked in the mirror and groaned. She looked terrible and she felt worse. Her body ached both inside and out. She had chills that caused her to shiver even though the day was quite warm. Her stomach was cramping and in the last few hours she had either been leaning over the porcelain throne, sitting on it, or curled next to it on the hard, cold floor. She knew there was not much she could do but let it run its course. However, she could do something about her comfort.

She slowly opened the door, and as the next wave of nausea swept over her, she took a deep breath to push it down. Looking out at the small hall outside the bathroom, she saw what looked like a linen closet. She gingerly walked down the hall and opened it. Inside were some linens and she gratefully reached for a blanket and pillow, taking them back with her to the bathroom. Before locking herself inside again, she pulled in the food and drink that Will had left for her. She wasn't sure she was ready for any of it yet, but when she was, she wanted it inside with her. She smiled weakly at Will's thoughtfulness… and the fact that he hadn't yet said, "I told you so!"

Elyssa dropped the pillow on the floor and wrapped the blanket around her, warding off a new round of shivers. Then she curled up on the floor, feeling more miserable than she had in a very long time.

Will found a small family run cafe a little over a block away and guiltily enjoyed a couple Guatemalan soft tacos. He ate quickly as he was anxious to return to the house. On the way back, he stopped at a small market and picked up a few items that might come in handy later.

When he returned, he put the food away and then went straight to the hall and stood outside the bathroom door to inform Elyssa that he had returned. He noticed that she had taken the food and drink in with her. He was relieved. Hopefully she was able to keep something down.

He tapped lightly on the door. "I'm back. Let me know if I can do anything for you."

He was answered with a long groan that admonished him to leave her alone. He stood outside the door silently wondering how long this would assail her body. He finally retreated back to the living room, picked up his book, and sat in the recliner chair, putting it in its most reclined position. He was here for the long haul -- whether she liked it or not!

Will had barely read a few more pages of his book when he quickly lost interest. Thoughts of Elyssa crowded out any comprehension of the written words on the page. He went from feeling concern for her well being, to joy at just being able to be with her, to disappointment that he had pretty much lost any opportunity that day to spend time in her company, to the smallest hope that things had begun to change between them.

He also had the anticipation of tomorrow, when Elyssa would surely begin to feel better. Although he was obliged to visit some of the coffee growers in the area, he trusted that Elyssa would wish to join him, although she still may not feel up to it. He didn't have much time left. As he contemplated these things, he became very drowsy and soon drifted off to sleep.

A very vivid dream beckoned him. He was not usually one to have dreams -- or at least remember them -- but in this dream, he saw Elyssa standing up in a boat on a lake. He was on shore and wondered how to get to her. She didn't seem in danger; she was just frustratingly out of reach. He ran along a dock that stretched far into the lake, but the farther he ran, the further the boat seemed to be. She looked everywhere but at him. He contemplated jumping in and going after her, but something prevented him from doing so. He wasn't sure if it was something sinister or was it just his own fear? He watched in dismay as the boat drifted away and faded from his sight.

~~*

Elyssa wasn't sure how long she had been in the bathroom, but she knew it had been several hours. Her body still swung tumultuously between chills, aches, nausea, and now, unsurprisingly, a throbbing headache. Whenever she suffered any sort of stomach ailment, she frequently experienced a splitting headache. When she was younger, she had always trusted Janet to sit by her side and gently rub her throbbing head until she was able to fall asleep. She always thought Janet would make an excellent nurse because she cared so much for people and was so compassionate. Unfortunately, Janet could not stand the sight of blood and therefore never aspired to being one. Tears began to sting Elyssa's eyes as she realized she would never have her sister's tender care again.

"Oh, Janet," she whispered. "Why can't you be here with me now?" Elyssa put her hand up to her forehead and rubbed it as she closed her eyes. "I know you would be able to help me feel better."

Once her silent tears had been shed, she slowly sat up. She waited to see if her stomach would rebel, but it didn't. She felt weak and a little dizzy, but other than that, she felt she would be able to stand up after a few minutes. She waited until the dizziness passed and pulled herself up. She leaned over the sink and splashed water on her face.

Elyssa took a washcloth from the towel bar, put it under the water, and cleaned around the sink and toilet. Then she sprayed some air freshener around the room. Just that little effort completely exhausted her, but she wanted the room to be clean if Will needed to come in here. She was sure at some point he would.

Elyssa knew she may have to come back in here in a moment's notice, but she was more than ready to remove herself from the bathroom. She *needed* to get out of this cold, confining room. All she wanted to do was to sleep, but she didn't want to fall asleep here on the floor.

Finally, garnering enough courage to lift her eyes to the mirror, she gasped at what she saw before her. Her hair was a tangle of snarls, her face was pale and her eyes were red. Her thoughts went to Will, who most likely was still out in the living room. Elyssa shook her head. *If the way I have treated him since his arriving here didn't cause him to run in the opposite direction, the sight of me right now certainly will!*

As she peered at her reflection, she wondered whether or not that mattered to her. Letting out a bemused huff, she decided she would tackle that issue when her mind was a little clearer.

Elyssa picked up the blanket and pillow from the floor, hugging them both tightly against her stomach as another wave of nausea threatened to delay her escape. She stood very still, taking slow, deep breaths until it passed. She closed her eyes as her head began to throb again with an occasional sharp pain arcing across her temple. She steadied herself by bracing her hand on the sink and was tempted to simply collapse back on the floor, but decided to brave her body's upheaval and move herself to the living room.

Before leaving the bathroom, Elyssa took another look at her reflection in the mirror. In disgust, she took the blanket and slung half of it over her head, so that it covered her like a hood. She wrapped the rest around her, keeping her pillow snug against her, and opened the door.

It was quiet when she stepped out. She wondered whether Will had finally tired of sitting around doing nothing. Had he finally gone to the pension and checked in? She rolled her eyes as she thought to herself, *Oh, I hope so!*

She quietly walked down the hall and at first didn't see him. A sigh of relief almost escaped, but stopped abruptly when she noticed a pair of shoeless feet stretching out from the recliner that faced away from her. She walked up to him and peered out through her blanket. He was fast asleep.

A weak smile touched Elyssa's lips as she looked down at Will. He looked quite *unlike* a driven corporate executive. Her fuzzy mind tried to comprehend this man who had gone from being a hated ruthless executive… to being a thorn in her flesh… to something of an enigma to her.

As she gazed down at him, one of his brows lifted and an eye slowly opened;

then the other. He stared at her for a moment trying to make sense of this woman with a blanket covering her face, and then shook his head to rid it of its grogginess and imagery from the dream.

"Well," he said, as he straightened up in the chair. "Have you at last come back from the dead?"

"Not quite," Elyssa answered from underneath the blanket. "All I want to do is sleep and the bathroom floor has just become a little too uncomfortable." She let out a breathy moan. "I feel lousy enough that I might not wake up for hours."

"Mmmm, it's that bad, is it?" Will stood up from the chair. "Come, Elyssa, if you need sleep that much, I insist you sleep in the bed."

Despite Elyssa's frail condition, she remained adamant. "No, the sofa will do."

Will shook his head in exasperation as she turned and threw the pillow down on one end of the sofa.

"Right now all I want to do is sleep and forget about the last five or six hours." Keeping the blanket covering her face and wrapped about her, she collapsed onto the sofa.

Will left the room and went into the bathroom where he picked up her stash of food and drink. Before taking it to her, he stopped by the kitchen and rummaged around for a big bucket. Unable to find one, he finally found a large cooking pot. Bringing them all back, he leaned down. "Have you tried eating or drinking anything? You really must."

She waved her hand. "I ate a cracker a little over and hour ago and sipped some 7Up before I came out."

"Well, it's here for you in case you get hungry. I'll leave it on the table. In addition," here he paused and stroked his chin, looking for a delicate way to say it. "I'll put this pot on the floor in case you can't make it to the bathroom in time."

Elyssa groaned, "Oh, thanks. And I don't want any more to eat." Barely able to speak another word, she mumbled, "You might as well check into the pension now, I won't be much company."

She turned away from him, covering herself completely with the blanket. Her head still ached, but the comfort of the sofa, although not quite long enough for her to completely stretch out upon, was much more preferable than the bathroom floor. She quickly found herself drifting away and although Will was saying something, it was completely lost to her.

"You know I'll not leave you like this, Elyssa. Don't you know that by now?"

Her breathing deepened and Will knew she had fallen asleep. It was close to six o'clock and he decided he would go into the kitchen and make a sandwich with some of the things he had purchased at the market.

After eating, he returned to the living room and stood over Elyssa. She seemed to be getting restless on the small sofa. He watched as she squirmed and moaned causing the blanket to slip down off her feet. He reached down and picked it up, putting it back over her. When he tucked it in around her shoulders, he became alarmed when he noticed how warm she felt.

He touched the back of his fingers to her forehead and realized she had a fever. When he went to remove his hand, however, he was taken by surprise when she suddenly grabbed it. "Elyssa, what is it?"

"My head… it hurts so much."

"Is there something…"

He was interrupted by Elyssa's slurred words, "Janet, rub my head."

Will tensed and tried to pull his hand away, but Elyssa tightened her grip and held it in its place. He began to gently rub her forehead and she seemed to settle down, but he was now quite alarmed. She obviously was feverous and thought he was Janet. He shook his head as he wondered what to do. He didn't know whether to try and shake her out of it or help make her as comfortable as she could be -- all the while Elyssa not truly realizing he was the one doing it!

Will carefully lifted up her head and sat down, placing the pillow on his lap, and then lowered her head back down on top of it. When he removed his hand from her, she seemed to writhe and groan until he returned it to its place and stroked it again. He enjoyed looking down at her sleeping face as his fingers kneaded circles around her forehead. They occasionally strayed and nestled deeply into her mane of thick, dark hair, massaging her scalp. He felt more than a little guilty pleasure in his actions.

As the evening wore on, he wondered whether Elyssa was actually getting any sleep, as anytime his hand stopped or he removed it, she seemed to notice it. He wasn't sure whether she knew it was him and not Janet, but she hadn't said anything since that last outburst.

One thing he was sure of, though, was that she would be much more comfortable in a bed and would probably get a better night's sleep there than she would on the sofa. He looked down the hall and tried to calculate whether she would be angrier at him for placing her in the Blakelys' bed or awaking and finding herself asleep on his lap.

He knew her stubbornness would rise up and challenge him for going against her wishes, but he knew it was for the best. He shook his head and ran his free hand through his hair. "You may not be happy about this, Elyssa," he said softly, "but I've got to do it for your own good." He chuckled. "Besides, I'm getting a little stiff sitting here and I need to get up!"

Being very gentle so as not to awaken her, Will extricated Elyssa from his lap and laid her head back down on the sofa while he stood up and stretched his legs. He went to the window and looked out. There was a small view of the lake and he saw that the sun was setting. The deep colors from the sunset spilled across the sky and as he looked back at Elyssa's sleeping form, he wished he could take her for a walk down to the lake's edge. He was quite sure she would have enjoyed it. He knew *he* would have enjoyed just having her by his side.

As if she knew he was watching, she dug her head deeply in her pillow and one of her legs dropped down the side of the sofa.

"That does it," he said softly. "You're going into the other room."

Will went into the bedroom and pulled back the covers. "It's not like Chad and Janet would be upset that you're sleeping in their bed! I'm sure they'd want you to!"

He walked back into the living room and Elyssa was moaning again. He decided it would be better for him to wait until she was in a deeper sleep so she wouldn't wake up as he carried her in. He sat down in the chair and waited until she had settled down.

Will drifted to sleep occasionally, waking whenever Elyssa let out a groan. Finally, at well past ten o'clock, Elyssa seemed to be back in a deep sleep and he went over to pick her up. He touched his fingers to her head again and breathed a sigh of relief that her temperature seemed to have gone down a little.

Lifting her up in his arms, he carried her back into the bedroom. When he placed her on the bed and began to pull the blankets snugly up over her, she reached out for his hand again. "My head…"

He sat on the edge of the bed next to her, leaning on his one arm while his hand went back to her forehead.

"This is just great, Elyssa. All I need is for you to wake up and find yourself in Chad and Janet's bed with *me* by your side! You're really intent on setting me up, aren't you?"

Each time he tried to remove his hand, Elyssa moaned or reached back for it. As the evening wore on, Will found himself more and more uncomfortable. Finally, he reached over for the other pillow that was on the bed and put it behind him. He was propped up at an awkward angle against the headboard, but at least he had some soft support behind him. He wouldn't be here very long, anyway. He would wait until she was fast asleep and then he would quietly leave and go back into the living room and sleep.

That was his very last thought.

Chapter 14

In the still of the night, Elyssa awoke just enough to try to adjust her sleeping position. Her mind was still foggy and she was barely able to even comprehend that something prevented her from freely stretching out and moving. She was finally able to squirm and turn onto her side against a solid form, maneuvering underneath something draped across her. In her dazed state she didn't question this presence, but instead, felt safe and warm. A vaguely familiar pleasant scent coupled with a rhythmic beating and soft purring sound aided her in falling back into a deep slumber.

Later that morning, Will slowly opened his eyes. It was dark except for a trickle of light coming into the room. His back and neck ached, and at first he wasn't quite sure where he was. In a moment's recollection, however, his eyes widened and he was shockingly alert!

He had fallen asleep next to Elyssa on the bed. His body, rebelling against a most uncomfortable position, yearned to stretch out, while at the same time it reveled in her presence. Looking down at her, his heart began pounding mercilessly at the sight of her turned toward him; her head snuggled against his chest. His arm was draped across her and a yearning to enfold her within both his arms and pull her closer fought against a rational voice telling him he was playing with fire and the prospect of her wrath the longer he stayed.

As much as he wanted to remain there and savor the moment, he deemed it more prudent to remove himself from this most compromising, but tantalizing, circumstance before she awakened. Even though she was under the covers and he was on top of them, if she were to wake now, she would in all probability accuse him of unsavory intentions. Not that the thought of being with her hadn't crossed his mind. He found that her nearness and touch threw him into a tumultuous turmoil. Giving in to an irrational desire and throwing caution to the wind, he leaned over and softly kissed the top of her head before he carefully, and begrudgingly, disentangled himself from her side.

Will slid both feet off the bed onto the floor and then slowly pulled away from her. A slight moan from her prompted him to halt his difficult maneuver and remain still until he was sure Elyssa was sound asleep again. He watched as she stretched out her hand to within inches of him. When she settled down, he quickly pulled himself off the bed, taking in a deep breath, and stood looking down at her.

"That was just a little too close for comfort," he said softly to himself. "Even in your sleep you're determined to put me in situations where you can find fault with me!"

The light coming into the room allowed him to see that the coloring had returned to her face. He smiled as he anticipated seeing her bright eyes and beautiful smile again. "And trust me, Elyssa, at this moment, I am *not* without fault!"

He went out into the living room and looked out the window. The sun was just barely peeking out over the crest of a mountain across the lake. The sky above declared loudly, with bright sunlight, the dawn of a new day. The water shimmered in the awakening rays of light, but the street outside the window was still cloaked in shadows.

Will took in a very satisfied breath. He had not felt such peace and contentment for several years. Looking back toward the bedroom his thoughts went to Elyssa, apprehending that just being in her presence filled a void that had long been empty.

He shook his head. Yesterday had been a loss in making any attempt to change her opinion of him. She had been ill for most of the day, secluded in the bathroom. Today he was committed to go out with Manuel to visit some of the coffee growers. He knew Elyssa would probably not feel up to accompanying them. He was quite sure she would be weak from yesterday's ordeal, and in addition to that, she still had to sort through Chad and Janet's belongings to determine what she wanted to take back with her. No, today did not look good either, and they would be returning to Guatemala City tomorrow.

He folded his arms and looked back out the window. He shuddered as he considered the possibility that she would remember him being with her on the bed. He could only imagine her fury and knew that it would most likely cement her estimation of him.

He went into the kitchen and began making a pot of coffee. As it began to percolate and its aroma began to waft through the house, Will decided to take a shower. Checking in on Elyssa first, he smiled at her sleeping form. She needed her rest and he knew that the longer she slept, the better she would feel.

After a quick shower, Will poured himself a large mug of coffee and returned to the living room to await Elyssa's rising and her possible wrath.

Elyssa finally stirred about an hour later. She opened her eyes slowly, taking in the room around her. Her lips pursed into a twisted smile. "Why that presumptuous man!" she whispered softly. "How dare he move me here without my knowledge and against my will?"

At the thought of Will, her hand slid across the bed in front of her and she wondered why it suddenly felt cold. She sat up slowly, waiting for any signs of residual effects from yesterday. Other than a little weakness, she felt fine.

Elyssa swung herself into a sitting position. She stretched out her toes to touch the floor and fingers to reach up to the ceiling. She had to admit that she had slept like a baby. Perhaps she had been irrational in not wanting to sleep in here. Taking in a deep breath, she wondered if Will was awake yet. She was fairly certain he wouldn't have left her to spend the night in the pension and figured he must be out in the living room.

Elyssa looked down at the clothes she was still wearing from yesterday. She was more than anxious to get out of them. A shower would feel wonderful and she looked forward to putting on something clean and possibly trying to eat a little. She stood up slowly and as her legs wobbled underneath her, she steadied herself by reaching down to touch the nightstand next to the bed. When she felt balanced, she walked over to her suitcase and pulled out some clean clothes.

Peering first out into the hallway, she then darted quickly into the bathroom before Will could see her.

Stepping into the shower felt wonderful. Elyssa felt as though she was washing off every ounce of sickness from the day before. Her fingers went up to her temple, where the slightest trace of a headache was the only reminder of yesterday's torment. As she gently rubbed her forehead with the tips of her fingers, she suddenly thought of Janet. A vague recollection of Janet rubbing her forehead teased her memory.

"Oh, Janet," she said to herself as the water pulsated down upon her. "It has been several years since you nursed one of my headaches and yet I feel as though it was just yesterday."

At that thought, she closed her eyes and lifted her face toward the spray, the water from the shower mingling with the few tears that began to fall.

Elyssa finally turned off the water and stepped out, drying herself off and slipping into her clean clothes. She combed through her wet hair and squeezed her naturally wavy locks to encourage the curls to appear on their own.

When Elyssa felt that she was tolerably presentable, she came out and walked into the living room. Will had a mug in his hand and when he noticed her walk in, he immediately put it down and stood up. He tried to erase the look of apprehension as he greeted her.

"Good morning, Elyssa. How do you feel this morning?"

Elyssa pursed her lips at the look of guilt on his face and couldn't help but want to put him through a little discomfort. "I feel fine, but you were terribly presumptuous last night, don't you think?"

"Elyssa, I'm... I..."

She waved her hand at him, shaking her head. "I truly cannot believe it."

Will looked down, letting out a huffy breath. "I really did not mean to..."

Suddenly Elyssa laughed. "I'm sorry. I just had to make things difficult for you. I want you to know I'm not angry about what you did last night."

Will looked back up at her; his eyes widened with surprise. "You... you're not angry at me, then?"

"No, I actually slept very soundly."

"I'm glad," he said with a cautious smile.

"I know I was being ridiculous and quite irrational not wanting to sleep in their bed. You were right. It was very silly of me."

Will slowly let out the breath he had been holding. "I... I never thought you were being silly." With a relieved laugh he added, "I'm glad you're not upset. I felt as though you would sleep better there."

"I did. Thank you."

Will kept his eyes upon her, trying to read her face to see if she recalled anything else. At the moment, at least, it appeared she didn't. He was grateful she had no memory of him sleeping by her side. "Let me make you some toast with just a little butter. See how your stomach reacts and if you're still feeling OK in a little while, I thought I'd make a cheese omelet, if that's all right with you. You'll want to stick with bland foods today."

"That sounds fine, but you don't really have to go to all this trouble."

"No trouble," he called as he entered the kitchen. He made the toast while Elyssa sat on the sofa thinking about all he was doing. She was hungry and still weak, and had to admit she rather enjoyed the pampering. When the toast was finished, he brought it to her on a plate. She glanced up and thanked him, gracing him with another irresistible smile.

"You're welcome. Would you care for some tea? It would probably be easier on the stomach than coffee."

"Yes, please, that sounds delicious.

Will walked back toward the kitchen, but paused just outside the door and looked at her. "Is your headache gone this morning?"

Elyssa looked up. "My headache? How did you know I had a headache?"

Will breathed in as if he was going to say something. Elyssa thought he looked uncomfortable again for some reason. Finally, he said, "Umm, you... you mentioned it last night."

"Oh," Elyssa said slowly. She really could not recall anything about last night after coming out into the living room. She certainly didn't remember any conversation with Will. "I still have a headache, but it's just a small one."

Will nodded and forced a smile, then quickly disappeared into the kitchen. Elyssa turned her attention back to her toast. It may have been a slight throbbing of her headache, or because they had just talked about it, but she brought her hand up to her head and began rubbing it. She then began to comb her fingers back into her scalp and massaged the top of her head, which always helped alleviate the pain. Suddenly, a very clear and vivid memory from the night before assaulted her thoughts.

Someone did rub my forehead last night! She looked back toward the kitchen door and another recollection intruded. *Not only do I remember someone rubbing my forehead...* Elyssa gulped. *I remember hands going through my hair and massaging my scalp!*

With widened eyes, she began to recall bits and pieces of the night before. She had been in no condition to fully comprehend all that went on, but she remembered waking on several occasions. Her stomach no longer ached, but her head had. It was about the only thing she was aware of, except for the gentle hands continually rubbing it. In her muddled mind, she had associated it with being Janet, but in all reality, it had been Will!

Elyssa finished her toast and dropped her head back against the sofa looking up at the ceiling. She then closed her eyes and asked herself, *Why must he continually prove himself to be so opposite of what I thought of him? Why is he taking such prodigiously good care of me?*

When he returned with her hot tea, she thanked him. As she reached out her hands to take it from him, the warmth of the cup and the feel of his fingers brushing against hers brought a most annoying and unwelcome blush to her cheeks. As he hovered close, feelings of vulnerability stirred in her again and she wasn't sure whether or not she liked it.

Elyssa decided to change the subject. "What are your plans for today?"

"Manuel and I are going to visit some of the coffee growers."

She slowly nodded her head. "That's right. I had forgotten."

"I thought you might like to go. I was hoping you would, but it will be a long afternoon and most likely there will be a lot of walking."

"I'd really like to go, but I'm not sure if I should. I'm still tired and feel somewhat weak and I need to give the house a good once-over before we leave to see if there's any thing else I'd like to bring home."

Will nodded. "Why don't you work on that this morning and then when Manuel comes by later, see how you feel? If you're not up to joining us the whole afternoon, perhaps we can stop back by later and take you to visit one or two families with us."

"I would like that."

"Good!" Will clasped his hands together. "Now, how is the toast settling in your stomach? Are you up to trying a Denton omelet?"

Elyssa smiled. "Right now I feel as though I could eat anything!"

Will stood up. "I don't really know whether to take that as a compliment or not, but I think you'll like it."

The sounds and smells of Will's cooking began to permeate the living room. Elyssa hadn't considered the fact that he might be a good cook. She rather expected that he had a hired chef to prepare all his meals or that he ate out a lot.

When he came in with the omelet, Elyssa was pleasantly surprised. It was light and fluffy with just the right amount of cheese in it. He handed her a plate and then he sat down beside her. His close proximity and the scent of his aftershave made her feel inexplicably drawn to him and for a while she did not trust herself to say anything, let alone look at him.

After taking a couple bites, though, she had to compliment him. She tilted her head and smiled at him. "This is very good, Will. Making the perfect omelet isn't that easy."

The combination of her twinkling eyes and smile directed at him, coupled with her words of appreciation resonated within him. He smiled back at her. "I'm flattered you think it's perfect! But truly, it's not that difficult to make."

"But from one who probably has a kitchen staff to prepare all your meals, it's pretty commendable."

He looked at her, surprised. "A kitchen staff?"

"Well, certainly it's either that or you go out for every meal."

Will laughed and shook his head. "I do go out to eat when it's for business, but you know I don't like to eat out alone."

Elyssa nodded. "So you told me." After a few more bites, she said, "So are you telling me you cook your own meals?"

"Actually, I do have an excellent cook, but she's leaving soon."

"Oh? Why is that?"

In a soft voice filled with admiration, he answered, "My sister, Gina. She loves to cook, but unfortunately she'll be leaving for college in the fall."

"Ah, yes. So will you hire someone to cook for you when she is gone?"

Will looked back down at his omelet. "Probably not. I'm not a picky eater and I can make a big batch of something and eat it as long as it lasts. With all the business luncheons that occur throughout the week, I get enough variety."

Elyssa peered at him out of the corner of her eye. "So how is it that you have been able to stay away from work this past week?"

"My cousin, who is the vice-president, is handling things while I'm away."

"And you trust him to do that?"

"Implicitly." He looked up and met her gaze. "There are some things I set into motion when I first arrived, but right now they are out of my hands. When we get back to Guatemala City, I'll need to see how they are progressing."

"Hmmm." Elyssa took a couple more bites of her omelet and then put the plate down. "It's very good, Will, but that's all I can eat."

"That's OK."

Will stood up and as she handed her plate to him, she said, "I appreciate everything you did to help me yesterday. I really did not even think about eating the fruit in that market place without washing it off first with the bottled water."

"I think everyone who has come down here with Pemberleo has had at least one bout with *Montezuma's Revenge*."

Elyssa laughed. "Including yourself?"

Will let out a chuckle. "Oh, yes, several times. I recall as a child, spending the whole night in the bathroom."

"And that taught you a lesson you never forgot?"

Will pursed his lips. "You'd think it would, but no. About a year ago I came down and it was terribly hot. I wanted something to drink and asked for a bottled water and ice in a glass."

Elyssa looked at him oddly. "And?"

"Well, I had the bottled water, but had forgotten that in most places, they make ice with tap water. It hit me about as bad as it hit you."

"Hmmm. From ice?"

Will nodded. "From ice."

Elyssa found herself growing weary and couldn't hold back a yawn. "Perhaps I ought to begin sorting through everything before I fall asleep."

"Would you care for any help?" Will asked.

"No, you've done enough already. I'll be OK."

"All right, but don't overdo it. You probably still need some rest."

Elyssa answered with a very soft, "OK."

As Elyssa walked into the back bedroom, Will sat in the chair, beaming. It had been a good morning and there had not been one argument between them. Fortunately, she had not been aware of the fact that he spent the night sleeping by her side. He felt a little guilty not confessing it to her, but for the moment, he wanted to savor her good opinion. *Maybe someday I'll tell her,* he thought to himself. *When we're old and gray and babysitting our grandchildren!*

Chapter 15

Elyssa spent a good part of the morning opening cabinets, closets, and drawers, looking for anything that she might want to take back with her. Other than a few pictures, she really didn't find anything that struck a sentimental chord. She felt that there were most likely many needy people here who could use those things more than she.

Will checked in on her occasionally, hoping he would not come upon her in a state of tears. He was grateful that she appeared to be in control of her feelings this time around. He was quite certain she was not yet over her grief, but things had improved. He also knew that there was one more thing she should do before they returned to Guatemala City which would undoubtedly unleash any residual grief. As much as he dreaded causing her any further pain, he knew it was something she would later be glad she did.

As the time approached for Manuel to come for Will, Elyssa grew more and more weary. She was seated upon the floor, looking through the bottom drawer of a dresser, and she could barely keep her eyes open any longer. She took the small stack of neatly folded clothes and placed them onto the carpet, then placed her head on the stack. Within minutes, she had fallen asleep.

It had been a while since Will heard anything from the back room. When he went back and looked in, he smiled at her sleeping form curled up on the floor. She looked very serene and he didn't wish to awaken her. He reached for a throw that lay tossed over a chair and spread it across her. He would let her sleep.

Manuel arrived shortly thereafter and Will left a note for Elyssa, saying they would return after a couple of hours. He hoped that she would feel up to visiting a family or two.

~~*

Later, Elyssa opened her eyes and stretched out the kink in her back as she sat up. The throw slipped down to her waist and as she eyed it, her fingers swept over the woven fabric. She knew it hadn't been there when she fell asleep. Her eyes went to the door and she wondered if Will had already left with Manuel.

Walking into the living room, she noticed Will's note and smiled at his consideration. *A throw and a note.* If he wasn't so controlling, he could be rather pleasant. Her eyebrows came together as she pondered her estimation of him. For some reason, controlling no longer seemed an accurate description.

Elyssa went to the front door and when she opened it, she took in a deep breath of the warm, moist air filled with the fragrance of flowers. From the porch she could see the lake's deep blue water glisten and a reflection of the mountain ridge on the other side shimmering down in the lake's depths. She looked out at the mountains that enclosed Atitlan. She could see two volcanoes from where she stood, but both were partially obscured by white, puffy clouds hovering around them.

Elyssa decided it would be most refreshing to sit outside for a while. Slipping back inside, she picked up a straight backed chair from the kitchen and carried it out to the porch. She decided that if this was their last day at the lake, she wanted to at least enjoy it a little.

Elyssa watched a variety of people walk by, smiling at those who occasionally looked up and acknowledged her. She had to chuckle when she became aware that she was rocking back and forth, almost as if she were on a porch swing. This would be a perfect place for one.

Will and Manuel returned about an hour later. Upon seeing Elyssa on the porch, Manuel rushed up the steps and reached for her hand.

"I am so sorry you took ill yesterday, Elyssa. Are you feeling better?"

"Yes, Manuel. Thank you. I was feeling tired earlier today, but I'm feeling much better now."

Will walked up the steps and his hand grasped the porch column. "We have one more family to visit, Elyssa. They live just up the block toward the hillside. Do you feel up to coming with us?"

A smile burst upon Elyssa's face. "I would love getting out."

"Good!" Manuel helped Elyssa to her feet. "I think you will like this family. Their oldest son, Pedro, even speaks a little English. If he is home, maybe you can talk with him."

Noticing Will's and Manuel's finer attire, Elyssa thought it would be best to put on something nicer. "Just give me a minute while I change."

The men waited out on the porch for her and both were surprised when she came out after only a couple of minutes. She wore a knee length flowing skirt and a light cotton blouse that she had loosely tucked in.

The three began to walk up the street away from the lake and toward the hillside. Manuel and Will told her of their earlier visits. Manuel enjoyed telling Elyssa how impressed the families were that *"El Presidente de Pemberleo"* was actually paying them a call and how proud they were of the coffee crop into which they poured their lives.

When they arrived at the house, Manuel walked up and knocked. An elderly lady, stooped over and wrinkled, opened the door. When the woman saw Manuel, she smiled and held out her arms wide to give him a hug.

Manuel introduced Will and Elyssa to her. She noticed the woman's eyes grow big when Will was introduced and she reached for his hand and enfolded it within her small, bony, fingers. At Elyssa's introduction, her eyes lit up and she smiled and drew her close into an embrace. She whispered something in her ear, but since Elyssa was clueless as to what she said, she merely smiled.

The woman sent one of her young daughters to go after her husband, who was out on the hill behind their house with their son. Within minutes, they both walked into the house.

The gentleman looked to be as old as the woman, with a dark, leathery face, and hair that was grayer than the black of his younger years.

Again Manuel made introductions and she watched as Will reached out his hand and exchanged a firm handshake with the elder gentleman, Miguel. Will seemed to have no trouble engaging the man in conversation. He truly seemed interested in what the gentleman had to say. They walked out toward the hillside and Elyssa glanced back at the young boy, Pedro, who remained with her.

He looked about 17 years old and Elyssa could see that he probably spent as much time out in the Guatemalan sun as his father did. He was taller than both his parents and had jet black hair. He smiled at her, somewhat shyly.

"I understand you speak a little English," Elyssa said to him.

He nodded. "Yes, a little."

"Where did you learn it?"

"I learn a little at school and then a man at my church speak English and teach me. I also go to Panajachel to the library when I have some free time."

"You speak very well, Pedro. What year in school are you?"

"Oh, no more school for me. Now I help my family farm."

"Oh, but Pedro! You must continue your education! There is so much you could do. You certainly are smart enough to go on to college!"

Pedro slowly shook his head. "No. I must help my father grow the best coffee beans for Pemberleo. He needs my help."

Elyssa could see the resignation in the young man's eyes as he told her of his family's expectation.

"If you could choose to do anything, Pedro, what would it be?"

Pedro took in a deep breath. "I would like to teach children here to read and write."

"Oh, Pedro, that is admirable!"

Pedro looked confused. "Excuse me, but, what does admirable mean?"

Elyssa smiled. "It means that is an excellent profession and you would be wonderful at it!"

Elyssa and Pedro continued to talk as they followed the men out to the hillside. She couldn't help but notice the shade of the soil seemed to permeate everything, from the darkness of the men's skin to the fabric of their clothing. Everything appeared to take on the same hue. She laughed as she considered her eye for color, and thought that this was carrying it a bit too far.

As she and Pedro approached the men, Elyssa watched Will stoop down and dig his hands into the soil, bringing some up to smell. She thought it odd that observing this simple gesture surprisingly made him seem more attractive. Here was this rich and powerful man not afraid of getting his hands dirty.

Miguel called his son over as he spoke with Will. Manuel then excused himself and joined Elyssa.

"Tell me, Manuel," Elyssa said as she looked about her. "I see very little farming equipment. Don't they have any equipment to help them farm?"

Manuel laughed and as he spoke, he extended his hand up toward the hillside. "Nothing is more efficient than a good mule and a handful of people on these slopes. There really isn't any comparable machine that could do the same thing."

"It seems as though they have to work so hard. Pedro says he is expected to remain at home with his family and farm. He seems fairly intelligent and would like to be a teacher. Isn't there some way he should be able to do that?"

"It would make things too difficult for his family. They wouldn't be able to afford the cost of a college education and they wouldn't be able to afford his absence. They need everyone in the family to help work the crop."

Elyssa let out a huff and folded her arms stiffly in front of her, which drew Will's attention.

"But it shouldn't be that way. He should have a chance to improve himself and do something else."

Will was standing close enough to hear their end of the conversation and knew from the determined look on her face and her firm stance, that Elyssa was seeing some injustice in this situation. He knew, from previous experience, that she was not reluctant to accuse him of something in front of others. She had done it earlier in the week around Manuel. Now he waited for her to lash out in front of Miguel and Pedro.

She turned to look at Will and their eyes met. This time, however, instead of flashing, challenging eyes, she had more of a questioning look. He was grateful -- and a little surprised -- that she said nothing further on the subject.

When they finished their visit, they all bid their farewells. Elyssa could see that the men all seemed to be satisfied with their time together.

As they walked back to the house, Will waited for that moment when Elyssa would blurt out all her feelings of unfairness. But instead, she walked ahead of the two men, stepping over to a large red flowering bush that was spilling over the fence of a home they passed. She leaned over to smell the flowers and Will mulled over what was going on in that pretty little head of hers.

"Mmmm," she said as she lifted her head. "These are beautiful and smell heavenly."

At the moment, it appeared to Will that she was not inclined to bring up the subject, but he was fairly certain she would when they were alone.

~~*

Manuel stayed only long enough to see them back to the house and make plans to come by tomorrow with his son to return to Guatemala City.

When he left, Will turned to Elyssa. "Are you hungry? Manuel pointed out some good places to eat close by."

"I think I would like that. My stomach does seem to be crying out for some nourishment."

"Good. Let's go."

They walked the few blocks to the restaurant, taking in the sights, sounds, and smells of this little village and saying very little to each other. Will's hand brushed against Elyssa's several times and it took all his restraint to keep from reaching out for it and cradling it in his. The sun was ahead of them, making an approach to the tips of the mountain ridge where it would soon disappear. The moist, warm air determinedly clung to them while a light breeze teased them with a fleeting cool relief.

They reached the small restaurant and stepped inside. Lively mariachi music was piped in through speakers. Colorful tablecloths and Guatemalan handicrafts dotted the walls of the room. It was crowded, but they were quickly seated and coffee was brought to them.

Will eyed Elyssa as she took the menu and began reading it. She had been more quiet than normal ever since leaving Miguel's. He knew there was nothing he could say that would pacify her -- except perhaps promising to provide for every family in Guatemala until his dying day. He knew, however, that he had to explain to her and that he would try.

Once they ordered, Will clasped his hands together and placed them in front of him on the table. "I gather the situation with Pedro having to stay home and work for the family farm does not sit well with you. I would imagine you feel we do not pay these farmers enough for their crops."

Elyssa tilted her head and slowly shook it back and forth as she spoke. "It's *your* business -- literally."

"Yes, but I want you to understand."

Elyssa shrugged, folded her arms across her, and leaned forward. "Okay. I'm listening."

Will picked up his cup of coffee and took a sip. He then held it out toward Elyssa. "How many coffee beans do you think it takes to make a pound of coffee?"

Elyssa laughed. "I don't know. 500 maybe."

"No," Will replied. "It takes 4000."

"That's a lot of beans."

Will nodded. "Yes it is, and the individual farmer is the one who does all the tending of the plant, picking, sorting, and drying. There's a lot to do to ensure a good cup of coffee. At this level it's mostly manual labor because there just aren't machines that can work as efficiently as humans."

"But surely they can be paid more. Pemberleo certainly isn't hurting for money."

Will met her gaze and carefully chose his words. "Elyssa, our growers are paid well above the market value. What you don't understand is that if they only have an acre of crop, even our price can make living difficult, especially if you have a large family."

He scrutinized Elyssa's face as she processed this. He had hoped to enjoy another day without an argument and waited to see what her response would be.

Elyssa took in a deep breath and blew it out through puffed cheeks. "It just doesn't seem fair that someone as bright as Pedro and with such noble dreams has no other option."

"Perhaps not, but I do believe what I pay my farmers for their coffee is very reasonable."

"But..."

Will put up his hand. "Trust me, Elyssa. They don't make much in comparison to our standard of living, but they do quite well. Unfortunately it is the farmers with only an acre or two and large families that suffer most. In all fairness, I can only pay them for the actual coffee beans that meet our standards. It doesn't matter how large or small the farm is. We can't use every bean that grows. Some coffee beans get infested with bugs, or damaged by too little or too much rain, or mold. There are a lot of variables."

Elyssa's sigh was accompanied by a resigned shrug of her shoulders and their conversation was halted by the arrival of their meal. When Elyssa inhaled the aroma of her food, she rejoiced that her stomach was more than eager to be filled. For the moment, she satisfied herself with a delicious dinner and they talked no further about Pedro.

When they finished eating, they stepped out of the restaurant and Will looked out toward the lake.

"Come," he said. "Let's walk down to the water's edge while it is still light. We really haven't had the chance to enjoy the lake."

When they reached the shore, they both began walking toward a sandy section of beach. Elyssa sat down and began to take off her shoes. She then stood up and squished the sand between her toes and a look of delight lit her face.

"Go ahead. Give it a try."

"What? Take my shoes off?"

Elyssa gave her head a firm nod and then skipped out to the water's edge. With her feet in the water up to her ankles, she turned and called out to him. "Come on! The water is great!"

"Yeah, but it can't be that clean!"

"Ohhh," Elyssa responded with a playful splash.

Will could not suppress the smile that came to his face nor calm his heartbeat that began to race as he watched Elyssa. *This is crazy!* he thought to himself as he took his shoes and socks off. He then decided it would be prudent for him to at least roll up the bottom of his pant legs.

Elyssa had turned away from Will to watch the colors in the skies change with each passing minute. Unbeknownst to Will, however, she had quite the smirk on her face as she contemplated seeing whether this man really did know how to have fun. He was really far too severe for her.

When he came up to her, she turned around and unsuccessfully tried to suppress a giggle. He was making such a concerted effort *not* to get wet.

Sorry, Will, Elyssa thought. *You're not going to stay dry for long!*

Without any warning, Elyssa dipped her hands into the water and began splashing him.

"Hey!" he cried out. "What did I do to deserve that?"

Instead of turning tail to run, as Elyssa expected he would, he began splashing her back. Her meager attempts were not as strong and efficient as his, and she was soon all the more drenched because of it.

Elyssa tried to back away from him, lifting up the hem of her skirt as the water got deeper and deeper. Her foot went down suddenly in what must have been a hole in the sand, and before she could regain her footing, she fell down and found herself sitting in about ten inches of water.

Will began to laugh. "That serves you right!"

Elyssa rolled her eyes. "Well, the least you can do is to help me up." She reached up her hand to him. "Who knows what all is in this water!"

Will trudged through the water and when he took her hand, instead of using it to pull herself up, she gave it a solid yank, toppling him into the water. He twisted his body just enough so he didn't land on top of her and when he came to a stop, found himself seated in the water next to her.

Elyssa could not stop laughing. "I'm sorry, Will. I couldn't resist. It looks like rolling up your pant legs isn't doing any good keeping your pants dry."

"Yeah, thanks to you."

He turned toward her and began drowning her with splashes, which she readily reciprocated. When they were both completely drenched, Will stood up.

"Now, are you willing to take my hand to help you up and not to pull me back in?"

Elyssa smiled and nodded. As Will stood over her, looking down into her face, he was sure her eyes were glistening as brightly as the lake. The vibrant color and expression on her face rivaled the sunset above for his attention. There was no question as to which he would rather look upon right now.

She took his hand and he slowly pulled her up, wishing this moment would go on forever. He didn't think he'd ever seen a woman more beautiful and gave her hand a slight tug as she rose to her feet. Without thinking of what he was doing, he scooped her up in his arms.

"What are you doing?" Elyssa screamed.

"Pay back is fair play," he answered as he began carrying her further out into the water.

"You wouldn't dare!" Elyssa wrapped her arms tightly around him, holding on for dear life.

Will smiled as he considered the possibility that as long as she thought he was going to throw her in, she'd hold on tightly to him. He rather enjoyed the feel of her in his arms and her arms wrapped tightly about his neck.

"Will, this is absolutely disgraceful. Look at you! What must the villagers think?"

"They think that you're about to be dropped in the water! Besides, you started it."

He released his grip slightly, just enough for her to think he was going to drop her. She clung even more fiercely to him.

In tightening her hold and drawing up against his chest, she inhaled his cologne. She hadn't noticed it before, but now, the scent teased her thoughts with a memory. A memory about last night.

The smile on Elyssa's face froze as the recollection of last night became clearer. She remembered awaking in the night and trying to move, but was prevented by something rather solid. Soft, yet solid... that scent... a sound... breathing!

"Put me down, Will! Now!"

He pulled back at the intensity of her tone. "Here?"

"No, no, back up on shore."

Will walked through the water and set her down on the beach. She turned away from him as her mind spun around in turmoil. She had earlier realized that he had spent the evening rubbing her forehead. Could he have merely fallen asleep next to her? Was it as innocent as that or did he have ulterior motives?

Elyssa shook her head, trying to find the answer. Why was he in her bed last night? Why was she finding it so difficult to think clearly around him? For goodness sake, where was that anger that used to accompany every thought about him?

Elyssa walked determinedly towards her shoes. She was more angry with herself for *not* being angry at *him*!

"Hey, wait up, Elyssa."

Will caught up to her and watched as she frantically attempted to put her shoes back on.

"I think we ought to get back."

"Sure," he eyed her with a little surprise, knowing something had brought about a change in her.

As he sat down beside her, Elyssa shivered. It wasn't so much the fact that she was wet and cold, but there was another reason for it. That reason was sitting right next to her.

When she finished getting her shoes on, she cast a sideways glance at Will. She had just had more fun with him than she ever had and the recollection about his sleeping next to her all night would have… *should have*… made her angry. But she could not find that seed of prejudice against him any longer. She now found herself facing a very real possibility. Could she be falling in love with him?

They walked back to the house and Will couldn't help but wonder if he had gone too far. Was she upset that he had gotten her so wet? Was she offended that he picked her up and held her so close?

When they reached the house and came into the living room, Will faced her. "I should go now and check into the pension, since I never got around to that yesterday. Will you be OK?"

"You really don't have to do that, Will."

"I don't?"

"No." It was a long pause before Elyssa continued. "I'll go ahead and sleep in the bedroom again, but…" Elyssa took in a deep breath and looked with all seriousness at Will. "As far as where you sleep, well, I just don't think it should be a… *repeat of last night."*

Will's face turned white and he coughed out a, "No, no, probably not."

Elyssa smiled at his discomfiture and then turned toward the hall. "I do claim the shower first, though."

Will didn't think he could breathe as he watched her leave the room. She did remember him sleeping next to her last night and she wasn't angry! She wasn't angry!

Will sat down in the recliner chair, soaking wet, quite elated, and very hopeful.

Chapter 16

The next morning, Will and Elyssa awoke early to pack up their belongings in preparation to return to Guatemala City. They were to meet Manuel and his son at the dock at seven o'clock.

As they passed the same flowering bush that Elyssa had stopped at the day before, Will reached over and picked a handful of bright red flowers.

"Here," he said. "You'll want these."

Elyssa's eyes widened and she brought them up to her nose, inhaling their fragrance. "Thank you!" She looked up and searched his face for an explanation.

"You'll want them for later."

"Later?"

Will only nodded and then he saw Manuel up ahead. "There's Manuel. It looks like the boat is here."

The four of them boarded the boat and were the only ones to make the trip back to Panajachel. When they reached the town, Manuel went to retrieve the car while the others waited at the dock.

When Manuel returned with the car, Will pulled him aside, speaking to him in Spanish. Elyssa thought this was unusual, especially noticing Manuel's reaction, but put all thoughts and questions about it aside.

As they drove away from the lake, Elyssa told a very astounded Manuel about the water fight she and Will had down at the lake the night before. While Will laughed a few times, he seemed preoccupied. She wondered whether he would leave the person he had become the past few days back at the lake and turn into the man she originally thought him to be. Had she truly been with the real man or had it been only a temporary transformation.

The car reached the top of the summit that overlooked the lake and they pulled on to the highway that would take them part of the way back. Elyssa settled in for a quiet car ride, as Will was definitely not in a talkative mood.

About a half an hour later, Manuel pulled over. He and Will spoke briefly in Spanish and Elyssa looked at them curiously.

"Is something wrong?" she asked, looking from one to the other.

Will took a deep breath. "You'll want to get out." After a pause he pulled out a handkerchief and pointed to the flowers, "And you'll want to bring these."

Something in Will's words and expression made Elyssa's chest tighten. She slowly turned toward the window on her side and looked out. There, on the side of the road, lay a rustic wooden cross with a few flowers at its base. Some of the flowers had begun to wither. Her hand suddenly reached for Will's and she gripped it tightly.

"This… this is where…" Tears and sobs came suddenly and prevented Elyssa from saying any more.

"Yes," he replied softly.

Manuel came around and opened the door for them. He stepped back as Elyssa walked dazedly toward the place where Janet and Chad had died; her shaking hands holding the flowers Will had picked earlier that morning. Will kept close behind her, ready to be a support if she needed it.

Elyssa stooped down as she lay the fresh flowers down at the base of the cross. Her breathing became ragged as her fingers trailed over the two pieces of wood that had Janet and Chad's names carved with simple, block letters on it. She brought the handkerchief up and buried her face in it as a fresh wave of grief rolled over her.

Will silently stood behind her until she started to rise. When he noticed her wobbling, he immediately came to her side to help her up. A new tremor of grief swept through her and she turned and buried her head in Will's chest. His arms went around her and tightened to keep her from crumbling to the ground.

"I'm sorry, Elyssa. I know this is very painful for you, but I thought you'd want to see what a few people have done here in their memory."

"No, no…" Elyssa waved her hand. "I'm glad you did. Thank you. Thank you."

She remained in the strong embrace of his arms, feeling a complete sense of solace there. Will thought back to the embrace yesterday. He hoped this one wouldn't overshadow the other, more pleasant one.

Elyssa finally pulled away and announced that she was ready to go.

"Are you sure?"

Elyssa nodded. She didn't try to shield her red eyes and tear-stained face from Will. He had seen it often enough. When they got back in the car, Elyssa asked, "Who did this? Who put the cross here and brings the flowers? They weren't that old."

It was Manuel who answered.

"A young lady named Maria. She lives just down the street from the townhouses and she and Janet often got together to work on Maria's English and Janet's Spanish. Maria faithfully takes the chicken bus every week up here, bringing fresh flowers to place here."

Elyssa took in a few trembling breaths. "I would like to meet her if we have time when we get back. Do you think that would be possible?" She looked from Manuel to Will and then back to Manuel.

"I'll check with Shelley. She can see if she's home and arrange a visit."

"Thank you, Manuel." Elyssa looked over at Will. "And thank you, again."

Will looked down and took one of Elyssa's hands. "I thought… I hoped you would be consoled with the fact that people here cared for them and remembered them." He lifted Elyssa's hand and gently squeezed it.

"Do you know any more about how it happened?"

Will shook his head. "Unfortunately there were no witnesses. We know it was raining pretty hard and visibility was poor. In those conditions anything could have happened. I ordered a complete check of the car and nothing was found that might have caused it. We may never know."

"No, we may never know."

Soon they were back maneuvering through the dizzying traffic of Guatemala City. When Will's phone rang, Elyssa found herself tense up and she wondered what she would hear. The last thing she wanted to hear was Will's dictatorial demands and angry outbursts that made up the first part of their time here.

The call was short and it was apparent to Elyssa that a meeting had been set up for first thing in the morning. A trace of irritation came through his voice, but for the most part, he was quite civil. When he hung up, he turned to her.

"Elyssa, tomorrow, when we fly out, there are a few things -- er, several things -- I would like to talk with you about."

Elyssa looked at him quizzically. "When *we* fly out? Are you on my flight?"

"No, I would like to fly you home on Pemberleo's jet."

"Oh," Elyssa shuddered. "I… I wouldn't want to inconvenience you."

"It won't be an inconvenience. I have a meeting at seven o'clock tomorrow morning. It should last no more than an hour or an hour and a half. We'll come by around nine o'clock to pick you up and we'll fly out by ten. Would that work for you?"

"Yes, my flight was at nine thirty, so I would have needed to be at the airport by seven thirty or eight. This will give me a little more time in the morning."

"Good. You'll get home much sooner, too. You won't have a lay over."

When they reached the townhouse, Will told Manuel he would take Elyssa's things in while Manuel went to the Walkers' home to find out about Maria.

When they walked in, Elyssa again thanked Will for everything he had done.

"Would you like to go out for something to eat before I leave?"

Elyssa shook her head. "No, I think I would like some time alone."

Will reached for her hand. "I understand." He looked around the room. "Do you have everything you want to take back with you?"

"Yes, it's all over there." She pointed to the corner of the room.

"I'll have Manuel take it with us now to get it boxed up with the things you brought back from the lake."

There was an awkward silence for a moment as he still held her one hand in his. When Manuel returned, Will released it. Manuel informed Elyssa that Shelley called Maria and she would be coming by in about fifteen minutes. He told her that she was really eager to meet her.

"Good. I'm anxious to meet her as well."

Will pointed to the items in the corner of the room, asking Manuel to take them out to the car and that he would come out shortly.

When Manuel left, Will turned back to Elyssa. "You'll be OK tonight?"

Elyssa nodded.

"Good. If my morning meeting goes as planned, good things should come out of it."

He took a step closer to her. She looked up into his face and saw a glint of admiration and determination in his eyes that made her pulse skip.

"I better go, now."

She watched his face draw nearer to hers, feeling as though she was watching something in slow motion. As he came to within inches of her face, he turned his head and kissed her softly on the cheek.

"I'll see you in the morning." The feel of his lips on her cheek lingered, and as he spoke, she could almost feel the warmth of his breath radiate all the way down to her toes.

"Yes," Elyssa answered unevenly.

He pulled away and seemed to examine every inch of her face. He then gave her a satisfied smile and turned away. "Good night, Elyssa. See you in the morning."

Elyssa stood motionless until he had walked out and closed the door behind him. Her fingers went up to the spot on her cheek where he had just kissed her. She found it difficult to catch her breath and her other hand went to cover her heart, but her racing pulse could be felt throughout her whole body.

Sitting back down in the chair, Elyssa didn't dare move. Her thoughts played over and over the moment when he kissed her. She looked about her as if in a dream. How could so much have changed since she first arrived here? Since *he* first arrived here?

She had not moved from the chair when there was a slight knock on the door about fifteen minutes later. She shook herself from her reverie and stood up to answer it. Standing at the door was a young Guatemalan woman. She looked to be in her early twenties and her apparent shyness was evidenced by her cast-down eyes.

"Hi," Elyssa greeted her. "You must be Maria."

The young lady nodded and Elyssa invited her in.

Maria was pretty with dark eyes that looked at everything but Elyssa. She walked in slowly and immediately tears filled her eyes. She dabbed at her eyes with a worn tissue and interspersed an apology between English and Spanish. "I am so sorry... lo siento... lo siento."

Elyssa took Maria's arm and guided her into the living room. "I appreciate your coming... and I wanted to let you know..."

Elyssa was halted in her words by Maria breaking down in heaving sobs. A string of unintelligible words poured forth from her mouth. All Elyssa could understand was an occasional, "I am sorry."

Elyssa reached for the young girl's hand. "It's all right, Maria. We're all sorry." Elyssa hoped a smile would ease the young girl's noticeable feelings of grief and loss.

"No... no..." Maria waved her hand excitedly. "It is my... my... oh, how do you say, *mi culpa*?"

Elyssa shook her head, "I'm sorry, Maria. I don't know what you're trying to say."

"Es mi... It is my... Oh, I am so sorry!"

Elyssa remained silent as she watched the grief and a look of fear come across the young girl's face. "It is because... of me."

Elyssa's eyes widened. "Are you saying it was your fault?"

Maria looked up and nodded. "Yes. It was my fault."

"Why would you think that, Maria?" Elyssa was concerned for this apparent blame she held.

Another string of Spanish and Elyssa had to wait until she had calmed down.

"I am sorry. I do not know how to say… I call Janet. I was upset."

"You mean you called Janet at the lake?"

Maria nodded.

"Why were you upset?"

Maria tightened her fists. "I am so ashamed. I loved him and thought he loved me."

"Who, Maria? Who did you love? What happened?"

A raspy sigh escaped and Maria continued. "I am too ashamed to say, but Janet warned me. That night I see him with another woman and he laugh in my face when I ask him what he is doing with her."

"Oh, Maria. I am so sorry."

"I called Janet. I told her not to come home that night… that I would be all right." Maria looked up into Elyssa's eyes. "It was raining hard. I did not want them to drive home, but Janet… Janet said she could not stay there while I was so upset."

Elyssa reached for Maria's hand. "Please don't blame yourself, Maria. The accident was not your fault!"

"But it was. If I had not called… if I had only listened to her warning… Janet and Chad…" Maria buried her face in her tissue. "I should never have called. I am so sorry."

Elyssa closed her eyes tightly. This poor girl had been blaming herself the past two months for Janet and Chad's deaths. She softly patted Maria's hand while she continued to cry.

Maria slowly looked up. "You are angry with me?"

"Oh, no, Maria. Please don't think that. And don't think that you are to blame. It was Janet's kindness that prompted her to decide to come home that night. You yourself said that you told her not to come. Please, don't blame yourself any longer. Will you do that for me?"

Maria looked up into Elyssa's understanding face and slowly nodded.

"Good. Now, I would like to tell you something."

Elyssa explained how they had stopped at the cross and she was so pleased that Maria was faithfully making the trip out there to place flowers at the site. "It means a lot to me, Maria, that people cared for her. It means a lot that you still care enough to keep her memory fresh."

A small smile appeared on Maria's face. "You are very kind, Elyssa. Thank you. Gracias."

Maria stood up, wiping her eyes one more time. "I must go. My family waits."

Elyssa escorted her to the door. "Thank you for stopping by, Maria. I am so glad I was able to meet you."

Maria smiled, and said softly, "And I am glad I came."

Elyssa let out a long sigh as she pondered how Maria could have been carrying that weight around all this time. She wondered whether anyone else knew.

Elyssa sat back down on the chair in the living room. She shook her head as she suddenly began to grasp just how unreasonable she had been in blaming Will for Chad and Jane's deaths. How easily she told Maria not to blame herself and yet she had clung tenaciously to the absurdity that somehow it was Will's fault. *How could he have treated me so cordially when I so tenaciously held him responsible?*

She looked back over the day. It had taken an emotional toll on her and she didn't think she could handle one more thing. She would rest a moment and then go visit Shelley. She needed to apprise someone of Maria's situation.

Elyssa leaned her head back and closed her eyes, but was prevented from any reprieve when the doorbell rang. The only person she could possibly want to see right now was Will. Her heart flip flopped at the thought that he may have returned, but in reality she suspected it was Maria who may have forgotten to tell her something.

When she opened the door, however, it wasn't Will. It wasn't Maria. It was George Westham.

Chapter 17

"Hello, George. How are you?" Elyssa stared at the man in front of her, strangely aware that she had barely thought of him in the past few days.

"Just fine. And yourself?"

"Fine, thank you. Come in. How was Colombia?"

"Thanks." George stepped in and shook his head. "Colombia was just as I suspected. There was nothing there that needed my attention as urgently as Will made it sound. The guy needs to get a life."

Elyssa raised her eyebrows at his critical spirit -- especially aimed at his boss. She was surprised that she hadn't paid attention to it before.

George walked into the living room and casually looked around. "So, you had a pretty good time at Lake Atitlan."

It sounded more like a statement than a question and it appeared as though George wasn't really expecting an answer. Elyssa replied anyway, "It was beautiful, just as you said."

"Yeah, I bet." George was holding some rolled up papers and he tapped them several times into the palm of his hand. He looked down at them briefly.

"What do you have there, George?"

"Oh, these?" A frown froze his features and he took in and let out a long, deep breath before he answered.

"Look, Elyssa," he said, an expression of concern accentuating his features. "I hate to be the one to show you these. But I think you ought to know."

"Know what? What are they?"

He slowly unfolded one of the papers, and as he handed it to Elyssa, she could see that it appeared to be a printed picture of a photograph from a web page. When she looked at it more closely, she recognized it as herself being carried by Will across the street in Panajachel during the downpour.

The picture was bad enough, but her eyes went down to the caption below it which read, *Pemberleo Coffee's wealthy and quite eligible president William Denton sweeping mystery woman off her feet in a downpour!*

"No!" she exclaimed. "Where did this come from? Who took it?"

George shook his head, as if in disgust. "It came from some internet site where people post pictures of celebrities they see."

"You have got to be kidding. Will's not a celebrity!"

George looked very somber. "You and I both know that! But he's got that ridiculous title of being one of the top 50 most eligible bachelors, so people with nothing better to do take notice."

Elyssa's voice shook as she asked, "Are *those* more pictures?"

George gripped them tightly. "Maybe you better sit down."

"I don't need to sit down, George! I want to see them!"

He handed her the next and she saw the two of them walking into the hotel in Panajachel. To her benefit, the picture had been taken from behind them, but with the other incriminating photo, there was no denying that it was them. The caption read, *William Denton checks into one of the finer hotels with brunette bombshell.*

Elyssa closed her eyes and looked away. "Why would anyone do this?"

"I am of the opinion they do it only for the money. Ridiculous if you ask me. They hope some magazine will see them and buy the rights to print them."

Elyssa spun her head toward George. "A magazine? These might end up in a magazine?"

"Not necessarily. They would have to feel there is a story here."

Elyssa felt sick. She could see by the stack of papers still in George's hand that there were several more. As she reached out for the next, her hand was shaking.

George remained gravely silent as he handed her the next.

Elyssa gasped as her eyes took in the next picture of her and Will on the balcony at the hotel the next morning. She was standing next to him in her robe and he was shirtless, with only a towel slung over his shoulders.

"No! This is not the way it was!"

She looked down at the caption. *It appears to have been a pleasant, cozy night for Will and his lady.*

"We were standing on separate balconies! He was in the room next to mine! There is a divider between us for goodness sake!"

George reached up and placed his hand upon her shoulder. "Unfortunately, it doesn't look like that."

The next picture was of the two of them on the boat to the village. Her eyes flashed at George. "The American on the boat! He had a camera and was taking pictures. I thought he was just a tourist taking pictures of the scenery!"

"He must have known who Will was. Probably some aspiring paparazzi."

Elyssa brought her hand up to her head. The beginnings of a headache were making themselves known.

"I think I *will* sit down."

"Look, Elyssa. You don't need to see any more of these. I just wanted you to be aware of what's out there."

When Elyssa was seated, she reached up her hand. "No, George. I want to see them all!"

With the next picture in her hand, Elyssa found herself looking at the two of them walking into Chad and Janet's small house. She cringed at the caption. *Very little was seen of Will and his lady once they checked into their private love cottage.*

She slammed the pictures down onto her lap. "This makes it sound like we… like we…" Elyssa could barely speak. "Nothing happened between us. Nothing happened! I was sick all afternoon Saturday and was still recovering Sunday morning. Nothing happened!"

George looked at her oddly. "You're really serious, aren't you?"

Elyssa nodded and held out her hand, but George held tightly to the last picture.

"I was hoping you didn't fall under the spell of the lake." George tilted his head as he eyed her doubtfully. "Or under the spell of the *man*!"

"No, George, I didn't fall under *any* spell," Elyssa rubbed her head.

George slowly extended the last picture out to her. "You still hate the guy?"

Taking the picture from George, Elyssa looked down at it and was quite sure that he probably already knew the answer to his question. In it, Will was holding Elyssa in his arms in the lake. Elyssa was clearly laughing and enjoying herself in the photo. She didn't even bother to read the caption.

"No, George, I no longer hate the man." Elyssa closed her eyes and shook her head. "But nothing happened."

George sat down next to her and leaned in. "You don't know how glad I am to hear that. I was really worried when I saw these pictures. But I had faith in you. I knew you weren't like all those other women who absolutely love to see their pictures in magazines with him by their side."

"No, I'm *not* like them," she said softly.

"His only concern is for his company. He rarely considers other people's feelings. I knew you were too smart to fall for a man like him. I knew you'd be able to see through him."

Unlike before, a strong yearning to defend Will rather than join in George's assault on him surfaced deep inside of her. As she opened her mouth to come to his defense, George began to shake his head slowly.

"I couldn't even imagine how you tolerated the man who tried to talk Chad out of marrying your very own sister."

Elyssa's jaw dropped and her eyes widened in shock at his revelation. "What?"

"I'm sorry. You mean you didn't know? Almost everybody else did!"

"Will tried to talk Chad out of marrying Janet?"

George looked down and stared at the floor.

"Yeah, nasty business. You gotta love Chad, but he often doubted his own judgment. For some unfathomable reason, he always checked things through with the big man. When he told Will he wanted to ask Janet to marry him, well, Will told him he didn't think he should. He was adamantly against their marriage."

George looked up and could see the pain etched in Elyssa's face. He had suspected that her feelings for Will must have changed when he saw the pictures. Now he was certain that she no longer viewed him as the monster she once thought he was.

"Why? Why would he do that?"

George laughed. "Oh, you may have spent three unbelievable days with the man in an exotic, romantic locale, but he still is a manipulator, obsessed with controlling other people's lives! Everything revolves around the company, whether it's this project or that! He doesn't care about anyone but himself and Pemberleo Coffee!" There was fire in George's eyes as he spoke.

Elyssa thought back to their day in Antigua when they were standing on opposite sides of the dome room in the monastery ruins. She overheard Will refer to her as a "project" to the man next to him. She shook her head violently.

"I can't believe it!"

"Well, believe it. You can even ask the Walkers. They knew. Once Chad talked with Will, he asked other people what they thought."

"But he didn't listen to Will," Elyssa protested. "He *did* ask Janet to marry him."

"And I give him credit for having the guts to defy him."

Elyssa looked down at the pictures in her hands. "How did you find out about these internet pictures, George?"

"I almost hate to say."

"Just tell me," Elyssa barely eked out.

"Some guy from a magazine called the office today while I was in. He wanted to know if we'd give them a name."

"He was from a magazine?"

"Yeah, I forget which one."

"And he wanted *my* name?"

"Yeah, Pemberleo won't give it out, but unfortunately, these guys can usually find a source who will divulge the information they're looking for in exchange for a little something in return."

Elyssa lowered her head into her hand and she dug her fingers into her scalp, trying to rub away the headache that was now throbbing. "George, I think I would like to be left alone."

"Yeah. Sure. Look, I'm really sorry I had to be the one to show you these. I wish that we... well, maybe if you ever come back, we can carry on where we left off."

Elyssa smiled. "Thanks, George. It's not your fault. My one consolation right now is that the only people who will see these pictures are ones who visit that website. If they appear in a magazine, well, I guess I'll have to deal with it then."

"You will, Elyssa. You're strong. Will always shrugs these things off. He's seen enough pictures of himself with women in magazines that it doesn't mean a thing to him anymore."

George walked slowly to the door. "I suppose your travel arrangements are all set for tomorrow?"

Elyssa stood up to see him out and glanced toward her luggage. "Yeah, everything's arranged."

"Well, then, until next time."

"Thanks, George."

George shook his head. "Yeah."

He turned to leave and then stopped. Looking back at Elyssa, he asked, "Hey, was that Maria that stopped by earlier?"

"Yes, it was."

"I didn't know you knew her."

"Oh, I only just met her today. I understood that she faithfully goes out each week and places flowers at the little memorial cross on the highway where Chad and Janet died. I wanted to meet her."

"Oh." George looked down and then back at Elyssa. "Sweet kid."

"Yes, she seems to be."

"Good night, Elyssa."

"Good night, George."

Elyssa shut the door and her hand tightened into a fist, crumpling the pictures. The tension and throbbing in her head echoed the new feelings of anguish in her stomach. Her mind and heart swirled with the insinuations from the website and the accusations George made about Will. She needed to talk to someone, but she needed to sort out her thoughts first.

She sank back down into the chair and wrapped her arms tightly about her. She tried to think, but her muddled mind wouldn't cooperate. *Just who exactly is Will?* Elyssa asked herself. *Why was I so sure about his character and prejudiced against him when I first came, how and when did that change, and now, why do I feel so confused?*

As her head began to throb, she lifted a hand to gently rub it. It was not long before she was reminded of an evening two nights ago when Will did the same. She crashed her hand back down into her lap.

Had she merely been a project in his eyes? If so, what kind? Did he dislike the fact that she didn't fall head over heels for him like every other woman? Elyssa let out a moan. Was he merely trying to make amends to her for his part in sending Chad and Janet here? Did his behavior reflect his true feelings for her or was he merely fulfilling an agenda?

Feelings clashed with reason as she tried to make sense of it all. George's words hit her as painfully as any spear piercing through to the depths of her.

Elyssa sat up with a start, suddenly remembering Janet's journal. She wasn't sure what her sister may have written about Will in it, but she could at least see if there appeared to be any sort of concern over his character or behavior.

Looking around the room, her eyes latched onto the corner of the room and her heart sank. She remembered that she had placed it with the stuff Manuel had taken to box up for her. She would have to wait until she got home to read through it.

A tear slowly made its way down Elyssa's face as she realized that she may have fallen in love with the laid-back, considerate man at the lake, but in reality, his behaviour these past few days was probably nothing like the driven, manipulative corporate president that characterized him elsewhere.

She needed some time away from him to reflect on everything more clearly. As she looked over at her luggage, she knew one thing for certain -- she could not fly home with him in his jet. She needed to distance herself from him to allow her to think judiciously -- and the sooner the better!

She knew she would be vulnerable just being in his presence, that her feelings for him would overrule any reasonable objection to him. No, she would somehow decline his offer to fly her home and take the time apart from him to sort out who she truly believed him to be.

Elyssa stood up and walked into the bathroom. Looking into the mirror, she splashed some water on her face to help wipe away the redness that stained her eyes and blotted her cheeks. Staring at the image looking back at her, she whispered, "I've got to talk to Shelley."

She took a few deep breaths to steady herself and walked through the complex to the Walkers' townhouse. Knocking on the door, she waited, her heart pounding thunderously in her chest.

The door opened and Shelley greeted Elyssa with a beaming smile. "I am so glad you came by! I was hoping to see you before you left!" She reached for Elyssa's hand and gave it a gentle tug. "Come in."

Elyssa stepped in and couldn't prevent herself from inhaling deeply the aromas filling the house. It was obvious Shelley was cooking.

"How was the lake? Did you think it was just beautiful?"

Elyssa nodded. "Yes, but unfortunately I was sick for a good part of it. I ate some fruit that I neglected to rinse in bottled water."

Shelley ushered Elyssa into the living room. "That will get you every time. Here, have a seat."

"No, no thank you, Shelley. I'll only stay for a minute. I had a couple questions I'd like to ask."

"Sure."

John walked in at that moment and Elyssa couldn't help smiling when she saw him wearing a large white apron. It was obvious that he was the chef this evening and she thought how nice it would be to have a husband who was willing to help out this way. A sudden pang of realization hit her that Will was too corporately ambitious to be this kind of man and husband.

"Hello, Elyssa," John smiled. "Are you staying for dinner?"

"Oh, no, I can't."

"Please do," encouraged Shelley. "We have plenty."

Elyssa shook her head. "Thank you both, but I have a lot to do before I leave in the morning."

"Are you sure?" John asked.

"Yes, but I do have a favor to ask."

"Anything," Shelley reached out and took her hand. "What is it?"

"My plane leaves at nine thirty in the morning and I wondered if I could get a ride to the airport at around seven thirty." She looked back and forth at each of them. "If it's not too much trouble."

"Sure, I can take you, but I thought... wasn't this already taken care of? I mean, isn't Will..."

"Will had a meeting come up in the morning," Elyssa quickly interjected.

"Well, sure. Come on by when you're ready."

"Thanks, Shelley."

Elyssa briskly rubbed the palms of her hands together while searching for the right words to her next question. Finally, she asked, "Do either of you know the details concerning Chad going to Will for advice about asking Janet to marry him?" A deep breath steadied her shaky voice. "Did Will really tell Chad he didn't think he should ask her to marry him?"

When Shelly and John stole a guarded glance at one another, Elyssa knew the answer immediately. He *had!*

"He did, didn't he?"

"Look, Elyssa, that was two years ago. Will only thought he was looking out for Chad's future with the company."

"As opposed to his happiness in life with Janet by his side as his wife!" Elyssa felt the throbbing in her head grow increasingly prominent and her ire against Will rising. "I can't believe he did that!"

John took a step toward Elyssa. "We can only assume it was because of the possibility of Chad being sent here to Guatemala. He may have wondered whether Janet would have been a hindrance."

Elyssa stood up and tried to smile. "I'm sorry. I didn't mean to sound so angry. I need to get back to the townhouse and get myself ready to leave tomorrow. I want to thank you both for all you did to help me out here. I really appreciate it."

Shelley stepped toward her and walked with her to the door. "If you can't eat with us, can I bring you a plate? John makes the best enchiladas!"

Elyssa smiled. "That does sound great. Thanks!"

"Good. I'll bring some over in about an hour. Besides, there is a matter I want to talk with you about."

Elyssa then recalled what Maria told her earlier and thought it would be best to tell Shelley about it when they were alone. "That reminds me, Shelley. There's something *I* would like to talk with *you* about. Don't let me forget."

After saying goodbye, Elyssa walked slowly back to the townhouse. Her hands were shaking, her stomach was churning with confusion, and her head was spinning. She knew she had seen and had been with a very different man the past few days, but didn't know whether Will could have changed so dramatically -- and completely -- in the two years since she first met him. How she wished she had Janet's journal!

One thing of which she was certain, though, was that she enjoyed her simple, country life and knew that a relationship with Will would require her to relocate to Chicago. She couldn't see herself making such a drastic move without the assurance that he was everything she wanted in a man.

A cold shiver passed through her, despite the warmth of the late afternoon. No, until she knew for a certainty who he really was, she would try to push aside all the thoughts and feelings that surfaced this past weekend towards him. She would return to her simple life in the Santa Ynez Valley and go on as if nothing ever happened between them.

Chapter 18

By the time Shelley arrived with the plate of food, Elyssa's stomach was growling from hunger, although she really wasn't sure if she felt like eating.

Shelley brought the foil-covered plate inside and took it into the kitchen, placing it on the counter. Her eyes were downcast for a moment before she finally looked up at Elyssa.

"I mentioned earlier that there was something I needed to tell you."

"Yes?"

Shelley looked down at her hands wringing together nervously. When she finally looked up, her face was drawn with concern. "We were notified today of some pictures, Elyssa, that have appeared on an Internet site."

"Unfortunately, I know."

"You do?"

Elyssa looked down and nodded. "I saw them."

Elyssa turned and walked over to the small table in the corner of the room. She began picking things up and rearranging them as if it was therapeutic for her. "I know it is best not to try and defend yourself when these things appear." Elyssa let out a sarcastic chuckle. "Not that I am used to this type of thing." She turned back and faced Shelley. "I know it doesn't really matter, but the pictures and comments suggest a very evocative weekend rendezvous, when actually, nothing happened."

Shelley stepped forward and grasped Elyssa's hands. "You don't need to explain anything to me, Elyssa. That's not why I came over to tell you."

"But I feel as though I do need to explain! That's why this is so frustrating! I want to tell everyone who sees those pictures and reads those captions that nothing happened between us!" Elyssa fought back the tears that welled up in her eyes.

Shelley released Elyssa's hands. "I told you how Will doesn't tolerate gossip and I am sure he will be infuriated by the insinuations. He takes no pleasure in this invasion of privacy and I know he won't be happy that people are getting the wrong impression about the two of you."

Elyssa's eyes shot up and she bit her lip. Shaking her head slowly, she said, "No, he wouldn't want that, would he?"

"I know it sounds trite, Elyssa, but everyone will have forgotten about these pictures in a very short time. Something more titillating will come along and these will be history."

Elyssa brought her hand up to her forehead and pressed her fingers deeply where it pulsated with pain. "Perhaps."

"I just want to let you know that Pemberleo is very sorry that this happened."

Elyssa forced a smile. "Thanks. I don't blame Pemberleo. It's not really their fault."

Shelley took Elyssa's hand. "Come sit down, Elyssa, and tell me what it was you wanted to talk with me about."

A wave of guilt swept over Elyssa as she realized that her problems had once again wiped Maria's situation from her mind. They sat down and Elyssa proceeded to tell Shelley what Maria had told her.

Shelley shook her head. "These young girls tend to latch on to any guy who pays attention to them. I didn't know she had been seeing anyone. She was much closer to Janet. I'll get together with her in a day or two to see how she's doing and make sure she's no longer holding on to any of those feelings of guilt. I can't believe she's blamed herself for so long."

"Thanks, Shelley."

"Sure. Let me know if you need anything else tonight. Otherwise, I'll see you in the morning."

When Shelley left, Elyssa sat down to her plate of food. The enchiladas were delicious, but she could hardly bring herself to eat even half of what they had given her. She felt overwhelmed by a tumultuous gnawing and couldn't reconcile anything that had transpired these past few days.

Her eyes drifted over to the corner table. She shook her head as she contemplated how easily she could rearrange the objects on a table or on the wall to make them more pleasing, yet at the moment she had no idea how to arrange the events of this past week into any semblance of order. Without giving it a second thought, she could rearrange a display so that it evoked a sense of peace rather than chaos, yet she couldn't arrange her thoughts and feelings so that they gave her even an iota of peace and harmony. She knew how to create a focal point in design, but knowing where and how to focus her thoughts on the man William Denton eluded her.

~~*

Elyssa awoke early the next morning with about as much anguish and inner turmoil as she had when she first arrived in Guatemala. But it was no longer because of losing her closest sister and friend. It was because she had allowed herself to fall for William Denton, a man she had once determined to loathe.

She was all packed and sat in the living room waiting for the clock to strike seven. She knew that Will would be in his meeting and decided she would call at that time and leave a message for him, telling him that she had decided to fly out using her own ticket. He wouldn't discover her change of plans until he got out of his meeting. By that time she would safely be in the boarding area at the airport where he would not be allowed to go.

Elyssa closed her eyes and took in a deep breath. She knew she was taking the easy way out, but she didn't even know what she would say if she had to make explanations to him. She was angry with him that he felt it was his duty to do things like interfering with Chad's decision to marry Janet, yet she couldn't dismiss what he had been like at the lake. How could she clearly explain to him her reasons for refusing his offer to fly her home in his jet when everything seemed so muddled?

Elyssa leaned her head back in the chair, but the last thing she wanted to do was sit. With each tick of the clock, her mind played the events of last night over and over. When Will left, he kissed her cheek. Without thinking, she reached up with her fingers and touched the area his lips had left their lasting imprint.

She thought about Maria, who had practically collapsed in Elyssa's arms as she blamed herself for Janet's death. Elyssa didn't understand all the details, but she hoped Shelley would see to it that she no longer carried around this false sense of guilt.

Elyssa dropped her head into her hands. *False sense of guilt!* Ever since Janet and Chad's deaths, she had clung tenaciously to a false sense of *blame* directed at Will. She knew now how foolish she had been. Their deaths were no more his fault than they were Maria's fault.

She admitted to herself that she had been wrong. But she couldn't dismiss George's startling accusation that Will tried to talk Chad out of marrying Janet. She closed her eyes as she considered what all she did *not* know about Will. Were there other things he had done as president of Pemberleo that made people sacrifice what was truly important to them?

She had spent the past two years harboring feelings of loathing and disdain for the man and his driven, controlling ways. Those feelings all seemingly vanished after spending less than a week with him in an exotic locale and seeing a kind and caring side of him. Which man was he? Was he the man she had just been with or the man she had known him to be all along. There was an unanswerable question that loomed ominously over her. Was this past weekend with him a side of his true character or merely an uncharacteristic display that was rarely exhibited?

To make matters even more convoluted, there were those incriminating pictures from the Internet. She knew Will was a man whose face might be recognizable to those who ravenously devour every word and scrutinize every picture of those deemed noteworthy. She would have never dreamed that their taking shelter in a hotel for the night -- in separate rooms -- would be shown for all the world to see. She only hoped the pictures would never appear in a magazine.

Her thoughts went back to Will telling her there were some things he wanted to talk with her about on the jet. She closed her eyes as she recalled how his eyes had searched her face, as if hoping for some sort of encouragement. A small smile had appeared just before he leaned over and kissed her cheek.

Elyssa shook her head determinedly as thoughts of her father intruded in her mind. From that first meeting with Will, she had considered him to be very much like her father's boss, who stole precious time away from her father that could have been spent with her and her family. She could not allow herself to fall for someone like him!

Elyssa let out a huff of exasperation, as she considered Will to be more of an enigma than ever.

Elyssa's breath faltered as tears filled her eyes. She knew something had happened between them; something unlike anything she had ever felt before. Her chest tightened as she realized those few days with Will would most likely have to be relegated to a cherished memory to warm her winter years. Some day she would be able to look back and laugh at her folly and be thankful she did not succumb to him. In years to come she would see that he was very much the dictatorial man she once thought him to be.

At about twenty minutes past seven, Elyssa summoned the courage and made the call she was dreading. A secretary dutifully took the message, asking Elyssa for more details than she was willing to give.

"Please express my thanks to Mr. Denton for his generous offer to fly me home on his jet," she told her. "But I must decline. I will be flying home on my scheduled flight. Shelley Walker is driving me to the airport in a few minutes."

"Is there anything wrong?" the woman asked.

"No, there's nothing wrong. Please, just tell Mr. Denton I am grateful for all he did for me while I was here."

Elyssa then gave instructions to have the items that Manuel had picked up the day before shipped to her home C.O.D.

When Elyssa replaced the phone on its base, she fought back the tears that were threatening. Looking around her, she knew she had to say goodbye. But it was more than just a goodbye to her sister.

~~*

The drive to the airport produced much anxiety for Elyssa, as they seemed to hit every red light, and at some points the drive proceeded at a crawl. Looking several times at her watch, Shelley reassured her that they would get to the airport in time and she wouldn't miss her flight.

A weak smile was directed at Shelley, as Elyssa's only concern was when Will might be told about her decision and what he would do about it.

They finally arrived at the airport and Shelley pulled up to the front. Once she had pulled her baggage from the car, Elyssa leaned in to Shelley and gave her a hug, thanking her for everything she had done to make her visit more pleasant. They exchanged farewells and then Elyssa turned to look at the crowd of people making their way into the Guatemala City airport. Her thoughts assessed the possibly that by now Will probably knew that she had decided to fly home on her own.

As she walked into the crowded check-in area, a wave of uneasiness passed through her stomach; this time it was not due to something she ate. She glanced about her for her airline's ticket counter and then was dismayed to see that it had the most people in line.

She turned to look again toward the doors where people were coming in and leaving the airport. This area was not confined to passengers only and she knew Will could easily find her here -- if he even chose to come.

Taking only a few tiny steps in the line as it slowly moved forward, she wished the checking in process would progress more rapidly. Her only consolation was that once she was past the security gate, Will would not be able to reach her.

She looked around at the other airline check-in counters and wished she hadn't booked on one of the larger airlines. If she was flying out on a smaller airline, she would have been checked in and walking toward her gate by now -- out of Will's reach.

For her own peace of mind, she decided to keep her eyes toward the counter. *He has no reason to come,* she told herself. *He's probably grateful I'm out of his hair.*

When she finally reached the counter, the agent did not seem to sympathize at all with Elyssa's desire to rush. Her flight was now a little less than an hour away and everything he did seemed to progress in slow motion.

When she finally had her boarding pass in hand, she rushed to the security gate, keeping her eyes directed straight ahead of her. *Just a few more steps,* she reassured herself.

She put her purse and small carry-on bag upon the moving ramp that would take them through the x-ray and awaited her turn to walk through the security check. Her heart pounded as the gentleman ahead of her set off the alarm. He searched his pockets, pulling out some loose change and walked through again. It was finally Elyssa's turn and without even a backwards glance, she stepped through, quickly picking up her things. She had finally made it!

She looked at the myriad of signs ahead of her for her gate number. Turning in the direction the arrow indicated, she quickly set off and didn't stop walking until she was there.

Elyssa took a seat away from other waiting passengers gathered for the flight. She wished to be left alone; preferring to lose herself in a book. As she attempted to concentrate on the words written on the page, voices filled her ears as people walked past her, conversing with one another or on their cell phones. It was like a dull hum as the foreign words meant little to her. Occasionally, she would hear a word she recognized in Spanish or someone walked past speaking English, but very little registered -- much like the written words her eyes scanned on the pages of the book in front of her.

She felt her eyes sting from the tears that were trying to push their way to the surface.

Why did I have to fall for such a man? The thought came with no warning; her cheeks flushed and her heart picked up its pace.

Her trembling hands formed into fists as George's words suddenly came to her. *I knew you were too smart to fall for a man like him. He's a manipulator and thrives on control. Look at how he tried to keep Chad from marrying your sister.*

How dare he interfere like that! she thought. *Chad and Janet loved each other very much!*

A yawn brought Elyssa's hand up to cover her mouth and for the first time this morning, her body reminded her just how tired she was. Last night afforded her very little sleep as her mind and heart fought for any sort of answer. *I am right in doing this,* she reassured herself. *I am right!*

Elyssa directed her eyes back to her book and tried to begin to read again. She had to reread each paragraph several times before she was able to tend to the words. Her mind insisted on diverting her thoughts to Will.

With each recollection of his uncharacteristic acts of kindness, his smile, his arms around her, the kiss he gently placed on her cheek, she forced herself to remember his acts of manipulation. She could not help but question his total focus on business and how his actions took Janet away. She recalled the wedding reception two years ago when she overheard his words about her. She thought back to his eulogy for Chad and how cold and unfeeling he was.

Elyssa took in a deep breath and closed her eyes. She felt them grow watery and she lifted a hand to gently wipe them away. *No,* she told herself. *He is not the kind of man with whom I would want to be involved.*

When she opened her eyes, she noticed someone standing in front of her.

She did not need to look up to see who it was. She could tell by the expertly tailored designer suit. Her heart pounded mercilessly as she forced herself to look up.

"What are *you* doing here?" she asked meekly.

She could see him strive for control as his jaw tightened. "Shouldn't I be asking *you* that question?"

"Didn't you get my message? Oh, I guess you must have received my message for you to be here. I decided it would be best to use my own ticket and I really didn't want to inconvenience you or for you to go out of your way." Elyssa knew she was rambling and found it difficult to look him in the eye.

Will looked at her incredulously and seemed to measure each word he spoke. "Don't you think *I* should be the one to determine whether or not flying you home on my jet was an inconvenience?"

Elyssa could see fire in his eyes, but it was coupled with something else that she couldn't quite pinpoint. Whatever that was, it made her feel vulnerable. To arm herself against such feelings, she quickly stood to her feet, crossing her arms tightly in front of her.

"Your offer to fly me home was generous and I thank you. But I cannot accept it."

"May I ask why?"

Elyssa drew in a deep breath while she formulated her answer. "Will, you must have known what my opinion of you was when you first arrived here. I certainly did not keep it hidden from you. In fact, my opinion of you had been formed when we first met at Janet and Chad's wedding rehearsal two years ago."

The expression on Will's face did not change. "Go on."

Elyssa glanced down, unable to meet his piercing eyes. "I saw evidence of a man consumed by his work, manipulative, and uncaring for the feelings of others."

"Did you really?" Will's voice shook with the anger and hurt coursing through him.

Elyssa nodded and looked up slowly. "I will admit that over the course of the week, my opinion of you did improve, and I confess I no longer hold you to blame for Chad and Janet's deaths."

"How very generous of you!" Will huffed out.

Elyssa's heart pounded wildly in her chest as she considered her next words.

"I am grateful for all you did this past week."

"Grateful?" he asked in disbelief.

"Yes," she answered determinedly. "I am grateful, but I think it would be best if we went our separate ways."

"Am I entitled to any explanation for this decision?" he demanded.

Elyssa looked down and then back at him. "Some things have come to light that have me wondering, Will, if my opinion of you was correct in the first place!"

"You mean your opinion that I am consumed by work, uncaring, and manipulative?"

Elyssa nodded slowly. "I've seen too many men who think of nothing but their careers. My father's boss was one and his unreasonable demands literally killed my father!"

"May I ask what these things are that have come to light?"

"For one, I understand that you advised Chad not to ask Janet to marry him. You told him you didn't think he should!"

As she pronounced these words, Will changed color, but any sort of prevailing emotion soon dissipated, and he listened without attempting to interrupt her while she continued.

"I have every reason in the world to think you overstepped your bounds, William Denton, even as Chad's employer. Chad and Janet loved one another and were perfectly suited to each other. Do you deny that you told him you didn't think he should propose?"

"I have no reason to deny it. I had my reasons."

"Your reasons! You care little for anything or anyone but your company. You manipulate people as if they were your puppets, with little thought or consideration for them. I can't help but wonder how many others in your employ have sacrificed happiness because of your interference!"

"You must believe there to be a multitude!"

"I know there is George Westham!"

An angry shudder coursed through him. "And what do you know of George Westham's concerns?" He practically spewed out the man's name.

"It's obvious you have something against the man. He told me how your father had promised him advancement within the company, seeing his potential. You chose, upon taking the company over, to send him off as a salesman to Guatemala. You broke your own father's promise to him!"

His eyes darkened even more. "Poor George, indeed!" He turned away and Elyssa could see that he was trying to maintain some semblance of control. A slight slumping of his shoulders and nod of his head inexplicably made Elyssa feel her defenses beginning to wear down. For a brief moment she had an impulsive desire to reach out to him. She quickly shook that away.

When he turned back to look at her, his rigid posture had returned and his head was held high. "And what, may I ask, do you think I think about *you*?"

Her heart lurched at his question and his eyes seemed to bore deeply within her. Moistening her lips, she finally uttered, "Two years ago, I believe your words describing me were something to the effect of *being naïve, opinionated, that everything revolves around me, and I have no idea how to run a business.* More recently, however, I overheard you refer to me as a *project*! Something to wheel and deal for whatever purposes you had in mind!" She looked down as her eyes began to well up with tears.

He stood still; his eyes fixed on her face. He seemed to catch her words with no less resentment than surprise. She noticed him wince when she mentioned his words from two years ago. His complexion became pale with anger and the disturbance of his mind was visible in every feature. He was struggling for the appearance of composure and would not open his lips, till he believed himself to have attained it.

Finally, he said, "So this is what you think of me! I thank you for explaining it to me so fully! I wonder how you endured my presence these last few days." He shifted his weight from one foot to another. "I see my coming here was a mistake."

Suddenly Elyssa's eyes narrowed. "Exactly how *did* you get past the security gate? No one can come back here without a ticket."

"I purchased one."

Elyssa met his gaze, suddenly alarmed. "You are on my flight?"

He let out a huff and shook his head. "No, rest assured, Elyssa, I am not on your flight. It was full. I purchased a seat on another." He tossed the ticket down. "Obviously I won't be using it and never intended to. I only came back here to…" He took in a shaky breath. "Well, never mind."

Elyssa fought back her tears as one last time she looked up at him. "I am sorry, Will, but we are two very different people who live in two worlds that are poles apart. I just need to go home and sort this all out."

Will's jaw tightened again as he looked down at Elyssa. "I'm sorry, too, Elyssa, but what is there for you to sort out? Your words certainly indicate that you have me all figured out. Goodbye. I hope you have a good flight home." With that, he turned and walked away.

Elyssa stood very still for some time, watching him take brisk strides through the crowd of people. She was all too familiar now with his confident gait. She told herself she ought to feel relief that he was now out of her life. Unfortunately, she felt anything but. The tears that had threatened earlier were now more demanding and soon spilled out. She collapsed into the chair in which she had been sitting, unable to move for quite some time.

She stared down at the ticket he had tossed at her. She wondered how much it had cost him to come find her. Why would he have done such a thing? Why had he even bothered to come down to Guatemala in the first place?

She could not, would not, answer that question, for if she did, she would have realized that for some explicable reason, William Denton had in fallen in love with her.

Chapter 19

Elyssa returned to her modest country home and within days after settling back in, she felt as though the previous week in Guatemala had merely been a dream; some of it a nightmare. Apart from the anguish and confusion in her heart, she could almost believe it had never happened.

She waited anxiously for the box Pemberleo was shipping to her. She was eager to get her hands back on Janet's journal, look again through the keepsakes from the Blakelys' belongings she sent back, and although she didn't want to admit it to herself, she was hoping Will had written a note to her and included it in the box.

She saw that the package had been delivered after returning home from work a few days later. The large box had been left on the porch and she struggled in vain to pick it up to bring it inside. She finally decided to open it out there and remove some of the items, making it possible for her to carry it in.

With each item she lifted out, she told herself that her one main objective was to find Janet's journal. But her eyes seemed to betray that intention as they searched instead for an envelope in which a letter may have been placed. When at last she found both, she gingerly pulled out the letter.

She opened it slowly and found herself looking at a typewritten letter. Her heart sunk when she glanced down at the bottom to see that it was from Will's secretary, Mrs. Reed. The letter informed her that the remainder of Chad and Janet's belongings had been given to several charities. It concluded with a statement that Pemberleo would be in further contact with her regarding a matter that was being finalized. A fleeting sense of curiosity caused her to wonder what that matter might be, but disappointment quickly took its place. If Will had any intention of contacting her again, he would have written this very first letter himself.

Despite the reasons she told herself and had lashed out to Will as to why they should go their separate ways that last day in Guatemala, she now found herself questioning her rationale. Since returning home, she found it more and more difficult to justify the assault on his character. Perhaps it was true, that with distance and the passage of time the faults of another grow dim.

She found herself frequently thinking about him and their time together in Guatemala. Just the recollection of him walking by her side filled her with regret. She thought of his most surprising, yet effective means to rid her of the blame she placed on him when he took her on the bumper cars. The memory of him carrying her across the rain swollen street made her yearn to be held in his arms. His attentive comfort when she was ill was not something she could easily dismiss. The look in his eyes and the gentle kiss he placed on her cheek began to appear more and more an indication that he had strong feelings for her.

She slowly pulled out Janet's journal. Holding it to her chest, she knew it would be difficult to read, but she knew she had to. Walking over to the swing, she sat down and drew her legs up underneath her. She opened the journal as the swing began swaying rhythmically to the beating of her heart.

As she began to read Janet's words, all her initial feelings of grief surfaced. It took Elyssa the remainder of the week to read through the journal and gradually she was able to push aside that grief and enjoy the story of the Blakelys' life together in Guatemala.

Most of Janet's entries dealt with her day to day routine. Elyssa cried at the description of her first day at the pre-school and how precious, but needy, the children were. She laughed at her sister's description of how crazy the drivers were in Guatemala and how Janet didn't think she would ever find the nerve to get behind the wheel.

Elyssa was touched by the warmth and admiration Janet had for Chad and how much she enjoyed supporting him in his work.

Elyssa devoured every word Janet wrote and upon turning each page, she found herself glancing down to see if there was any mention about Will. While Janet didn't mention him all that often, when she did, it was always in a positive light.

The only reference she could find that gave Elyssa any indication that Janet knew of Will's interference came in an entry where Janet had the most to say about him.

She wrote,

Will joined us for dinner this evening. He had been in meetings all day. I couldn't help thinking how tired he looked. He must have enjoyed himself, though, because he stayed fairly late and commented several times how pleasant it was to be able to come home to a family and eat a home cooked meal. I thought how sad it must be that the only family he has is Gina and she will be going off to college soon. He always asks me how my family is, asking about each one by name if I forget to mention anyone, and I think he's truly interested in what I tell him. It's funny. Even though he is Chad's boss and I know what he did, I've never felt any censure from him. I actually think he enjoys being in our company! Imagine that!

Chad says he has seen a change in him. Not a drastic, sudden change, but one that has come about slowly. He's known him since university days and has spent a lot of time with him. While he can't put his finger on what the change is, he thinks it's for the better.

Elyssa read and reread that entry. She was grateful that Janet never picked up any antagonism toward her on Will's part. Perhaps he came to believe that Janet had been good for Chad. Elyssa couldn't help but wonder whether he ever admitted to himself -- or Chad -- that he had been wrong. Could he have truly changed from the man she met two years ago?

As Elyssa read Janet's entries, she came to truly appreciate the genuine spirit of charity Janet had toward others and how she only had kind things to say about everyone and everything. Elyssa was surprised, then, when she came across some entries toward the end of the journal. The entries dealt with Maria's visits and how the young girl had become enamored with someone. That someone was George Westham.

Elyssa felt sick when she read Janet's words describing how George was an unscrupulous womanizer and not to be trusted. Janet wrote how she had tried to warn the young girl about his character, but Maria loved him and felt certain that George loved her. When Elyssa read Janet's very last entry that dealt with George, she practically grew sick.

Janet wrote,

I don't know why Will has allowed GW to continue to work for Pemberleo. I know he has his reasons; I think in part he is trying to honor his father's wishes. But GW is a liar, cheat, and manipulator. I hope he doesn't hurt Maria. I really hope he doesn't, but deep down inside I know that he will. He knows no other way!

Immediately after reading that part, Elyssa sent off a letter to Shelley, enlightening her that it was George who caused Maria such grief. Shelley may have talked to Maria already and knew George was the man in question, but in case Maria was too ashamed to tell her, Elyssa thought Shelley ought to know.

Elyssa should have trusted her initial instincts about the man, but when he showed up that last night with his pictures and accusations, suspicion about his character was the last thing on her mind.

When the weekend came, Elyssa took some of the items from the box down with her to Los Angeles to give to her mother and sister. She had planned a short visit with them knowing they would want to hear more about her trip. She also brought along some things for her Aunt and Uncle Garner, whom she was really looking forward to seeing.

She was disappointed to find out that her aunt and uncle would not be there, as they were traveling the country with their children. Apparently they were looking to relocate to the Midwest, where they once lived and where Maddy had grown up. They thought it would be preferable to raise their young family there.

The weekend she spent with her family was just as she expected. She felt very little rapport with her mother, who was always eager to express her grave concern about one thing or another. There was always something for her to worry about. Her younger sister was so different than her that it made her miss Janet all the more.

The weekend concluded with a visit with Charlene. Elyssa always enjoyed Charlene and her wild, impulsive ways. Her personality was very much suited for the lifestyle there. She was doing well in the entertainment industry, but presently was between jobs.

"I'm on board to do the set design for a Western, but it's in pre-production stage right now. They're trying to agree on the budget and until I know what it is, I can't do a thing other than dream. I'd love to have you by my side when it comes time to begin work on it, Elyssa, but it may be months before anything can be done."

Elyssa thanked her, but declined. "I don't think Western is my thing, but thanks, Charlene. I do so appreciate it."

"You know I hand out your business cards everywhere I go. Have you never received an offer of a design job from one of them?"

Elyssa laughed. "You hand them out everywhere but where I live! No one is going to call me when they have no idea who I am, especially if they live on the other side of the country!"

Charlene smiled. "Well all that's needed is to get your business card into the right person's hands!"

The two friends shared a few more laughs and some cries together reminiscing about Janet, and then Elyssa made the drive home. She loved the part of the drive where she drove along the coast and could see the blue waters of the Pacific Ocean before she headed inland. She always stopped at the last turnout to give herself a rest and enjoy the ocean breeze and the sound of the endlessly pounding waves.

She decided this time to get out and walk along the beach a bit and then sit for awhile on the sand. She pulled out a small blanket she kept in her car and walked toward the beach. Taking her shoes off, she stepped into the soft sand and squished her toes into it. As she walked closer to the water, she thought of the day at the lake when she and Will ended up soaking wet. A smile crept upon her face as she recalled the fun they had. She stepped into the water up to her ankles and turned to walk along the coastline.

When she came back, she spread out her blanket and sat down, looking out at the reflection of the sun as it approached the horizon. There were no volcanoes looking back at her, but she couldn't help but think again about Will. She closed her eyes as she began to lie down upon the blanket. Her fists pounded into the sand on either side of her and she wondered if she would ever be able to forget him.

~~*

The next month passed quickly for Elyssa. She was sitting one day at the table in the kitchen looking over her bank statement. Her checking account was dwindling to almost nothing and her savings had grown only a few cents from the interest. Her job at the library barely paid for her living expenses and she began to fret over whether she'd ever get another decorating job while living so far out here in the country. She began to despair that she might have to move back to the big city and go to work with Charlene. It was something she swore she would never do.

Elyssa walked out to her mailbox and pulled out a stack of envelopes. As she flipped through them, she was thrilled to see a letter from her Aunt and Uncle Garner. Elyssa began to rip it open as she walked back to the house.

Her Aunt Maddy began the letter with her usual greeting. She told her how much she missed her and what a wonderful time they had been having. The letter then went on to inform Elyssa that they had found the perfect home in Lamstone, Illinois, a small town about 45 miles from Chicago. Elyssa delighted in her aunt's description of this quaint little town with rolling hills and thick woods. A lake was only a few miles away, tempting Edward with his favorite pastime --

fishing. Lamstone was close enough to Chicago to have all the amenities of a big city, but it still had a small town feel. She was sure Elyssa would love it.

An invitation was extended to Elyssa to come any time. While Elyssa would gladly make a visit to see her aunt and uncle and cousins, another person came foremost to her mind. Will would only be about 45 miles away.

She tucked the letter back into her desk drawer. Now was not the best time for her to go, as she desperately needed some income to help pay her bills. She knew, however, that as soon as she could afford to go, she would. As she wrote down her expenses for the remainder of the month and worked at saving here so she could spend there, her phone rang.

"Please be someone with a design job!" she said as she looked up to the heavens.

"Hello?"

The voice on the other end was soft spoken. "Hello. Is this Elyssa Barnett?"

Elyssa smiled. She didn't recognize the voice and thought that perhaps this could be her big break. "Yes, this is Elyssa Barnett," she said with the most professional sounding voice. "May I help you?"

"Yes. My name is Gina Denton."

Elyssa was grateful the caller could not see her reaction, for her jaw dropped and she shook her head in disbelief. "Gina Denton?"

"Yes, I am William Denton's sister."

Elyssa took in a deep breath and steadied herself. "Yes, I know. I mean he told me about you. What can I do for you?"

"I am in the area and would like to know if you were free for me to stop by today. There is something I would like to discuss with you."

Elyssa's eyes narrowed as she tried to determine what the young girl wished to talk to her about. "I am free all day today. When would you like to come by?"

"Would an hour from now be convenient?"

"An hour from now would be fine."

Gina asked Elyssa for directions to her house and they hung up. She wondered whether Gina had been sent to discuss the matter that Mrs. Reed had mentioned in the letter.

Elyssa went outside onto her porch and sat down on the swing to wait for Gina. She knew that Gina's visit today was a very strong indication that Will chose not to have any further interaction with her. She really couldn't blame him.

Almost exactly an hour from the time they had hung up, a car pulled up front.

Elyssa stood up from the swing and walked over to the steps, watching the blond haired girl come toward her.

"Hi," said Elyssa. "You must be Gina."

"Yes, I am," the young girl answered.

"Please come in."

"Thank you."

The two came into the house and Elyssa eyed her curiously. She saw very little resemblance between Gina and her brother. With fair hair and skin, blue eyes, and a rather thin build, they seemed rather to be opposites.

Elyssa ushered the young girl into the living room and offered her a seat, still fighting a desperate curiosity to know why she was there.

"I understand you attend Stanford."

"Yes. But I was actually in Solvang with friends for the weekend. It's beautiful country around here."

"Yes, it is. I love it! Are you enjoying Solvang?"

"Yes, very much. I've been there a couple of times and every time I go, someone always assumes I am Scandinavian because of my coloring. I particularly love the Danish pastries!"

"They are scrumptious, aren't they?"

Elyssa smiled, waiting for the young girl to state her business. She could see that Gina was rather shy and she took the time to gather her thoughts before she spoke. It seemed as though there was one area where Gina and Will were similar; neither were excessive talkers. But she was nothing like what Elyssa had expected.

"You have a beautifully decorated home, Elyssa. Did you do it yourself?"

Elyssa nodded. "I have a degree in interior design, but unfortunately my business is slow in taking off."

"I like how you have incorporated different styles and fabrics. You do it well." The young girl walked over to a table. "I recognize the runner here as Guatemalan."

"Yes, I brought that back from my visit."

"I like it." Gina said.

"Thank you." Elyssa watched as Gina began fidgeting and looked down. She waited for the girl to continue.

Gina slowly turned toward her and stood tall. Elyssa chuckled under her breath as she figured Gina must have been one of those privileged girls who had been sent to charm school to learn how to walk and talk in the most poised manner.

"First of all, I wanted to express my condolences to you in the loss of your sister and her husband. I know it must have been very difficult for you."

Elyssa felt compassion herself for the young girl; for she was struggling for the right words and Elyssa wanted to reassure her. "Thank you, Gina. While it was very difficult at first, and I still miss her terribly, I am getting through it."

Gina smiled and a small burst of uninhibited enthusiasm escaped. "How wonderful to have had a sister you were so close with. I only have Will and while there could not be a finer brother, I have often wished I had a sister."

At her words, Elyssa felt another pang of regret at her remarks to Will, but said, "It can be wonderful to have a sister! Janet and I had something special."

Gina looked down. "It must make it that much more difficult."

Elyssa nodded, and murmured an affirmative.

Wanting to change the subject, Elyssa asked, "So are you and your brother close?" She hoped she was not being too nosy.

"Even though he is 12 years older, I couldn't ask for a more wonderful brother."

"And just what makes him so wonderful?" Elyssa was more curious than just making conversation.

"I don't know. I guess I've always looked up to him. Being such an older brother, we never had that sibling rivalry between us. I can't imagine what it would have been like when our father died for him to suddenly be my guardian if I hadn't liked and respected him."

Elyssa found it sweet that both Will and Gina seemed to brighten up and talk openly of the other when given the opportunity.

Gina paused reflectively. "I think my going away to college has been hard on him. He has warned me that he is going to fly out and visit me at least twice a month because he will miss me so much."

Elyssa was rather surprised by that. "Don't you feel he's being a little overprotective by his visiting so often? Don't you want a little freedom now that you're in college?"

Gina laughed. "I wouldn't call him overprotective, just caring. He knows how shy I am and he only wants to make sure I don't spend every weekend sheltered in my room studying. I'm really not the partying type, so I honestly will look forward to his visits."

"I see," were the only words Elyssa could eke out. "And your visit to Solvang this weekend? He's not with you, is he?"

"No. I'm actually here for a class I am taking." Gina suddenly looked guilty and a sly smile appeared. "Don't mention this to Will, but I am taking a cooking class."

"A cooking class?"

"Yes. My major is business, but what I really want to do is bake. I'm taking a class near the university three nights a week and they suggested we make a trip to Solvang. One of the restaurants there allows us to come in and observe them for training. I had a couple of hours off this afternoon, so I thought I'd come by and see you."

"And your brother doesn't know?"

Gina smiled. "I think he suspects something. My fondest desire is to run a bed-and-breakfast. I can't help but think the Santa Ynez Valley would be the perfect area. But you mustn't say anything to Will."

Elyssa let out a soft chuckle. "I really don't think we'll be talking. But would he not approve?"

Gina tilted her head back and forth as if she was not quite certain. "We've always both assumed I would work for Pemberleo, but I don't think I have the passion for it."

"Like the passion your brother has for it?"

"William has a passion for doing things excellently. Right now that involves running the family business. I think if other things presented themselves, he would enter into them with the same passion and Pemberleo would take a back burner."

A part of Elyssa wondered whether that was indeed true. "So you never felt that he put Pemberleo before you?"

Gina laughed. "Well, there is one thing he puts before me and that's his board meetings. I know that I am never to call him during a board meeting because that is the one time he does not want to be disturbed. It would have to be quite an emergency to get him to leave before it's finished." Gina paused and smiled. "No, I never felt neglected by him -- or my father."

Elyssa smiled. "I can tell."

"Anyway," Gina brushed back a strand of hair that had fallen across her face. "The reason I came by was to tell you that Pemberleo Coffee would like to set up a memorial for Janet with money given in her memory to be used to build a park adjacent to the pre-school she worked at."

Elyssa's eyes widened. "A park by the pre-school?"

Gina nodded. "Yes. William said that he noticed the abandoned, boarded up buildings adjacent to it when you visited and there was really no place for neighborhood children to play but in the street. He spoke briefly to the woman who runs the preschool about the possibility of putting a park and playground there. He said he even put in a call to the Guatemala office while you were still at the facility to see if they could get things into motion as quickly as possible."

Elyssa thought back to her accusatory look at Will when he walked away carrying on a conversation on his mobile phone, thinking he was doing business as usual. In reality, he was setting into motion the plans for a park for the children.

"He never said anything to me about it."

"I don't think he wanted to get your hopes up. Several things had to be checked into and approved before we could even move on this." Gina laughed. "Finding the owner and contacting him was apparently not the easiest thing. Getting him to agree on a price was a whole other matter."

Gina folded her hands in front of her. "Is this something that you would approve of, Elyssa? Would you like Janet to be remembered in this way?"

Tears pooled in Elyssa's eyes and she nodded. "I can't think of anything that would have made Janet happier."

Gina reached over and took Elyssa's hand. "I understand she spent a lot of time at the pre-school."

Elyssa nodded, reaching for a tissue and she wiped her eyes. "Yes. When Will and I went to visit it, I was so touched by the children. I know they were very special to Janet."

"I'm quite certain Will thought so too. With your approval, Pemberleo will set up the memorial and we will match any amount given towards it. But to get the memorial started, we will purchase the land, clear it, and put in grass. Basically, any additional money given will be used for playground equipment."

"That is so generous. Thank you."

Gina's smile broadened. "No need to thank me; my brother made all the plans. I am merely the messenger."

Elyssa nodded her head, knowing all too well what that meant.

Chapter 20

Elyssa mulled over Gina's last remark. The fact that Will sent Gina to relay the message instead of communicating with her himself clearly indicated his disinclination to see her or to have any further contact with her again.

Gina stood up and walked over to a small table that had a wood carving on it and picked it up. "Did you get this in Guatemala?"

Elyssa nodded. "Yes, at Lake Atitlan in the market place."

"Oh, that reminds me," she said as she turned around. "Pemberleo has also established a memorial for Chad."

Elyssa's eyes widened. "I'm so glad! What will it be?"

"A scholarship is being set up in Chad's name. One will be made available each year for a young man or woman whose family grows coffee beans for Pemberleo Coffee to enable him or her to further their education. A stipend will also be given to help the family hire others to replace the work that their child would have done. I believe the first is going to a young man named Pedro."

"Pedro?" Elyssa exclaimed. "Oh, I know he will appreciate it!"

Elyssa's joy at hearing what Will had done was tinged by the shame she felt by her presumptions and the heated words she lashed out at him at the airport. She was silent for a while and Gina asked if she was all right.

Elyssa laughed remorsefully. "I just can't believe that Will did all this."

"Does it surprise you?"

"I confess it does. I guess I..." Elyssa stopped. She knew she would be dredging up her original opinion of him and suddenly felt uncomfortable speaking so critically of Will to his sister.

Gina's eyebrows lifted as she encouraged Elyssa to finish.

"I'm sorry, Gina, but sometimes I've wondered whether he even had the ability to consider other people or their feelings." Elyssa shook her head. "There were times he seemed to care little for anything else but Pemberleo."

Gina winced and sat back down. "Oh, my brother!" she said in a soft whisper. "You're not the only one who sees him that way, Elyssa, and it's true that a couple of years ago he was consumed by the company. I think he felt he was honoring our father by putting his whole self into it. He never neglected me and has always had the greatest regard for our family, but he struggles with showing compassion for others. I don't think he lacks compassion, but he never really knew how to show it. I believe he is changing for the better, though."

Elyssa took a deep breath as she recalled Janet's similar reference, but there was still so much she needed to know. "Gina, do you know anything about your brother trying to talk Chad out of asking my sister to marry him?"

Gina sighed. "Yes, as a matter of fact I do know he advised Chad that way."

"Do you know why?"

Gina looked down as though she were thinking. When she looked up, she said softly, "From what I understand of the situation, when Chad came to him, Will was already making plans to offer him the promotion. That meant he would be moving him to Guatemala. He didn't want to mention the promotion to Chad, as he wasn't yet sure of the particulars."

Elyssa interjected, "How could he justify his advice when he didn't even know Janet that well?"

Gina let out a sigh and smiled softly. "He did know Chad. He knew Chad was very easy going and would adapt anywhere. Not many people can pick up and go live in a foreign country. From what he saw of Janet, I believe he wondered whether she would be homesick the first month and talk him into coming back home. Perhaps she would have talked him out of accepting the promotion at all. Will knew Chad was perfect for the job and... well, yes, he was putting Pemberleo's welfare before his friend's."

"I just have a difficult time believing Will had any right to do that," Elyssa lamented in frustration.

Gina nodded. "Perhaps he was wrong, but I believe that it was merely a suggestion, Elyssa. What he was about to offer Chad was going to directly affect Janet if they married, but he was not able to explain his reasoning at the time. Besides, I don't think Chad was offended by it. He still asked William to be his best man at his wedding."

"Sometimes your brother's behavior is so incomprehensible to me!"

Gina looked at Elyssa and smiled; her eyes sparkling a knowing gleam.

"What?" asked Elyssa. "You look as if you know something."

Gina let out a breathy chuckle. "When my father took Will and me to Guatemala when we were younger, he used to say that I was like the beautiful flowers that dotted the landscape and Will was like the coffee beans."

Now it was Elyssa's turn to laugh. "Coffee beans! I thought of him more as one of those volcanoes!"

Gina tilted her head at Elyssa. "Really? A volcano?" A gleam sparkled in Gina's eyes, followed by a sweet, hearty laugh. "A dormant volcano, perhaps!"

Gina's hand went directly to cover her mouth and her eyes widened in surprise. "Oh, I can't believe I just said that!"

Elyssa reached out and touched the young girl's shoulder. "I'll never tell, Gina. But why do you say that?"

"Because he's always so controlled, holding his emotions in check. There's nothing I gain more satisfaction from than seeing him really enjoy himself when we're together. I've always longed for the day he meets someone who can bring that out in him. Not too many people have even seen him really laugh."

Elyssa thought back to their time at Lake Atitlan and how he seemed to really enjoy himself. Those first few times she saw him really smile -- and laugh -- warmed her heart. *That* was when she found herself drawn to him.

Elyssa turned her attention back to Gina. "Now, tell me, what's this about him being like a coffee bean?"

"I think my father meant that life came too easy for him."

"Too easy?"

"Easy yes, satisfying no. I've only just truly begun to understand what my father was trying to say. Mind you, I have always held my brother in the highest esteem; he is a man of the highest integrity. But my father knew Will would need to go through a good amount of testing to round out his character. He needs some sort of challenge in his life that will force him to fight for what he wants."

Gina bit her lip as she looked intently at Elyssa. "A flower easily and readily blooms into something beautiful with very little effort. I personally think my father was being a little too gracious towards me, but did you know, Elyssa, that the coffee bean needs to be dried, roasted, and ground up before it can truly be enjoyed? I think my father knew that Will would always have his wealth and position literally handed to him; even his popularity. He never had to work at making and keeping friends."

Gina paused and took in a deep breath. "When our father died, it was difficult for William, but he has such a natural talent for business that he stepped into the role without too much trouble. Of course he grieved our father's loss terribly, but he threw himself into work -- I think to help him get through it."

Gina sighed deeply and her body trembled slightly. Elyssa reached out her hand and gently touched the young girl's shoulder, encouraging her to continue. The thought that Will dealt with his grief this way had never occurred to her.

Gina continued, "I think he needs to be shaken up a bit more. He can tackle anything on a business level, but is somewhat at a loss if something happens to him personally. Friendships came easy to him because he was looked up to; but not because he had an engaging personality or an abundance of enthusiasm. It was because he was a good athlete, a good student, good looking, or wealthy. Even the women who have attached themselves to him have never really brought out that spark that makes him want to work at the relationship. I think he has always been more suspicious of their professions of love because he wondered if they really ever got to know the real William Denton."

Gina smiled softly. "While any sort of testing would be difficult to go through, I believe it would do him a world of good. He's only just learning there are things he will have to fight for, but he doesn't even know how. He's never had to before."

Elyssa gave Gina a shrewd smile. "Perhaps I put him through more than a little drying, roasting, and grinding while we were in Guatemala."

Gina looked over and met Elyssa's eyes. "Yes, Elyssa. Perhaps you did -- in more ways than you imagine." Gina then looked down and a slight blush crossed her face. Very softly, she said, "I think we both did."

"We *both* did?" Elyssa asked.

Gina did not answer for some time. Finally, she said, "Yes. Unfortunately mine has to do with George Westham."

"George Westham?" Elyssa was stunned.

Gina stood up and turned, looking down at her nervously fidgeting fingers. "George's father worked alongside our father for as long as I remember. Our families did a lot together. I feel as though I have known him all my life; that he is as close as a brother."

"He told me a little about that."

Gina turned back and somberly faced Elyssa. "But what he probably didn't tell you was that about a month before you went down to Guatemala, he did something that overstepped his bounds."

Elyssa looked at Gina thoughtfully. "What did he do?"

"My brother and I had gone down to Guatemala. Will found himself in meetings one day from morning to night with some of the staff. It was a warm day and I remember I was just sitting outside around the pool when George came by. He said it was such a beautiful day and asked me if I would like to take a short drive out to Lake Atitlan. He called it the most romantic place in the world. What infatuated girl wouldn't accept?"

Elyssa closed her eyes tightly, remembering his words to her as well.

"I'd always had a childhood crush on George and was more than willing to go with him. As we drove out, he started to pour on the charm. He told me how much he had always cared for me; how I had turned into such an attractive young lady. Of course I was flattered with his attention."

Elyssa stood up and walked over to Gina, putting up her hand to stop her. "Gina, I don't need to hear anymore."

"No, please. Let me continue. We had eaten lunch at a restaurant in a hotel overlooking the lake. He left for a short while and when he returned, he told me he had secured a room." Gina looked down as a blush tinted her cheeks again

"He told me it was so that we could go swimming in the lake and then come back and change before we drove home."

"Did you really believe that was his sole motive?"

Gina shook her head. "I don't think I ever thought about whether I could trust him or not. When my cell phone rang, George told me not to answer it. I felt wrong about that, especially when I saw that it was Will. I knew he was probably looking for me. I answered my phone and, needless to say, my brother was furious when I told him where I was and who I was with. He had me put George on the phone and warned him that he better not lay a finger on me and that he wanted him to leave me right where I was and we were to wait until he arrived." Gina looked at Elyssa with pain filling her eyes. "I should have known better."

"But why does he still work for your brother if he did this?" Elyssa asked in aggravation. "Why wasn't he fired?"

Gina let out a breath of relief. "He finally has been. William fired him a week or two ago. I think he originally let him continue working because he thought he could better keep his eye on him that way. He knew where he was and where I was. My silly little heart still held out feelings for him and I think George knew it."

"And now, Gina? How is your heart now?"

"Grown up these past two months. I have seen George for who he is and my brother knows he no longer has to worry about me doing something immature like running off with him."

Elyssa shook her head in frustration. "I am so glad he was fired. I recently discovered that Maria, a young friend of Janet's in Guatemala City, had become pretty enamored with him."

Gina reached out and took Elyssa's hand. "Shelley was able to get the whole story from Maria. Apparently she saw George with another woman one night and he laughed at her when he saw she was so visibly upset." Gina lowered her eyes and shook her head. "All she could think to do was call Janet. When no one answered the phone at the Blakelys' home, she called Janet's cell phone. They were at the lake. Maria was so upset by the whole incident, Janet insisted that they would come home immediately."

Elyssa began to shake with anger and grief and fell back into her chair. "That's when the accident happened."

Gina nodded. "Part of Maria's guilt was due to George planting that in her head. He told her the accident was all her fault because she acted so childishly in calling Janet. Unfortunately she chose to believe him."

Elyssa tightened her fingers around the armrests of the chair. "How could he do such a thing?" she cried.

"Elyssa," Gina said as she grew more somber. "That's not all."

"What?" Elyssa asked with trepidation as she drew her hand to her chest.

Gina knit her eyebrows together. "Will discovered that George was involved in hiring the man who took pictures of the two of you at Lake Atitlan."

Elyssa could feel her heart lurch as she tried to comprehend the fact that the very man who most apologetically showed her the pictures had been the one behind them all along.

"He was responsible for those pictures on the internet?" Elyssa felt her head begin to pound and brought up her fingers to massage her temple.

"When Will found out about the pictures, he thought it was highly unusual for someone to have recognized him there. Several celebrities frequent Panajachel, but Will would not be the most recognizable or that sought after. He hired an investigator to trace the photographs to the photographer and from there linked him to George."

"How can someone be so cruel? Is there no end to the man's madness?" She turned to Gina. "I feel like… like wringing his neck!"

Gina let out a sigh. "So did Will. I think someone had to physically restrain my brother when he confronted him. He had literally reached his breaking point."

"I don't blame him! How could someone do something like that?"

"Definitely not the kind of person my brother wants working for Pemberleo. You'll be pleased to hear that George is long gone and the pictures will not appear in any magazine. They have been destroyed and are off the internet site."

"I'm certainly relieved about that, but that pales in light of everything else he did and all the pain he has caused!"

Gina looked intently at Elyssa. "I'm sorry. I know what I've had to say has not all been easy to hear."

Elyssa clasped her hands and brought them up under her chin. She gave Gina a weak smile. "But you also brought very pleasant news and I will try to dwell on that."

"Thanks. I'd best be off. The others in Solvang will worry about me if I get back late." She smiled and extended her hand. "I have really enjoyed getting to know you, Elyssa."

Elyssa rose to her feet and grasped Gina's hand in both of hers. "Me, too. I do hope we meet again."

With a fervent look of expectation in her eyes, Gina replied, "I do too, Elyssa. I do too."

~~*

For the next few days, Elyssa couldn't get Gina's words out of her mind. Her heart swelled with appreciation for what Will had done, while it revolted against George's contempt for others. Elyssa felt sick as she recalled how deceived she had been by him.

That first night she arrived in Guatemala, she had fallen into a heap of tears. George had let her pour out her disdain for the man she blamed for Chad and Janet's deaths, while all along it was *he* that was truly responsible. If anyone was guilty of not caring for others, it was George. Will was only guilty of not knowing how to show others he cared.

From what Elyssa read in Janet's journal and what Gina told her about Will, she couldn't get him out of her heart and mind. Those feelings that had begun to grow more favorable toward him in Guatemala were pushing their way to the surface again now that she knew a little more about him.

Elyssa knew she had to thank Will for what he did. She was fairly certain he wouldn't want to be thanked, but thank him she must. Several times she picked up the phone to call, but was never satisfied with the meager words she had prepared in advance. She picked up pen and paper more than once, but the finished letters all ended up in a crumpled heap in the waste basket.

She determined that she needed to tell him to his face. A visit to her aunt and uncle in Lamstone would give her the opportunity. She just wasn't sure when she would be able to afford to go and she didn't want to burden them with the financial responsibility of flying her out.

A telephone call the very next week seemed to provide the perfect answer.

When the phone rang, Elyssa picked it up, thinking it was some friend or family member. Instead, a woman introduced herself as Emily Brownwood, from Regency Home Management Company. She explained that she was acting as manager for someone who had built a new home and wanted to have a designer come in and do the finishing work and decorate it.

When Elyssa asked how she heard that she was a designer, the woman told Elyssa that the owner of the house had been given her business card from someone named Charlene.

"Charlene!" Elyssa's eyes looked up toward heaven as she laughed at this unbelievable news. "They received my business card from Charlene and want to hire me?"

Emily cautioned her that there were several designers being contacted, but that the owner was looking for someone outside the area. She told Elyssa that they would like her to send them a designer board with samples of fabrics, tiles, wood stains, and pictures of room layouts so they could get an idea of her preferences. Once they received hers and the others, they would make the determination of who got the job.

When Elyssa took down the address of the management company, her hand began to shake. It was in Illinois.

"Where in Illinois is this?" Elyssa asked, almost afraid to hear her answer.

"We're about 50 miles south of Chicago. We have access to everything you need close by, but the transportation system into Chicago is exceptional, with the buses, commuter trains, and the 'L'. If you fly in, Midway Airport would be closest if you can get a flight into there. O'Hare is a little bit farther."

"And do you know if you are very close to Lamstone?" Elyssa asked.

"Yes!" the woman replied. "My office is about ten miles away, but the house you will be working on is not five miles from Lamstone. Are you familiar with it?"

Elyssa could barely formulate the answer as her excitement was building. "My aunt and uncle just purchased a house there and I had plans to visit them. This would work out tremendously if I got the job!"

"Well that's a plus in your favor, then," Emily assured her with a chuckle. "We won't have to worry about putting you up in a hotel, although money is not really an issue."

"Is there a budget I am to work with?" Elyssa suddenly thought to ask.

"No, not really. You will be able to do whatever you want to do!"

Elyssa's mouth opened, but nothing came out. She couldn't imagine working on a house where there was no concern for a budget.

After a few moments, Elyssa was finally able to say, "I have a designer board already made up from my senior project which I can send to you right away, if that's all right. It really is a true reflection of who I am and what I like to do!"

"That sounds fine. Of course once you see the house, you'll be able to do whatever you want with it. You won't be bound to what's on the board."

"And who is the owner of the house?" Elyssa wanted to know.

"The owner is... I have the contact name of Richard Fitzpatrick. But you will pretty much work through me. Mr. Fitzpatrick doesn't want to be involved in any of the decision making other than approving the design."

"That's pretty surprising. I am used to people hovering over me, ready to give their opinion on all my ideas. I'll go along with it, though, if that's what he wants."

"Good. You'll be hearing from us as soon as the designer is chosen."

A squeal was let loose from Elyssa when she hung up the phone. "I might have a job!"

She scrambled out to her garage and began looking through the mélange of things she had accumulated in her few years here. She pulled out her senior project designer board and hoped it wasn't damaged or too outdated. When she looked at it, she smiled. *Yes!* she thought. *I have to admit that this is really pretty good!*

She carefully wrapped it up and sent it out the very next day with a big prayer that the eyes that saw this would also see the potential she had.

She called her aunt and they talked excitedly about the possibility of her coming out -- with a major job! She asked Maddy to do some checking on the Regency Home Management Company. Maddy called her back within the hour to inform Elyssa that it had an excellent reputation.

Elyssa received the call three days later that she had landed the job and she was ecstatic. A check to cover all her initial expenses including airfare would be sent immediately and the sooner she could fly out, the better.

Elyssa clasped her hands over her heart as she considered the ramifications of this journey. She couldn't be more thrilled that she had a job and would be seeing her aunt and uncle, but a tinge of apprehension lingered as she wondered how, or if, Will would receive her.

Chapter 21

When the check arrived from the Regency Home Management Company, Elyssa couldn't believe her eyes. It was in the amount of $1,000 which was to be used for any expenses she incurred getting to Chicago. When she checked airline prices, they were fairly high, considering she wanted to leave with only a few days' notice. She called a friend of hers who was a travel agent and they found the best deal.

She arranged for her paper to stop being delivered and her mail to be forwarded to her aunt and uncle's. She really had no idea how long she would be there.

Elyssa made good use of her three days before flying out by going online and finding stores that sold designer fabrics and other home decorating supplies. She had only a vague idea about what would be required of her, but she wanted to be prepared. She knew which manufacturers she preferred to work with and wrote down several addresses of businesses that carried their product, marking them with a black "X" on a map she purchased of Chicago and the surrounding area.

In addition to the different stores, there was one other location on the map that she had circled. It was the home offices of Pemberleo Coffee.

In all the details that required her attention before leaving, she never once forgot about Will. Her mind raced with scenarios on how she would see him again; what she would say. She wasn't even sure he would want to see her, but she knew she had to take a chance. She needed to offer him an apology as well as thank him for the memorials. It was just a matter of when and how.

~~*

Elyssa was able to get a non-stop flight and purchased a few home decorating magazines to look through on the journey out. She wanted to be ready for anything in case this Richard Fitzpatrick had any special preferences. She cringed at some of the decorating styles she saw, but folded down the corners of the pages that had ideas that appealed to her. She really couldn't do any planning, though, until she saw the house. She believed a house had a very definite character of its own and that the design would automatically flow from it. She would need to take that into consideration before making any decisions.

When the plane landed at Midway Airport, she walked briskly toward the baggage claim area, where her aunt and uncle would be waiting. The airport bustled with people coming and going and the energy swirling about her filled her with immeasurable eagerness. A tinge of nervousness invaded her thoughts as she considered both the enormity of this particular design job and the state of

Will's feelings for her. She wondered whether her message of thanks, appreciation, and offer of apology would be the extent of their contact.

The Garners waved enthusiastically when she finally made her way out to the open area of the airport. Elyssa greeted her aunt and uncle with a fervent hug and then reached out for Lillian, the youngest. With her free had, she patted Frederick, the oldest, on the head.

"It is so good to see all of you! I have missed you so much!" Elyssa was beaming from ear to ear and gave Lillian a gentle squeeze.

"And how fortunate for you to be able to combine a visit with a design job! You must be excited, Elyssa. I can see it in your face!" Maddy observed.

"I am excited," Elyssa concurred. "I couldn't have planned this out better myself if I tried."

"Are you hungry?" her uncle asked as they turned to walk toward the baggage carousel unloading luggage from her flight.

"A little. But I'm willing to fit right into your schedule. We have the weekend to enjoy each other's company. So I'll let you set the pace. Monday, however, I'll be a little more consumed with work."

They made it to the baggage area and kept their eyes open for Elyssa's two suitcases. When she pointed them out, her uncle easily picked them up and they walked to the car.

As they drove away from the airport, Maddy and Edward apprised Elyssa on all that had happened the weeks since they had last seen one another. Elyssa told them all about her trip to Guatemala, leaving out one major detail -- William Denton. She didn't feel up to talking about him, especially to her most discerning aunt. Maddy would easily pick up on the slightest quiver of voice or downward glance and know the leaning of her niece's heart. Elyssa would wait until she knew what his reception of her would be before she told her anything. The only mention she made of him, as well as to her family, was of the memorials he and Pemberleo established for Janet and Chad.

The time flew by quickly and the city soon gave way to the suburbs with gentle rolling hills and wooded areas. It almost reminded her of the Santa Ynez Valley. When Edward kept going straight instead of turning at the sign indicating that Lamstone was to the right, Elyssa questioned where they were going.

"Well," her uncle answered, "we thought we would drive you past the house you will be working on."

Elyssa clasped her hands together. "Do you know where it is?" she asked.

Maddy turned around from the front seat of the car to face her. "I talked to Emily Brownwood at the management company and asked her for the address, telling her I was your aunt. Edward and I drove past it a few days ago."

"And?" Elyssa's eyes widened with curiosity.

Her uncle waved his hand across the air. "A real fixer upper. I hope you're not too disappointed when you see it." A sly glance and wink at his wife told Elyssa he was teasing.

"I saw that wink, Uncle Edward. You've probably found the most run down piece of property and that's where you're taking me."

They drove about five more miles and finally turned onto a winding road that was lined with trees.

"Are you sure you know where you're going?" Elyssa asked as she looked around her. "This road seems to go on forever!"

"This is the driveway!" Maddy exclaimed. "This is the beginning of the property!"

They drove on in silence, Elyssa taking in the wooded area around her. "It is beautiful here, but for heaven's sake, are we ever going to reach the house?"

As they made a final turn on the gently curving road, Elyssa gasped. Situated across a small pond so that its reflection was mirrored, was a beautiful home. It reminded her somewhat of the English estates she had studied in her design classes, although it was smaller.

"Oh my!" Elyssa exclaimed. "I don't think that I've ever seen a more beautiful home or such picturesque surroundings." It looked as though no landscaping had been done, but it had a natural beauty to it. She wondered if anyone had ever lived in the home.

"What do you think, dear?" Maddy asked.

Elyssa looked at the beautiful stone façade that covered the main floor of the house and her eyes went up to the Tudor style of the top floor. "I can't believe I actually get to decorate this! For the first time since getting this job, I'm feeling just a little nervous!" She leaned over and reached for her aunt's hand. "Look, my hands are shaking!"

"You'll do fine, Elyssa. Just trust your instincts and your natural talent!"

Elyssa rested her chin on the front seat, unable to take her eyes off the house. "Do you think it odd that someone… this Richard Fitzpatrick… is willing to entrust his house to someone he's never met; that there is no budget and I pretty much have free rein to do as I please?"

Maddy shook her head. "It's probably someone who knows nothing about decorating and really doesn't care. All he wants is a nice house."

Her uncle chimed in. "I wouldn't be surprised if it's someone who isn't going to live here all the time. Maybe it's just a summer home."

"Well I can tell you one thing," Maddy said. "This Richard guy can't possibly be married. I don't think any woman would allow someone else to decorate their house without some input."

Elyssa let out a dreamy sigh. "Just look at that grand wrap-around porch. Do you know what the first thing I want to buy for it is?"

Maddy and Edward looked at her and together answered, "A porch swing!"

Elyssa's eyes twinkled. "How did you ever guess?"

They drove home and Elyssa felt as though she were in a dream. She would never have imagined anything so grand and her heart beat ferociously. She even surprised herself when she realized she had not thought about Will once since setting her eyes on the house.

Elyssa enjoyed the weekend with the Garners. They took her to a couple of nice restaurants, she and her aunt enjoyed a chick flick at the movies while Edward stayed home with the children, and they spent some good, relaxing time in their home. In every free moment, however, Elyssa and Maddy spread out the home design magazines and began to plan and dream.

~~*

On Monday morning, Elyssa drove the car her aunt loaned her to Regency Home Management Company. It was on the main highway, so it was easy to find. Dressed in her most professional outfit and carrying her brand new briefcase, Elyssa wanted to make a good impression.

When she pulled into the parking lot and got out of the car, she smoothed out her skirt and pulled her jacket taut. Then she took a deep breath and walked in.

A friendly looking woman greeted her. "Hi! I'm Emily Brownwood. May I help you?"

Elyssa reached out her hand. "Hello Emily. I'm Elyssa Barnett."

"Oh, Elyssa! I just knew it was you! How do you do?"

The two exchanged pleasantries and then got down to business.

"Here, come into my office and I'll show you what you have to work with."

Once in her office, Emily produced a floor plan of the living room and kitchen. She spread it open and the two looked down at it.

"This is what you'll begin with. It's a fairly good sized home, but I hope that doesn't intimidate you. The living room and the kitchen are the two rooms you are to work on first. Then we'll talk about whether you want to stay on and do the rest of the home."

"That sounds reasonable," Elyssa affirmed.

Emily picked up an envelope from her desk. She reached in and pulled out a photograph. "I don't know if this will make it easier or more difficult, but this is the only thing he insists on putting in the house. You know how some people are. You will see the real thing there."

When Elyssa looked down at the photograph, she saw a painting of a large manor, much like one would see in England. She could definitely see a little resemblance to the house she saw yesterday. "It's a beautiful painting."

"It is an estate that was in the family several hundred years ago. You can do whatever you want with furniture and fabrics, but this has to be incorporated."

Elyssa looked at it and smiled. She wondered if she would ever be able to meet the owner, but already decided that he held his family, even those long gone, as important and dear.

Emily pulled out the designer board Elyssa had sent earlier. "We really liked how you fashioned your board, dear. We would like you to do the same thing with your plans for the two rooms, giving us fabric samples and furniture styles. I'll pass it on for approval. On the floor plan, he will want to see how you will arrange the furniture you buy for the house."

Elyssa nodded. "And you said there is no budget?"

Emily shook her head and reached into the envelope again. "No, and to make it easier for you, we'll order all the paint, floor coverings, counter tops, and that sort of thing from here. I have a list of approved sub-contractors who will do the work. Just pick out the materials and tell us what you want to do with it."

"That's great!"

"You'll be responsible to order any furnishings for the house yourself, but you can charge them to me. I have an account with most of the major stores around here."

Emily reached into the envelope again and pulled out some papers. "Here's my card, business license number, and a letter of authorization from me that will enable you to charge it to me. If you run into any problems, I'll write a check for the amount."

Emily handed the envelope to Elyssa. "Inside is a sheet of paper with some of the stores close by and in Chicago that you might want to check out. I have included home design stores, wallpaper, paint, and tile stores, and some of the finer furniture stores. But don't feel as though you have to stick with only them."

Emily turned to face Elyssa. "Do you have any questions?"

"Not yet, but I'm sure I will."

"Good. Would you like to go see the house?"

Elyssa beamed. "I would like nothing more!"

~~*

Elyssa followed Emily in her car to the house, purposely neglecting to tell her that her aunt and uncle had already driven her out there. Even though it was her second time out, Elyssa's heart still lurched when she drove around that last bend and beheld it in all its grandeur.

When they walked up the porch, Emily handed Elyssa the key. "This is yours, dear, as I'm sure you will be coming and going throughout the day."

She stepped back and let Elyssa open the door. It swung open slowly and Elyssa's mouth dropped at the sight before her.

They entered into an expansive foyer that seemed to travel forever. Emily pointed off to the right and they stepped through an opened set of carved wooden double doors.

Entering into the living room, Elyssa took a great liking to its spaciousness and its tall ceilings. Glistening wood floors seemed to stretch out in every direction. An unfinished fireplace with a heavy mantel dominated one side of the living room. Elyssa knew it would be up to her to decide whether to finish it with stone, tile, wood, or a combination. Large paned windows let in light from every direction.

"What do you think?" Emily asked Elyssa.

"It is beautiful. There are so many possible directions to go."

"Come, over here is the painting."

The painting was protected by a heavy cloth draped over the front. Elyssa was astounded at the size. It had been difficult to ascertain how large the painting was merely from the photograph. Emily pulled the cloth down and Elyssa stood even more dumbfounded as she cast her eyes over the most magnificent oil painting she had ever seen.

"This is absolutely beautiful!" she exclaimed. "I'd love something like this in *my* house!"

"It truly is a beauty. The only thing I can think of that might come close to its beauty is the real home itself. I believe it was somewhere in England."

Elyssa walked up more closely to study it. "It definitely has hints of taupe, apricot, and spruce green. I could use any of those as my primary color." Her eyes swept over it again. "But then again, there is mustard, ice blue, mauve, and ivory."

Emily tilted her head. "I think you have your work cut out for you, my dear. Just deciding on the colors to use in this place would have me in quite a state!"

Elyssa looked around her, beginning to feel the enormity of the task before her.

She turned back to look at the painting. "I think that having this painting as the focal point will actually help me. It will definitely dictate the mood that I will want to create in the room."

"Good. The wall above the fireplace will be where it is to be hung. Those are really the only instructions."

Emily clasped her hands. "Now, if you need anything, feel free to give me a call. My work number and cell phone number are on my business card. Do you have a cell phone in case I need to reach you?"

Elyssa reached into her purse. "Yes," she exclaimed, proudly pulling it out. "I actually purchased it before I came out here. I must confess I tend to drag my feet when it comes to modern technology."

Emily laughed as Elyssa wrote down the number for her. "I'm sure you will soon wonder how you ever survived without one!"

"You're probably right."

"Well, Elyssa, I guess we're pretty much finished here, unless there's something else you need."

Elyssa chuckled and looked inquiringly up at Emily. "Do you mind if I ask you about the owner? I mean it may affect the direction I go if he is married or has children."

"Mmm. Yes, I can understand that. No, he is not married, but I think he most definitely has a wish to be married someday and have a family live here."

"Well there goes my idea of a bachelor's pad!" Elyssa laughed. "Seriously, though, that really helps."

"If there's nothing more, then I guess I'll leave you to begin."

When Emily left, Elyssa walked over to her briefcase and pulled out a large drawing pad and a fan deck of paint colors. The pad would be the place to jot down and sketch her ideas. She then walked to the very center of the room and began to turn slowly. As she did, her mind played through various scenes of furniture styles and arrangements, colors and textures. After she had done that, she walked to the edge of the room and paced along each wall, playing the same scenes over in her mind, with a few new ones added in and a few being tossed out. This style would work; this one wouldn't. This color would be great with that color; no, that one wouldn't do well. She took notes as she did this, as well as drew some ideas for furniture arrangements. Then she walked to each door that entered the room and imagined what would be pleasing to the eye.

When she finished doing that, she sat down on the hardwood floor to get a final view. She had to laugh as she considered that her whole house would probably fit in this room alone.

She drew a couple more sketches and jotted down a few more ideas. She had a fairly good idea of what she would like, although she wouldn't know precisely what it was until she saw it. She needed to visit fabric and furniture stores and hoped that what she saw there would harmonize with the character she envisioned for this room.

She then took the fan deck of paint colors over to the large oil painting. Thumbing through the medley of hues, she selected several that matched the colors in the canvas. She marked them, not really knowing which ones she would go with. She figured she would know when she saw the fabrics she wanted to use.

Before leaving to go into the city to check out some stores, she had to see the rest of the house, even though there was the possibility she might only end up doing the living room and kitchen. She gave herself a quick tour, opening doors and imagining what she would do with the plethora of rooms. She ran upstairs and found four bedrooms plus an immense master suite. She walked in and immediately was drawn to the large bay window that overlooked the front. She sighed at what her eyes took in. *Oh, I could very easily wake up to this view every morning!*

The window overlooked the small pond she had seen in front. She knew there had to be houses nearby, but from this vantage point, she could not seen any evidence of them.

She walked to the window on the other wall and saw that it overlooked a dense wooded area. In her active designer's mind, Elyssa could foresee a small garden in a clearing down there and thought a little landscaping would certainly add some color. "But not too much!" she caught herself saying aloud. "I don't think you can improve too much on its natural beauty."

When Elyssa returned to the car, she pulled out her map. Just looking at it began to overwhelm her. She was grateful that her aunt told her she would accompany her into Chicago when she was ready and would happily give her pointers on getting around using the transportation system.

Elyssa looked down at the map at every little "x" and the one circle. She didn't want to put off another day to stop by the Pemberleo offices and express her appreciation to Will. She knew the sooner she got this over with the better off she would feel. Her heart picked up its pace as she simply mulled it over. One way or another, by the end of the day she would know how William Denton felt about seeing her again.

Chapter 22

Elyssa drove slowly back out the winding drive. Her gaze drifted from right to left and up the towering trees about her, taking in all the beauty. She hoped that her job responsibilities wouldn't preclude her from taking some leisurely walks through the woods while she was here.

She drove the five short miles to her aunt's home and they ate a quick lunch before setting out. They walked Lillian and Frederick to Maddy's neighbor, who had two children around the same age of her two. She and Maddy often traded baby sitting responsibilities.

As her aunt drove to the commuter train station, Elyssa spoke with unabated excitement about her morning and gushed over details about the house and its one sole accessory. "Aunt Maddy, you must see this painting! It's beautiful!"

The look of amusement in her aunt's eyes did not escape Elyssa's notice.

"I know that look, Maddy. You think I'm carrying on as usual!"

Maddy reached over and grasped Elyssa's hand, giving it a squeeze. "No, my dearest niece. It just warms my heart to see you truly happy again. Your uncle and I have been worried sick about you."

Elyssa smiled. "It has been a difficult few months. There were times when I felt completely weighed down with grief. When I think I've finally made it through, when I least expect it, something will happen that will trigger a memory and just drown me in sadness."

Maddy patted Elyssa's hand before returning it to the steering wheel. "And most likely it will continue to do so. Prayerfully, though, you will find your waves of grief lessen with time and someday you will be able to think of Janet with joyous memories alone."

It was silent in the car as Elyssa considered the reality of her aunt's statement. When she first arrived in Guatemala, she had been frequently overcome with grief. As the week went on, though, she found herself enjoying the things Janet had enjoyed. A soft moan escaped as she recalled how her sorrow and pain had actually eased in Will's presence and had been replaced with feelings of joy and delight -- in him.

Maddy looked over at her. "Are you all right?"

Elyssa nodded. She knew her aunt could read her so well and for that reason, she could not tell her about her feelings for Will until she knew for certain how he felt. She did not want to give Maddy something *else* to worry about and hoped that if she did indeed experience a broken heart while here, she would be able to keep it from her aunt.

"I have been thinking about what Pemberleo did in establishing the memorials for Janet and Chad. I wanted to wait to thank them until I arrived and could do it in person. When we get into the city the first thing I want to do… I need to do… is go there and thank them."

"And face that dreadful Mr. Denton?" Her aunt gave Elyssa a smile.

Elyssa turned her head to look out the window, a little too quickly for her own peace of mind. Elyssa let out a forced chuckle. "I guess he's not all that dreadful since he is the one who came up with such a perfect memorial for them both."

"No, perhaps he's not, but I can't help but recall how upset he made you."

Elyssa guiltily looked down and wished she could correct her aunt's estimation of him. At length, whatever the outcome of her meeting with him, she would tell her what he is truly like.

When they reached the commuter train station, they had several minutes to wait before the train arrived. Maddy explained to her a little about how the Chicago transportation system worked, the different types of trains, and how often they ran.

Elyssa pulled out her map and they talked about which stores they wanted to visit. There were an unlimited number of wholesale stores in the Merchandise Mart, but Elyssa decided against going there today as they wouldn't have time to see even a fraction of the shops. There were a few other stores not too far from the Pemberleo offices, and they decided to stop in as many of them as they could today after her visit with Will.

The train finally arrived and they boarded. As they rode into the city, Elyssa watched the scenery pass. It seemed a very short distance before they were outside the tranquil country feel of the suburbs and saw signs of the looming city before them.

Upon arriving into Chicago, Elyssa felt her heartbeat grow increasingly stronger. She wasn't afraid to see Will -- in fact she was looking forward to being in his presence again. She was amazed at how much she missed him, but she wondered whether he would be willing to forgive her for the words she lashed out at him at the airport.

As the commuter train came to a stop, Elyssa and Maddy stood up and walked to the door, waiting for it to open.

The two ladies kept pace with the crowd of people also exiting as they made their way down to the street. Having taken another look at the map, her aunt knew they had could either hail a cab or enjoy a brisk walk of a couple blocks to reach Pemberleo's office building.

Both Elyssa and her aunt opted for the walk. It was a beautiful day and Elyssa wanted to get a real feel for the city. Along the way, they passed one beautiful building after another and Elyssa was in awe at the splendor of all the architecture that surrounded them. She had never seen anything like it and her eyes darted from the addresses of each building they passed and then upwards toward the sky as they passed the tall edifices.

Elyssa's feet came to an abrupt stop and unwittingly her hand went up to her heart when they finally came to the Pemberleo Offices building looking out over Lake Michigan. As her eyes traveled up, she couldn't help but wonder which floor Will was on. She figured his office was probably on the lake side of the building and had a wonderful view.

Maddy looked at her and smiled. "Now I'm sure he won't be all that bad, Elyssa. Just tell him you appreciate what he's done. You'll do fine."

Elyssa looked quizzically at her aunt. "Excuse me?"

"Mr. Denton. I'm sure he will be most accommodating to you, dear."

Elyssa reached out and placed her hand gently on her aunt's shoulder to reassure her. "I'm sure he will, but if you don't mind, Maddy, I should like to go up there alone. There are some things I need to say to him and I wondered if you wouldn't mind waiting for me down in the lobby."

"Of course I don't mind, Elyssa. Take as long as you need."

They stepped into a large, beautiful lobby and Elyssa felt her chest tighten so dreadfully that she had to force herself to take each breath. As they walked across the marble floor, she believed she could almost feel his presence. Maddy pointed to some benches in the corner. "I'll wait for you over there."

Elyssa walked over to the office directory and saw that Pemberleo occupied five floors of the building with the executive offices being on the eighteenth floor. Seeing his name, William Denton, President, sent shivers of anticipation through her.

She joined a few others at the elevators and waited for one to come down to the lobby and open. There were three elevators in all, and when one of them finally opened, it quickly emptied. If Elyssa had any second thoughts about getting on, the push from the crowd around her would have made the decision for her. Once inside, floor buttons were pushed and Elyssa didn't know whether she was grateful or not that there would be several stops before she reached the eighteenth floor.

As she stood in the elevator, however, she couldn't help but overhear the conversation between two gentlemen.

"I hear he anticipates being gone the whole week. Some problems arose in Guatemala that needed his attention. I don't think he was too keen on having to make the trip."

When she heard Guatemala, her ears tuned in to their conversation.

"When did he leave?" the other gentleman asked.

"Took the jet this morning. I thought it was odd that Will never seems to be bothered by having to make these unexpected trips, but he seemed rather distressed to have to leave this time."

"You don't suppose he had some rendezvous he had to cancel?" The man chuckled.

"William Denton?" The two men cast laughing glances at each other.

"No!" They both said at once.

The two men got off on the seventeenth floor, leaving Elyssa and another young woman on the elevator. At the eighteenth floor, Elyssa felt as though she had to step out, but she knew she would have to put off facing Will until he returned next week. She decided against even going in and leaving a message. She needed to speak to him to his face.

She cautiously stepped off, gratefully finding herself in a hall. Her eyes took in the length of it and she smiled at the Guatemalan artifacts they had decorated it with. She pushed the elevator button to take her back down and as she waited, she looked just behind her at the door that was marked with his name.

"Another day, Will," she said softly to herself. The elevator finally opened and she returned downstairs to her aunt.

When she stepped back out into the lobby, her aunt seemed rather surprised to see her return so quickly.

"Oh, dear. It was terrible, wasn't it? Did he just brush you off or did he not even see you?"

Elyssa put up her hand. "No, apparently he left this morning for Guatemala. He'll be gone the whole week."

"Oh, that's too bad. But look. I saw this while I was waiting."

The two walked over to a small sign indicating that Pemberleo offered tours of their coffee plant on Fridays at eleven in the morning and one and three in the afternoon.

"That might be fun, wouldn't it Elyssa? Edward will be off in the afternoon and if I can find someone to watch the children, why don't we come back into Chicago and take the tour? Apparently the plant isn't too far from here."

"Oh, I don't know," Elyssa said. "I might be really busy at the house."

"We can combine a shopping trip with it. That way you won't feel so guilty about taking some time for yourself. Come on, what do you say?"

Elyssa laughed. "Well since I saw one side of the coffee production in Guatemala, I guess it would be interesting to see the rest of the process."

"Good!" Maddy clasped her hands. "I think it will be interesting. Edward always enjoys things like that."

They walked out of the building and Maddy turned to Elyssa. "Now, where were those stores you wanted to check out today?"

They consulted their map again and plotted out their course. The first store they stopped in appeared to be very up-scale and Elyssa felt as though the salespeople looked down their noses at her because she didn't work for a well-known design firm and they didn't know who she was. They left after merely looking at a few items.

After feeling the same way in each of the first three stores they came to, Elyssa turned to her aunt. "If only they knew what a big sale they could have made if they had treated us with a little more respect!"

"I'm sure they would have changed their tone if they knew about the house you are working on. They might even know the name Richard Fitzpatrick."

"Well I'm not inclined to inform them of that just to garner their approval. If they can't accept some independent designer from California, I won't do business with them!"

They walked to another store that Elyssa had circled on the map. It was a few blocks away and Elyssa knew from the information she had taken from the internet that it would be smaller than the ones they had just been in.

They finally reached the other store and walked in. An older gentleman greeted them and told them that his wife was out ill and he was minding the store. As Elyssa glanced about her, she wondered if they would have anything at all of interest to her.

"Now," he continued. "I can help you with a few things, but my wife's the real expert. Hopefully, she'll be back tomorrow."

"That's OK," Elyssa said. "I would like to look at some samples of designer fabrics, if you have some."

"Oh, yes. That we do!"

He took her to a small room off the main floor where there were rows and rows of fabrics. They were meticulously sorted by texture, color, and company. "Just let me know if I can help you. My name is Curtis Jones, by the way."

"Thanks, Mr. Jones!" Elyssa said. "I'm Elyssa Barnett and this is my aunt, Madeline Garner. Do you, by any chance, allow people to take some of the samples out of the store to see if they work well?"

"We certainly do! Take home as many as you want. But let me warn you. If you take any samples down from the rod and then change your mind, just leave 'em. My wife has a very particular sorting system that even I don't understand."

Elyssa laughed. "I can see she is very well organized!"

"I have some coffee brewing over here and some cookies if you like. Can I bring you some?"

"Thanks. That sounds great!"

He took their coffee orders and returned with a plate of cookies. When Elyssa took a sip, she knew immediately that it was Pemberleo Coffee.

Elyssa spent at least an hour going through the fabrics, matching tints and hues to the paint colors she had marked and occasionally asking for her aunt's opinion. When she finished, she had a pile of fabrics that was as diverse as a sampler box of candy. Knowing she needed to scale down her selection, she then went through that pile, pulling out ones she wanted to take with her, leaving the others for Mrs. Jones to put away.

Elyssa laughed as she held up one of the samples, admiring its color and running her fingers across the heavily textured fabric. "Maddy, I can't help but feel as though this Fitzpatrick character is going to get his house decorated exactly according to my own personal preference, unless he decides he really doesn't care for what I select." She picked up one of the fabrics she discarded. "Do you think I should throw in some bizarre pieces just to see what he does?"

Maddy smiled. "I think he is very fortunate to have chosen you, my dear, and you must trust your instincts about this. You were chosen because of the designer board you submitted and he must have appreciated your partiality toward the traditional look. Personally, I think too many people go a bit overboard just to be different. I have a feeling he just wants something nice that will stand the test of time."

Elyssa leaned over and whispered to her aunt. "I hope Mr. Fitzpatrick won't be upset, but even though there isn't a budget to worry about, I'm not planning to buy from the most expensive stores. I think I can get the same items from a place like this for half the cost and I like the service much better."

"If he doesn't appreciate your financial prudence, I certainly do. No sense in throwing away money just to be able to say the house was furnished by a particular store."

They gathered up the fabric samples and Elyssa took them to Mr. Jones. She gave him her driver's and decorator's licenses and Emily's letter and business card so he could complete the check-out form. As she stood at the counter, she looked around her, admiring the eclectic array of both antique and modern furniture and accessories.

She suddenly had a thought. "Do you have any porch swings here or do you know where I can find some nice ones?"

"As a matter of fact, we do have one! Follow me!"

He placed the fabric samples in a bag and handed them to Elyssa, then took them to a back corner of the store. "We picked this up a few days ago at an estate sale. It needs a little sanding and refinishing, which I had planned to do myself, but other than that, it's in great condition. If you want it, just tell me what you want done and I can have it for you in a couple of days. Refinishing is my specialty! Most of the antiques you see here I have restored."

"And I can see that you do an excellent job," Elyssa commended him.

Elyssa turned her eyes back on the swing and smiled as she ran her fingers lightly over the wood. I think it will look striking with a dark wooden stain. Can you do that?"

"That's what I had planned to do with it. I need to replace the chain and I'll throw in the fixtures to hang it up. Would Thursday be soon enough for you?"

"That's great!" Elyssa said and exchanged a grin with her aunt. She made arrangements to have it delivered directly to the house.

She liked this store. She was eager to come back and leisurely walk through, looking at the selection of furniture they had in stock and glean any ideas they may have. She appreciated the kindness of Mr. Jones, who told her he could order anything that the larger stores carried. Elyssa was anxious to meet his wife and knew she would be coming back here.

Despite her disappointment at not being able to see Will earlier that day, and knowing it would be a week before she did, Elyssa couldn't help but feel elation. The joy and fulfillment she felt in actually doing work that she enjoyed surprised even her.

She and her aunt talked all the way home about their afternoon. Now that Elyssa was actually "getting her feet wet" in the actual design process, her excitement mounted. When her uncle returned home from work that evening, he graciously and patiently listened to a recap of Elyssa's first day as a designer.

~~*

Elyssa spent the rest of the week choosing color for the paint, tile and flagstone to finish the living room and fireplace, and went back a couple more times to the little store. With each decision she made, she passed it on to Emily, who in turn, passed it to Richard Fitzpatrick. She always received an OK on it by the next day.

On Thursday, Elyssa stayed at the house all day, awaiting the arrival of the porch swing. After thoughtful consideration, she decided she would put it at an angle at the corner of the porch so a view of the front and the side of the house could be enjoyed. She was almost as excited about the porch swing as anything.

Another delivery that Mr. Jones brought along with him was a large area rug that Elyssa had selected from his store. It was one of the finer brands and had all the colors in it that she had chosen to work with. Once he had the rug down on the beautiful hardwood floors and the swing was installed, Elyssa felt as though that was all that was needed to give the house a warm and welcoming look.

She found herself in new territory, though, ensuring that the sub-contractors were doing everything exactly as she desired, checking each order that arrived to make sure it was accurate, and then having to deal with some difficult people when things didn't arrive on time or as ordered. By Thursday night she was tired and decided taking the tour of Pemberleo Coffee on Friday would be a diversion she could well justify.

Chapter 23

On Friday, Elyssa and Maddy planned to meet Edward in Chicago at the Pemberleo plant for the one o'clock tour. He was working at a job nearby in the city and decided that rather than come all the way home and go back, he would meet up with them there.

Elyssa was required to be at the house that morning to oversee some work that should have taken only an hour or two to finish. When some mistakes were made, she insisted that it be redone and she called to tell her aunt she wasn't sure when she'd get back. A quick call to Edward alerted him to the delay and so he decided he would run some errands and then join them for the three o'clock tour.

It wasn't until almost one o'clock that Elyssa finally walked through her aunt's door. She had never been so glad to finally get away. It hadn't been so much a problem of poor workmanship, but of not fully understanding what she wanted. She hated the fact that she had inconvenienced her uncle, but her aunt assured her he had plenty to keep him busy in the city as he waited their arrival.

"Don't worry about it, Elyssa," her aunt assured her. "He's used to being flexible. I change my mind so often that he doesn't put anything on his calendar until after it happens!"

Elyssa laughed as she considered how different her aunt and uncle were from each other, yet they complimented one another wonderfully. "I have enjoyed being with you so much this past week. I can't imagine what it would have been like doing this job here without really knowing anyone. It's nice to come home after a full day's work and relax and laugh with people you really care about."

"I'm glad we were here for you, too, Elyssa. Although if we weren't," her aunt gave her a teasing smile, "you know there would always be Mr. Denton." Maddy chuckled. "He certainly is a handsome man -- he must have *some* redeeming qualities. Perhaps once you have paid your visit and thanked him, you'll actually find yourself totally smitten with him."

Elyssa tried to sound genuine as she joined her aunt in a laugh. "Perhaps," was all she could mutter as she turned and looked away.

A crinkle in Maddy's brow suggested that she had begun to ponder why it was that each time Mr. Denton's name was mentioned, Elyssa behaved so uncharacteristically. She shook away any conjecture on the subject, though.

Elyssa and Maddy planned their departure so they would arrive at the plant at two thirty. That would give them plenty of time and allow for any delays. They kept in touch with Edward by cell phone to let him know where they were and when they were close to arriving.

When they came upon Pemberleo's manufacturing plant, Elyssa was surprised at how modern and clean it looked. A sign on the door in front instructed those coming for the tour to step in and remain in the waiting room until it was time to begin. Edward was already inside.

The room was dotted with photographs, and Elyssa recognized several as being from Guatemala. She walked around with her aunt and uncle showing them places she visited and telling them a little bit about them.

They came to a picture of Lake Atitlan, and Elyssa could tell from the finer buildings around it, that it was taken at Panajachel.

She laughed as she began to tell her aunt, "This is Panajachel at Lake Atitlan. It's a beautiful place, but Will and I got caught in a most torrential downpour there."

Both Maddy and Edward looked at her and asked simultaneously, "Will?"

Elyssa's breath caught as she realized she hadn't told a soul about his coming down to Guatemala while she was there. Before she could command herself to calm down, her fingers intertwined and she nervously began rubbing her thumbs together.

An uncharacteristic blush tinted her cheeks as she answered as nonchalantly as she could, "Will... William Denton came down to Guatemala while I was there."

Maddy and Edward raised their eyebrows in unison at this news. As they walked on, they came to photographs of the line of Dentons who had held the esteemed position of President of Pemberleo.

The last picture was of Will, and as Elyssa gazed upon it, she almost felt as though his eyes looked back at her.

The overprotective side of Edward was aroused and he said, "I certainly hope he behaved himself around you. I can't say I trust a man around my Elyssa who claims to be one of the top 50 bachelors in the country."

A nervous laugh betrayed Elyssa's composure. "I don't think he owns up to that claim. I rather believe it's been more of a nuisance to him."

"Elyssa," her aunt turned to her, "why didn't you tell us you saw him down in Guatemala? Do you still find him reprehensible?"

Elyssa let out the breath she found she had been holding. "No, not really." A remorseful laugh brought a longing look to her eyes. "But he still has the uncanny ability to unsettle me with some of the things he says or does!"

Maddy was prevented from asking anything further about one William Denton when a tour guide appeared and called the group together. She introduced herself as Patty and told them she had been with the company for over twenty years. She informed them that the tour would take about an hour, concluding with an opportunity to enjoy some Pemberleo coffee and pastry in their visitor's lounge.

Before walking out into the plant, the group of about fourteen listened with interest as Patty explained how the coffee beans were grown and harvested by small farmers, some of whom only farmed an acre of land. She shared how these farmers did almost everything themselves, sometimes with only the help of their family. She told how after harvesting, they dried the beans on large slabs of concrete for a few days before they were shipped to America.

Elyssa couldn't help but think of Pedro's family.

The tour group followed Patty out the door and down a hall. The first area they came upon was a room that they could look into through a large glass window. A handful of people were manually picking out coffee beans from a conveyor belt. In front of the window was a plaque giving a description of what could be seen in the room. Elyssa looked down to read it as Patty began to speak.

"Most of the farmers sort through the beans before they arrive here, removing the ones of inferior quality, but inevitably some get through. Our employees know exactly what to look for and pick out the bad ones."

"Isn't that terribly boring work?" asked someone on the tour.

"Yes, and that's why we rotate that position. We figure about an hour is about all anyone can take at a time before they begin to lose focus. We try to vary the jobs so an employee doesn't become totally bored. When that happens, you end up with an unhappy employee and a less than superior coffee product."

After answering a few more questions, Patty moved the group on. They watched the conveyor belt carry the beans into the next area where they went through the roasters. Patty told everyone how the beans were subject to a variety of temperatures as they were roasted to perfection.

As the group traversed down a long hallway, one of the women asked, "Is William Denton one of the highlights of the tour?"

Patty laughed as though she had heard this question many times. "Well, if you had been on the one o'clock tour, you would have had the pleasure of seeing him. He was down in the tasting and packaging room. He rarely comes down to the plant so it was a surprise, but I doubt he is still there now."

Upon hearing this, Elyssa inhaled sharply and a look of concern colored her features. Her hand went up to the wall, as if she needed a little added support.

Maddy looked curiously at Elyssa as several of the ladies expressed their disappointment with a round of regretful sighs.

As the group walked toward the tasting room, everyone's curiosity about William Denton was piqued.

"So what is it like to have him as your boss?" the same woman asked.

Patty stopped and turned around. "There are some who say that he is difficult to work for and that he is very demanding, but I don't think there could be a finer boss."

"Yeah, and handsome, too!" called out another.

Patty laughed. "Yes, even a woman my age can appreciate his fine features. But there is more to him than that. He truly cares for the company and its reputation of distinction. The ones who bemoan him usually are the ones who aren't committed to excellence in their work." With a shake of her head she continued, "They probably would complain wherever they worked."

Patty pointed up ahead. "Now, if there are no further questions about William Denton, let us continue on and we'll see where samples of the coffee are tasted and packaged."

As they walked toward the next room, Elyssa couldn't help but consider the fact that they had originally planned to be on the one o'clock tour. She wondered what would have happened if Will had seen her there. Obviously he had returned from Guatemala and he would have no idea that she was here.

The tour group came to a standstill in front of a large glass window that looked out over a group of people who truly seemed to be enjoying themselves. It was very apparent to Elyssa that they were actually sampling cups of coffee.

"In this room," explained Patty, "a small pot of coffee is made randomly from a batch of coffee beans and then it is tasted." She turned to the group with a smile on her face. "This certainly has got to be the toughest part of the whole job!" Everyone laughed.

Patty continued. "Each batch of coffee is brewed and tested for taste, aroma, and texture. Anything that doesn't meet our standards is discarded. If it does pass our exacting criterion, the coffee beans are then packaged in those machines in the back, both as full beans and ground."

Elyssa noticed a group of people who were gathered in a small circle. One person held a clipboard and was writing down what the others were saying. She then turned her attention to the sign below the window and began reading.

A door opened in the tasting room and Elyssa's eyes darted up as a gentleman walked in. Her quickening heart slowed, however, when she saw that it wasn't Will.

She shook her head. Obviously he was gone. She could finish the tour in peace, but she didn't know whether she felt disappointment or relief.

The door had begun to slowly close when it stopped and began to open again. Elyssa looked up as another person strode through. She took a small step backward into the crowd of people behind her when she realized it was Will.

He was intently staring at a clipboard and when he lifted his hand to summon someone's attention, his eyes casually drifted to the glass window. He came to an abrupt halt as he saw Elyssa on the other side.

The small group of people on the tour pressed in around Elyssa as their tour guide exclaimed, "Oh, look, William Denton *is* still here!"

Elyssa was too stunned to even move. She couldn't bring herself to smile, nod, or even mouth a "hello."

Will seemed to be taken aback at seeing her, but directed a nominal nod in her direction. He then turned and ripped off the white apron he had over his suit. As he hurriedly walked out of the room, Elyssa closed her eyes as she wondered what he must be thinking about seeing her. Their last meeting had not been the most cordial.

"Well, that was a treat, wasn't it? Twice in one day!" Patty said. "He is a very busy man, though, and must have had something urgent come up to make him leave like that."

"Oh, I think he is so much more handsome in person!" said a lady who was standing behind Elyssa.

Patty laughed. "I think he would be positively embarrassed if he heard the remarks about him that I hear from the ladies on the tours."

Elyssa was eager to move on and leave the plant. It was apparent that he was not happy to see her there.

Patty explained about the final steps involved preparing the coffee to be shipped to stores and shops around the country. When she finished, she asked if there were any more questions, and when there were none, she directed the group into the lounge for their coffee and pastry.

As Elyssa stepped through the door, she couldn't prevent her eyes from searching for Will, thinking that out of politeness he might join them. When she saw that he was not anywhere to be seen, her heart sank in disappointment.

"You're welcome to stay here until five o'clock if you like," Patty told them. "At that time, the lounge will close for the day. Thank you all for coming on the Pemberleo tour. I hope you enjoyed it. We, at Pemberleo Coffee, hope you will always look for our coffee when you shop, and if your store doesn't carry it, we hope you will ask for it by name."

Elyssa felt numb as she followed the others into the small eating area. She was barely aware that Maddy had gently wrapped her hand through Elyssa's arm, giving her a little support as they followed Edward to a table.

When they sat down, a young lady came by with good-sized coffee mugs, plates, and silverware. She asked whether everyone wanted coffee, and when they all answered in the affirmative, she asked whether they preferred regular or decaf. She then told them that she would bring out a pot of coffee for them and a tray of pastries shortly.

Elyssa was grateful that her uncle knew her tastes and answered for her, for she couldn't quite concentrate on the conversation. Her attention was drawn to the door in the back of the room. Each time it opened, she turned to see who was coming in or going out.

"Very interesting tour, don't you think?" Edward exclaimed when the server left. "Now I know I'll appreciate each and every good cup of coffee I drink."

The door opened again and Elyssa turned her eyes in its direction.

"Yes, it was, dear," his wife answered, giving Edward a concerned look as she tilted her head toward Elyssa. He gave his shoulders a small shrug.

Elyssa pushed down a sense of anger -- whether it was directed at Will or herself she was not sure -- as she realized he was not going to come out to see them. Even though her heart ached, right now anger was easier for her to hide from her aunt and uncle. She decided it would be prudent for her to attend to them and their conversation.

Edward commented with enthusiasm on what he had learned anew about the process of making coffee. His wife agreed as she tried to keep a pulse on Elyssa's demeanor. Even though Elyssa was now paying attention, sometimes nodding her head to what her uncle said and other times only murmuring an agreement, Maddy could see something was most definitely wrong and she was fairly certain it had to do with William Denton.

As Maddy watched Elyssa, she thought back to the few times since her niece's arrival that the subject of William Denton came up. At first she believed her niece still held him responsible for her sister's death. Now, as she furtively examined Elyssa's features, she had to conclude it wasn't anger that she was dealing with. It was something just as powerful, though.

Elyssa sensed her aunt's scrutiny, so she sat up tall, squared her shoulders, and smiled. "Well, we have the weekend before us, Aunt. What shall we do?"

Maddy smiled at Elyssa's attempt to act as though nothing was wrong. "Well, we can see if there are any good movies out. Or would you rather sit around the house and relax?"

"A movie would be fine. Perhaps some exciting adventure movie."

Maddy pursed her lips together as she thought it odd that Elyssa would opt for an adventure movie when her greatest preference was romantic chick flicks.

At length, her uncle finally said, "Ah, here comes the young lady with our coffee, now." A wide grin appeared on his face and his said, "Well! Isn't *this* a treat?"

"Oh, my! He's bringing it over himself!" exclaimed Maddy.

When Elyssa looked up at her aunt and uncle, both were looking beyond her, with fervent smiles on their faces.

She heard footsteps behind her and her heart took a faltering leap when a very warm, familiar voice spoke.

"Hello. I believe you all wanted regular coffee?"

Elyssa didn't even have time to turn around. Will was suddenly standing next to her at their table with a pot of coffee in one hand and a small tray of pastries in another. He put the tray down on the table and began pouring the coffee.

Casting a faltering glance down at her, he said. "Hello, Elyssa."

She had to swallow before she could answer. "Hello, Will."

When he had filled all three mugs with coffee, Edward stood up and reached out his hand. "I'm Edward Garner, Elyssa's uncle, and this is my wife, Maddy."

Will took the extended hand into his in a firm grip. "It's a pleasure to meet you, Mr. Garner, Mrs. Garner. I'm William Denton."

"Mr. Denton, won't you join us?"

Will looked over at Elyssa as if securing her permission to join them. A gentle smile and nod from her gave him the assurance that she would accept his company.

He looked back at Edward. "Thank you for the invitation, but I will join you only if you call me Will."

Edward laughed. "I will if you call me Edward."

"It's a deal."

Will pulled out the one empty chair and sat down. The dynamics that occurred at that moment around the table was not difficult for Maddy to discern. She brought her hand up to her face and covered an emerging smirk with her fingers as she noticed repeatedly the furtive glances that her niece and Will cast at each other. It was almost as if each was carefully testing the waters.

"How is your family, Elyssa?"

"They are fine, thank you," she replied, just as a young lady came up alongside of them and snatched a picture.

Will appeared a little flustered, but answered, "I'm glad to hear that."

As the murmurs in the lounge increased, Elyssa couldn't help looking around at everyone. All the eyes were on the gentleman who had just joined them.

Tapping his fingers against the table, Will finally asked, "Would you mind terribly if we continue this in our private lounge?" He shifted his eyes to Elyssa and then back to the Garners. "I get a little uncomfortable around people with cameras. Do you mind?"

Elyssa looked down at his remark, a blush coloring her cheeks. She knew exactly what he meant.

Edward stood up. "That would certainly be a pleasure." He began to pick up his coffee and plate, but Will stopped him.

"I'll have someone bring all this in for us."

"I'm going to go out the door I came in to ensure we can have a little privacy. Your server will come in and show you to the private lounge in a minute or two."

When he departed, both Maddy and Edward looked at each other and let out a delighted laugh.

"This must be because of you, Elyssa," Maddy said. "I'm sure he doesn't often give people on the tour this special attention!"

Edward chimed in, "He must be a busy man!"

Elyssa's thoughts had begun racing as quickly as her heart was beating. Her aunt didn't miss the look of anticipation that swept across her face.

The young girl came with a tray and picked up their coffee cups and plates. "Follow me, please." Elyssa was grateful for her prompt arrival, which negated her having to compose a response to them.

All eyes in the room watched as the threesome followed their server out of the room.

They came into the plush lounge and she seated them at a small table in the corner. Will walked in and joined them.

"Thanks," he said. "I just didn't want a lot of interruptions."

"No problem!" laughed Edward. "And if you heard what some of the ladies said about you during our tour, you would have had several come by and want their picture taken with you."

Will seemed uncomfortable by this comment, but turned to Elyssa, hoping to change the subject. "What brings you to Chicago, Elyssa?"

"I have a design job here."

"Do you really?"

Elyssa nodded.

Will turned his attention back to Edward and Maddy. "Do the two of you live in Chicago?"

Maddy answered. "We live in Lamstone."

"Lamstone! Why that's just fi…" Will's voice trailed off and he looked awkwardly at Elyssa. "That's a very fine little town."

"Yes, we truly love it. We only moved here about a month ago."

"Have you explored all the walking and biking paths out there yet?"

"No, we really haven't had the time," Edward said. "But what I'm really anxious to find is some good fishing spots."

"Oh, I can recommend several that are fairly close to you."

"You know the area, then?" he asked.

Will paused before answering, as if carefully considering his words. "I know a little about it. I don't often get out that way, though."

Edward engaged Will in conversation about the many opportunities for recreation around the area. Maddy was impressed with the attention Will was paying them. She couldn't help but recall his stoic demeanor a few months back at the funeral. Even at the wedding two years ago, he seemed aloof. It was obvious that something had changed.

Knowing that Elyssa hadn't had the opportunity to thank Will for what he did for Janet and Chad, Maddy drew Elyssa's attention and slightly nodded her head toward him. Bringing her hand up to the side of her nose as if to scratch it, she mouthed the words so Will couldn't see or hear, "Thank him!"

Elyssa pursed her lips together, feeling as though she were a little girl who had just been admonished for forgetting her manners.

Edward mentioned to Will that Elyssa had just informed them that he had been down in Guatemala with her. He turned to her and they both looked awkwardly at each other.

"Well, yes, I was. I wanted to make sure she had everything she needed and was well taken care of. I knew how difficult it had been for her."

Elyssa met his eyes as he turned toward her and she smiled. There was so much she wanted to say to him, but she couldn't right here -- right now. She hoped he could read in her eyes her appreciation and her apology for all that had happened.

"Well, we certainly appreciate that," interjected Edward, "and we know Elyssa must feel the same way!"

"Yes... yes, I do. I do appreciate... everything!"

When Will gave her a penetrating look with his deep brown eyes, Elyssa needed to take in a deep breath to calm her nerves. "I do want to thank you, Will, for the memorials that Pemberleo... that *you* set up for Janet and Chad. They were so perfect for them. That was very kind of you."

Will looked down and then back up to her, his eyes filled with admiration and longing. "There is no need to thank me."

"But I must! This means so much to me and it would have meant so much to them!" Elyssa's eyes pleaded with him to acknowledge her thanks.

Will brought his hand up to his chin and began to rub it. He couldn't believe that Elyssa was right here; he had been waiting for this moment for a long time. The circumstances, however, did not allow him to discern her true feelings for him. "I am... pleased... that you appreciate it."

Will leaned back in the chair and seemed to relax a little as he said, "I just returned yesterday from Guatemala and took pictures of the progress at the park. It's coming along quite well. I don't have the photos on me, but I would like for you to see them."

He turned and looked intently at Elyssa. "Would it be possible for you to come by my office one day next week so I can show them to you? Or I could bring them out myself to Lamstone."

Elyssa swallowed; her mouth suddenly completely dry. "I would very much like to see them and I need to return to the city next week. Is there any day that would work best for you?"

Will shook his head and stood up. "No, you come at your convenience. Unfortunately, I have a business dinner shortly that I must leave for. It was a pleasure meeting you both," he said to the Garners and then turned to Elyssa.

"I'll see you next week, then?"

Elyssa nodded and smiled, her heart vacillating in its beat.

Will turned to walk away and Maddy couldn't stop herself from gushing once he had stepped through the door. "Oh, Elyssa, he is the most amiable man I have ever met! How could any of us have believed him to be such a tyrant?"

Elyssa let out a sigh. "I guess we're all entitled to be wrong once in a while." At the moment, Elyssa could not bring herself to tell her aunt and uncle just how wrong she had been. She could only hope that Will's congeniality today was an indication that he would readily forgive her.

Chapter 24

As Elyssa sat in the backseat of her uncle's car as they drove home from Chicago, she couldn't help but feel an overwhelming sense of optimism. The mere fact that Will had made a point of coming out to see her and meet her aunt and uncle was almost too much for her to comprehend. He could have very easily left the plant and avoided them altogether.

It also provided quite a distraction for Edward and Maddy, as they couldn't get over how completely gracious and well-mannered he was towards them. They talked non-stop all the way home about how honored they were by his visit.

"I think you were right, Elyssa," her uncle looked in the rear view mirror at his niece. "I think being named one of the top bachelors is more of a nuisance to him than anything else."

"Can you imagine what it would be like to go through life having complete strangers coming up to you wanting to take your picture?" her aunt asked. "At least he's not likely to be readily recognized anywhere outside of Chicago."

Elyssa closed her eyes and took in a deep breath. She shook her head as she thought of those pictures from Panajachel.

"You know what the man needs?" Edward laughed heartily. "It would solve all his problems."

"What, dear?" Maddy asked.

"All he needs to do is get a wife! That will take care of the whole bothersome business!"

"I wouldn't be surprised if he already has someone in mind," Maddy said coyly.

As Edward and Maddy laughed unreservedly, Elyssa slouched down in the seat and leaned her head back. *That is all I need,* thought Elyssa to herself, *to come all this way only to find out he already has a special woman in his life!*

~~*

After much contemplation, Elyssa decided that more than anything else, she preferred to relax that weekend. Her reasoning to Maddy was that she wanted to recuperate from a very busy and demanding week and prepare herself for the next. Her reasoning to herself was that she wanted to think through Will's every word and expression to try and ascertain what his feelings toward her were in anticipation of their meeting together next week.

There were moments when she recalled a look and was flooded with emotion. His smiles, although not as fervent and unrestrained as they had been at the lake, emanated warmth. By the end of the weekend, she was fairly certain he would forgive her and perhaps he already had. She had even bolstered her confidence that perhaps there *could* be something more between them.

Several times her aunt and uncle remarked that they would like to invite him over. Elyssa was quite certain that Maddy knew her true feelings for Will, although she hadn't outright confirmed her aunt's suspicions. Maddy was too considerate to mention it to Elyssa before her niece said anything about it first.

Elyssa had a very busy Monday and Tuesday. Several times during the day, when she found herself completely frustrated by one thing or another, she sought refuge on the porch swing. As she let her eyes wander out to the furthest thing she could see, she was able to clear her thoughts of all but that which was important.

Elyssa looked forward to the end of the day when, after all the workers had departed, she could retreat to the swing. She often pondered just what kind of man this Richard Fitzpatrick was. She would like to meet him. She felt that if she knew him, she would have a much better idea of what he wanted in his home. She shook her head, though, when she considered that he had given his approval on everything she had submitted.

On Tuesday afternoon, Elyssa sat on the swing enjoying the sun paint the sky with a palette of hues as it set. It had been a long, busy day and as the swing swayed softly, she felt herself unwind. The breeze rustled the few leaves that had begun to lazily drift down from the trees in anticipation of autumn. She felt she could sit here for another couple of hours.

As Elyssa sat on the swing that afternoon, she decided to call Emily and let her know how strongly she wished to meet Mr. Fitzpatrick. When she called, Elyssa encouraged her to see if he could come by some time when she was at the house. She told Emily that it would help her immensely if she could speak to him directly. All Emily could promise was that she would see what she could do.

It wasn't until Wednesday that Elyssa was able to get back into the city. A stop by what had become her favorite store was in order as well as the Merchandise Mart. Mr. Jones' wife, Janelle, had encouraged her to look through this massive building if nothing but for the experience. If she needed any ideas or inspiration, this was the place to go. After a visit there, she would stop by the Pemberleo offices.

Elyssa ventured into Chicago on her own and congratulated herself that she had easily and quickly mastered the transportation system. She was grateful that her aunt hadn't accompanied her. If she found Will wanted nothing more than merely to show her the photographs, she would need the time alone to absorb the implications.

Elyssa chose to stop at the Jones' store first. She and Janelle had developed an easy friendship and she found that between her and her husband, Elyssa could get just about anything and get it the way she wanted. Today she had come to see an antique English sideboard that they had picked up over the weekend. If it was in the excellent condition they claimed it to be in, Elyssa knew she would want it and knew exactly where she would put it. She thought this piece of furniture would add just the right touch in complimenting the painting.

Upon her close scrutiny when she arrived, she knew they had stumbled across a wonderful antique. It needed some simple restoration work, but other than that, it looked almost as good as new -- even though it was so old! She took a picture of it to turn it in for approval, but told Mr. Jones he could deliver it when he finished working on it. She had come to expect all her ideas to be approved.

From there she took a bus to the Merchandise Mart. A massive structure stood before her and Elyssa had to laugh when she realized she would barely make a dent in seeing all that was inside. Armed with her designer's license and a pad of paper to jot down notes and ideas, she decided to allow herself one hour to find out what this place offered.

The hour swept by before she knew it and Elyssa, finding it difficult to leave, remained another hour. She picked up business cards and samples, wrote some ideas down from displays and pictures she saw, and was grateful that Janelle had encouraged her to go. She knew another visit was simply indispensable.

When she stepped outside the mart, she slipped off the sweater she had put on earlier. A cool breeze and gathering clouds this morning had teased her of autumn's approach, but now the sun shone steady and it was very warm. She knew, however, that if she didn't complete the two rooms in a month or two, she could be in for a very cold, harsh winter. Elyssa shivered as she considered just how cold it would be if she found that Will didn't return her regard.

She walked to Pemberleo's office building, enjoying the journey. Stepping inside the lobby, she walked over to the elevator and waited for it to come.

When the doors opened, Elyssa stepped in and as it traveled upwards, so did her thoughts. She didn't even know what she was going to say to Will. She only hoped he would realize her feelings were nothing like they had been when she left Guatemala. She was so consumed with her thoughts that it seemed the elevator reached her destination in no time. Her pulse quickened as she stepped out and heard the doors close behind her. Bringing her fingers up to her hair, she tried to repair the wayward strands that had been jostled by her walk.

Elyssa walked over to the door that went into the Pemberleo executive offices and stepped in.

An older woman greeted Elyssa as she walked toward the desk. Elyssa recognized the name of Mrs. Reed on a nameplate on her desk.

"May I help you?"

"Yes, I wondered if I could see Mr. Denton."

"Oh, I'm sorry, but he's in his board meeting at present. It is likely to go on through the afternoon. Can I help you with something or give him a message when he comes out?"

Elyssa could not masquerade the feeling of disappointment that surged through her, recalling Gina's words that her brother was never to be disturbed when in his board meeting.

"My name is Elyssa Barnett and…"

"Of course!" Mrs. Reed exclaimed. "I thought you looked familiar. You're Janet's sister."

Elyssa nodded.

"You have our deepest sympathy, Miss Barnett."

"Thank you." Elyssa took a deep breath. "Will… er, Mr. Denton told me he had some pictures to show me of the park in Guatemala City. Perhaps I should return tomorrow."

Mrs. Reed stood up. "No sense in making another trip up here. Come, would you follow me, please?"

Elyssa halfheartedly followed Mrs. Reed into an open office. The woman was graciously doing her job, but Elyssa felt frustrated nonetheless. She knew that if she left without seeing him today, she would have to come up with another plan."

"You may have a seat here and I'll see about those pictures."

"Thank you," Elyssa replied softly.

As Elyssa turned her gaze to the pictures, awards, and diplomas adorning the wall, she knew for a certainty that she was in Will's office. Instead of taking the proffered seat, she walked over to the window and looked out. The glistening waters of Lake Michigan provided an excellent view from his office, just as she had suspected.

She stepped to the side and carefully began inspecting a few of the framed pieces on the wall. She knew Mrs. Reed would likely be back shortly with the pictures, but curiosity prompted her to see just what this man was made of.

Elyssa was rather impressed with all his awards for excellence, the honors he received at the university, and his apparent regard for his family, for photos were interspersed among all the framed documents.

She saw a picture of a very young William Denton with Gina and a very striking gentleman that she presumed to be his father. She could see in their faces the closeness they all felt. Elyssa smiled as she looked at another picture of a young boy with both his father and his mother, who was holding a baby. She knew for a certainty it was the Denton family. She leaned in closely to the photograph, trying to make out the detail of William Denton as a little boy.

Scanning the wall, her attention was drawn to a young man in a baseball uniform. Walking up to it, she knew immediately that the dark curly hair and eyes of this young man could only belong to Will. He looked young enough for it to have been taken in high school. Her fingers went up as if she wanted to gently stroke his cheek. He looked…

"Hello, Elyssa. I'm glad you were able to come."

Elyssa spun her head around; her jaw dropping in astonishment as Will came through the door. "I thought… I thought you were in your board meeting." She took the picture in both hands and straightened it, as if it had been crooked.

"I was, but Mrs. Reed informed me you were here."

He stepped over to her and looked at the photograph she had been looking at. "I was never much of a football player, but I did love baseball. They actually let me play on the team because I was great at stealing bases."

Elyssa's mind raced with conflicting thoughts. What did he think when he came upon her reaching out for his picture, and why would he come out of his meeting for her?

"Well," she nervously laughed as she made every attempt at composing herself, "I am familiar enough with the game of baseball to know you have to be able to hit a ball to get on a base before you can steal it!"

"True," he said unassumingly. He turned and picked up a picture from his desk. "Did you see this one?"

Elyssa turned around and saw that Will was holding a picture of Gina, grateful that he was making this easy for her. "She is certainly a beautiful young girl. I really enjoyed my visit with her."

Will's eyes went from the picture to Elyssa. "I'm glad. She said she enjoyed getting to know you, as well."

"You must be very proud of her."

"Just a little," he said with a smile.

A heavy silence hung over them for a moment. Elyssa could barely breathe.

"Would you like to see the plans for the park?" Will said, finally breaking the silence.

"Yes, if you want to just give them to me, I'll look at them on my own so you can get back to your meeting."

Will shook his head. "They're perfectly capable of handling things without me. My cousin is in there keeping them all in line."

Will walked around and opened a drawer in his desk, pulling out a folder. He then came back around and sat on the corner of the bench next to where Elyssa was standing.

As he began to reach in for the pictures, Elyssa nervously reached out and gently touched his arm. Her heart was beating so fiercely that she felt it was up in her throat. "Will, first there is something I would like to say."

Will drew in a ragged breath and his hands dropped down into his lap. He looked down at the folder he was still holding and then at her hand resting upon his arm. He slowly turned to look at Elyssa.

"You have no need to thank me, again."

Elyssa shook her head from side to side. "I wish it were something as easy as that." Elyssa removed her hand and began nervously intertwining her fingers together. "I wanted to apologize for the words I lashed out at you at the airport in Guatemala. It was very wrong of me."

"Elyssa, you don't need to apologize."

"Oh, but I do! It was inexcusable of me. I am truly sorry."

"What did you say to me that I didn't deserve?" The look he gave her pierced her very core.

"Well you certainly didn't deserve a tongue-lashing from me. It was very wrong for me to say such unkind things about you that weren't true."

Will placed his large hand over Elyssa's clasped hands. "Very much of what you said that day *was* true."

"No, Will. I saw a very different side of you in Guatemala. I just had a lot of presumptions about you and didn't know whether I could trust what I saw."

They sat in silence for a few moments. The only thing either was aware of was Will's hand covering Elyssa's.

Elyssa turned her face toward him. "Will you please forgive me?"

Will let out a breathy chuckle. "Yes, I forgive you, but now you must also forgive me for behaving so abominably."

"When did you ever behave abominably?"

"Well, for starters, when I insulted you at the wedding reception."

Now it was Elyssa's turn to laugh. "All right. You do have a point. That was abominable. But yes, I do forgive you."

Elyssa looked down at Will's hand as he gave her hands a quick, gentle squeeze. "Now, would you like to see the pictures?"

"I'd love to see them." Elyssa felt as though a massive weight had been lifted from her.

Will pulled some photographs out of the folder and showed Elyssa how the area had been cleared and sod had been put down. He showed her where sand would be hauled in and playground equipment set up.

He then pulled out a landscape drawing of what the finished park would look like. He handed it to Elyssa. "I thought you'd enjoy seeing the artist's rendition of what it hopefully will look like when it's done."

Elyssa took in a sharp breath as her eyes took it all in. "This is beautiful!"

He pointed to a plaque at the very front. "This is where we will have an inscribed memorial to Janet. It will say a little about who she was, what she did, and how much she cared for the children."

Elyssa felt that all too familiar sense of heartache flood through her as she looked at the beautiful drawing. She knew this would be a place the children would immensely enjoy. As tears began to pool in her eyes, however, she realized they were tears of joy and not pain. She could actually take delight in what Will was telling her.

As Elyssa looked at every detail in the drawing, Will pulled out pictures of the playground equipment that had been ordered for the children.

Elyssa stared at everything in front of her. What an oasis this would be for the children in that neighborhood! She let her tears of joy spill down her face as she thought how much Janet would have appreciated this.

She swallowed hard and whispered a very soft, "This will be so wonderful! Thanks so much, Will."

"Is there anything else you can think of that it should have?"

Will looked over at Elyssa and she turned to meet his gaze. With a smile that lit up her face, she answered, "Yes! Children!"

As Will watched her, he became more convinced that he could not live without this woman. His ploy had brought her to Chicago and now his mind scrambled as to how he should best garner her affections. He also had the monumental task of figuring out when and how he should tell her the truth about the job that brought her here.

Suddenly a man burst through the door, prompting Will to abandon all reflection.

"Will, I'm sorry to interrupt, but we need a decision in there before we can proceed any further."

Will stood up. "Sure." He glanced back and forth between the gentleman and Elyssa as he made introductions.

"Richard, this is Janet Blakely's sister, Elyssa Barnett. Elyssa, this is my cousin, Richard Fi..."

"Hi!" the other man interrupted and walked toward her with an extended hand. "I am so pleased to meet you. You have my deepest condolences. Chad and Janet were so well liked around here."

"Thank you, and it's a pleasure to meet you too, Richard."

He turned back to Will and the two men exchanged guarded looks. "I hate to interrupt, but we have kind of a stand-off in there, Will, that requires your perceptive finesse and diplomatic hand."

Will narrowed his eyes at his cousin and told him, "I'll be right in. I was just showing Elyssa the plans for the park."

"Ahh!" Richard exclaimed as he turned to Elyssa. "You would not have believed this man when we went out looking for everything to put in the park. He had to try out each of the pieces of playground equipment! He was having too good a time, but was quite undignified, if you ask me!"

Will gave his cousin a look of mock disgust. "I'm sure Elyssa doesn't believe one word you're saying."

Richard smiled at Elyssa and then said, "It was a pleasure meeting you, Elyssa. I must get back to the men." He winked as he said to her, "They're not used to being left to their own devices!"

"I'm sorry, Elyssa," Will said. "I do have to get back in there, too. I'd offer to take you home, but I wouldn't want you to have to wait the two to three hours we have left. Can I have a driver take you home?"

"Oh, no! It is too beautiful outdoors! I love to walk and I've quite mastered the transportation system."

"Are you sure?"

Elyssa nodded. "Unless, of course it's Manuel. I'd love to talk to him, again."

"No, it's not Manuel."

Elyssa chuckled. "I didn't think so."

Will was determined that before she left today, he would make some plans to see her again.

"Elyssa," he said, somewhat apprehensively. "Do you think it would be possible for me to come by and see the house you're working on? I'd really like to see it."

"Oh," Elyssa could barely contain her pleasure. "Certainly, but it's not anywhere near finished. I've only just begun working on the living room."

"I'd like to see it anyway."

"I'm sure that will be fine. I'm usually there Monday through Friday unless I go out to some of the designer stores."

"Then I'll come by the house one day this week to see you," Will said as if to confirm it with Elyssa. As he turned to go out the door, he looked back and said, "I'm glad you came by today."

Elyssa smiled and Will stepped out.

"But don't you want to know where it is?" Elyssa asked suddenly.

Will stopped abruptly and gave a nervous laugh. "Yes, I suppose that will help."

Will walked back to his desk and picked up a scratch piece of paper, giving it to Elyssa along with a pen.

Elyssa quickly did some scribbling and then handed it back to him. "There! I've also included my cell phone number in case you need to reach me. Do you think you'll be able to find it?"

"Sure," he said as he looked at the address. "No problem. Thanks, Elyssa."

Will walked out, chiding himself for the two times he almost slipped up. He was not used to this kind of pretense and he wasn't good at it at all!

Elyssa turned back to give one last glance around his office. She let out a sigh of relief and delight. She didn't think her meeting with him could have ended any better. He was actually going to come out to see her!

Chapter 25

As the board members walked out of the office conference room, Richard Fitzpatrick thanked each one for the excellent input and direction they always give to the company. When the last one stepped through the door, Richard closed it and turned around, his hands casually tucked inside his slacks pockets.

Sauntering back toward Will, he said, "So that was the legendary Elyssa Barnett, the one woman who finally has been able to find the chink in the Denton armor." He let out a few huffs as he added, "Quite unknowingly, I must add."

Will stood alongside the large conference table, placing some papers inside his briefcase. As he closed the lid, his eyes lifted to his cousin who had come to stand directly opposite him.

Will looked back down. "I know what you're thinking."

Richard took his hands out of his pockets and braced them on the tabletop in front of him. "No, my most respected and honorable cousin. You have *no* idea what I am thinking!"

Will let out a groan. "Go on. Get it out of your system."

Richard leaned across the table toward Will. "As Vice-President of Pemberleo Coffee, I find it necessary to exert a heavy hand upon you for this act of deceit and pretense which I have recently become informed about. Now, if the President, William Denton, were *truly* here, the task would fall to him, but since I have no idea where *that* man is, I must step into his shoes."

Will grimaced as he listened to Richard's mocking words. "I know it seems out of character for me, but…"

Shaking his index finger firmly at his cousin, Richard continued. "Will, first of all, you almost blew it back there when you started to introduce me. You were not made for this kind of thing, ol' man! It's not in your fabric to be deceitful."

Will swallowed. "Offering her the job under your name was the only way I knew to get her here. If she knew the house was mine, she might never have come."

"You can't be serious! You pride yourself on the integrity of the company, the honesty and loyalty of the employees, and yet you choose to carry off this conniving scheme! You are the one who abhors any sort of disguise. You do realize, don't you, that if you discovered that someone in your employ had done something of this magnitude, you would have come down harshly on them?"

"You're right," Will said softly.

"And why you had to drag my name into this whole thing, I'll never know."

"When I gave your name, I had no idea that she'd even come."

"And so you didn't think beyond that."

"I only hoped she would."

Richard shook his head. "I still don't understand how you got her to come out here for a design job."

"While we were in Guatemala, Elyssa told me that her friend, Charlene, hands out her business cards to people in the hopes of getting her clients."

"And you've met this Charlene and were given one of Elyssa's cards?"

Will forced a smile. "No, I don't have one of her cards, but she doesn't know that. She only thinks Richard Fitzpatrick -- *you* -- were given one. I arranged to have Emily work with me on this since she works for a reputable company. I didn't want Elyssa to worry about accepting a job from some guy she's never met."

"Boy, you thought of everything."

Will shrugged his shoulders sheepishly.

"Except," continued Richard, "What happens when she finds out you own the house. I suggest you inform her of the truth of the situation before she discovers it on her own."

"I intend to, but just not yet." Will collapsed in the chair and leaned over the table, his fingers raking through his hair. "It's too soon."

Richard threw his hands up in the air. "Too soon for what? To be truthful?" Richard turned around and leaned against the table, his back to Will. "Let's see, what was that word you said she accused you of being? I believe it started with an 'M'."

Will grunted.

Richard abruptly stood up and began walking around the room, rubbing his jaw as if he were trying to remember. "I don't believe it was *marvelous*. No, that doesn't sound right. Perhaps it was *mediocre*. No, that's not it either. Let's see…" He came up alongside Will and leaned over, looking him squarely in the eye. "I believe it was… *manipulative*."

Will fisted his hand and pounded his chin as Richard continued. "Now this couldn't be an accurate description of William Denton, could it? My good cousin and President of Pemberleo? Let's see, has he ever been manipulative?"

"Richard…"

Richard sat down in the chair next to Will. "Look. She seems like a fine lady and I couldn't be happier that you think you've found the woman of your dreams. But why, in heaven's name, are you carrying on this charade? What do you think she's going to do when she finds out?"

"She'll be angry."

"Yeah!" Richard laughed sarcastically. "But you have this lame-brained scheme to win her over with deceit."

"I'm not trying to win her by deceit. The only deceit is in what brought her here."

"Well, far be it for me to tell you how to live your life. Goodness knows you run an impeccable company…" He poked his finger at Will for emphasis as he continued, "that prides itself on its integrity and honor."

Will let out a breath he had been holding. "You've said that already. I just can't tell her yet."

"Would you be so kind as to tell me why?"

"If I tell her the house is mine right now, she'll have one of two responses, both of which are not what I want."

Richard peered at his cousin through squinted eyes, shaking his head slowly. "That just reeks of manipulation. So what do you think she'd do?"

Will brought up a hand and rubbed his forehead, before looking at his cousin. "If I tell her now, she would either get very angry and leave immediately…"

"That's the only thing you've said about this whole thing that rings true!' Richard folded his arms across his chest. "Or?"

"Or she will have fallen so madly in love with the house that she'd accept my attentions and want to marry me just to have the house of her dreams."

"And no, you wouldn't want to have her love based on material things."

"I could have any woman's love based on material things."

"Well, maybe that wouldn't be too bad. Perhaps she'd grow to love you, too."

Will slouched in his chair. "No, because she'd never do that. Marrying for material things is not in Elyssa's makeup."

"So that leaves only the possibility that she'll get angry at you and leave… just like she did in Guatemala!"

"That's right."

Richard laughed. "Well, I am so glad you have that all figured out, because I am totally clueless as to what you think is going to happen when you finally tell her."

Will leaned his head back and stared off into space. "My hope is that if I can spend some time with her that she may begin to like me for me. Then, by the time I tell her, she will not see it as manipulation but as giving us another chance."

"Look, Will. I give you credit for pursuing this relationship when she completely lambasted you at the airport. *I* wouldn't be so gracious to a woman who did that to me. Goodness knows I've been waiting for the day when you find someone you can love and trust. You deserve someone great!"

Will looked up at his cousin. "Elyssa *is* great!"

Richard unfolded his arms and grasped Will's shoulder, giving it a gentle shake. "Look, Will. I'm only saying this because you're my cousin and I love you! I'm concerned about you. I can't forget, though, what you were like when you returned from Guatemala. I'd never seen you so miserable. I don't want to see you go through that again. Do you truly believe there is even the remotest chance she will ever return your affections?"

Will nodded his head. "There was a connection between us in Guatemala. Once she got over blaming me for Chad and Janet's deaths, we really enjoyed ourselves."

"You do realize, don't you, just how much you have going against you?" Richard laughed. "She blamed you for their deaths and yet you think there is a remote possibility that her feelings toward you will change?"

"I'm willing to give it a try."

"You're sure of this?"

Will lifted up his head and looked at his cousin. "For the first time in my life

I felt as though there was something more important to me than Pemberleo."

"Yeah, you had people wondering what happened to you when they suddenly couldn't reach you by cell phone down there."

"I just came to realize that when I was around her, I didn't want to be interrupted."

"It also helped that Manuel gave you a heads up that Elyssa didn't take too kindly to all your cell phone calls."

Will looked sharply up at his cousin. "Where did you hear that?"

"Manuel told me when I was in Guatemala a while back. The man isn't blind. He could very easily see what was going on in both yours and Elyssa's heads."

"I guess I need to have a talk with Manuel."

"Ha!" Richard laughed. "He tells me everything! I pay him off, you know."

Will barely smiled at his cousin's teasing. "I have never felt strongly enough about any woman to put all my work aside when I was in her presence. When I first arrived in Guatemala, I tried to dismiss my feelings for Elyssa. She was so angry at me I thought it was useless. But the longer I was with her, the more I wanted her to shed that anger she had toward me. I thought if I could show her in just this one way that she was important to me, perhaps she'd notice."

"There is hope for you yet!"

"She accused me of being consumed by my job and she was correct. Pemberleo *had* become my whole life, and now I'm ready for a change." Will turned and looked intently at his cousin. "I want more than just coming home to an empty house and continuing my workday there every night."

Will paused and took in a deep breath, his eyes growing soft. "I felt so much pain and anguish when I returned from Guatemala. I've never felt so much *anything* in my life. I didn't know how to handle it."

"Well, you certainly had Gina and me worried."

Will shook his head somberly. "I don't know what I'd do without Gina. She sat me down and refused to budge until I told her everything that happened."

"So you poured out your heart to Gina?"

Will nodded. "She encouraged me to try to fight for what I wanted. I guess I really didn't even know how to go about doing that."

Richard walked over and sat down at the table next to Will. "So was it your idea or hers to send her to see Elyssa?"

Will tapped his fingernails against the table. "Well, I needed to let Elyssa know about the memorials. I thought it would be the perfect opportunity for Gina to pay her a visit to tell her since she left soon after for California."

"And it didn't hurt that she idolizes you and would put in some good words about you to her."

"I didn't tell her what to say to Elyssa."

"But you did tell her how you wished you could have a second chance with Elyssa."

"Something to that effect."

Suddenly Richard started laughing.

"What?" Will asked as he looked suspiciously at his cousin.

"Boy, you know how protective Gina is of you? If she hadn't liked Elyssa, she could have very easily influenced her the other way."

"I knew that was a possibility, but I also knew Elyssa. I was fairly certain they'd get along nicely."

"So, fortunately for you, Gina thought Elyssa was wonderful and ran interference for you. And what did she report back to you about Elyssa?"

Will clasped his hands together and rested his chin on them. "She felt Elyssa was no longer angry at me and saw some things in a different light." Will paused and his jaw tightened. "Especially when it came to George Westham and the things he told her."

"Blast that George! How he can ruin so many lives and have no remorse is beyond me!"

"Fortunately, Gina was able to convince Elyssa of George's true nature." He tilted his head at his cousin. "I know she must have trusted Elyssa, because she told me that she confessed everything to her. You know how shy Gina is. I didn't think she'd ever share that with anyone!"

"She told Elyssa everything?"

Will nodded. "I believe she did."

Richard pursed his lips together. "That is surprising."

He slapped his hands against the table and stood up. "Well, cousin, I don't know about you, but I've got to get going."

"Wait," Will reached out his arm. "I have a slight dilemma that I just became aware of earlier today."

"Only a slight one? I'd say you have a major dilemma, but what is it?"

"Emily told me that Elyssa would really like to meet the owner of the house and wants her to set up a time for you to come meet her."

"Oh, great! Now that she has met me, what are we to do? I can't show up at the house. She'd figure it out right away!" Richard turned around and threw his hands up in the air. "Good grief! Now I sound just like you!"

Will swallowed. "We'll simply buy some time. I'll tell Emily to let Elyssa know you're planning to come by on a particular day and then you can call and say something came up."

"All right, Will. You have this whole scheme planned out, but I have one question for you." He leaned in to his cousin. "What is your strategy for winning Elyssa's heart? What are your plans to make her fall for you?"

"What do you mean?"

"Look, I do love you like a brother, but I hate to tell you, when you're around people, you're rather stiff and boring. Elyssa didn't seem like the type that would be naturally drawn to the strong, brooding, silent type."

Will rolled his eyes. "I figured we'd just do some things together."

"Will, are you sure you know what to do on a date. All you've ever done recently was attend one of those gala affairs or posh extravaganzas that you're obliged to attend with a lady attached to your arm."

"I've got some ideas."

"You better. After all, you're one of the top 50 bachelors in the whole US!"

"Not that I ever desired that title!"

"No, not you. Now me? Hey look, I'm the confirmed bachelor! Why didn't they ever give me some consideration?"

"I'd gladly pass it over to you."

Will pushed his chair back and stood up. Walking over to the window and looking out at the lake, he said, "I just want to go out on a regular date with her. I mean, well, something simple, but maybe not ordinary."

Richard picked up his briefcase. "I'm sure you'll figure something out!"

"Thanks, Richard. Thanks for understanding."

Richard held up his hand to stop him. "I never said I understood, but I do have one more question, Will."

Will raised his eyebrows. "I can hardly wait."

"Have you gone by the house to see it? I mean, of course, when she's not there. How do you know she's not designing it with some appalling décor?"

"I trust Elyssa's taste. Besides, I haven't wanted to take the chance that she'd show up and see me there. I did just talk with her about my going out to see her and the house. I'm planning to go by some time this week."

An expression on Will's face suggested to Richard that he had done something foolish.

"What was that look for?" Richard asked.

"I almost blew it again after you walked out. I asked Elyssa if I could see the house and then didn't ask for the address. Fortunately, she reminded me. It would have been terribly awkward showing up and her realizing she hadn't given it to me."

Richard laughed. "Like I said, Will, you're not made for this kind of thing. I suggest you tell her before she finds out some other way!"

Richard raised his eyebrows and turned to walk out. As he passed through the door, he yelled, "But I don't want to be anywhere near you two when she discovers the truth! You've experienced her wrath before; I suggest you prepare for it again!"

Chapter 26

Elyssa could barely contain her joy as she took the trains back to Lamstone. She was fairly certain that her smile never left her face. Holding the folder with the pictures and plans for the memorial tightly against her chest, she couldn't help but feel gratitude and admiration for Will Denton.

As she scrutinized her feelings, she wondered also if there was something more. Her one hand slid up to her neck and as it rested there, she could feel the pulsating of her heart as she considered whether she had fallen in love with him.

She was rather surprised to realize such strong, unexplainable feelings had been with her for quite a while. A soft chuckle escaped as she pondered exactly when this ailment called love had overtaken her.

Was it when he dragged her out to the bumper cars so she could take out all her anger against him? Or was it when he lifted her out of the rain-swollen street and carried her to the other side before running off after her wayward sandal?

Her smile deepened as she thought of how he had cared for her when she had taken ill, but she cringed when she recalled her conduct at the airport. Although he had graciously forgiven her, she still felt the shame of her actions.

Elyssa leaned her head back and closed her eyes as the rattling and swaying motion of the train tried to lull her to sleep. It proved futile, however, as her mind actively sought an explanation to what she considered this most unlikely happenstance. She had fallen in love with the one man she had once been so determined to hate!

When the train stopped at Lamstone, Elyssa hopped off and hurried to the car she had left at the station earlier. She was anxious to get to her aunt and uncle's home and relay to them the events of the day. She pulled her sweater tightly around her as a blast of cool air teased her as she walked across the parking lot. She hurriedly slipped into the car and drove the short distance back.

When she arrived, she burst through the door, her eyes bright and smile endless.

"I'm back!"

"I'm in here," her aunt replied from the kitchen.

As Elyssa walked in, Maddy looked up from chopping some celery. "How was your day?"

Elyssa picked up a piece and sat down with it. "Fine," she said as she took a bite.

Her aunt tilted her head toward Elyssa and smiled. "Is that all? Just fine?"

Elyssa stood up and walked to her aunt, giving her a hug. "I guess you could say it was wonderful. Let me freshen up and then I'll come back and help you with dinner. I'll tell you all about it once Uncle Edward comes home."

Over dinner that night, she told her aunt and uncle about her visit to the Jones' store and the Merchandise Mart. They sat patiently and listened, waiting eagerly to hear about her visit to the Pemberleo offices.

Elyssa finally pulled out the packet of pictures and conveyed to them all that had been done and would be done, as Will had related to her.

They poured over every picture with profuse words of admiration. Elyssa waited for the right time and the right words to tell them what all had transpired between her and Will. She didn't have to wait long, however, for her aunt, provided her with the opportune opening.

"And how was William Denton?"

Elyssa inwardly chided herself for the blush that most infuriatingly appeared. She was quite certain both her aunt and uncle noticed.

She turned quickly to distract herself with little Lillian, helping her with her meal as both Edward and Maddy kept their eyes on Elyssa.

"Well, there is much to say on that matter. I guess I need to tell you a little about what happened in Guatemala."

As if on cue, they put down their forks with a clang and sat back in their chairs, eager for a confirmation of their suspicions.

Elyssa cleared her throat and began. "When he came down to Guatemala, he did a lot for me. Of course, I was loath to see him -- at first. I did everything in my power to convince myself and him that his meager attempts to appease his guilt -- and my indictment against him -- were useless."

Elyssa looked up sheepishly to see that Edward and Maddy were both leaning toward her now, as if wanting to hear more. "I assumed that was why he had come all the way down to Guatemala. I felt certain he must have felt a great deal of guilt, for he certainly wouldn't have come down there just to pay me a friendly visit. Before he arrived, I had made plans to visit some of the sights around Guatemala City and when he showed up, he took it upon himself to accompany me."

Elyssa softly laughed. "I was quite discourteous to him on more than one occasion, but I found myself -- at times -- enjoying his company. In fact, by the end of my time there, I think…" Elyssa paused and took in a deep breath, causing Edward and Maddy to hold theirs.

"I think I had fallen in love with him."

Maddy clasped her hands together. "I just knew it! Elyssa, I knew there was something between you. And Will? How does he feel?"

Elyssa winced. "Well, that's where it gets a little tricky. You see, I did something rather foolish the day I came home."

"What was that, dear?" Edward asked.

Elyssa looked down at her plate of food, stirring a mound of mashed potatoes with her fork. She finally answered, "I adamantly refused his offer to fly home in the company jet and accused him of all sorts of horrid things."

"But why?" Maddy's face exhibited the shock she felt.

Elyssa shook her head. "I was misinformed and mislead. Anyway, needless to say, in addition to going today to see what he was doing with the memorials, I needed to go see him alone so that I could apologize."

"And?" her aunt asked.

With teasing eyes, Elyssa scooped up some mashed potatoes and slowly brought the fork up to her mouth. Just as she was about to take a bite, her uncle put up his hand and stopped her.

"Don't you dare take that bite until you tell us what we're dying to know!"

Feigning ignorance, Elyssa shook her head. "What do you want to know?"

"What happened!" they both declared at the same time.

Elyssa smiled as she put down the fork. "I think things went well. He doesn't seem to be harboring any anger or resentment toward me. He even asked if he could come out and see me at the house I'm working on."

Elyssa waited to share a little more about her time with Will for later in the evening while she was alone with her aunt. She gave her a more detailed explanation of what had happened in Guatemala, and in particular, about George Westham and how she had been deceived by him.

When Elyssa went to bed that night, she was kept awake by a rapidly beating heart and a mind full of anticipation about the next time she would see William Denton.

~~*

The week proved to be a very demanding and frustrating time for Elyssa at the house. As work continued and more furniture and accessories were delivered, she found her days quite full. The one consolation that kept her going was anticipating Will's visit. He had called and told her he would stop by on Thursday. She wanted as much accomplished by then so she would be ready for his visit.

Elyssa was one who paid attention to detail and therefore she insisted that work be redone if it didn't satisfy her. By Wednesday, when two suppliers had not been able to meet her shipping deadline, something had been delivered wrong, and a painting job had not been done to her expectations, she was ready to pull her hair out.

She had come to the house that morning truly hoping for a respite. She desired for nothing more than for something to go right! She tied up her hair in a ponytail with a bandana and put on an old oversized shirt that had been in her uncle's give away pile. She was planning to use a lot of her own elbow grease as she added some texture to a couple of the walls that had been painted to give them an aged look.

It was an exceptionally busy day with sub-contractors coming and going. At one time she must have counted at least twelve in the house, side-stepping one another. Occasionally, she had to answer a question or give some helpful, yet firm, direction to the workers.

As Elyssa painstakingly began working with the paint, glaze, and some other tools of her trade, she hoped there would be no further interruptions.

She had just put the final touches on the wall when a worker called out that there was someone to see her. She wiped her face with her shirtsleeve, brushing back some wayward strands of hair that had escaped from her bandana. A few splotches of paint dotted her face, but the delivery man certainly wouldn't care.

When she walked toward the front, the worker told her he was outside on the porch.

"Thanks!" Elyssa called, wiping her hands on an old paint-laden rag that she carried tucked in her jeans pocket.

When she stepped out, her eyes looked out on the long, circular drive for a delivery truck. When all she saw were cars, her gaze drifted down the long porch.

Elyssa froze when she saw that the *someone* to see her was Will and he was now seated on the porch swing. She reached for the doorframe to give herself support as she pondered why he had come a day early. Despite the fact that she was not expecting him and knew that everything from her clothes to her hair was in disarray, she had the most incomprehensible feeling that he belonged there. He was the last person she expected to see right now, but oddly, it seemed so right.

As Elyssa watched him, his long legs stretched out before him gently propelling the swing to sway, he seemed a most contradictory subject. Elyssa knew he had to be a busy man; she had determined early on in their acquaintance that Pemberleo was his whole life. Yet here he was, idly sitting in the porch swing as if he had nothing better to do. She smiled at the picture he made and she finally willed her feet to move and walked toward him.

As she drew close, he heard her footsteps and turned, quickly bringing himself to his feet. "Hello, Elyssa."

"Hi!" she answered as she continued toward him. She ran her fingers up to her hair and upon feeling the bandana, she quickly pulled it off, and shook her head to loosen her hair. "How are you?"

"I'm fine. I was just enjoying the view. I like how the swing is positioned in the corner here so you can look out both directions. Most swings would be either looking directly to the front or to the back."

"Well it helps that it's a wrap-around porch," Elyssa laughed as she waved her hand in a partial circle.

She tilted her head at him. "I didn't expect you until tomorrow."

"I hope it's not an inconvenience. I see that you're pretty busy in there. I was coming out this way and thought I'd stop by. I left you a message on your phone."

Elyssa reached into the pocket of her large shirt and pulled out her phone. "I've been on my cell phone so often today that I neglected to check whether I had any messages. Someday I'll get used to having one of these things." As she looked down, a sharp huff escaped. "It appears I have *three* messages."

"Do you want to check them? I only left one of them, so you've got two others to deal with."

"No, that's OK. They can wait."

Will extended his hand to the swing. "Would you care to sit down?"

"Sure, but don't you want to see the house?"

He smiled. "We've got time."

She sat down next to him and let him guide the swaying of the swing with his feet. He seemed content to enjoy the view and the silent camaraderie between them.

"Are you enjoying the work?" he finally asked.

"Oh, yes! At times, however, it can be quite a monumental task overseeing everyone and everything." Elyssa couldn't stop herself from looking down at her phone as she wondered what those other two calls were.

"I can certainly relate," Will assured her.

As much as Elyssa was enjoying the reprieve from her work and most certainly, Will's company, she felt restless, going over in her mind what needed to be done and whether or not the workers inside were doing what they needed to do. She looked down at the phone again, held tightly in her hand.

Will looked over at her. "Are you sure you don't want to check on those calls?"

"Do you mind? I've had a few problems that I'm trying to iron out."

"Go ahead."

Elyssa stood up and walked over to the edge of the porch as she retrieved her first call. She rolled her eyes and a look of exasperation permeated her features. As she pressed for the second call, she relaxed and a smile appeared. She turned to Will. "This is your message."

Elyssa felt a wave of giddiness flood her as she listened to his voice. She turned away from him so he wouldn't be able to see the delighted smile on her face. *How silly!* she thought, to be feeling this way over a simple phone message when he was sitting no more than a few feet away!

She rather liked the way he said her name, however, and smiled as she furtively pressed "save," so she could listen to his voice at a later time.

Unfortunately, the final message brought back the scowl to her face.

When she had finished, Will asked, "More bad news?"

Elyssa sat back down, determined to enjoy her visit with him. "I am having trouble with one particular vendor. The store I ordered from has been so helpful, trying to get to the bottom of it. This last call was Janelle, who owns the store with her husband. She has been trying to track down something I ordered. She told me that she wasn't getting anywhere with the company; that they didn't seem to have a knowledgeable person anywhere that she could talk to."

Elyssa pocketed her phone and folded her hands in her lap. Will had stretched out one arm along the back of the swing and she could feel its presence touching softly behind her head. He appeared so calm and serene and the mere presence of his arm near her had a calming effect on her. As they fell into an easy conversation of light topics, Elyssa became more relaxed.

"Are you encountering a lot of problems on the job?" Will asked, somewhat apprehensively.

"It's like a dream job, but it hasn't gone as smoothly as I would have liked."

"I'm sorry to hear that," Will commented as Elyssa's phone rang.

She offered a quick, "Excuse me," and reached for it.

"Hello? This is Elyssa Barnett."

Will watched and listened silently as Elyssa grew more frustrated. Her tone and color heightened as she stood up and walked to the edge of the porch, leaning against the rail. As she began to demand immediate resolution to the problem, she turned and noticed Will watching her.

She stopped in mid-sentence as she wondered what he must be thinking of her. She couldn't help but recall their time in Guatemala and how irritated she was at him when he took all those phone calls and sounded so harsh.

Her voice immediately softened. "Please just try to right this situation as quickly as possible. Thank you."

Elyssa ended the call and sat down again next to him. He said nothing and that made her feel more ashamed.

"I guess it's easy to get a little… consumed by a job," she said haltingly.

"When you want it done right, sometimes people need a little… prodding." Will stood up and reached for her hand. "Why don't we take a look inside the house, now?"

Elyssa lifted her hand to his and he gave it a gentle tug, helping her out of the swing. As she came to her feet and he turned to walk toward the front door, his hand fully surrounded hers. She didn't remember taking any steps; she was quite sure she was floating.

When they reached the front door, she realized that Will just now had the perfect opportunity to defend himself against her accusations that he was consumed with his work -- and yet he didn't. He merely offered that when you want a job done right, you need to put a little effort into it. She wondered how she had come to deserve even his friendship. It was something she was beginning to treasure.

Once they stepped indoors, Elyssa's attention was drawn away from him by one of the workers needing her advice on something. Will took it upon himself to wander around the living room, looking at everything with great interest.

He was very pleased with what he saw. It had been difficult for him to envision a home when this house was being built, but even with only a portion of it finished, he felt a sense of belonging in it. She had done a brilliant job and he wouldn't have wanted anything different. As he waited for Elyssa, he walked over to the corner of the room where a collection of furniture had been delivered and was out of the way of the workers. As he examined it, he appreciated that she had ordered furnishings that were practical as well as pleasing to the eye. She had incorporated a mixture of fabrics, dark woods, and an occasional touch of suede or leather.

He knew that, God forbid, if she chose to return to her life in Santa Ynez without him, this house would still suit him perfectly. He knew it would be because Elyssa had been the one to decorate it. Now in seeing it, he truly appreciated her and her talent. But more than that, he hoped she would stay.

He walked over to a large reclining chair and sat down to wait until Elyssa returned. He gave in to the urge to lean back and stretch out in it, bringing his hands together and clasping them under his head.

He momentarily closed his eyes, and when Elyssa returned, she laughed to herself when she saw where he was. It was, after all, the memory of him in the recliner at the village that prompted her to buy this one. She walked over and he opened one eye.

"Caught me sleeping on the job!" he teased.

"I'm sorry, Will. This must truly bore you."

Will brought the chair to its upright position and stood up. "You couldn't be more wrong."

The look he gave her sent shivers throughout.

"So what do you think?" she forced herself to ask him.

While keeping his eyes on her, he answered, "I like what I see very much."

It took every ounce of strength for Elyssa to mutter, "I'm glad you like it."

Their attention was solely fixed on one another, but the movement of the workers inside suddenly caught Will's attention.

Will took Elyssa's arm. "Come. Let's step back outside."

They walked out and when they came to the steps of the front porch, Will stopped and turned to Elyssa.

Taking in a large gulp of air and an even bigger step of faith, Will asked, "Would you like to go out with me on Friday night?"

Elyssa turned and looked up at him, her eyes widened in surprise. "You mean on a date?"

Will let out a nervous chuckle. "If that's what they still call it these days, then yes, a date."

"Oh," Elyssa said softly, her mind having difficulty comprehending this.

Elyssa's pause gave Will reason to experience a slight alarm, but he quickly added, "I thought we could go to Old Town, eat dinner and take in a movie. Nothing fancy."

"Sounds wonderful. I'd like that very much," Elyssa said as she broke into a disarming smile.

Will breathed out a sigh of relief. "I'm very glad to hear that. I debated between that and bumper cars." A smile widened on his face, matching Elyssa's, and they both chuckled.

"I'll come by and pick you up at your aunt and uncle's around seven o'clock, if that's OK. Can you give me their address?" At least he remembered to ask for the address. He really did need it this time, although he'd be able to find out easily enough merely by asking Emily for it.

Elyssa wrote it down for him and he tucked it into his shirt pocket. "I'll see you on Friday, then."

Elyssa nodded. "Yes, Friday."

The two stood staring at each other, neither seeming to want to move. Will only managed to take one step backwards down the first step of the porch.

"Well," said Will finally, "I suppose you ought to get back to work."

Elyssa sighed. "Yes, I suppose I should."

When Elyssa still didn't move, Will reached out and took her hand. He drew it towards him, prompting her to take a small step forward. He looked down as his fingers closed around it.

With a pensive gleam, he lifted his eyes back up to Elyssa and they stared silently at each other, the warmth of his hand enfolding hers. Ever so slowly, he brought her hand up, bending his head slightly as he brushed the very tip of her fingers with his lips.

He smiled at her and reluctantly released her hand. "I couldn't be happier that you are here, Elyssa. I couldn't be happier." He reached out and with the back of his fingers, he gently stroked her cheek. "I'll see you on Friday."

He turned to walk to his car and Elyssa couldn't move as she watched him leave, reaching out for the porch rail to keep her balance. She brought her hand up and pressed her fingertips against her cheek, feeling a lingering warmth from his kiss and touch that pervaded deep within her very soul.

Chapter 27

Elyssa worked with a new joy and determination for the remainder of the week, looking with much anticipation to Friday. There were, unfortunately, a few more problems, but instead of causing her frustration, the mere expectation of her date with Will eased her troubled mind. In the midst of receiving a problematic phone call or encountering an unexpected delay, she was able to keep a smile on her face and a skip to her stride.

Elyssa left work early on Friday to get ready for her evening out with Will. Each time she thought of it, she would shamelessly giggle.

Her aunt joined her in her bedroom as she put on the finishing touches to her makeup and she took Elyssa's hand. "Your uncle and I are so happy for you! We both feel that he is a very good man!"

Elyssa laughed. "You don't have to worry about how I feel about him anymore, Maddy. I've changed. My opinion of him has changed." She turned and gave her aunt a smile. "And I think *he* has changed."

"Good. Now just relax and enjoy yourself, tonight."

"If I can just get rid of these first-date jitters. I'm too old for this!"

"You never felt nervous around him before, did you?" her aunt asked.

"No," Elyssa couldn't repress a nervous chuckle. "I was too angry at him most of the time and making sure he felt every ounce of blame I directed at him!" As she gave her hair a final brushing, she said, "A mere two months ago he was truly the last man in the world that I would ever have wanted to go out with!"

As the time drew nearer to seven, Elyssa grew more and more nervous, pacing back and forth and checking the clock.

"Seven o'clock will be here when seven o'clock comes," her uncle teased. "Not any sooner and not any later."

"Do I look OK?" she asked for the umpteenth time.

"Elyssa, you look beautiful. Besides, you really don't have to worry about how you look tonight," Edward stated emphatically, a teasing glint in his eye.

Elyssa directed her eyes at him. "Why do you say that?"

Edward laughed. "Because if he was willing to ask you out despite the way you looked at the house on Wednesday, he can have no objection to your appearance tonight!"

"Oh!" Elyssa pounded her fists to her side. "Don't remind me how terrible I looked that day!"

A car's headlights shining into the window gave everyone an early announcement of Will's arrival.

Elyssa stood up and began to walk to the back of the house. "I'll be doing some last minute touch-ups. You may announce me in a minute or two," Elyssa gave a dipping curtsey and then scurried off.

Edward and Maddy glanced at each other with raised eyebrows. Their niece certainly had it bad and if William Denton was willing to overlook the way Elyssa treated him, he certainly was not one to let get away. They eagerly anticipated having a few moments with the man all to themselves.

Edward answered the door when Will knocked and gave him a cheerful greeting. "Well, my good man, it is a pleasure to see you again!"

"Thank you, Sir. It's a pleasure to see you."

Will stepped in and Edward ushered him into the living room. "Come, have a seat. Elyssa will be ready in a minute."

As he walked in, Maddy could not suppress the smile on her face. He looked almost as nervous as Elyssa had. "Good evening, Will."

"Hello, Mrs. Garner."

"Call me Maddy; everyone does."

Will nodded as he sat down. He brought his hands together and tapped the edges of his fingers against each other. Looking about him, he said, "You have a nice home here. This is a very pleasant area."

"Thank you. We like it." Maddy smiled as she considered their house was probably much smaller than what he was used to. She supposed he had a grand house north of Chicago, probably along the lake, where most of the exclusive mansions were located.

"We've really enjoyed exploring the different parks and lakes around here," Edward said. "If the weather holds up, we are all going to have a picnic tomorrow. It's supposed to be one of the last pleasant days before the cool days of autumn come upon us. I hope to find a lake and do some fishing."

"Can't think of anything that sounds nicer," Will said, his hands now clasped together tightly.

"Would you care to tag along?" Edward asked. "You did say you could show me some good fishing spots around here."

"I did, didn't I?" responded Will with a smile.

"If you aren't too busy," Maddy added, "we would love to have you join us."

Will nodded his head. "I think I would like that. I could suggest a few places if you like." He looked over at Edward. "I know of a few lakes that are very well-stocked, in fact."

Edward leaned back and clasped his hands together. "Wonderful!"

"Can I bring anything?" Will looked to Maddy.

"No, no," Maddy waved her hand in the air. "Just bring yourself. Why don't you come by a little before eleven. We thought we would leave before noon to give us time to find a nice place to have lunch."

As Will thought about this, he couldn't think of a better time to tell Elyssa about the house. He didn't want to tell her tonight. He wanted to have at least one whole evening with her without there being anything that would ruin it. He was fairly certain that she was beginning to enjoy his company. The picnic tomorrow might provide the perfect opportunity to tell her -- at least when the picnic was over and he had some time with her by herself. Maybe afterwards, he would take her over to the house and tell her there.

Maddy stood up. "Let me tell Elyssa you're here."

As she started to walk out, Elyssa stepped into the hallway. An exchanged look between aunt and niece let each other know everything was just fine.

Will turned and saw Elyssa step into view. As she walked toward him with a smile directed specifically at him, his heart leapt. "Hello, Elyssa. You look very nice."

"Thank you. Let me get my coat."

Will told the Garners he would have Elyssa home by about one or two. Elyssa thought that was sweet of him and Edward responded as if he expected nothing less.

"We appreciate that, Will." Edward gave him a firm pat on the shoulder. "Not that we are over-protective of her or anything, but our niece is very dear to us and it is good to know when to expect her home."

Elyssa grabbed her coat and they walked to the door.

"Here, let me help you with that," Will offered. "It's getting chilly out there."

Once she had her coat on, they walked out and the Garners offered their wishes for a good evening.

~~*

A very congenial atmosphere surrounded the two as they left the home. Elyssa was happily surprised, after just a few minutes, to find that her jitters had ceased. She realized with a start that there was little more she could do to disappoint him. No more than two months ago, she had done everything within her power to push him away. She had accused and abused him and yet he still had been willing to ask her out on a date!

He had seen the very worst of her. No, she had no reason to be nervous. She chuckled as she also considered that the plush interior and smooth riding of his small luxury car helped relax her immeasurably.

Will asked Elyssa if she liked Mediterranean food. When she replied in the affirmative, he suggested they eat at a place fairly close by, rather than drive all the way into Chicago. He claimed that it had some of the best food around.

As they walked in, she found herself admiring the décor. It had a very intimate and welcoming ambiance. Will was greeted by name and they were taken to a table back in the corner.

Will described his favorite entrees to Elyssa, and trusting his judgment, she asked him to order for her. He ordered two different meals and when they came, they ended up splitting each in half and shared.

Over the course of the meal, they talked about the picnic the following day and how he was looking forward to it. Will updated her on the progress of the memorials. Elyssa asked him about Gina and how she was enjoying her first semester at college.

"She says she enjoys it. It's been a little lonely not having her around. I wonder whether she misses me as much as I do her."

Elyssa looked down as she suddenly thought about how much she missed

Janet. Tears didn't begin to spill, but she did take in a steadying breath.

Will extended his hand and placed it over hers. "I'm sorry. I just wasn't thinking."

"No, it's OK, really." She felt strengthened by the touch of his hand. "It's only natural for you to miss her. So how often have you gone out to visit her?"

Will looked at her. "What do you mean?"

Elyssa shook her head playfully. "She told me that you planned to come out every other weekend to make sure she was studying instead of out partying."

Will narrowed his eyes at Elyssa as he watched her try to wipe the smile from her face. "She didn't really tell you that, did she?"

Elyssa laughed. "Oh, yes! She said you were quite overprotective and she was looking forward to finally being out from under your strict control."

Will glanced down with a grimace and then back up, only to see Elyssa laughing. "I'm teasing, Will. She actually told me you would probably visit her just to make sure she was getting out and not locking herself in her room studying all the time."

"You had me worried, Elyssa. I wondered whether I even knew my own sister."

When they had finished their meal, Will reached over for Elyssa's hand. "After the picnic tomorrow, would you have some time to go somewhere with me? I have something I want to show you."

Elyssa saw a hint of apprehension cloud his eyes, but she quickly dismissed it. "I don't have any plans tomorrow other than the picnic, Will. I would love to. What is it?"

Giving her hand a squeeze, a hesitant smile touched his lips. "You'll see."

Elyssa smiled. "The last time you were this secretive, it was an afternoon of bumper cars."

"Not this time," Will replied somberly.

After dinner, they drove into Chicago and Elyssa found Will easy to talk with. He was never inclined to dominate the conversation, but always had intelligent comments or wise insights to contribute. He was also always eager to discover Elyssa's views on things.

As they made their way into Chicago, Elyssa was quite surprised how quickly the time passed despite the distance and traffic. When they came into Old Town, Will easily maneuvered into a parking garage and they set out to walk.

They ambled down streets filled with eclectic shops and restaurants, peeking in windows and commenting to one another on the window displays. When they reached a home decorating store, Elyssa insisted they go in.

Filled with everything from antiques to classics to modern, Elyssa knew this was just the type of place to find that one thing that would add a special something to a room. As they walked in, they were welcomed in by the owner.

"Are you looking for anything in particular?" he asked.

"I'll know it when I see it, "Elyssa responded.

Will walked somewhat behind her as she closely inspected a few items. Her fingers trailed lightly over the wooden pieces and she opened drawers to see the quality of workmanship. As she walked through the store, Will's eye settled on a collection of rare, collectable books in a beautiful antique bookcase. He pulled a book out and carefully opened it.

He could easily see that the binding was in perfect condition and it seemed as though the pages, although fragile, were completely intact.

The owner walked over. "This is a rare find, indeed. The gentleman who owned them died recently and his family sold them at an estate sale. We thought it would be nice to keep the books with the bookcase, so we're selling them together. I know it's a fairly high price. If we can't sell them that way, we'll have to begin to sell them individually."

Elyssa walked over and looked at the book in Will's hand and the ones in the case.

"Are they all in such excellent shape?" she asked.

The owner nodded. "We wondered if they had ever been read!"

"Hmmm!" Will said, glancing down at the price. "This is certainly something I'll have to consider."

Elyssa didn't say anything to Will, but she thought it would look great in the den of the house she was working on. Even though she wasn't hired to finish that room -- yet -- she'd keep the books and bookcase in mind. She may even have to conspire to get it before Will did.

By the time they left the store, Elyssa had made several mental notes of things there that she might like to come back out and buy for the house.

Elyssa was really enjoying herself. The atmosphere and the variety of stores and the buildings that housed them did not cease to keep her interest. She was pleasantly surprised to discover that Will had very similar tastes to her own.

The street became more and more crowded with people. Will reached out for Elyssa's hand and as his fingers closed around hers, he smiled as he felt her fingers close gently around his.

They walked for some time up one side of the street and down the other. When they were almost to the garage where his car was parked, he suggested they drive to the Film Center so they would get there more quickly. They returned to the car and were soon on their way to the theater.

When they arrived, the title of the movie was spelled out on the marquee. Elyssa didn't recognize the language, but felt reassured that it must be a good movie because of the number of people in line.

When they walked past the people in line and toward the ticket taker, Elyssa looked at him curiously.

"I already have the tickets," he said, as he reached into his pocket.

They walked in and he handed the tickets to the man at the door. They were directed to go the opposite direction that everyone else was going.

"That's odd," Elyssa said. "Everyone else is going into *that* theater."

"Well, it does have two theaters. This one is smaller, I think."

Elyssa briefly raised her eyebrows in surprise and followed Will, still clinging to his hand.

When they entered the theater, Elyssa was surprised to see that it was empty. "Oh, goodness! Are you sure we're in the right place?"

"Yes," he said confidently. "Where would you prefer to sit?"

"How about right in the center of the theater?"

"Here?" Will asked as they came to a row that fit Elyssa's description.

"This looks great."

They walked toward the middle of the row and sat down. "Do you want some popcorn or a drink?"

"No," Elyssa answered as she looked around her again. "I'm fine."

Elyssa was just about to ask Will again if he was sure they were in the right theater when the lights dimmed. As the name of the movie appeared and the music played in the background, Elyssa gasped.

"The Umbrellas of Cherbourg!" she exclaimed.

"No, I believe that says, *Les Parapluies de Cherbourg.*" The French words flowed smoothly out of his mouth. "Have you seen it before? If you have, we can leave."

"Yes, but no! I don't want to leave," she declared as she realized he probably could speak French as well as Spanish.

She suddenly began digging in her purse.

"What are you looking for?" Will asked.

"A tissue! Oh, why can I never find one when I need one?"

Will reached into his coat pocket for a handkerchief. "Here. Take my handkerchief, but do you really think you'll need one?"

"Most definitely!"

Elyssa looked around her again. I can't imagine why no one else wants to watch this movie! It's wonderful!"

"So you think it's good?"

Elyssa let out a big sigh. "Words can't describe it. Just be prepared, Will. They sing throughout the whole movie. Look," she said, as she pointed to the screen. "Even the mechanics in the garage sing their lines."

Will lifted his eyebrows to that, smiling to himself over Elyssa's enthusiasm. He then reached over for her hand.

Very quickly Elyssa forgot that they were the only ones in the theater. She was lost in the sights and sounds of this movie that she and Janet used to love to watch. It was one thing to watch it on TV, but on a full screen it was so much more enjoyable. She was also very much aware of her hand in his as occasionally he would stroke it with his thumb or give it a gentle squeeze.

Will smiled when he'd catch Elyssa humming the tune to a familiar sounding song -- the song, "I Will Wait For You" that he heard her sing in Guatemala. The song and its words had haunted him, and he had wondered just how long he would have to wait for her. He felt a little more confident that things were going well, but he still had that major hurdle before him when he'd tell her the house was his. But not tonight. He cast a sideways glance at her and hoped that when he told her tomorrow, she would understand.

The story of a young couple in love was very sentimental. Both struggled financially and made some decisions based on that.

As it neared the end, Will realized it was not ending the way he would have wished and began to realize why Elyssa needed a tissue.

As Elyssa wiped her eyes, Will fought back the swelling up of heartache that he began to feel for this couple. He couldn't help but wonder if this would be his and Elyssa's fate. He held on tightly to Elyssa's hand as the movie came to an end.

"Wasn't that the most beautiful movie you've ever seen?"

"I can think of some that end a little happier," Will tried to joke.

"I think that's what makes it so special. It's like real life. We have no guarantees."

"No, we don't," he answered a little somberly. He had no guarantee that his plan to bring Elyssa here would sit well with her once she was told the truth.

They stepped out from their row of seats and again Elyssa looked about her. "People just don't know what they're missing!"

When they came into the lobby, Elyssa excused herself to go to the ladies room. While inside, she touched up her makeup and brushed through her long, dark hair. *It has been fun,* she thought with a smile as she looked at her reflection in the mirror. *Who would ever have imagined this?*

As she walked out, she looked around for Will. Not seeing him, she began walking toward the front. A small sign caught her attention.

Theaters available for rental. See management.

Her eyes widened and she let out an audible gasp. "Oh my goodness! That's the only reasonable explanation why we sat in an empty theater!"

She looked ahead and saw Will leaning with his back against a wall up ahead. As she walked toward him, she asked herself, *How did he know this is one of my favorite movies? How did he know?*

"All set?" he asked as she came up to him.

"Yes, I think so."

They returned to the car and drove a short distance before Will pulled over. "I know it's late," he said, "but it's such a beautiful night. Would you like to walk along the river?"

"I'd love to," Elyssa answered.

They walked along Michigan Avenue. As they looked down toward the river, the shimmering lights from the city danced across the water. Coming to the Michigan Avenue Bridge, they began to walk across it.

"It's beautiful here, Will."

"They have dinner cruises along here and architectural tours. I thought maybe we could come back and do that someday."

Elyssa stopped and looked out over the water. "I'd really like that." Then she turned and leaned her back up against the rail, looking up at Will. "Thank you for a wonderful evening," With a crooked smile and the raising of one eyebrow she added, "I don't believe I've ever had anyone rent a theater for me before."

Will inhaled slowly at Elyssa's acknowledgment and glanced toward the ground. Softly, he said, "I must confess that I've never rented a theater for anyone before tonight." A gnawing at the back of his mind reminded him that there was something else he had done that he needed to tell her. Pushing it down so their evening together would end on a pleasant note, he said, "I'm glad you've enjoyed yourself."

He looked back up at Elyssa and despite the beauty of the city around them and the glistening water below, all he could see was her.

He reached out and fingered a lock of Elyssa's hair, running his fingers down its length. He seemed reluctant to release the curl as a ringlet at the end wound around his finger.

Elyssa remained motionless, barely able to breathe, as she watched him lift his eyes to hers and ever so slowly lean in toward her. She closed her eyes as she felt his lips kiss her cheek.

Will pulled back slightly after a moment to gauge her response. When he found her eyes closed, he brought his hand up to her chin and with his fingers, he tenderly turned her head just enough so that he could easily press his lips to hers.

Elyssa moved in closer and slipped her arms around his waist, latching them together behind him.

When at last they pulled away, words seemed difficult to come by.

Later, when he drove into the Garners' driveway, he stopped the car and turned to Elyssa, taking her hand in his. "Elyssa, I enjoyed being with you tonight."

"Me too," she replied.

He sat quietly for a moment, simply watching her face in the darkness of the car; the only light being from the porch. He finally opened his door and got out of the car and walked around to let Elyssa out. When he took her hand, he kept a firm grasp on it as they walked to the front door. As they stepped up on the porch, he clasped his other hand over hers.

His eyes traveled down to their entwined hands as he began to stroke hers. He only wished he could impart the depth of his feelings to her so that she would not respond to his confession tomorrow with anger. He finally released her hand and pulled her close, wrapping his arms around her. When he felt her arms go around his waist, he turned his head and lowered it, resting his cheek on the top of her head. As he inhaled the fragrance of her hair, he wished with all his might that he could make the time stand still to this very moment. Finally, he drew back and lowered his head, kissing her gently.

"Good night, Elyssa. I'll see you tomorrow."

Elyssa said good night and stepped inside, closing the door behind her. Will stood looking at it for several moments. He took in a deep breath as he realized this evening with her had been perfect. He could not have enjoyed himself more. As he fingered his set of keys, looking for the right one, he contemplated what tomorrow would bring. He could only hope she would understand.

Chapter 28

Elyssa closed the door behind her as she came in from her date with Will and collapsed against it. She brought her hand up over her heart as she felt its clamorous beating and took in a few breaths that were sorely needed. When she finally garnered her strength and pulled herself away from the door, she turned and took a quick peek out the peephole. She saw Will fingering his set of keys before he turned and walked to his car.

Elyssa knew she wouldn't be able to sleep until she told her aunt a little about their evening. She tiptoed down the hall and softly tapped on the door to their room. Maddy promptly got out of bed and put on a robe. She stepped out and closed the door so the two of them could talk and not awaken Edward.

Elyssa didn't know where to begin, but began in hurried, excited whispers. "Maddy, from the moment we were together in the car, I felt so at ease. I really enjoyed his company. We went to a restaurant fairly close by. You'll have to try it. Then we drove into Chicago. We walked through Old Town, going into an occasional store and looking through the display windows. Then you won't believe what he did!"

Maddy took in a deep breath as if she were exhausted just listening to her. "What did he do?" she asked with eager anticipation.

"We went to a theater -- actually he called it a film center -- where they show foreign and classic films. There were a lot of people there, but when we walked into the theater, we were the only ones in it!"

"Really? Did anyone else ever come?"

"No! And that's not the only incredible thing. The movie was "Umbrellas of Cherbourg!"

"My! That's one of your favorites!"

"I thought that perhaps the other theater was just showing something everyone wanted to see, but after the movie I saw a sign that stated theaters were available for rental. Maddy," Elyssa said as she took her aunt's hands in hers and inhaled deeply. "He rented the whole theater just for us and arranged for them to show that movie!"

"Had you told him you liked it?"

Elyssa shook her head. "The only thing I can think is that while we were in Guatemala, I sang 'I Will Wait For You.' He must have remembered and either knew that's what movie it was from or he found out."

Maddy gave her niece a knowing nod. "He's a very successful businessman, Elyssa. He is probably very good at remembering things that will help him at a later time."

"I guess!" Now that a condensed version of her date had been relayed to her aunt, Elyssa relaxed and suddenly felt all the weariness of the late hour. She yawned and stretched out her arms. "I'm tired. What time do you want me to get up in the morning to help you get lunch ready for the picnic?"

"Don't you worry about a thing! I prepared most of it this evening while you were out. Now you go to bed and get a good night's sleep!"

"I'll try. Good night, Maddy."

~~*

Elyssa had just begun stirring the next morning when her cell phone rang. She blinked a couple times, trying to get her bearings and reached aimlessly for the phone.

When she picked it up, she looked down and saw that it was Will.

"Hello?"

"Hi, Elyssa. I didn't waken you, did I?"

"Oh, no." Elyssa yawned. "I was just lying in bed trying to find the strength to get up."

There was a pause on Will's end.

"Is everything all right?" Elyssa asked.

"I don't know, yet."

"What is it?"

Elyssa heard Will take in a deep breath. "I received a call this morning from Guatemala. There has been a lot of rain and the villages are having some problem with flooding. Some of our farmers may have lost fields and possibly homes. I'm actually on my jet now heading down there."

"You're on your way to Guatemala?"

"Yes." Will paused a moment. "I'm sorry, Elyssa, but I won't make it to the picnic today."

Elyssa felt a wave of disappointment flood her, but she also felt a deep concern for the villagers. "Do you know which villages were affected?"

"Unfortunately, no. Communication has been slow in coming from the area. I'll call you when I know something."

"I would appreciate that."

"Elyssa, I…" A deep breath swallowed up any additional words.

"Yes?"

"I… uh… I really enjoyed myself last night."

"Me too."

"Well, the jet's about to take off. Hopefully I'll be home in a couple of days. I will want to see you as soon as I return."

"I'll be looking forward to it. Please be careful, OK?"

"I'll be careful." Will turned off his phone and looked out the window of the plane. This was not how he had expected to spend the day, but he needed to go and assess the damage -- not just to the crops -- but possibly to a farmer's whole livelihood. A few more days waiting to tell Elyssa wouldn't hurt.

~~*

Although Elyssa enjoyed the picnic with her aunt and uncle and their children, her heart was somewhere else. She thought about how much she would have enjoyed Will being with them and frequently wondered where he might be and what he might be doing.

She finally heard from him Sunday afternoon and he told her the village that he and Elyssa had visited had not been heavily damaged. He was now setting out for a village on the north side of Lake Atitlan. He didn't know what he would find when he got there. Again, he made a point of telling her that he wanted to see her when he returned and hoped he would be back by the end of the week.

When she started work on Monday, her one consolation was that the living room was almost finished. The furniture and accessories had all arrived and now it was up to her to arrange it. Fortunately, she had a few burly men who could easily move the furniture back and forth until it was exactly as she wanted it.

As they moved the recliner from where it had been to where she wanted it, a small slip of paper fell away. She leaned down to pick it up and was quite surprised to find that it was a parking garage stub from the same one they parked in while walking around Old Town. As she looked at the stamped date and time, she wondered for a moment at the coincidence of someone else being down there at the same time that she and Will were, but was interrupted in her thoughts by the men looking to her for their next set of instructions. She stuffed the stub into her jeans pocket.

She kept tabs on the work going on in the kitchen in between moving things around or hanging something on the wall in the living room. When that room was exactly as she wanted it, she went into the kitchen to talk with the cabinetry man about the center island he was installing. One of the other workers came in with a concerned look on his face.

"Elyssa, there's someone here to see you."

"Oh. Is it a delivery person?"

"Uh, I really don't think so." He skewed up his face. "It's a woman who is demanding to know who's in charge here."

Elyssa gave a questioning raise of her eyebrows. "Did she give her name?"

Catherine something. I didn't quite get her last name."

Elyssa shrugged her shoulders. "Thanks, I'll be out in a minute."

She finished what she was doing and stepped out into the living room to find a somewhat older, very fashionably dressed woman. She was snooping around, looking intently at the furnishings.

"May I help you?" Elyssa asked.

"Exactly what is going on here?" The booming voice of the woman must have penetrated every room and floor of the house.

Elyssa looked at the tall, rather imposing woman who unceremoniously strutted toward her. She came to a stop a mere foot from Elyssa and propped her hands up against her waist, gripping it tightly.

"May I help you?" Elyssa asked again.

"And who are you?" the woman asked contemptuously.

"My name is Elyssa Barnett. What can I do for you?"

"Are you in charge of this travesty?"

Elyssa tensed, not really sure who the lady was or why she was so upset.

"I am the designer, if that's what you would like to know. And you are?"

"I am Catherine Deboer." She spoke as if everyone ought to know that.

"Well, Ms. Deboer, is there something I can help you with?"

She shook her head and let out a huff. "You must know how much this seriously displeases me. It is not at all as it should be."

Elyssa felt a wave of anger sweep over her. "I'm sorry that you feel that way. Are you a relative or acquaintance of Richard Fitzpatrick?"

The lady held her head high and looked down her nose at Elyssa. "Richard Fitzpatrick? Of course I am! I am his aunt!" She leaned in and narrowed her eyes as she spoke. "What has *he* to do with all of this?"

"He hired me, of course."

"Richard?" She leaned in closer as if giving Elyssa a meticulous inspection. "Why would he do that?"

Elyssa shrugged her shoulders. "The house needed to be decorated and he hired me to do it."

"This cannot be! It is impossible! It is not up to him to decide who designs this house. Besides, it was decided from the start that my daughter, Anne, would be the designer!"

"I'm sorry," Elyssa answered apologetically, "but I know nothing about that."

Ms. Deboer turned her head, looking from one thing to another. "She would have done a much more superior job."

Elyssa was quickly losing her composure, but took in a deep breath. "I am sure your daughter would have done a fine job, but for some reason, Mr. Fitzpatrick hired me."

"I still don't understand why! But never mind that. What design firm are you with?"

"Excuse me?"

"I wish to know who you work for! What your credentials are!"

"I work for myself."

"For yourself? How absurd! Where is your place of business? What are your references?"

"I live and work in the Santa Ynez Valley in California."

"Whose homes have you decorated there?"

"You wouldn't recognize anyone's name, Ms. Deboer. But I do have a degree and am just as capable as your daughter would have been!"

Catherine Deboer's hand flew up to her forehead. "This is not acceptable! My nephew knew that my daughter has been interning with the most prestigious design company in Kent, Ohio. The least he could have done was to have consulted with her. But no, instead, he hires some nobody from the middle of nowhere! Look what you have done to this place!"

Elyssa turned to look at the room. To her eye, it was most pleasing.

"I am sorry you feel that way, Ms. Deboer, but everything I have done has been approved by your nephew."

Ms. Deboer gave a sweep with her hand around the room. "Where did you purchase these furniture pieces?"

Elyssa gave her the names of a few of the small shops she bought most of them from. The stern woman shook her finger at Elyssa. "Those stores have no standing with our family! Don't you know who we are? Don't you know that it is expected that we buy from the most esteemed stores?"

Elyssa shook her head. "I am sorry, Ms. Deboer, but I was told that I could design this house the way I saw fit. I thought it was odd that I never met with your nephew, but he has approved everything I have done here."

"My nephew! I am shocked and astonished! How dare he allow some upstart to decorate the house when all along my daughter had been promised the job?" She waved her finger back and forth at Elyssa. "Don't do another thing to this house! I'm going to speak to him at once."

Catherine Deboer turned to look up at the painting hung over the fireplace. "Even that painting of Pemberleigh Manor is wrong! It should have been hung higher! That's the only thing in this room that belongs and even *it* is wrong!"

Elyssa felt her chest tighten. "What did you say?"

"I said, even *it* is wrong!"

"No, you mentioned a name of the painting."

"Pemberleigh. This is Pemberleigh Manor. In England, of course!"

Elyssa felt herself grow dizzy. "Is there… is there any connection between this place Pemberleigh and Pemberleo Coffee?"

Catherine's eyes bore down into Elyssa as if she were an alien. "Pemberleigh is not just some place! And anybody who is anybody knows they both belong to the Denton family!"

Elyssa abruptly turned away as she felt her face flush with confusion. She gripped the back of the chair she was standing aside to help steady her. She reached into both pockets, searching for that parking garage stub she had found earlier. As she pulled it out and stared at the time on it, she found it difficult to formulate a coherent thought.

She turned back to the woman, her voice shaking. "When you said you didn't understand why Richard Fitzpatrick would have hired me, what did you mean?"

"He has nothing to do with this house! It belongs to my nephew William Denton! He owns it. He's the one building the house and I don't know why he would have given his cousin permission to hire you! I must get to the bottom of this!"

Elyssa watched in shock as Ms. Deboer stormed from the house. She collapsed into the chair and leaned her head back closing her eyes. Softly, she said, "You will not find him. He has gone to Guatemala."

Elyssa felt the room spinning around her. *This is Will's house?* She felt as though she could barely breathe. *Why didn't he tell me?*

She buried her head in her hands as she tried to fathom the news she had just received. A worker stepped out from the kitchen and asked if she was all right.

"Yes, I'm fine. I just need to sit down a moment."

"Miss Barnett," he said, "I wouldn't pay any attention to what that lady said. She doesn't know anything. We all think you're doing a spectacular job!"

It was obvious that everyone heard the woman's tirade. Elyssa looked up and attempted to reassure him with a forced smile. "Thanks. I appreciate that."

She sat motionless in the chair as she attempted to think through this whole pretense. Obviously he had driven here last night to sleep instead of going all the way back into Chicago. He dropped her off, and without saying a word to her about the house, he came here.

She could barely bring herself to look around the room as it all seemed so different now. It was one thing to design it for someone she didn't even know, but to find out she'd been designing it for Will -- she didn't know what to think!

Her eyes burned as she held back the tears that were building up, recalling the callous words of Will's aunt and her scathing appraisal of the house. How could she have known how it was to be decorated if she had never met the owner? But she *had* met the owner and he had every opportunity to tell her -- yet he didn't!

Her fists tightened as she wondered why he had kept it a secret from her. Was he laughing to himself when he walked through here the other day? Did he think this was some kind of practical joke? Was this his way of getting even with her for the words she lashed out at him?

Elyssa found a measure of composure and pushed herself up out of the chair to walk into the kitchen. She called out to the men who were working and announced that they could finish up what they were doing and leave. She wanted to lock things up and go home.

Once the last workman had left, she felt the tears begin to pool in her eyes. She looked around her at the finished living room. It was beautiful. Catherine Deboer could say whatever she wanted about the room! Elyssa thought she had done as excellent a job as any prestigious designer could have done!

As she wiped her eyes with the back of her hand, she contemplated Will's actions… his deception… his silence… his manipulation! Elyssa thought of their evening together the other night and could not deny that it was the most wonderful night of her life, but he had said nothing!

She recalled Maddy's words that Will probably remembered and knew how to use information given to him. He must have remembered her casually mentioning how Charlene handed out her business cards to spur her business opportunities. He used that information to bring her here unsuspectingly.

A surge of disappointment crept up within her. Would he always do things so underhandedly with her? Would he always want to have the upper hand?

She found it more and more difficult to think and even breathe inside this house. She needed to get out.

Elyssa walked briskly from room to room, ensuring that everything was locked up before leaving. This time she practically felt Will's presence in each room. She walked to the front door and stepped out, locking it behind her. As she turned, her eyes fastened onto the porch swing. She suddenly recalled her thoughts when she had seen him sitting there last week. She remembered thinking that he looked as though he belonged in it.

Elyssa turned and ran to the car, sliding in and slamming the door. With both hands gripping the steering wheel, she leaned her head over and let her tears spill out.

~~*

When she finally walked into the Garners' home, the door slammed a little harder and her steps were more strident than usual. She walked into the living room where her aunt was reading to her children.

Maddy recognized instantly the look of distress on Elyssa's face. She stood up and placed the children on the floor with the book and told Frederick to turn the pages for Lillian.

Walking over to her niece, she asked, "What is it, Elyssa? What's wrong?" Putting her arm around her, she exclaimed, "You've been crying!"

"I need to sit down."

Maddy walked Elyssa into the dining room, away from the children.

"Tell me what has happened."

In a shaky voice, Elyssa told her what had happened when Will's aunt came by and what she found out from her.

"My word, Elyssa! Will owns the house?"

Elyssa nodded slowly.

"And you're upset?"

"Of course I'm upset! He didn't even have the decency to tell me!"

Maddy patted her arm. "I'm sure that he was planning to, Elyssa." Shaking her head firmly, she added, "I don't think Will kept it a secret to deceive you. Let's give him the benefit of the doubt, here."

"He conveniently lied to bring me here. He knows all too well what I think of manipulation!"

Maddy took Elyssa's hand. "My dear, perhaps it's not as bad as it seems."

Taking a few deep breaths, Elyssa looked up into her aunt's eyes. "I feel so confused right now. I think I hurt more than anything. I hurt because he didn't feel as though he could be forthright with me. I hurt because I thought we had something special between us. I'm angry, though, too. I'm angry that he brought me here through deception and I'm angry because I felt like a fool in front of his aunt who in no uncertain terms denounced my work!"

"Elyssa," her aunt said her name tenderly, "I know this is difficult for you, but don't judge Will too harshly until you hear his side of the story. I can't believe he would have intentionally done anything that would cause you pain."

Elyssa lowered her head into her hands. "You know, a couple of months ago I would have expected this from him."

"But you don't now, do you? The two of you have come so far."

"I think it would be easier to be angry at him. It's not as..." she looked up to her aunt. "It's not as painful."

"I think, young lady, *that* is because you have fallen in love with him."

Elyssa was silent for a while as she looked down at her fingers knitting together.

"And if I may be so bold, Elyssa, I believe he may be in love with you. Love does propel us to do all kinds of things."

"Like hire someone to decorate your home and neglect to tell them you own it?"

Maddy gave her niece a crooked smile and nodded.

"Oh!" Elyssa pounded her fists down on the table. "Is love always this confusing?"

"Sometimes."

Maddy stretched out her arm and placed it over Elyssa's shoulder. "Is there any chance I can see that smile of yours again?"

Elyssa obliged her aunt and gave her a small smile.

"Now, when you talk to him again, will you promise me you will allow him to defend himself before you thrash him with accusations? Will you try to forgive him? I mean, look at the job opportunity he provided you with!"

Elyssa's face drained of all color as she looked at her aunt with eyes widened. "This wonderful job opportunity to further my career as an interior designer has been nothing but a fraud!"

"Now, Elyssa…"

With eyes narrowing, and a sudden realization of the full implications of Will's deceit, she said, "All along I thought I had been chosen to decorate this beautiful home because of my talent; that I had been chosen from a small group of designers on the basis of the designs I submitted, but it wasn't based on my ability at all!"

Maddy reached out her hand and gently covered Elyssa's hand. "I'm sure that he truly appreciates your gift for design."

Elyssa shook her head and looked down. "How am I to know that for certain?" She slowly lifted her head. "Without my knowing it, he's been paying me to stay here! Even though the checks have been signed by Emily, he's the one behind every one of those most generous paychecks!" Tears filled Elyssa's eyes. "Do you know how that makes me feel?"

For the first time in her life, Maddy didn't know how to answer her niece.

As they sat there, Elyssa's cell phone rang. She pulled it out of her purse and looked at the readout. "It's Will."

As she put it back in her purse, Maddy asked, "Aren't you going to answer it? Give him the chance to answer your questions."

"No. I can't talk to him now," Elyssa said as she shook her head, tears streaming down her face. "I assume he has heard from his aunt so he knows I know the truth. I've suffered enough pain. I think I'll let him suffer just a little before I talk to him."

She looked down as the phone's muffled ring continued from inside her purse. "If I do mean anything to him, let him squirm a little as he wonders what I'm thinking right now. Let him go through just a little fear and trepidation about what his actions may have cost him!"

Maddy cocked her head at her niece. "Now don't go and do anything that will ruin things, Elyssa. I think you should answer the phone."

"When I'm ready to talk to him, Aunt, I'll answer."

Chapter 29

If Elyssa had any regrets not answering Will's call, she didn't show it. She patiently waited a few minutes before listening to the message he left on her cell phone. As she listened, she could tell that he wasn't quite sure whether or not she knew the truth.

Hello, Elyssa? This is Will. I... uh... I just... How are you? I was wondering how you were and would like you to call me. I've got my phone, so call me back on this number. I need to talk to you. It doesn't matter how late it is, I need to talk to you.

There was a long pause and a breathy huff. *Call me, Elyssa. Please. Bye.*

An hour later, Will called again. Elyssa reached for the phone and her thumb hovered over the button half tempted to answer it. She abruptly shook her head of any such notion, reminding herself that the secret he kept from her hurt her immeasurably. She waited a few moments before listening to his message.

As she played back that message, Elyssa could readily detect that he was quite a bit more concerned.

Elyssa, this is Will again. All right, I guess now you know. My cousin just called a few minutes ago. Our aunt paid him an unexpected visit and he told me he was fairly certain you know that I own the house and not him -- not Richard Fitzpatrick. Earlier when I called, I had just received a call from my aunt who was very angry and quite incoherent. All I could gather from my conversation with her was that she went to the house and was infuriated with the designer. I'm sorry, Elyssa. I'm sorry for everything. I'm sorry for not telling you and I'm sorry for everything she said. Knowing her as I do, I can only imagine her words. Please call me. I need to talk to you. I was going to tell you about the house after the picnic. Honestly I was. I just hope... I hope you're not angry, but I'm getting a little concerned that you haven't called me back. It doesn't matter what time it is. I'll wait up. Goodbye.

Elyssa turned off the phone in case he called any more that night and she went to bed wondering if she truly knew the real Will.

~~*

Will was in a small village with two other men from Pemberleo as they assessed the damage to a farmer's crop. A thin layer of topsoil had washed down the mountain as the rains pelted the region. Fortunately, this farmer had not suffered much damage.

He received the call from his aunt while ankle deep in mud. He glanced down at his phone when it rang and when he saw who it was he recoiled with distress. She was the last person he was in the mood to talk to. He plucked his feet out of the mud and walked away from the other men before answering, knowing that she was the one person who could cause him to lose his temper. It didn't matter how many times he told her something, if she had her mind set elsewhere, she would rarely let it go.

Girding himself for whatever she was calling about, he answered the phone.

"This is William Denton." He rolled his eyes as he answered this way, but hoped it would pacify his aunt somewhat that he was a successful businessman and not a young, immature boy who needed her counsel.

"William! What have you done?"

Taking a deep breath and contemplating what it was she was angry about this time, he asked, "What do you mean?"

"I mean about this girl who claims to be a designer! You know she can't be experienced! Why was she hired when all along Anne was supposed to get that job? I insist upon knowing!"

Will's jaw dropped as he realized the import of her words. Making a vain attempt to calm himself, he asked very pointedly, "You went out to my house?"

"I most certainly did and you must know how gravely upset I was to see the travesty of this decorating job! You must get rid of that girl!"

"Did you speak…"

"What was this she kept saying about Richard? She made no sense at all."

Letting out a frustrated huff, he clenched his jaw and whispered harshly, "You *did* speak to her!"

Speaking directly into the phone, he asked, "What did you say to her?" He wanted answers and he wanted them fast.

"I told her what you should have told her -- that I was extremely dissatisfied with the work she had done! How could you, William! How could you hire this nobody and give no notice to little Anne, your very own cousin?"

"Did you…"

"You must release her from any further work," Catherine interrupted again. "I told her not to do another thing. I hope she has the sense to leave. Let her go back to California! I can have Anne here in a week or two. She'll make all the improvements you need and fix what that impostor has done. I'm sure Anne won't charge you much at all and you'll get the most superior decorating!"

His aunt spoke so fast and considering her anger as she spoke and his anger as he tried to listen, he wasn't sure he caught all of her words.

Will's hands shook with so much fury that he could barely hold the phone still. "Did you say anything about me?"

"About you? Of course, I did, nephew! I told her that you were out of your mind hiring her! But why did she keep mentioning Richard? I swear, William, that girl didn't seem to know what she was talking about!"

Will was beside himself as she continued to rant and he was finally able to end the call by telling her someone needed to talk to him. He dug his fingers across his scalp as he considered what Elyssa probably went through when his aunt stopped by the house and hurled her accusations against her. He was sure Elyssa endured a scathing assault and wondered if the subject of who owned the house had come up.

Will immediately called Elyssa, not knowing whether or not she had been told by his aunt about him owning the house. He figured he would know once he heard her voice. When she didn't answer the phone, he hoped it was only because she was busy, and he left a friendly, but urgent, request for her to call him back.

When she hadn't returned his call about an hour later, he began to get concerned. When his phone rang and it was his cousin Richard, he quickly answered it.

"Hi, Richard. What can I do for you?"

"You can save me from our aunt!"

"Sorry, no one can do that. You've talked to her?"

"Yeah, and... well, you better do some quick thinking here, man. You need to know that she went to the house and talked to Elyssa!"

Will looked at the ground and scuffed his shoe into the mud. "Unfortunately, I gathered that from a conversation I just had with her. Do you think Elyssa knows?"

"I don't *think* she knows, I *know* she knows!"

A tightening of his chest made it difficult to breathe as he heard his cousin's words. "What did Catherine say?" he demanded, taking several deep breaths.

"She said Elyssa kept mentioning *my* name and Catherine didn't understand what I had to do with hiring her. She was upset about everything -- the stores that Elyssa shopped in, the things she bought, the colors she used -- everything! She was even upset that the picture of Pemberleigh Manor was hung too high and our most diplomatic aunt told her so."

Will closed his eyes as he listened to his cousin. "Do you know exactly what she said to Elyssa?"

"Not exactly, but she said something to the effect that she couldn't believe this girl didn't seem to know anything about Pemberleigh and the Denton family!"

Will let out a frustrated groan. "So she knows."

"Yep, she knows. I hate to say I told you so..."

"Yeah, thanks, Richard. Look, we're heading out to another village in the morning. I'll keep in touch with you. Right now, though, I've got to try and call Elyssa again and hopefully make things right with her."

When Will called Elyssa and got her voice mail again, he decided to tell all, although it wasn't exactly the way he wanted to do it. Doing it this way was not going to win him any points -- not that *any* way would have won him points. He decided to be honest with her and hope for the best.

He and the other two men returned to the small pension they had checked into earlier. It was more primitive than anything he had ever stayed in and having to share a bathroom down the hall did nothing to facilitate the removal of the mud that caked his body. There were several waiting in line to shower and Will decided to do the best he could to clean up with the slow dripping sink in his room. After a while he decided that the water coming from it only spread the mud around and barely removed it.

As he looked at himself in the dingy mirror, he suddenly had a picture of what Elyssa probably thought he was on the inside. Bracing his arms against the sink, he lowered his head and the thought crossed his mind that he didn't deserve her. He wouldn't be surprised if he found out she had returned home, forever grateful to be out of his presence.

He suddenly had a memory of his father telling him he was like a coffee bean. Will shook his head with a mock laugh as he remembered his father admonishing him to take care and not treat his personal life as he would his business. His father used to praise him for his business savvy, but told him he had a lot to learn on a personal level.

"You will not be content with what comes easy to you, William. You must be like the coffee bean that is plucked from its vine, dried, roasted, and ground up in order to be at its best. You will find there are some things not easily won, but well worth the sacrifice fighting for."

Will had been fighting from the very beginning to secure Elyssa's affections. He felt very strongly that Elyssa was worth any sacrifice, but perhaps he had gone about it all wrong. He wondered if his actions had just cost him everything.

Will was grateful he had his own room in the pension because he was too agitated to sleep. He listened as the rain began to fall and thought to himself that nothing was going right. The last thing this place needed was more rain and the only thing he needed was to get through to Elyssa. He tried calling her one more time just after midnight, but his call went straight to her voice mail. She had most likely turned off the phone and his only hope now was that she would listen to his message as he poured his heart out to her.

At five the next morning, when he still could get little sleep, he decided to get up and call one more time. They were leaving for the small village shortly and he wanted to let her know. He didn't know whether she even cared, but he called and told her of his plans all the same.

~~*

A restless night afforded little slumber for Elyssa as her body and mind continued to toss and turn relentlessly. Will's deceptive actions and his silence had stunned and hurt her. She couldn't help but consider all the implications and ramifications of the fact that Will owned the house she had been decorating. She also couldn't push aside his aunt's tirade. While she didn't doubt her designing ability and was quite satisfied with what she had done with the house, the woman's words had hurt just as much as Will's silence had.

When she awoke the next morning after just a couple hours of sleep, she snatched up her phone and saw that Will had called two more times after that last call. He had called a little after midnight and at five in the morning. A sly smile indicated Elyssa's satisfaction that he had not slept well, either.

She listened to the third message.

Ok, Elyssa. I know that you must be angry since you're not calling me back and I don't blame you. But you must believe me when I say that this whole thing was done because I care for you. No, it's more than just caring. I... I love you. I think I've loved you from the moment you lashed out at me at the wedding rehearsal dinner when I announced I was sending Chad and Janet to

Guatemala. I know that sounds ridiculous, but it's true. When we were in Guatemala, I savored each day with you -- even when you were ruthlessly angry with me! Elyssa, I couldn't think of any other way to bring us back together. More than anything else, I wanted you here and I wasn't sure you would come if I just outright asked you. Please believe me and I beg you to forgive me, Elyssa. Please call.

Elyssa could barely move as she listened to his words. Her heart pounded with increased measure as he expressed his feelings for her. A tinge of guilt swept over her as she listened to his pleading voice and his heartfelt confession.

"He loves me!" she said softly with a smile and quickly hit the key to listen to his final message.

Hi, Elyssa. I know you're probably sleeping, but I can't. It's begun to rain here in the village again, which isn't good, because the land and hillsides are saturated. I'm going to be leaving with two others soon to travel to a village that had some of the worse flooding in the area to see if we can help in any way with the rescues and recovery. Will paused and Elyssa could hear him take a deep breath. *I love you.*

Again Elyssa smiled at his words of love, but this time she felt a little concern. He didn't speak at all in this last message about the house. She suddenly realized his voice had an urgency to it; almost as if he was going to be putting himself at risk.

Elyssa listened to his last two messages several more times. His words -- his very voice, in fact -- soothed her aggrieved heart and helped bolster her confidence that he had done it all because he loved her. His justification for his actions didn't necessarily make them right, but they certainly did help ease her critical mindset. She sat down on her bed, looking down at her phone, feeling a bit sheepish for the way she felt and acted last night. She was grateful she hadn't called him, however, for she may have said some things that she would have later regretted.

Maddy had also told her the night before that she believed Will loved her, but coming from her aunt had not been as reassuring. Even with all of the indications that Will cared, from his helping her in Guatemala to renting the theater for just the two of them, Elyssa realized she had a difficult time believing *she* was the one he loved.

Why me? she asked herself.

She was interrupted from her speculations by a tapping on her door.

"Yes?"

Maddy peered in. "Edward is watching the morning world news in the other room. He said there's a special news report from Guatemala on next!"

Elyssa threw on a robe and quickly came into the living room, her aunt following on her heels. They waited while several tedious commercials played before their eyes. When the news returned, the picture on the television was like an arrow piercing through Elyssa's heart as she saw people wading through mud. The newscaster's voice was ominous.

"Heavy rains overnight have caused several areas in the remote villages around Lake Atitlan to suffer landslides as the ground had already become heavily saturated from rains last week. Numerous rescue teams have set out for one small village that seems to be hardest hit. We have a breaking news report about a team of three Americans who set out for one of the villages early this morning and are presently missing. It is believed that a road may have been washed away and their whereabouts are uncertain. The names have not been released and everything is being done to find them as well as aid those who have lost homes and property. We will keep you updated."

Elyssa couldn't move as she stared at the television screen. A cold fear spread throughout her body as she imagined the worse. Maddy immediately went to her niece as she noticed Elyssa's face grow extremely pale.

In barely a whisper, Elyssa said, "Will left me a message at five this morning saying that he and two others were setting out for a village that had suffered a lot of damage from the flooding."

Putting an arm around her for support, Maddy encouraged her with, "We have no reason to believe it's Will."

She slowly turned and looked at her aunt. Tears filled her eyes as she said, "But what if it is him? I'll never be able to forgive myself!"

Elyssa ran out of the room and her aunt and uncle looked at each other. They knew it was highly unlikely that Will was one of the ones missing, but as long as they didn't know for certain, Elyssa would be beside herself.

Elyssa closed the door to her room and dialed Will's number. It began ringing and with each ring, she said a prayer that he would answer. She had no idea what she would say. She no longer cared that he hadn't told her about owning the house. She only wanted to make sure he was all right.

She finally heard a click and her heart leapt with relief when she heard him say, "This is William Denton."

"Hi, Will. This is…"

"I am sorry that I missed your call. Please leave your name and number and I will return your call as soon as possible."

Elyssa's heart sank as she realized her call had gone to his voice mail.

When she heard the beep to leave her message, she desperately searched her mind for the right words to say. "Will, this is Elyssa. I'm sorry I didn't call you back last night. Please call me and let me know you're all right. We heard news this morning about flooding and landslides down there. I won't have any peace of mind until I know you're all right. Please call me as soon as you are able!"

Elyssa sat for a few moments with her eyes watching the phone intently as if willing it to ring. She lifted her shaking hand and raked it through her tousled hair. Her heart beat thunderously as she considered how foolish she had been last evening in not answering his call. She could have at least given him a chance to explain. Now what if… Elyssa couldn't even bring herself to think of what she would do if Will was one of those missing.

~~*

Elyssa hoped that the busyness of work at the house -- at Will's house -- would provide an escape from her persistent thoughts and worry. She kept her phone with her and turned on at all times in case he called. She tried several more times herself during the day to reach him, but still reached his voice mail.

"All right, Will, you're paying me back for what I did to you. Please either answer my call or call me back! I don't care why you did what you did! I only want to know you're safe!" Elyssa paused as a tear fell down her cheek. "I love you," she whispered.

That was the most desperate she had sounded in the few messages she had left. She didn't care. She knew that she loved him and didn't know how she would ever forgive herself if something had happened to him before she could talk to him.

When things slowed down at the house, Elyssa decided she would stop by and see Emily. She knew that Emily probably knew all along and wanted to get her perspective on this whole matter. Elyssa hoped that she might have word from Will.

When she walked into Emily's office, Emily waved her in. Emily could tell from the expression on Elyssa's face that she was upset -- and she knew precisely the cause of it.

"Hello, Elyssa. I was planning to come by today. Have a seat."

Elyssa sat down wearily.

"I heard you had a visitor at the house yesterday."

Elyssa looked up quickly. "Word gets around. I suppose one of the workers mentioned it to you. Her outburst was heard by everyone, I'm sure."

"No, it wasn't one of the workers who told me. It was my mother."

"Your mother?"

"Yes. My mother is Barbara Reed." Emily's fingers tapped nervously on the table. "She is William Denton's personal assistant."

"Ahh, so there's the connection."

Emily nodded. "I'm sorry, Elyssa. If it weren't for the fact that we think so highly of Will, we would have never done such a thing. The guy was desperate to bring you out here. I was assured that he would tell you as soon as possible."

"I feel like such a fool! Did *everyone* know?"

"No. In fact, it really hasn't even been widely known in the community here that he's the one building the house. His name is pretty well recognized all over Chicago, but he's been able to keep that a secret." Emily smiled. "I think that's one secret he is entitled to keep."

"So how did your mother find out about his aunt coming by yesterday?"

"Catherine stormed into the offices. She expected to see Will, and my mother had a difficult time convincing her that Will really wasn't there. Apparently she drove in from Kent, Ohio, and the house was on the way, so she stopped there first. She never calls ahead to let anyone know she's coming. Everyone tries to run the other way when they hear she's here."

"So she told your mother she had been at the house?"

"Yes. My mom knew Richard was going to be returning shortly and kept her there until he came. She knew Richard would be able to find out exactly what happened when she encountered you at the house. My mom was very concerned for you -- not so much because of what Will did, but because his aunt can say such unkind things."

"So your mother wasn't worried how I would take Will's deception?"

"She knew that at first you'd question why he did it, but then my mother idolizes the man and doesn't know how anyone can *not* like him. If I were ten years younger, I would have set my sights on him. Goodness knows, the man is so oblivious to how handsome he is, and money means nothing to him."

Emily folded her hands and leaned toward Elyssa. "The poor guy has not been himself since coming home from Guatemala. If you blame him for anything, blame him for being deeply in love with you. Perhaps I shouldn't be saying this, but…" Emily took in a deep breath. "We often wondered whether any young lady would ever capture his heart and we were all very pleased when it seemed he was smitten." Emily chuckled and her eyes lit up. "My mother can easily detect any change in that man and she was quite amused when she noticed things about him whenever the subject of Elyssa Barnett came up."

Elyssa blushed and looked down. "I guess I've been pretty hard on him."

Emily waved her hand through the air. "Oh, it's been good for him. Everything has always come too easily for him."

Elyssa's face sobered. "Emily, he left me a message early this morning that he and two other men were heading out to a village around Lake Atitlan that suffered a lot of damage. This morning on the news there was a report of three Americans missing. I know it's probably not him, but I haven't been able to get through on his cell phone. Do you think you could call your mother and find out if he's been in contact with anyone? I would feel so much better."

"Sure. Hold on."

Elyssa watched as Emily called and talked to her mom. With a smile on Emily's face, the two talked a few moments about what they each were doing. She then told her mother that Elyssa was there with her, asking about Will. The smile quickly left her face and her voice became more concerned.

"Really… when was that… he hasn't… all right, I will. Love ya! Bye."

As she hung up the phone, it was a moment before she turned and looked at Elyssa. "It's probably nothing, but no one has been able to reach any of the guys. Now it's probably because communication is down and they're so far out in the middle of nowhere. Heavens, it could be that there's no way they can recharge their phones."

Elyssa's hand slowly went up and covered her mouth. "Are they doing anything to try and find them?"

"They're doing all they can. My mom said she'll call as soon as they know something."

Elyssa fought back tears as she said, "Please let me know immediately when someone hears something. Please!"

"I will, Elyssa. I will."

Chapter 30

Elyssa left Emily's office and returned to Will's house, feeling little inclination to do much of anything. She walked through the completed living room and checked on the finishing work being done in the kitchen. This was all she had been hired to do, but in actuality, as she had spent the last few weeks walking through the whole dwelling, she had begun to envision just what she would like to do in the other rooms -- even before she had known it belonged to Will.

As she walked through the house, she came into his study. *Will's* study. Suddenly she could see him seated at a large desk with built-in bookshelves stained a deep, rich brown, lining two of the walls. She looked over at a third wall and thought how nicely that antique bookcase and books would look there.

Two men were cleaning up in the kitchen after putting down tile on the counters and backsplash. They gathered up their things as Elyssa came in and inspected it. They had done a superb job and Elyssa thanked them.

Once the men were gone, Elyssa went around the house to make sure it was locked up as she normally did before she left. As she walked toward the front door, however, she stopped. She didn't want to leave. She wanted to stay in the house a little longer by herself.

She walked around slowly, eyeing everything she had done and imagining what more she wanted to do. She looked over at the reclining chair and remembered coming upon Will stretched out in it. She sat down on it herself, closing her eyes. She could almost feel his presence from the other night.

She reached for her phone and tried calling Will again. She wasn't sure how many times she had tried and how many different ways she had pleaded, but nothing seemed to get through to him. As she listened to the ring go over to the now ever so familiar voice mail, she opened her mouth to speak, but couldn't. A cold fear swept over her, taunting her with the words of the newscaster that morning. *A team of three Americans who set out for one of the villages early this morning are presently missing.*

"No!" Elyssa cried out and pounded her fist onto the arm of the chair. "I won't let myself believe it was him! I won't!"

Taking a deep breath to stifle the tears, she knew she had to do something to ensure his safe return. She knew it was silly, but she decided that if she bought that antique bookcase and books that they had seen together, he would have to come back. He would *have* to!

Elyssa reached into her purse and pulled out her checkbook. She looked at the deposits she had recently made from her paychecks. She had been paid extremely well and had very few expenses herself while here. She had taken her aunt and uncle out to dinner a couple of times because they refused to accept any rent from her. A nice balance had accrued, and it should be sufficient to pay for those things without putting them on her credit card.

The thought of spending so much for something ran against her grain, but she decided he was worth it. She wasn't going to charge it to Emily -- thus, Will -- she was going to buy this for him with her own money.

Elyssa looked at her watch and realized the store might be closed by the time she got there. She couldn't recall the name of it to call and ask what their weekday hours were, so she decided she would stop by there first thing in the morning.

When she finally returned to her aunt and uncle's, she was met with bolstering words of care and comfort, but no further news on the missing men. Having not heard from Emily or anyone from Pemberleo, she assumed no one else had heard from him either. That thought alone caused a rising dread within her.

~~*

The next morning came too soon for Elyssa. Thoughts of Will -- and where he might be -- troubled her and she hadn't been able to sleep. She remembered looking at the clock at three in the morning and it seemed the next thing she knew, her alarm was sounding at seven. Reaching over and turning it off, she couldn't bring herself to get up just yet.

Elyssa stayed in bed an hour longer, and when she came out, Edward had already left for work. She asked Maddy if there had been any update on the missing Americans and she was told there wasn't.

She called Emily and told her she would be out most of the day. Elyssa wasn't expecting any workers today, but if someone did need to stop by, she asked Emily if she could let them in. With a brief inquiry as to whether Emily knew if there had been any word from Will yet, she was told there hadn't been and she ended the call with increasing concern.

Elyssa moved slowly that morning and drank several cups of coffee to help awaken her. With each sip of Pemberleo's morning blend, she thought of Will in some small village in Guatemala trying to help out -- or trying to get out. She wondered why he had felt so strongly that he needed to be there. Was it because he was only interested in his precious coffee beans or was he truly concerned about the people? Whatever the reason, no one seemed to know where he was.

Elyssa finally left for the city a little before noon. The leaves on some of the trees had begun to turn varying shades of red with the autumn days growing shorter and cooler. Elyssa easily made her way to the antique store, amazed at how beautiful everything was when she felt so wretched inside. She suddenly wished that Will could be there with her so she could fully appreciate the beauty.

Elyssa took in a deep breath filling her lungs with the cool air. Hugging her sweater tightly around her, she marched with determination to the store. She felt all the tenseness of the past day ease slightly as she set her mind to this task as if it would ensure Will's safe return.

While in the store, she looked around more thoroughly and purchased not only the bookcase and books, but an antique area rug, desk lamp, and a frame. She thought a picture of Lake Atitlan would look nice in it. Handing over her credit card, she knew her bank would probably wonder what had gotten into her, but she didn't care. The items she purchased had exceeded the amount in her checking account, but she was resolute about doing this.

She arranged to have everything delivered the next morning at nine o'clock.

From there she proceeded to Janelle's store. It had been over a week since her last visit and Elyssa wanted to see if they had anything new.

Elyssa was grateful that no one else was in the store when she arrived. Janelle was pleased to see her and she poured Elyssa a cup of coffee and the two sat down to catch up. Their conversation centered on some of the new things Janelle had recently picked up for the store and other things she had seen at a trade show.

Elyssa then told her about William Denton owning the house she was decorating.

"Why, Elyssa! You sly one! You never told me you knew him!"

"I guess that's because as far as I knew, we were just passing acquaintances." A slight shrug told Janelle there was more to this than Elyssa was telling.

"So you've been decorating his house, but didn't know it was his?" Janelle shook her head in amazement. "He hired you because he wanted you here!"

Elyssa shrugged her shoulders. "Hard to believe, isn't is?"

Janelle clapped her hands together and leaned back in laughter. "Why that has to be the most romantic thing I have ever heard!"

"Romantic?" Elyssa exclaimed. "He didn't even have the decency to tell me! We were together the whole evening the other night and… and… it just happened to slip his mind?"

"Oh, but Elyssa, if you only knew how many ladies in this town would love to be in your shoes!"

"Well, even though I was very distraught and confused when I first found out, I guess I have come to see things in a little different light." Elyssa paused and skewed her face in a wince. "Janelle, he's gone to Guatemala because of the flooding there and no one has heard from him since early yesterday morning."

"I heard about the flooding," Janelle said sympathetically. "He's there?"

Elyssa slowly nodded her head. "We've heard there are some Americans missing. I just hope he's not one of them."

Janelle reached out and took Elyssa's hand. "I'm sure he's not, honey. We'll just have to have faith that he's not."

After they finished their coffee, Janelle showed Elyssa some of the new pieces she had acquired. Elyssa left shortly thereafter with the promise that she would let her know when she received word that Will was safe.

~~*

Elyssa sat in the train staring out the window as it made its way out of Chicago and back into the suburbs. She had been doing a lot of thinking the past two days; thinking about herself and thinking about Will. She pondered why she acted the way she did around him. Why was she always ready to question his motives? Why did she always have to attack his character? This morning she had even wondered of his motive for going to Guatemala!

Everyone she had talked to that knew him well -- from Gina to Emily to Mrs. Reed -- all thought him above reproach. Elyssa let out a groan as she considered how many times she lashed out at him in Guatemala and yet he never held it against her. Now, because she thought him manipulative in bringing her here under false pretenses, when in fact he loved her, had she gone too far and lost him forever?

When the train stopped at Elyssa's station, she trudged off, the weight of her conviction and anguish bearing down upon her. She walked mechanically to her car and got in, not really knowing where she wanted to go. In a way she wanted to go back to his house and immerse herself in what was his. On the other hand, she also felt she needed the compassion and reassurances that only her aunt and uncle could give. A nice quiet evening with them and their children would help take her mind off her anxiety.

The evening with the Garners did boost her spirits and she was often encouraged by her aunt's smile or her uncle's occasional hug.

There was still no further word on the missing Americans. More details had come in that a car with three Americans had stopped to inquire about directions to a particular village. The road to the village had been washed out and no one knew the identity of the Americans, where they were, whether they made it to the village or whether they had just turned around and left. Due to the damage in the area, very little information was coming out. Elyssa knew in her head that the odds of it being him were slim, but in her heart she couldn't help but agonize over the possibility.

For the third night in a row, Elyssa was afforded very little sleep.

~~*

Well before the sun began spreading its rays over the horizon, Elyssa slipped out of bed. When she finished showering and had dressed, the sunlight was just beginning to lighten the skies.

She peered out the window to see a cloudless sky and the bright glowing orb coming into view. To her native Californian eye, it would seem to promise a pleasant day. She was in Chicago, however, and this fall day was to be close to freezing. She shuddered in the warmth of the house as she thought how much colder it would be if she received any distressing news.

When she came out to the living room, Edward was already up, reading the newspaper and watching television.

"Any news?" Elyssa asked.

"Lots, honey, but not the kind you're anxious about."

The sound and smell of coffee percolating seemed to soothe Elyssa's nerves. She walked into the kitchen and waited for it to finish, and then poured herself and her uncle a cup. She brought them both into the living room and they drank and watched the news in silence.

Shortly after, her aunt came out and Elyssa announced she was leaving to go to the house.

"Isn't it awfully early, Elyssa?" her aunt asked.

"I'm expecting a delivery this morning and I want to make sure everything is ready for it." Elyssa gave her aunt a meager smile in hopes it would convince her she was all right.

"You know, it might be a good idea for you to take a little break. Why don't you think about it? You've been under a lot of stress lately."

"Thanks. Maybe this afternoon. Goodbye!" She kissed her aunt and waved to her uncle. "See you later!"

As she closed the door, Maddy looked at Edward. "If Elyssa doesn't hear from Will soon, I'm not sure she will be able to take much more."

~~*

There really wasn't that much to do to get ready for the delivery of her purchases. She just wanted to come back to the house and be alone for awhile.

She walked through the living room and into the kitchen. A large bay window faced the wooded part of the property behind and the sky -- ablaze with colors -- could be seen through the trees, which also filtered the brightness of the sun.

How beautiful! thought Elyssa. *I wonder if Will knew how perfect this room would be to greet the sunrise!*

She glanced around her at the tile on the floor and the tile design on the walls and for the first time she realized that it almost had a Guatemalan feel to it. She was shocked when she realized this. It wasn't something that just anyone would know, but having been there and seen their designs, one could almost believe she had chosen it with that in mind.

Elyssa shook her head. "I didn't even know he owned this house!" she said to herself. "And yet…" She looked around and suddenly saw touches of it everywhere in the design and color. It wasn't overt, just here and there. But it definitely was there.

To pass the time, Elyssa began to walk through the house. She went upstairs and peered into each room, designing it in her mind's eye. When she came to the master bedroom, she looked around her. Nothing came to her mind.

Her eyes drifted from one wall to the next and she found it difficult to envision anything. A fear gripped her that perhaps there was a reason.

"No! I will not allow myself to think like that! He *is* coming back!"

She shook off her dread and decided to go back downstairs to wait for the delivery.

Precisely at nine o'clock, there was a knock at the door. Elyssa jumped up and greeted the two delivery men.

"Are you Elyssa Barnett?"

"Yes," she answered.

"We have an antique bookcase, some antique books, a lamp, a frame, and an area rug to deliver."

"Yes, this is the right place. I'll have you bring them over here into the study."

One of the men, holding the lamp and frame, stepped inside. "Just show me where you want these."

"Actually," Elyssa said, "Why don't you leave them out here?"

The young man set them down and joined the other to walk back to the truck. They returned, each carrying one end of the rolled up antique area rug. It was fairly large and bulky, and when they unrolled it in the study, it extended to within about 6 inches of the wall. They then went out to bring in the bookcase.

As they struggled with the heavy piece of furniture, Elyssa helped them navigate. They stepped into the room and Elyssa pointed to the wall she wanted it up against.

As she was directing the men, another voice from behind her asked, "Where would you like these books?"

Stunned by the familiarity of the voice, Elyssa spun around, expecting to see another delivery man; yet *hoping* to see someone else. She gasped as she found herself looking into Will's weary, partially bearded, but ever so handsome face, carrying a large box.

Elyssa's mouth went dry and she couldn't bring herself to move or to answer.

"I hope you know this guy," the one delivery man joked. "He asked us out there if he could carry in the box of books." He walked over and took the box out of Will's hands and placed it next to the bookcase.

"Yes… yes, I know him," she said slowly, unable to take her eyes off of him and wanting so much to run into his arms.

"If you'll just sign this, then, we'll be on our way."

Elyssa willed herself to look down to the clipboard as she took the pen from the delivery man. She could barely hold it steady as she attempted to sign her name. The two men excused themselves and left as Will and Elyssa were frozen in a grip of a myriad of emotions, unsure of what the other was feeling.

As soon as the men walked out of the house, Elyssa took a small step toward Will and then unexpectedly ran toward him, flinging her arms around his neck.

Will hesitantly, but most willingly, drew his arms around Elyssa and locked them behind her waist, grateful for at least this moment of tenderness between them. A short moment later, he asked, "Isn't there something we need to talk about, Elyssa?"

Hanging on tightly, she cried out, "Yes! We didn't know where you were! After you went out to the village, no one could reach you and you didn't call anyone! There were news reports of Americans missing. I worried that it might be you!"

The expression on Will's face, unseen by Elyssa, displayed his surprise. "We weren't missing. At least, *we* knew where we were. I lost my phone in a river of mud. There were no cell towers around so no one was getting reception and the village had no power or telephone lines that worked. They suffered quite a bit of damage from the flood. We weren't able to communicate with anyone, but we also didn't realize people were worried."

"We were… *I* was!" Elyssa said as she held him tighter.

"Elyssa," Will said softly, gently removing himself from Elyssa's embrace and taking a small step away from her. "There *are* a couple of things we really need to address."

"Oh, *that.*"

"How can I ever convince you how truly sorry I am?"

"No, I understand, Will. It's all right!"

Will resolutely crossed his arms together in front of him and laughed. "Oh, no! I'm not going to get off that easy! You were angry with me and we need to talk about this. I would like the opportunity to explain my actions to you."

Elyssa took in a shaky breath. "You explained in your phone calls."

"But you didn't return my calls. The only thing I could assume was that you were angry with me -- or that you never received them and I still need to explain."

Elyssa gave him a weak smile. "I did get your calls. I didn't answer them because I was... well, I wasn't so much angry with you, Will, as I was hurt."

Will's face grew somber. "Hurt?"

"Yes, I was hurt that you didn't feel as though you could tell me the house was yours."

Will pursed his lips together and his nostrils flared as he drew in a deep breath. "I'm sorry I hurt you, Elyssa. I never meant for that to happen. Can you ever forgive me?"

Elyssa took his hands in each of hers and gave them a squeeze. "I guess you have the advantage of seeing me after a couple days of mulling it all over." Elyssa tilted her head and then added, "And worrying with absolute fright about your welfare!"

"I called you four times that first night and never heard back from you once."

"I did call, Will; just not until the next morning. I left you several messages, in fact."

'Hmmm. Probably after I lost my phone."

He slid his hands around to encase Elyssa's. "It seems as though *you* have the advantage over me here, because you heard *my* messages, but I didn't hear *yours*. Be honest now. What did you say to me? I'm sure you raked me over the coals in a way that I most definitely deserved."

Elyssa could not help but laugh. "No, I didn't do that at all! I was quite…" she paused and looked into his eyes. "I only wanted to hear that you were safe."

"Sure! I know you well enough to know you're not afraid to tell me off quite effectively!" he laughed. "You expect me to believe that you didn't tell me what you thought of me when you found out I hadn't told you the truth *and* after my aunt showed up and mercilessly attacked you and your work? Unfortunately, she is a woman who cares nothing for the feelings of others and only for herself."

Elyssa looked down. "She was quite unmerciful, but in my messages I wanted to let you know that… well, that my feelings for you are quite the same as the feelings you professed in your message."

Will leaned in to her. "Which means…?"

"Well, I believe you told me in the message you left me that you…love me."

A smile spread across Will's face. "I did, indeed. And?"

"And, well, I love you. I love you very much."

Will didn't hesitate to pull her back close to him. "You don't know how long

I've wanted to hear you say that. I've loved you a very long time."

They stood still, looking into each other's face, and then Will leaned down and kissed her fervently, neither wanting to let go or for the kiss to end.

~~*

When at last they parted, Elyssa looked at him slyly. "So why didn't you think you could tell me about the house belonging to you?"

"Elyssa, you must believe that I intended to tell you after the picnic. I didn't tell you sooner because I wanted our first real date, from beginning to end, to be special. I didn't want to do or say anything that would upset you."

Elyssa fingered the collar of his shirt. "That's sweet," she said, her eyes shining in recollection of their evening together. "It *was* very special."

Will reached up and took her hand, bringing it to his lips to kiss the back of it. "I had no idea I would be leaving for Guatemala the very next day or that my aunt would show up here, abusing you with her behavior and shocking you with the news about the house."

Suddenly Elyssa thought about everyone else who had been concerned about him. "Have you called anyone else to let them know you're all right?"

"We didn't get back to Guatemala City until about one o'clock in the morning. I called the pilot who was staying in a hotel there and had him meet me at the airport. I figured there was no sense calling anyone here and waking them up. The only call I made was to Gina and to the offices here where I left a message. They'll have received it by now. Other than that, I slept the whole way home on the jet, just cleaning myself up a little so you wouldn't think some barbarian had come to see you."

Elyssa pulled back some and inspected his face with a smile. "I think I rather like the rugged mountain man look."

Will raised his eyes and rubbed his chin. "I'll have to remember that, but it is somewhat itchy."

Elyssa leaned her head in against his chest. "I'm really glad you're home."

"I am too. I really missed you and hated what I had done to you. I hated that my aunt abused you to your face."

"I don't blame you for your aunt's actions, but what about your cousin, Anne?"

Will let out a huff. "What did she say about Anne?"

"That *she* was supposed to design the house."

After a long, drawn out groan, Will said, "If she had designed this house, I would have refused to step foot in it. She's one of those peculiar people that have bizarre ideas and uses wild colors and… well, nothing I would want in my house."

Elyssa laughed.

"Now," Will looked at her seriously, "about the *other* thing we need to talk about."

Elyssa looked at him curiously. "What other thing?"

Will walked over to the bookcase. "I don't remember approving the purchase of this…" he then waved his hand around the room. "Or any of these."

Elyssa propped her arms against her waist and gave him a stern look. "And you won't, either."

"Now, Elyssa, you know everything you bought was first to have been approved by me."

"No, it was to be approved by Richard Fitzpatrick, but as it is, I bought these without any approval."

"I don't know if I can accept that," he said with a teasing glint in his eyes.

Elyssa narrowed her eyes at him. "You can't tell me that you actually saw everything I submitted and gave it your approval?"

"Well, no, not everything, but this is a pretty major purchase and we haven't yet talked about whether you'll even do any more rooms in the house."

"First of all, I didn't submit this purchase because I bought it with my own money!"

"You didn't! Elyssa, do you know how expensive this was?"

"Yes," she said mockingly. "I bought it, didn't I?"

Will took a step forward. "With your *own* money?"

"Well, consider it bought with money you paid me to stay here."

Will took in a sharp breath. "Elyssa, I wasn't paying you to stay here."

"No?"

"Well, no, not really! You didn't think that, did you?"

"I've had a couple days to think of a lot of different things, Will. At first, maybe I did."

"I was paying you to design my house with the hope…" He paused and ran his hands across his bearded face.

"Yes?"

"With the hope that it would someday be *our* house."

Elyssa's eyes widened. "Will, is this a… you're not asking me…"

Will shook his head. "No, not exactly, but don't think I haven't been thinking about it for a long time. Consider it more of me stating my intentions."

A teasing smile displayed a reclusive dimple on his cheek. "I *would* propose right now, however, if I knew it would mean we would never have another misunderstanding that couldn't be resolved immediately."

Will reached out with one hand and ran his fingers through Elyssa's hair, coming to rest on her shoulder. "Look, Elyssa, I know that we've only had one evening together that was, well, without any turmoil. I think, for your sake, I'd like us to try and have a few more of those before I ask you to commit to marriage with someone like me."

"Someone like you?" Elyssa laughed. "Whatever do you mean? *I'm* the one who spoke so horridly to you, accusing you of things I had no right to."

"What did you say to me that I didn't deserve? Much of what you said to me *was* true in one way or another."

Despite Will's reassurances, Elyssa felt anew all the shame of the words she had lashed out at him and cast her eyes down. "I just can't believe you were willing to give me another try after all I did and said in Guatemala. I was heartless!"

Will placed two of his fingers under Elyssa's chin and lifted it up so she was looking up at him. "But it was also in Guatemala that I learned what it was to really want something and have to work hard to get it. I became more determined than ever to take the words to the song you sang there to heart."

"The words…?"

"I was determined that no matter how long it was going to take -- even if it took forever -- I would wait for you."

Suddenly everything was clear to Elyssa; how Will had come to Guatemala because he wanted to be with her and see her again; why he refused to be discouraged or disturbed by her rude behavior; and why he had arranged for the two of them to see *Umbrellas of Cherbourg*.

She had no idea when they were in the ruins of the convent and she was singing, that Will was actually experiencing what the words to the song said.

With his fingers still lightly under her chin, she brought her hands around his neck, this time pulling him down toward her as she rose up on her toes. Just before his lips touched hers, she whispered, "I believe your wait is over."

Chapter 31

Will and Elyssa did not seem inclined to end the kiss too quickly. But they soon parted and Elyssa rested her head against his chest, her arms wrapping around to circle his waist. Will responded in kind by draping his arms across her shoulders and locking his hands behind her.

They held tightly onto one another, each in an overwhelming state of disbelief that they were in such an ardent embrace. For Will, he could barely comprehend that both he and Elyssa had declared their feelings of love for the other. A surge of relief swept through Elyssa knowing that Will had returned unharmed and she had been able to acknowledge her feelings to him.

Finally Will pulled himself away and raised his eyebrows as he asked, "Do you think we both have an accurate understanding of all that has transpired between us now? Have we talked about everything we need to discuss?"

Elyssa lifted her eyes to look at him and slowly shook her head. "Not quite."

Will stepped back. "What?"

Elyssa lifted her hand and motioned with her finger for him to follow her. They came into the living room and Elyssa turned around. "Would you care to tell me about this painting -- Pemberleigh, I believe, is the name of the culprit."

"Culprit?"

Elyssa nodded. "Yes, it is the culprit, you know. It's all because of this painting that I realized you owned the house. When your aunt was... well, *critiquing* my design work, she mentioned that the painting of Pemberleigh Manor was too high -- or too low -- I don't remember."

"And the names Pemberleo and Pemberleigh were just too close to be a coincidence and you became suspicious."

"I asked your aunt if Pemberleigh had anything to do with Pemberleo Coffee. Your aunt told me..." Elyssa then told him in a high pitched, harsh voice that mimicked his aunt, "...anybody who is *anybody* knows they both belong to the Denton family."

Will rolled his eyes and shook his head. Elyssa did an exaggerated imitation of his aunt too well. It sounded exactly like her and was precisely what he expected her to say.

Elyssa turned back to look at the painting and asked seriously. "Don't tell me you own an estate in England, too."

Will let out a long breath and came up to stand behind, looking up at the painting. "Well, I'm afraid it does belong to the Denton family."

He placed his hands on Elyssa's shoulders and leaned over to speak softly in her ear. "But it's owned by a gentleman who is something like a third cousin twice removed."

Elyssa turned around slowly. "Oh, you don't own it, then?"

Will shook his head, "No. You're disappointed?"

"Well, you know my emphasis in interior design was historical decor from the nineteenth century. I studied both English and American."

"We'll have to see what we can do about that. Actually, in the 1800s, my great-great-great-grandfather was the second son born in the Denton family. His older brother was the one who would inherit the estate. He had a fairly good monetary inheritance, had a flair for business, and the taste for adventure. He decided to take his inheritance, come to America, and invest in something, although he really didn't know what that would be."

"How did he end up getting into coffee?"

"He met a man on the ship who had traveled down to Guatemala and gone into some of the small villages that lie on the hillsides of dormant volcanoes and had found the coffee beans to be dark and rich. With this man's help and encouragement, he decided then and there that's where he wanted to invest his money."

"And he started a company, naming it Pemberleo after his home in England."

Will nodded. "He didn't think Pemberleigh had the right sound for a company importing coffee beans from Latin America, so he changed it to Pemberleo."

"And the painting?"

"After he had been here several years, he commissioned someone to paint Pemberleigh and had it shipped over here. I think he missed his home."

"Did he ever go back?"

"Only once, I believe."

"Have you ever been there?"

"My father took Gina and me over there about ten years ago. Unfortunately, it's been pretty modernized and has little left of any historical significance."

"That's too bad."

Will nodded. "Now, can I ask *you* something?"

Elyssa turned around to face him.

"Of course."

"You haven't fallen in love with me because of the house, have you? I mean, you didn't tell me you loved me until after you knew I owned it!" A smile betrayed his teasing manner.

Elyssa thought for a moment that this type of banter was highly uncharacteristic of Will, but decided she could play the game, too. "You know that can be the *only* reason. On more than one occasion I laid out your faults to you, but if I had known about *this*," she said with a sweep of her arm, "I would have been putty in your hands."

"Mmmm," he said, as he pulled her close again. "Perhaps I should have told you sooner."

Later, after much insistence from Elyssa, Will began calling people to tell them he was all right and was with her. The concern of his close family and friends over losing contact with him was suddenly overcome by their curiosity about how Elyssa had responded to the news about the house.

He assured everyone that they had worked everything out.

~~*

The news traveled quickly about Will and this young lady, and for once, Will didn't care about his firm 'no gossip' policy within the company. He would be more than willing to pose for any pictures with Elyssa if it would remove him from the *Most Eligible Bachelors* list. Even though he wasn't actually married or even engaged, he knew he would no longer be of interest to the media.

He consulted with Elyssa about this first. He told her that if she could endure a few magazine photo shoots, after that the story would be gone. It actually turned out quite beneficial for Elyssa. When the photographers came to the house, most were more interested in the interior design and the work Elyssa had done.

Once Elyssa started gaining some recognition of her talent, Will's aunt seemed to do a complete turnaround and began praising her work. On the one occasion when Elyssa saw her before she returned to Kent, Catherine subtly hinted that perhaps she and Anne could form a partnership. Will adamantly and not so subtly advised Elyssa not to agree to any such thing.

She couldn't accept any further jobs until she finished designing Will's house, but Elyssa and Emily did work out an agreement for any job offers to go through her agency and Emily could weed them out, promising to get back to the ones that she deemed profitable once Elyssa was available.

Elyssa came to appreciate more and more the benefit of Will bringing her out to Chicago. Will soon took up residence in his house, bringing over a few things of his own until Elyssa completed designing and furnishing it. She was able to see what his demands at work were truly like and was pleasantly surprised that he often joined her at the end of the day either at his home or at her aunt and uncle's.

For the first month, Saturdays were spent together with the Garners and their children, playing games with them in the evening after a light supper. It was Fridays that Will reserved for Elyssa alone, and it was then that he lavished her with visits to the finest restaurants, theaters, and a myriad of cultural events that the city of Chicago had to offer.

They usually ate out first, giving them ample time to converse before going on to some other form of entertainment. He seemed to relish finding out all there was to know about her. He discovered she loved to read anything she could get her hands on; she enjoyed walking and bike riding; had never been on a horse; she loved Ferris wheels and steel roller coasters, but hated wooden ones, and she had just recently added bumper cars to her list of favorite amusement park rides. She loved watching baseball but was never good at playing it; loved going to the beach; was closer to her aunt than her mother; she had been closer to Janet than her younger sister; and she had loved to sing from the time she was three.

When Elyssa turned the tables on Will, she discovered that he loved to read in his leisure time; liked to walk and ride horses, but hadn't been on a bike in quite some time; he loved all kinds of roller coasters and, like Elyssa, also had a fondness for bumper cars; he loved watching *and* playing baseball; he loved the beaches and mountains; he was close to his sister and his cousin; and he couldn't carry a tune if he tried.

Elyssa saw in him a man who wasn't pretentious about who he was and was very kind and considerate. She had heard enough from those who knew him well that he was truly a good man. She knew that from the way he treated her little cousins and the children back at the pre-school in Guatemala, that he would be a great father someday. Having completely changed in her opinion of him, she now looked forward with great anticipation to the day he would propose.

It was with that in mind that she readied herself for a Friday evening out with him about a month later. He had told her they would be going to a gala fund-raising event at the Navy Pier Grand Ballroom. It was a formal affair that would include a banquet, art show and silent auction, and symphony orchestra with guest musicians. She wondered whether this would be the evening when he asked for her hand.

She and her aunt went out to buy a dress, as Elyssa hadn't brought anything along with her that would be suitable for such a fashionable event. She found a dark burgundy floor-length dress with a halter top that accentuated her figure nicely. She bought a pair of heels to wear, but borrowed an evening purse, some jewelry, and an evening stole from her aunt, which completed the ensemble.

When Will arrived that evening, he was wearing a tuxedo and Elyssa could barely catch her breath when she saw him step inside the door. He brought her a dozen deep red roses, which Elyssa noticed matched the color of her gown perfectly. She handed them to Maddy who promptly put them in a large vase. They talked with the Garners a bit before Will and Elyssa walked out the door.

As they drove into Chicago, Elyssa couldn't keep from wondering whether he would propose tonight. Nervously, she kept rubbing her left hand, specifically around her ring finger, and then would force herself to stop. They were going to be at a table with eight others, mostly from Pemberleo. She would know Emily, Mrs. Reed, and his cousin, Richard. It certainly wouldn't be an intimate affair, but she still felt that this might be the night.

She had to repeatedly tell herself to relax; and at one point, turned to look at Will. He certainly looked handsome. But then she thought of all the different ways she had seen him and a soft chuckle escaped as a thought crossed her mind.

"What was that all about?" Will asked, as he glanced over.

"Oh, nothing," Elyssa answered, turning her head to look out her side of the window.

"No, you definitely chuckled. I want to know why."

Elyssa turned back toward him, clasping her hands together and very decisively dropping them into her lap. "All right, if you insist." Elyssa tilted her head.

"I am having a bit of a struggle deciding something about you."

"Oh, dear. This sounds serious."

"Oh yes, it is!" Elyssa said gravely. "You see, I have seen you in a nicely tailored designer suit -- which I promptly made you change out of before going to the pre-school, in case you forgot…"

"I haven't forgotten."

"Then there were the jeans and T-shirt, but soon after they became a *drenched* pair of jeans and T-shirt when you rescued my sandal."

Will tilted his head as Elyssa gave this curious account of his wardrobe.

"Then there was the day you showed up at the house returning from Guatemala looking in a way that could only be deemed *scruffy*."

"Scruffy?"

"Oh, yes. Definitely scruffy." Elyssa let out a long sigh. "But you promptly shaved and cleaned up, and now you're in a tuxedo, although I did see you in a tuxedo at Chad and Janet's wedding, but that doesn't count, because, well, you know how I felt about you back then."

Will shook his head. "No, of course that doesn't count." He quickly turned his eyes to Elyssa, who seemed to be a little more animated than normal. "Doesn't count for what?"

"I can't decide how I like you best. You have so many different looks and quite frankly, I think I like them all."

She saw him squirm; followed by a little self-conscious grimace he made that told her he was far from being vain about his looks. She had come to the conclusion that he felt they were a detriment rather than a benefit to him.

He was quiet for a minute as he absorbed her words. Without any warning, he said, "Scruffy, huh? You included scruffy in that list?"

"I told you I liked it when you came by that day."

"No, I believe your exact words were 'rugged, mountain man look.' There is a big difference."

Elyssa crossed her arms in front of her and shook her head authoritatively. "I'm sorry, Will. You'll just have to face it. I like you scruffy and expect to see you -- on occasion -- sporting a couple days' growth now and then, combined with a T-shirt and jeans. You might even want to surprise everyone down at the office some day. Do you have a 'jeans' day? Every office needs one. Helps keep everyone relaxed."

Elyssa turned to Will and was met with his gaze. "That's something I won't promise to do, but I will consider it." He smiled as he thought that she seemed more nervous than usual, that perhaps she was nervous about going to a rather large gala affair. Perhaps she had never attended anything like this. Or perhaps she suspected something else.

They came into town and Will easily maneuvered the streets that took them to the edge of Lake Michigan. As Elyssa gazed out the window in awe at the sights around them, Will pulled into a parking garage. He followed the arrows for valet parking and soon he stopped the car and there were two uniformed gentlemen eager to help them both out.

As they walked out to the pier toward the Grand Ballroom, Elyssa admired and commented on everything around her. The lights glistening in Lake Michigan were beautiful, but the one thing that caught her attention was the Ferris wheel.

"Oh, look, Will! A Ferris wheel! Do you think we can ride it?"

"Dressed like this?" he asked as he pointed down to their wardrobe.

"I don't think they have a dress code," Elyssa answered without batting an eye. "Come on; let's go take a closer look."

They walked up toward the Ferris wheel and read that it closed at ten.

"We better get on now," Elyssa said. "These fund-raising things could go till midnight."

Will shook his head. "We really should get inside. That line is too long and Richard is waiting for us. The banquet will be starting soon."

Elyssa wrapped her hand tightly around his arm. "Do you think we can sneak out just before ten?"

"We'll see."

Elyssa pulled back a little on his arm to stop him. "Now look here, Will. I went with you on those bumper cars in Guatemala. The least you can do is ride on this little Ferris wheel with me."

Will laughed. "It doesn't look too little to me. It's fifteen stories high! If you insist, though, we'll try later. I'll leave it up to you to keep track of the time. Don't blame me if you suddenly realize it's after ten."

That satisfied Elyssa and they walked toward the Grand Ballroom, passing a carousel and a few other rides that were being enjoyed by young and old alike on this unusually mild autumn evening. They did look out of place in their formal clothes among the young revelers enjoying the rides. The closer they got to the Ballroom, however, the more their attire blended in with others around them. Soon they had joined a throng of people dressed in their finest, heading toward a large building with a domed roof.

As they walked in, Will leaned over. "Look for Richard. We have a table for ten and he's probably here by now."

"You mean Richard as in Richard Fitzpatrick, owner of the house I'm designing?" Elyssa teased.

"Well, yes… and no."

Suddenly Will pointed, "Look, he's over there."

As they walked through the ballroom, Elyssa gazed about her. It was beautiful. She didn't think she had ever seen anything quite like it before.

When they reached the table, Elyssa was greeted by the same smiling face she had met in Will's office. "Hello, Elyssa! It's good to see you again!" He paused and gave a teasing glance at his cousin. "This time not under false pretenses!"

Will rolled his eyes and shook his head as Elyssa greeted his cousin.

"Hello, Richard. How are you?" She then turned to the others at their table. "Hello, Emily. Hello Mrs. Reed."

"Hello, Elyssa," both ladies responded at once.

Emily introduced her husband to Elyssa. "Elyssa, this is my husband, Dwight. Dwight, this is Elyssa."

They exchanged greetings and Elyssa sat down next to Emily.

Will and Richard took their seats and suddenly Richard whispered to Will, "Here she comes. In the pink dress. What do you think?"

Will let out a muffled grunt and whispered back, "She looks just like all the others you've ever dated."

The two men stood up and Richard introduced Tiffany to everyone seated around the table. She was tall and blond and wore an excessive amount of makeup and seemed to giggle a lot. Elyssa hated to make quick judgments of people, but this young girl's manner was simply too tempting. She was a dumb blond. No, probably a dumb *bleached* blond. Now Elyssa knew several intelligent blondes, but this young girl was not one of them. Hearing Will's remark to his cousin about his taste in women, she suddenly had a much clearer picture of Richard, too.

The evening was enjoyable. Their table of ten included three more people from Pemberleo and they enjoyed a delicious meal, an art show and auction, and beautiful music from the symphony orchestra and soloists. Will and Elyssa took some time to peruse the art show and bid on a couple of works of art that they both agreed would look wonderful in the house.

Elyssa was enjoying herself so much that she practically forgot about the Ferris wheel.

It was at about five minutes before ten that she noticed Will glance at his watch and she suddenly remembered. She tugged at Will's sleeve. "Will, it's almost ten."

"Yes, are you ready to leave?"

"No! We have to get to the Ferris wheel."

"Oh, that. You really want to do that?"

Elyssa nodded.

"We could always come back another day and take a ride on it."

She gave a little more fervent tug on his sleeve. "No, winter is coming and by then it might be too cold! Tonight's perfect, but we have to hurry!"

"All right." He looked around the table and thanked everyone for coming and excused himself and Elyssa.

As they walked out, Elyssa said, "We can always come back after the ride, if you prefer."

Will shook his head. "They're just winding things up in there. The music is over and now there will just be some speakers who will finish up the evening. We'll do this and go home."

As they were approaching the Ferris wheel, Elyssa gasped as she saw that the lights went out.

"Oh no!" she said as she grabbed Will's arm and began to run as best she could in her gown and heels. "Come on! Maybe they'll open it up for us."

"I doubt it," Will replied nonchalantly.

As they came up to the attendant, who was closing things down, Will didn't have to say a thing. Elyssa began begging and pleading for just one time around. "Please?" she asked with her eyes wide and childlike.

"Well, OK, but just once -- and it's gotta be quick! I'm off duty!"

They climbed into a small gondola that was large enough to seat up to six people, three on a side. Will stepped in after Elyssa and slid over next to her.

As the ride began, Elyssa felt her stomach lurch as they went up and up. Soon they were going over the top and back down. Disappointment surged through Elyssa as she realized the ride was going to be over before it had hardly begun if they only got to go around once.

Instead of coming to a stop at the bottom, however, it kept going, and this time around, not having started from a standstill, the motion prompted Elyssa to grab on tightly to Will and she let out a scream.

"I thought you liked Ferris wheels."

"I do, but I don't think I've ever been on one this big!" she shrieked as they came around again.

"Do you want to get off?"

"No!" she squealed with a laugh. "This is too much fun!"

As it came up around to the top the second time, Elyssa readied herself for the plunge down. Instead they came to an abrupt stop, suspended at the top.

The gondola rocked from the momentum. After her initial joy and shock, she looked around, in awe of the view.

She turned and looked out across the water. "Look at the view, Will! It's beautiful. The lights are just dancing across Lake Michigan!"

"It is beautiful up here, Elyssa, but it's not just the lights. You are the most beautiful thing I see."

Elyssa shuddered as she gazed at his intense eyes. Looking down, she said, "You are too kind."

Elyssa leaned across Will to look out over the city of Chicago on his side, placing her hand against his chest, feeling his heart pound. Very softly, she said, "Who would have thought that day you took me on the bumper cars in Guatemala -- and I pummeled you to death -- that four months later we'd be sitting at the top of a Ferris wheel together?"

He covered her hand with his and Elyssa felt his fingers gently tighten around her hand; just enough to know she needed to remain silent and let him say what was on his mind.

"Who would have thought on that day we rode those bumper cars, that…" Will took in a deep breath and paused. He brought her hands up toward his lips. "…that four months later…" Will reached into his pocket and pulled out a small box. He slipped down off the seat and knelt on the floor of the gondola. Elyssa failed to notice the rocking and swaying his movement caused. "…we would be sitting at the top of a Ferris wheel and I would be asking you… to marry me and be my wife?"

Elyssa could barely move as she watched Will slowly open the box. She looked down and beheld a beautiful diamond and sapphire ring.

"Elyssa, will you marry me?"

Will bent his head over and kissed her hand, then lifted his eyes to wait for Elyssa's answer.

A smile crept across her face. "Who would have believed that day we rode the bumper cars, that four months later I would be on the top of a Ferris wheel *accepting* your proposal to be your wife? Yes I will!"

Will pulled the ring out of the box and his shaking hands took hold of Elyssa's shaking hand, slipping the ring on her finger. Elyssa's eyes were as wide as could be as she looked down at it. Suddenly the lights sparkling in the lake were dim compared to this.

He brought himself back up on the seat and wrapped his arms around her neck, leaning his forehead in against hers and let out a deep sigh. "You have made me so happy, Elyssa."

Suddenly the ride began again, as if it somehow knew everything was settled between them.

As they approached the ground and it slowed down, Elyssa thought their ride was over. But she noticed Will nod at the attendant and soon they were soaring up again. Elyssa gasped to catch her breath.

Once again, they came to the top and stopped. Elyssa snuggled up closely next to Will. "You know, Will," she said, "I took you on quite the roller coaster ride in our relationship, didn't I?"

"Roller coaster?" Will shook his head. "Not at all! I would call it more like a *House of Mirrors*. I wondered whether I would ever find my way out of the labyrinth I was in!" He looked at her and smiled, poking her nose with his finger. "It seems I kept seeing you right in front of me, but when I'd try to reach you, I'd run smack into a dead-end!"

She wrapped her arms around him and rested her head against his shoulder. "Well I'm here now, right in front of you."

Will completely encased her with his arms. "And don't think I'm ever going to let you go."

They started to move again, this time more slowly and Elyssa thought she could hear the sound of music playing.

"What's that?" she asked. "It sounds like it's right below us!"

Will shrugged his shoulders as they drew near the ground. Elyssa gripped Will tightly and looked up to him. "They're playing *I Will Wait for You*!" She released him and slid over to the edge of the seat, trying to look down.

As they reached the point at the back of the ride, where they could look down ahead of them, Elyssa gasped as she saw a small orchestra seated in a semi-circle of folding chairs below them. Everyone from their table at the banquet was now standing off to the side cheering and applauding, and then she saw that her aunt and uncle were down there as well, holding the dozen roses he had brought her earlier.

Tears began to flow. "You had all this planned! Will, how did you do it?"

"A lot of planning and prayer," he said as he laughed. "I was quite sure you'd insist on riding the Ferris wheel. If you hadn't, I would have been the one insisting."

They stepped off the ride to the snapping of pictures, hugs, and offers of "Congratulations" from everyone.

She looked to her aunt and uncle. "You knew about this all along?"

They both nodded as her aunt handed her the roses and her uncle remarked, "He couldn't very well ask you to marry him without asking *my* permission first, could he?"

Elyssa laughed and looked around her in awe.

Richard leaned forward and announced to the two that they had won the bid on the two pieces of artwork they wanted.

"I told him not to bid so high. He more than tripled their value!" Elyssa said in mock frustration.

Will shrugged his shoulders. "The proceeds are going to a good cause and we get two nice paintings out of it."

The small orchestra finished playing and Elyssa surmised that the musicians were most likely a handful of the ones who had performed at the benefit they just came from. She was touched that Will invited them to come and play especially for them and that he had extended the invitation to the others to join them at the bottom of the Ferris wheel. It was only for a short time, however, for they all quickly excused themselves and Will and Elyssa were left alone.

"Do you like it?" he asked as they walked to the car arm in arm. Will looked down at Elyssa by his side. She held out her hand in front of her, admiring her ring.

"It's perfect, Will. Everything tonight was perfect. I don't know how you organized all of this!"

"I'm glad you're pleased," he said, and then he stopped. "You don't mind, then, that I had to keep a few things a secret tonight? You don't mind that everyone else knew and you didn't?"

Elyssa slowly turned her head toward him. "If all your secrets are as special as this was tonight, I don't think I'll ever complain again!"

With roses still in her hand, she flung her arms tightly around the man she was to marry, intensely aware and forever grateful for his willingness to overlook and forgive all she had done and said to him in the past, and to finally see for herself, the man who William Denton truly was.

Chapter 32

As Elyssa stepped out onto the end of the aisle on her uncle's arm, a smile lit up her face when she saw Will standing up at the front of the church. He looked much like he had three years ago when he stood at the side of Chad at his friend's wedding to Janet, but now she could see the man he truly was. Certainly, he had changed, but a great deal of her perception of him had changed, as well.

Elyssa and Will wanted a more intimate gathering of close friends and family and thus had chosen to be married in this small Chicago church, smaller than the one the Blakelys were married in. After a brief one month engagement, they chose to marry over the Thanksgiving weekend to make it easier for people who had to come in from other areas. Gina had cooked a wonderful Thanksgiving dinner on Thursday for all the out-of-town guests. On Friday, most of the out-of-towners were able to go out and see the sights while Elyssa, her aunt, and her mother tied up all the final details of the wedding.

Now, as Elyssa made her way toward the front, she caught a glimpse of her mother in the front row fanning herself. It had been an interesting week having her there. Will had confided to Elyssa that he could easily see why she was drawn to her aunt. Her aunt was calm and reassuring while her mother was unsteady and easily fretted about anything. More than once Elyssa caught Will grimacing over something her mother said or did. They were both very grateful that they were going to live halfway across the country from her.

As Elyssa drew up next to Will and he took her hand in his, she felt all the strength of character he had and was willing to share with her.

~~*

Will had been waiting patiently up at the front of the church for the first glimpse of his bride. He took in a sharp breath when Elyssa first stepped out onto the center aisle of the church on her uncle's arm. Her dark hair and eyes contrasted with the white of the dress and ivory tone of her skin. She looked radiant, and he suddenly recalled the day when she walked down another aisle, in a beautiful teal dress, and he couldn't keep his eyes off of her. That was at Chad and Janet's wedding, and he had been fairly certain that as much as he found her exasperatingly attractive, she would never be his.

Today, with each step Elyssa took toward him, he recalled the little steps she took as she gradually warmed to him. The day he took her on the bumper cars was a turning point for them. He could thank his good father for planting that idea in his head. He often thought he might be able to use it someday with his *own* son; he had no idea he would use it with a woman he loved.

When they went out to the village, their ease in conversing together was a pleasant surprise. Not one to engage in profuse conversation, he found himself wanting to hear her thoughts and ideas and learn more about her. She seemed to enjoy their conversation, as well.

Staying with her in the house when she was ill, even though he had not planned it, provided him with the opportunity to show her he cared. As they drove back to Guatemala City that day, he was quite confident that they had crossed a major milestone. If it hadn't been for George Westham, he was fairly certain they would have flown home together, not wanting to part.

Will watched Elyssa glide to within an easy arm's reach from him. He could see every detail of her beautiful face and stunning dress; everything else that had taken place in the past few days getting ready for the wedding was now but a blur.

She stood before him now and Edward Garner handed her off to him. Will could barely comprehend that the eyes that he had found so fine that very first night he met her, were now gazing at him in love. He took her hand and the two turned to face the reverend who would marry them and pronounce them man and wife.

They stood together, eagerly waiting to speak their vows and promise their complete love and devotion, anticipating a lifetime of happiness.

~~*

As might be expected, Will and Elyssa flew to Guatemala on the company jet for their honeymoon. Once in Guatemala City, they were immediately whisked away to Lake Atitlan by Manuel, who was waiting for them at the airport when they arrived. There would be enough time on the way back to visit the Pemberleo staff that had not been able to make it to the wedding. A special reception was planned for them when they returned from the lake.

They spent several nights in the Panajachel hotel where they had previously shared separate suites. This time there was need for only one, no need for a connecting door, and no need to worry whether anyone was taking pictures of the two of them. They had enough leisure time to take in more of the sites around Panajachel before setting out for the village.

Manuel again made all the arrangements and escorted them to the house in the village before setting off to see his family again. As they walked up to the house, Elyssa could barely contain herself when she saw what was on the porch.

"Look!" she said as she tugged Will's sleeve. "Someone has put up a porch swing!"

"So it seems," he said softly.

Elyssa looked up into Will's face. "Did you do that when you were here last? You did, didn't you?"

Will looked down at Elyssa with a sheepish grin. "Well, I didn't actually put it up, but I did arrange to have it hung."

As they walked up the steps to the house, Will asked, "Do you like it?"

"Of course! That afternoon when you and Manuel had gone out and I was feeling a little better, I brought a chair out here and sat. I thought to myself how much nicer it would be if there was a porch swing."

When they came into the house, Elyssa could also see that things had been changed. Some pieces of furniture had been replaced, walls painted, and new window coverings hung. Will wanted to make sure that memories of Chad and Janet didn't completely overshadow their time there, but there were just enough of their belongings remaining so they were not completely forgotten. He also wanted to make the home available for anyone from the company who needed a break, so he had arranged to have it furnished very nicely. He wanted to surprise Elyssa and therefore didn't consult her with the design. Although it was simple, it was very nice. Will reassured her that if she was not happy with anything, she could make improvements while they were there -- but only if she wanted to. They were there to enjoy themselves and relax, not work.

Their time at the village was very special; Elyssa saw Will really loosen up there much like he had before. She encouraged him to grow that "scruffy" look again and although the weather was cooler than their previous visit, it was mild enough to walk barefoot along the shore of the lake and get their feet wet.

Will had not expected it, but Elyssa wanted to venture out to see some of the villages that had sustained damage in the flood. He knew they would have to get into some pretty primitive conditions and didn't want to put her through that on their honeymoon, but she insisted and he finally relented. He was pleasantly surprised again to find out that she was really a trooper and was not put out at all by having to "rough it" for a couple days. They were both ready, though, to get back to modern civilization. A small reception back in Guatemala City attended by employees and others who had come to know Will over the years concluded their time there and they returned to Chicago, eager to begin their life together there.

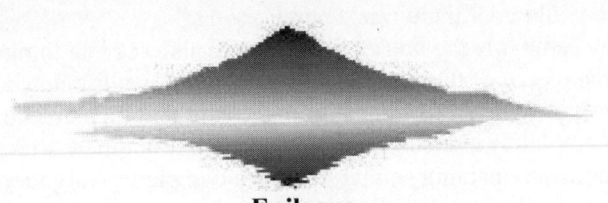

Epilogue

Five years later

Will sat contentedly on the porch swing, his legs stretched out and his heels and toes giving movement so it would gently sway. Elyssa leaned up against him reading from a book. Will's arms were wrapped around her now greatly expanded stomach, hoping to feel a small movement every once in a while.

"Here's a good name," she said. "Emma. I think Emma Janet Denton is nice."

Will nodded. "What does it mean?"

"Let's see…" Elyssa looked down into the book. *"Healer of the universe."*

Will tilted his head as he considered the name. "Sounds a bit overwhelming for a little girl. I still like Amanda, *worthy of being loved.*"

Elyssa turned her head to look out at the small playground they had built at the side of the house. Her cousin, Lillian, now 8, was playing with Nicholas.

"Be careful, Lillian. Remember, Nicky's only 2." She turned back to Will. "I think I like it, too. Mandy Denton."

"No, not Mandy. Amanda. I will not have you shorten it!"

Elyssa laughed. "Just like we never call Nicholas Nick or Nicky?"

"Well, I prefer they grow accustomed to their full names."

"We can do everything we can to keep their names full, but you know it's their friends who will win out in the end. If Nicholas wants to be called Nick and Amanda wants to be called Mandy, we'll just have to deal with it."

Their son, upon hearing his mother's voice, toddled back over to them and crawled up the steps, making his way to the swing.

"Come here, Nicky," Will said, scooping him up and placing him on his lap.

"Nicholas," his wife reminded him. "Nicholas Chad. Our little *victory of the people.*" She laughed. "Talk about overwhelming!"

Bouncing Nicholas on his knee, Will remarked, "It demands respect!"

Elyssa sat up and looked at her watch. "And you're going to be *losing* respect from everyone if you don't get yourself to work! What kind of example are you setting not going in until after noon?"

Will lifted up Nicholas and put him carefully on Elyssa's lap. "I suppose you're right, but as Fridays are casual day, I figure I can just amble on in any time I want." He leaned over and kissed Nicholas on the nose and then Elyssa on the cheek. "I don't think anyone is going to complain that I wanted to spend the morning with my wife and son."

He leaned over and patted Elyssa's belly. "And little Amanda."

Elyssa watched Will walk away in his jeans and polo shirt. He didn't always conform to the "casual day" attire that he established a couple of years ago. If he had any scheduled business meetings, he usually wore a suit. By the way he was dressed today, Elyssa could see he was anticipating a light day at work and that he most likely would be home within a few hours.

Elyssa stood up and brought Nicholas and Lillian into the house to give them lunch. As she looked around their beautiful home, she let out a sigh of appreciation. She had so much, and that included her own design business.

Almost immediately after Will and Elyssa were married, her decorating business boomed. She loved working with Emily and the sub-contractors she used. She also found the she could purchase almost anything through the Jones' little store and Elyssa and Janelle became close friends.

Once she had Nicholas, she intentionally cut back on the number of clients she took, and mainly did design consulting. She worked a lot at home, looking for products on the internet and then buying them from Janelle if at all possible. Emily worked with her in arranging the sub-contractors to do the work.

Now with Amanda coming in a few months, she knew she would be putting all design jobs here on hold. She did not want to be away from her children and knew the need to be home and more available would be greater with two.

Elyssa set Nicholas down with some books that Lillian wanted to read to him. She glanced up at the painting of Pemberleigh Manor and studied it a while. Then she walked back into the room that had become her design studio.

Despite putting her career on hold in Chicago, there was one design job offer that she had wholeheartedly accepted. She walked over to the plans that were spread out across a large work table and leaned over to study them. As inspiration came to her, she would jot down notes. She was excited about this project that had been presented to her by Will and Gina just about the time she learned she was expecting another baby.

Gina had graduated from Stanford a year earlier with a degree in hotel management. Along with her required classes, she had also continued attending cooking school and was ready to fulfill her dream to open a bed and breakfast. It pleased Elyssa greatly that her sister-in-law loved the Santa Ynez Valley and had found a perfect place to build, about 20 miles from where Elyssa had lived.

Part of Gina's inheritance along with some money Will put up as a partner set things in motion to buy the property that would give Gina *her* Pemberleigh.

The plans for an exact replica of the Denton estate in England were drawn up and Elyssa was asked to decorate *Pemberleigh Bed and Breakfast* in nineteenth century design. It would be a major project and with much enthusiasm, Elyssa began researching and dreaming even before they broke ground.

In perusing the plans for the large manor, Elyssa had to consider how many rooms would be used for guests and which rooms would be reserved for private use. Gina didn't need a large suite, but if she married and had a family, she would want more. They needed a few small suites for live-in staff and then a suite for Will and Elyssa and their family when they came to visit.

Elyssa wanted to do as much as she could before little Amanda was born. She ordered furniture and fabric and wallpaper from Janelle and had things held until the structure was far enough along for the items to be shipped and stored.

She knew that this little dream of Gina's would be gradual in its growth, which was just fine for Elyssa. She began by designing the main rooms and just a few bedroom suites. It would grow as Gina found herself able to handle it.

There was one more thing Will did once he and Elyssa got married that tapped into Elyssa's creative and giving side. He gave her a position within Pemberleo. It wasn't so much a job where she had to go in to work everyday. He knew very well that she loved designing and was doing well at it, but he knew something was missing at Pemberleo.

He put Elyssa in charge of the company's benevolent division, discerning the needs in Guatemala that they could meet and working to bring that about. One of the first things she did was to add a tutoring building to the pre-school so children of all ages could get the additional help they needed to succeed in school and beyond. Tutors were hired and some computers were purchased so skills could be taught. As the years went on, the pre-school was the recipient of a great deal of assistance through Elyssa's efforts.

Once *Pemberleigh Bed and Breakfast* was finished, Will and Elyssa went out often. Elyssa loved leaving the coldest months of winter in Chicago and spending them in a more mild climate. Visits to Guatemala and their own townhouse in the Pemberleo complex became a third home for them.

There were still times when Elyssa ached for her sister and missed her so much. She wanted to tell her how happy she was being married to Will. She wanted to share little Nicholas and sweet Amanda. The dream that she and Janet had shared to be close to one another's children could never be, but her sisterly feelings toward Gina grew with each visit and conversation.

Elyssa often thought back to what Janet said to her before they walked down the aisle at her sister's wedding. She told her that she had picked the teal color for the bridesmaid dresses because that was the best color on Elyssa and thought if there were any irresistible, single men there, they would not be able to take their eyes off of her. Elyssa often wondered whether Janet had Will in mind.

She'd never know for sure, but if it hadn't been for Janet, she would have never met Will. Elyssa couldn't even bring herself to ponder whether she and Will would have ended up together if Janet and Chad hadn't died. That tragedy inexplicably threw the two of them together in a way that otherwise might not have been. She simply accepted fate and how everything worked out.

Will would occasionally walk in on Elyssa as she read Janet's diary. It was her constant connection to her dearest sister. She could read through it now without constantly shedding a tear, and Will knew that when Elyssa began to talk about her, he needed to sit quietly and listen.

Will's life, which had once been so driven by his work, had taken a turn for the best when he met Elyssa. It hadn't always been easy on their bumpy road to love, but he did not regret all the lessons he learned while attempting to take on those things she wanted in a man and discarding those things she didn't. With prevailing resolve and a rather large dose of humility, he had persevered to the end and was rewarded with Elyssa's love.

Neither expected it, but both came to embrace it with a good measure of *drive and determination.*

~The End ~

Kara Louise lives in Kansas with her husband.
They share their 10 acres with
an ever changing menagerie of animals.
They have one married son who also likes to write.

Other published books by Kara Louise
"Pemberley's Promise"

Visit her website,
www.ahhhs.net
where you will find the novels
"Assumed Engagement"
"Assumed Obligation"
and
"Master Under Good Regulation"
and a variety of other stories
written by her and Australian author, Sharni.

Printed in Great Britain by
Amazon.co.uk, Ltd.,
Marston Gate.